Blaze

Dear Reader,

Ten years is a blink in the eyes of a Blaze heroine, who lives in the moment and takes what she can from every opportunity. I remember the day very well when my editor, Brenda Chin, called to talk about a book I already had contracted for publication as a Temptation Blaze, the precursor to the stand-alone Blaze series that is now celebrating a decade in print. I'd already started writing the book and had planned for it to be short and character-focused, like all my Temptations were. But Brenda was offering me a chance to do something spectacular and unheard of for a relatively new author: be a part of the Blaze launch! I could not turn her down.

The resulting book, *Exposed,* became one of my favorites. I learned to broaden the scope of the stories I wanted to tell, introduce more plot elements and delve more deeply into secondary characters. I learned so much and had a great time writing it! I'm thrilled beyond measure that readers will have an opportunity to revisit the start of Blaze as well as see how far we've come! I'm proud to still be around after ten years and still doing something new. This book, *Too Hot to Touch,* is the first in my Legendary Lovers series, which also happens to be my first back-to-back trilogy for Blaze.

I consider myself so fortunate to have had an opportunity not only to write a book for the launch of Blaze, but also for the line's tenth anniversary. If I can continue to write these supersexy, sassy books for another ten years and beyond, I'll be living a dream!

Happy reading,

Julie

Julie Leto

TOO HOT TO TOUCH
EXPOSED

Harlequin®

TORONTO NEW YORK LONDON
AMSTERDAM PARIS SYDNEY HAMBURG
STOCKHOLM ATHENS TOKYO MILAN MADRID
PRAGUE WARSAW BUDAPEST AUCKLAND

ISBN-13: 978-0-373-79635-9

TOO HOT TO TOUCH
Copyright © 2011 by Harlequin Books S.A.

The publisher acknowledges the
copyright holders of the individual works
as follows:

TOO HOT TO TOUCH
Copyright © 2011 by Book Goddess, LLC

EXPOSED
Copyright © 2001 by Julie Leto Klapka

Recycling programs
for this product may
not exist in your area.

This edition published by arrangement with Harlequin Books S.A.

For questions and comments about the quality of this book
please contact us at Customer_eCare@Harlequin.ca.

® and TM are trademarks of the publisher. Trademarks indicated with ® are registered in the United States Patent and Trademark Office, the Canadian Trade Marks Office and in other countries.

www.Harlequin.com

Printed in U.S.A.

CONTENTS

ABOUT THE AUTHOR

Over the course of her career, *New York Times* and *USA TODAY* bestselling author Julie Leto has published more than forty books—all of them sexy and all of them romances at heart. She shares a popular blog—www.plotmonkeys.com—with her best friends Carly Phillips, Janelle Denison and Leslie Kelly and would love for you to follow her on Twitter, where she goes by @JulieLeto. She's a born and bred Floridian homeschooling mom with a love for her family, her friends, her dachshund, her lynx-point Siamese and supersexy stories with a guaranteed happy ending.

Books by Julie Leto

HARLEQUIN BLAZE

To get the inside scoop on Harlequin Blaze and its talented writers, be sure to check out blazeauthors.com.

Don't miss any of our special offers. Write to us at the following address for information on our newest releases.

Harlequin Reader Service
U.S.: 3010 Walden Ave., P.O. Box 1325, Buffalo, NY 14269
Canadian: P.O. Box 609, Fort Erie, Ont. L2A 5X3

TOO HOT TO TOUCH

To the loyal readers of Harlequin Blaze—
thank you for ten years of joy.

And to Brenda Chin—for the same and more!

My dearest son, Miguel,

My death has come after a hard but full life. Your mother knows how desperately I loved her and I hope you know I loved you, too.

Unfortunately, I cannot say the same for your brothers. Daniel is lost. I have no doubt that Alejandro has just as many reasons for hating me, but he is a fine, upstanding man. He will want to know you, and I want you to know him.

I do not ask you to justify my sins to him—there is no justifiation. All that I ask is that you reach out to him as his brother and give him the legacy that he, as my oldest son, is due. The Murrieta ring must pass to my firstborn.

I know you don't believe in its power. I know you only humored my when I told you how the ring influenced my life and gave me the strength to change my ways. Alejandro is trapped by expectations that keep him from living his life with passion. The ring will free him, of this I am sure.

Do not allow him to refuse this, my last request.

I am proud of you, Miguel. Though I cannot give you the gift of the ring, I hope to give you something more valuable—a brother with whom to share our pride in the infamous Murrieta name.

With all my heart,
Ramon

1

"LUCIENNE, MAY I have a word?"

Standing between his office and the main gallery of El Dorado Auction House, Alejandro Aguilar crossed his arms, blocking the uncharacteristic nervousness attempting to sneak past his defenses. He wasn't a sixteen-year-old schoolboy. He was a grown man, a titan in the art world. He assigned prices to priceless artifacts and exposed fraudulent fakes in museums and private collections worldwide. By design, his name had become synonymous with honor, integrity and control.

And yet, the woman sitting at her desk in the gallery, typing determinedly on her computer without a glance in his direction, had reduced him to a twisted mass of raw, exposed wiring in a structure marked "condemned." Any minute, a spark could flare. One accidental touch, one misread innuendo and he'd go up in flames.

For six weeks, he and Lucienne Bonet had worked side by side to prepare El Dorado's inventory for liquidation. He'd come to San Francisco from Spain specifically to handle the auction because the man who'd collected the pieces, his father, had died.

The death had meant nothing to him. Alex had not seen Ramon Murrieta since he'd walked out on Alex's mother when he was three years old. But Ramon's passing had given Alex something he'd never had before—a brother. One who worked for the FBI and had no idea what to do with their deceased father's business holdings. At his invitation, Alex had traveled halfway across the world, expecting to spend two months getting to know his surprise sibling while breaking up the collection his fickle father had built.

What he had not expected was meeting a woman he could no longer resist.

"Lucienne?"

Her fingers continued to fly across her keyboard. She'd touched him just as quickly this morning, when they'd both reached for a diamond bracelet, one of the last items left for appraisal.

The contact had lasted less than a split second, but the effect had been like the strike of a match. Her smile over his wry retort had stoked a barely banked flame. Alex had endured yearlong love affairs with less incendiary power than this.

Of course, he'd slept with those women. The quickest way to burn out a fire was to smother it. But Lucienne was, at the moment, his employee. And since he never mixed business with pleasure, he'd had to suffer the conflagration.

Unless he changed the circumstances, which was what he aimed to do.

He opened his mouth to call to her again, but then thought better of it. He had no idea how she'd react to the indecent proposal he was about to set forth—for all he knew, she'd slap him soundly and walk out. As he wasn't a man who embraced risk, he opted instead to watch her work for a minute more.

Without sound, she mouthed the words as she typed, drawing his attention to her lips. She glossed them with a dark purple color that reminded him of a cabernet sauvignon or a fine Spanish riojo. Would her flesh taste as rich, as deep, as intoxicating?

That intimate question, among others, had driven him to this decision. For the first time in his life, he'd decided to put his personal needs above his professional ones.

It was insane.

But he was still going to do it.

He called her name again, louder this time. She looked up from her laptop, her gaze momentarily unfocused until she spotted him. She popped out the earbuds hidden beneath her luscious brown hair and gave her head a little shake—a shake that he felt from across the room.

"I'm sorry, Señor Aguilar, did you need something?"

"Sí," he responded, disconcerted by the rasped quality of his voice and the content of her question.

Yes, he needed something. He needed her.

He cleared his throat. "Could we speak in the office for a moment?"

"Of course," she replied, then turned back to her computer long enough to click her mouse and save her work. "I'm sorry I didn't hear you. I was caught up in transcribing the last interview for the catalogue. It was brilliant of you to suggest that we include first-person narratives about the pieces for the Hollywood collection. The stories are fascinating. The added text will undoubtedly double the expected opening bids."

Her grin lit her face from those seemingly delicious lips to her wide brown eyes, intensifying the tightness in Alex's chest. She reacted to the prospect of fetching a higher-than-estimated price for an auction item like another woman might react to diamonds and chocolates and roses.

Another man might have suspected he was in love. Alex, however, knew himself well enough to realize this was only lust, plain and unadorned.

Sometimes, even he appreciated the simple things in life.

"Actually, the narratives were your idea," he replied.

Her delectable mouth arched into a smile that reduced his insides to ash.

He really had it bad.

"It was a team effort," she said, her accent round and lush with a European lilt she'd undoubtedly picked up on her extensive travels. But when she crossed the room, her stride was sensual and confident and bold, as if she'd spent her time in ballet studios rather than stuffy museums or private collections, as her résumé indicated. Despite the countless hours they'd spent together working on the auction, he knew next to nothing about her beyond what was listed on that impressive document.

But he meant to find out.

"You're being generous," he concluded.

She batted her lashes with exaggerated coyness—and nearly knocked the wind out of him.

"Perhaps," she demurred. "But the bottom line remains. The auction is going to be a huge success."

Standing in the threshold between his office and the gallery, she shimmied with barely contained excitement, causing the tendons in his knees to quake. She was inches away from him, her skin flushed by the prospect of huge profits.

Lust just wasn't a sufficient word.

A long moment elapsed before he realized he was blocking her from entering his office. She moistened her lips. Slowly.

Patiently.

The move was innocent—just a pink tongue sliding over dry lips while she waited for him to step aside.

Only her lips weren't dry—they were slick and full and enticing.

He swallowed thickly and took a step back.

The auction house vibrated with silence, the only sound coming from the tap of Lucienne's sharp stiletto heels on the polished wood floor. In the distant background, the air conditioner hummed, protecting the antiquities and collectibles by regulating the temperature and humidity so that it remained steady and cool and dry.

So why was he feeling as if he'd just walked into a tropical rainforest?

"Please, have a seat," he invited.

Watching her manipulate her glorious backside—enhanced today by a camel-colored pencil skirt that had quickly become one of his favorite pieces—into the chair was performance art of the finest quality. He couldn't help but wonder if she was at all aware of the sensuality of her movements or if her body simply followed an intrinsic rhythm.

With any luck, he'd soon find out.

"Do you have questions about the estimations?" she asked, gesturing toward the spiral-bound report she'd delivered to him two days ahead of schedule.

"Not exactly," he replied, crossing to the chair behind his desk and ignoring, per usual, the *affresco* portrait of his father painted on the wall.

If not for the portrait behind the desk, Alex would not have known what Ramon Murrieta looked like—and yet, he generally avoided the old man's piercing black eyes, dark skin and roguishly wavy hair. Unfortunately, with his father perched over his shoulder, every single person who came into the room remarked on how much Alex resembled him.

Even Lucienne had made the comparison—but only once. Though he'd never shared any of his resentment toward his father with her, she must have sensed it because she rarely, if ever, mentioned his name. Not an easy feat, either, considering the reason fate had brought them together.

For six solid weeks, they'd spent hours alone together, the auction expert and the appraiser, picking through items his father had amassed—items that evoked stories best shared by lovers. They'd handled the fourteen fur coats owned by a Hollywood starlet who'd slept her way to an Oscar nomination, the bed used by a notorious predepression entrepreneur who'd reportedly seduced an equal number of men and women before dying of autoerotic asphyxia and a collection of gold and crystal phalluses created by a female artist in New York city during the era of free love, who had, it was said, personally tested out both her live models and her creations over the span of a forty-year career.

Unlike House of Aguilar, the auction house run by his mother's family in Madrid, El Dorado, specialized in the scandalous and notorious. At first, Alex had been appalled by the inventory, which ranged from the sensual to the shady to the macabre. But going through the collection with Lucienne had taken the edge off his inflated sense of artistic superiority and honed his libido instead, which was now sharp enough to cut through steel.

"Your report was perfect," he said.

"Thank you," she replied. "That is what you're paying me for."

"Yes, well," he said, unconsciously patting his jacket pocket. "I cannot complain about the job you've done here, especially under the circumstances."

"I confess…" She lowered her voice and scooted forward as if she didn't want to be overheard, even though they were, thanks to him, entirely alone. "I was surprised when you fired all of Ramon's staff. Their knowledge base could have been valuable."

"And they also might have robbed us blind. Their loyalty was to Ramon, if they had any at all. Besides, working alone, just the two of us…"

She arched a brow. Her mouth puckered, slightly, just enough for him to imagine those sweet, plump lips on his.

Whatever thought he'd been about to express dissipated on his tongue.

Luckily, she picked up the slack. "It's been a unique experience," she said, her voice throaty. "I've never worked in such an…intimate environment before."

She shifted in her chair, leaning forward just enough so that his gaze dropped from her eyes to her breasts. But only for a split second. Until he'd taken care of the business he'd called her into the office to discuss, this could go no further.

She was still his employee—and until she wasn't, he would keep his gaze—and his hands—off the merchandise.

He slapped his palm down on the cover of her report, more loudly than he'd planned. "Thanks to the quiet, we've completed our work in record time. Now that we have solid estimates and opening bid figures for next week's auction, it's time that we moved—"

He reached into his jacket to retrieve the paperwork he'd carefully prepared when the buzzer from the outer door crashed into the silence.

They both jumped. She fumbled to hit the button on his phone to activate the intercom, but he reached it first.

The shock of her hand on his nearly zapped the practiced words out of his brain. In fact, he answered first in Spanish, then repeated the greeting in English.

"El Dorado Auction House is currently closed."

"Yeah, no kidding," replied the voice Alex instantly recognized as his brother, Michael. "Let me in."

Lucienne had not removed her hand from Alex's. Her touch was tentative, her sharp intake of breath held in throat. Their eyes locked for a split second—long enough for him to catch a glimpse of what he'd been searching so valiantly for over the past six weeks.

Desire.

"I'm in the middle of something," he told Michael, willing Lucienne not to take her hand away.

"This is important," Michael insisted.

Before Alex could form a coherent response, Lucienne scrambled into the gallery. Her heels clicked a quick tattoo against the polished floor that matched the sudden, rapid pounding of his heartbeat.

He cursed, then punched in the code that would unlock the front door.

"He knows his way in," Alex called, but Lucienne had already disappeared. She didn't need to greet his brother, but she had needed to get away.

Maybe he hadn't seen desire in her eyes. Maybe that had been wishful thinking.

He remained at his desk, stewing over the interruption when Michael charged into the room.

"Maybe manners are different here than they are in Madrid, but a call ahead of time would have been appreciated," Alex snapped.

Not surprisingly, his half brother met his ire with an unrepentant grin.

"Was that a skirt I saw disappearing around the corner when we walked in?" he asked.

"We?"

Michael leaned back so Alex could see that his brother had not come alone. Special Agent Ruby Dawson, one of the members of Michael's team, was strolling around the gallery, her hands hooked behind her back as she lingered by the tables lined with trays of necklaces, rings and bracelets.

Lucienne was nowhere to be seen.

"My appraiser," Alex said.

"Ah, yes, the mysterious Lucienne Bonet."

"What do you mean *mysterious?*"

Michael shrugged. "You've mentioned her quite a few times, but she never seems to be around when I am."

Alex glanced through the doorway again. Why had Lucienne left in such a hurry if not to show his brother into the office? Of course, Michael had grown up at El Dorado and had inherited the auction house, along with his mother, so he hardly needed an escort.

"She's very busy," Alex snapped. "You know, working. A concept you generally understand on most days."

Michael snickered. "Sorry to interrupt your busy day, but a case I'm working just took a turn and I might have to leave town before the auction. And since I know you have to return to Madrid right afterward, I decided it's time for us to take care of some important business."

Alex sat up straighter, an unfamiliar pang of worry driving deep into his stomach. He wasn't used to having anyone in his family with a dangerous career. His mother, grandfather, uncle and several cousins worked at the auction house in Spain. He had an aunt who was the executive assistant for the head of a security firm, but he doubted she did more than answer phones and arrange appointments. She certainly never jetted off to cities unknown to catch elusive, terrifying criminals.

Michael, however, did this all the time—a fact that hadn't hit Alex until right this moment.

"What kind of business?"

Michael smirked. "You know I can't say. Not yet, anyway. But look, I didn't come here to discuss my case. I have to ask you something important."

Alex motioned for Michael to shut the door, which he did. But instead of taking the seat on the other side of the desk that Lucienne had just vacated, he crossed to the space behind their father's desk and dropped to one knee.

The tension in Alex's midsection evaporated with a laugh. "Are you proposing?"

Michael shoved Alex's chair so that it rolled back into the bookshelf behind him, dislodging several books that knocked him in the shoulder. While he slid the books back into place, Michael ran a finger over a groove in the polished floor where the chair had been and then pressed down so that the slat levered up on the other side.

"What is this?"

Michael's smile was only half-cocked and he suddenly looked more like their father than he did on first glance. Unlike Alex, who'd inherited his father's dark looks, Michael favored his all-American mother with his lapis lazuli irises and light brown hair, which had undoubtedly been blond in his youth.

When his mouth curved up with salacious intentions, however, he was all Ramon.

One tug on the lever and a section of the floor dropped and slid to the side, revealing a safe hidden underneath. It was old and dusty and the tumblers clicked loudly as Michael twirled in the combination, but it opened with barely a creak. From inside, he pulled out a tattered wooden box and a sheaf of papers, bound in a leather portfolio that smelled of age.

Michael put the documents on the desk, but handed Alex the box.

The minute he had his hands on it, he recognized the style. Eighteenth century, definitely Spanish design, but likely crafted in the new world, as evidenced by the selection of wood. He imagined a noblewoman had purchased or commissioned the piece to keep her trinkets or jewels in.

The lock, though discolored, was fashioned from tempered steel and coated with eighteen-karat gold.

Alex eyed his brother warily. He and Lucienne had individually searched through every inch of the building that housed the auction house. Neither had found the floor safe—though admittedly, Alex hadn't thought to look—or any reference in Ramon's meticulous notes to indicate he was keeping something hidden in his office floor.

Of course, making a record would have cancelled out the need to hide something so well.

"I ask again," he said. "What is this?"

"Open it," Michael instructed. "The key hasn't worked for over a century."

Michael finally took Lucienne's abandoned chair, giving Alex room to scoot in and flip on the retractable magnifying lamp attached to the side of the desk. He did as his brother instructed, somewhat surprised to find the inside of the box in worse condition than the outside.

The torn, faded silk, which he suspected had once been a brilliant red, was washed out and pocked with unsightly watermarks. And the large emerald-centered man's ring sitting atop a carved prong had clearly seen better days.

While the black opals flanking the main stone glowed with vivid blues and greens, the gold was worn and the center stone, while large and vibrant, had an unsightly scratch that looked like a crude number *2.*

Or perhaps a *Z?*

"This is hardly up to our father's usual standards for his inventory," he commented. The history of Ramon's collection was salacious, but even Alex had to admit that the quality was usually impeccable.

"This isn't part of the auction house's catalogue."

Michael's gaze flicked over Alex's shoulder. Alex followed the stare, his eyes lighting on their father's *affresco* portrait. Ramon had posed wearing a charcoal black suit and stark white shirt, the only splash of color coming from his thin red tie and the stunning green of his ring.

The ring in the box Alex now held.

"He wasn't buried with it?" Alex asked.

Michael shook his head. "That ring has been in our family for centuries. It passes from father to son. And it's your turn."

Alex dropped the box. The ring jostled off the prong and tipped onto the moth-eaten silk lining. From the side, he could see that the gold near the back was thin and had been repaired several times.

The condition did not surprise him. Any ring that had been around for as long as Michael claimed would have sustained a great deal of wear and tear, particularly if it was actually worn and not kept locked away. What shocked the hell out of him was that Michael wanted him to have it.

"I can't take your father's ring."

"He was your father, too."

"Genetically."

"He wanted you to have it."

"That's absurd!"

He hated the way his voice tipped up in disbelief, but the idea was incomprehensible. Why would Ramon bequeath a family heirloom to the son he'd abandoned over thirty years ago?

"It's the truth." Michael paced in front of the desk, his arms crossed and his gaze wary. "He told me he meant for you to have it. Right after he first told me about you."

Alex shook his head. As difficult as it had been, he and Michael had managed to keep their discussions about Ramon to a minimum. Alex could not begrudge his brother's happy childhood, but that didn't mean he wanted to hear all the white-picket-fence details.

"We don't need to discuss this," Alex said, sliding the box across the desk so that it sat in front of Michael instead of him.

"Actually, we do. A few years ago, when I was new at the Bureau, a case came up that Pop got caught up in. It was an art heist. The thief cut himself on a metal frame and left behind some DNA evidence. The techs ran it through the system and got a hit—me."

Alex arched a brow. His brother? A thief?

"You stole a painting?"

Michael rolled his eyes. "Of course not, but as an FBI agent, my DNA was in the system. It wasn't a perfect match, but the science indicated that I was directly related to whoever had cut himself on that frame. That led the FBI to Pop."

Alex's throat tightened. He scanned the inventory around him. His mother had always accused his father of being unprincipled and despicable, but had he amassed his collection through illegal trade?

"I don't know what—"

"But he didn't steal the painting, either," Michael said emphatically.

Alex did a poor job of hiding his doubt. "How can you be sure?"

"He allowed the FBI to do more DNA testing, and again, it wasn't a perfect match. But the likelihood that the thief was related to him was even higher. The squints said the blood likely came from a son. That's when he told me about you."

Alex stood, outraged. "I was a suspect in a burglary?"

"No, not with your reputation. I mean, not after we did our research."

Alex's incensed stare did not waver. He had worked his entire adult life to ensure that his father's disreputable past never reflected badly on him. Now he learned that the American justice system had suspected him of a crime?

Michael raised both hands and signaled Alex to sit. "You were eliminated almost immediately, thanks to Pop. He pulled up a society page from a Spanish newspaper that had a picture of you at a charity function in Barcelona the night of the theft."

Alex lowered himself back into the chair. He wasn't certain what shocked him more—the fact that he'd been, albeit briefly, suspected of a brazen robbery or that the father who'd never once called or sent so much as a birthday card had followed his movements and activities.

When he'd decided to accept Michael's invitation to the United States, he knew he would be forced to cut open the wound of his father's abandonment. But now that the man was dead and buried, Alex had thought he could handle the pain and resentment. He had, after all, had a great life. A mother who cherished him. A grandfather who had defied old age and illness to live past ninety to make sure his grandson had a father figure. His childhood had been filled with family, the finest schools and boundless possibilities.

The only thing his father had given him was DNA that had nearly caught him up in a crime investigation—and an old, battered ring.

"He wasn't proud of leaving you the way he did, Alejandro," Michael confessed. "I mean, he never shared many details, but he did say that he was a different man then. And I believe he was. He didn't have the ring until after he came back to the States."

"What does this ridiculous bauble have to do with anything?"

Michael's shoulders sagged. He was a strong man, his brother, but the emotions of this conversation were wearing him down. Alex understood. His stomach ached, as if someone had just punched him in the gut. He was learning more about his father than he'd ever wanted to know. It was much easier to maintain a steady hatred for the man when all he'd known about him was that he'd left his first-born son and never looked back.

But since he'd arrived in San Francisco, Alex couldn't help but learn more. Getting to know Michael—realizing how honorable he was—reflected on his upbringing. How could a man who'd abandoned one son raise another to be strong, principled and comfortable in his own skin?

"Put it on." Michael slid the box back toward him.

"What? No."

Michael opened the box, took out the ring and practically shoved it in Alex's face.

"Put it on, Alejandro. Once you do, you'll understand."

"SO PEOPLE PAY A LOT of money for this stuff, huh?"

Caught, Lucy cursed under her breath, then came out of the storeroom as if she'd only darted inside to put something away rather than to hide. Michael must not have recognized her—if he had, he wouldn't have left her out here to chitchat with the federal agent who'd come along with him.

"Some do," she replied.

The agent lifted up a diamond-encrusted dagger said to have been the murder weapon of choice for an infamous Renaissance assassin.

"How much would something like this go for?"

Lucy curved her body around the edge of her desk, her back to Alejandro's office. From behind her, the heat of a stare prickled against her skin. The feeling was familiar, as if yet again, Alejandro was checking out her ass. She didn't mind. What was the point of having an oversize backside that made it hell to find a good pair of jeans if a hot-blooded man couldn't appreciate it?

And Alejandro's appreciation had its advantages. Not only did his attention to her bottom keep him distracted enough to not realize, after six weeks, that she was not exactly the woman he thought she was, but it also gave her ego a much-needed boost. The man was a torrent of simmering passion capped like steam in a radiator—and with him, she wouldn't mind getting burned.

Getting burned by Michael Murrieta or his partner was another situation entirely. One that could result in jail time. But if Michael had not seen through her disguise—and really, why would he when they'd only met briefly once before—he'd expect her to be a worldly intellectual like Alejandro, not nervous and jumpy like a girl pretending to be someone she wasn't.

Lucy slipped on a pair of thin cotton gloves and turned her attention back to Michael's partner. "We're expecting the dagger will bring in close to fifty thousand."

"Dollars? For a letter opener?" The woman's voice was pitched high in disbelief.

Lucy risked a laugh. "This particular dagger dispatched the enemies of a particularly bloodthirsty pope, if rumors are to be believed."

With her insides quaking, Lucy's European-influenced accent, meant to support her claims of boundless world travel during an exciting childhood abroad, slipped a bit. In truth, she'd only left the States three times in the past six years—each time on a passport faked by one of the best pros money could buy.

Lucy inhaled deeply. She had to get herself together. She'd worked too hard and had risked too much to let one unexpected visit from federal law enforcement trip her up.

Wasn't like she hadn't played the role of sophisticated, overeducated Lucienne Bonet before. This was her favorite persona—the skin she slipped into whenever the fires got too hot around Lucy Burnett, a well-known fence who specialized in hard-to-get *objets d'art*. As Lucienne, snotty museum curators and puffed-up private collectors had invited her to examine their priceless artifacts and antiques, to run her hands over their rare books and centuries-old tapestries until she'd learned just as much about the art world as she had about pawnshops and black market traders.

The FBI agent, who seemed to be around forty, with skin that reminded Lucy of the luscious caramel that she loved to drizzle over chocolate ice cream, placed the weapon gently on Lucy's palm. Lucy turned it over as if examining it for the first time, when in reality, she'd already appraised this piece two weeks ago.

The woman grabbed a tissue from a box on Lucy's desk, then gingerly took the knife back, this time holding it under the lamp. "That looks like dried blood."

Lucy pretended she hadn't noticed that detail before. "Really? The price just went up to seventy-five."

The special agent's dark eyes widened, then narrowed with her smile. "You're playing me."

Lucy's grin twitched. "Maybe just a little."

From behind them, male voices rose not in volume, but in intensity. The men had shut the door. Whatever Michael had come to discuss with Alejandro was not good news. Had Michael's partner not been here to distract her, Lucy would have found a way to hear what they were saying. She'd slipped a listening device into Alejandro's potted palm on the day of her interview and had tapped his cell phone when he'd left her alone to complete her employment papers. But neither avenue was any use with the FBI agent watching her every move. Had Michael recognized her? Outed her to Alejandro? She'd been so careful to make herself scarce whenever the fed was around, but this time, he'd shown up without an appointment.

And yet, if he had identified her, she probably wouldn't

still be standing around discussing the cost of daggers with his partner. She'd be in handcuffs, at the very least.

At worst, she'd be sequestered in some dank, moldy interrogation room, answering questions about Daniel, the third Murrieta brother, who up until now—as far as Lucy was aware—Alejandro knew nothing about.

"I'm Ruby, by the way," the agent said. "Special Agent Ruby Dawes."

Lucy extended her hand. "Lucienne Bonet."

The other woman's handshake was quick, but powerful. If she was trying to size Lucy up, she was doing a great job of hiding it.

Special Agent Dawes returned the dagger to the display case and took a sweeping look around the room that gave Lucy an excuse to return to her desk.

"So, have you worked here long?" Ruby asked.

Dawes flapped the lapels of her boxy suit jacket. Right before the FBI had arrived, Lucy had raised the thermostat so that the temperature in the auction house would, over the course of the day, spike a little. It wasn't good for the inventory, but she'd wanted an excuse to lift her hair off her nape and sport a soft sheen of sweat when she met with Alejandro. She wanted the man thinking about sex, not wondering whether the woman he trusted with his auction was actually there to steal his most valuable possession.

If she could find the damned thing.

"Less than two months," she replied.

"And you'll stay until the collection is sold off?"

"I expect so. Señor Aguilar dismissed most of the original staff when he took over. He kept only a few warehouse workers to do the heavy lifting, but mostly, it's just the two of us."

"That's cozy."

Lucy allowed only a minimal smile, but the situation had not been nearly as cozy as se would have liked—for both professional and personal reasons.

She'd come to El Dorado Auction House with one goal in mind—to find the ring Ramon Murrieta had worn every single day of his adult life. The ring that would keep Daniel Burnett, her adopted brother, alive.

She didn't know how or why a piece of jewelry could pull off such a magical feat while Danny was in jail for a crime he didn't commit, but it wasn't her job to ask questions. Danny was the mastermind. He planned and executed the heists; she sold the goods for maximum price and minimum risk of exposure. The symbiotic relationship had worked well for years because she'd trusted Danny enough to do what he asked without second-guessing him.

But this time, he'd asked her to do the stealing, and so far, she'd come up empty. She'd searched through every inch of the considerable collection. She'd even met with several of Ramon's top clients under the guise of gauging their interest in the upcoming auction and had learned that Ramon had not been wearing the ring during his open casket funeral.

Last week, she'd talked her way into the Murrieta home to look for some apocryphal paperwork while Ramon's widow was baking cookies for the four-year-olds at her preschool. In between tea and chats, Lucy had given the place a thorough search. If Michael's mother had the ring, she'd hidden it well. Lucy had found no documentation to show that Ramon or his wife had ever owned a safe deposit box in a bank. More than likely, their valuables had been kept in the high-security safes at El Dorado—safes she'd searched extensively.

And if Michael had it—well, he wasn't wearing it. She'd taken the time to check that much. But she had no plans to break into his condo. It was one thing to bypass the privacy of a nursery school teacher. It was something else to break and enter the residence of a federal agent.

Thievery was not her area, but as a fence for one of the top cat burglars in the business, she'd picked up a little knowledge. And Daniel needed her help. If she didn't find the ring soon, he was going to pay a price higher than the sum of all the valuables in the building.

Special Agent Dawes continued the stroll through the gallery, examining, but not touching, the items laid out on long velvet-lined tables. Lucy wondered if the agent knew about Daniel. She hadn't been with Michael when he'd gone to the jail the day red-haired, green-eyed Lucy's path had crossed with his. She doubted Michael had even told Alejandro that he had a second half brother, one born to a mother who'd kept her pregnancy a secret from Ramon and who'd ultimately abandoned her son to foster care.

Lucy's bond with Daniel, forged when her family had taken him in, was stronger than any blood connection he'd ever have to any of the Murrietas—particularly since both of his brothers seemed to adhere to strict guidelines about rules and honor. Daniel might have that whole "honor among thieves" thing going on, but that was about his limit.

Well, except when it came to her. In all his many scrapes with the law, he'd never once implicated her. Because of Daniel's militant protection of her, she'd never spent a second in an interrogation room or a jail cell.

She owed him. He was the closest thing to a sibling that she'd ever known—and since her parents took in foster kids by the dozens, that was saying a lot.

She checked the clock on her computer. Alejandro had called her into his office earlier for some unknown reason, but in five minutes, they had a meeting they'd scheduled last week. The man was a slave to his calendar, so she figured he'd be kicking Michael out fairly soon.

Maybe until then, she could pump Michael's partner for information. If he had the ring, Dawes might have seen it.

"Perhaps there's something in the collection you'd like me to set aside for you before the big auction," Lucy said, waving the woman toward an impressive collection of jewelry retrieved from the estate of a notorious gangster's moll. "What month were you born?"

"May," Dawes replied.

Thank you, Lady Luck.

"Ooh, then, how about this?"

She lifted an emerald encrusted necklace from the red-velvet-lined tray and held it up against Dawes's neck. "That's spectacular on you."

Dawes turned toward the mirror and spent a few seconds admiring the effect of the bright jewels on her dark skin. "Yeah, I'm sure the guys would love it if I wore this to an interrogation."

Lucy made a face, as if she agreed with the inappropriateness of the magnificent piece for such an occasion. "Maybe something a little more subtle."

She pawed through the tray, pretending she didn't know the exact location of the items she searched for. She successfully faked a surprised "Oh!" and then pulled out emerald and opal earrings.

"Try them on," she encouraged.

Special Agent Dawes frowned, opting only to hold the studs up to her ears, which were currently devoid of jewelry.

"These probably cost more than my annual salary," she groused.

"Perhaps, but that combination of emerald and opal is

spectacular with your complexion. It's not a pairing we see very often. Emeralds and opals are both so delicate."

Lucy had billed herself as an expert, and Dawes seemed to buy the explanation without question.

"Michael's father had a ring with an emerald and opals," Dawes volunteered.

Bingo.

"The ring in the painting?" Lucy asked, pointing toward the office's closed door. "That was real? Sometimes, when someone has a portrait of themselves done, they often… embellish."

Dawes put the earrings back onto the tray. "Not Ramon. He was every bit as larger-than-life as that painting. Of course, I only met him once. He didn't seem comfortable around Michael's law enforcement friends."

Again, Lucy feigned ignorance. "Why not?"

Dawes's sculpted eyebrows knitted together for a second, then relaxed. "Oh, right. You're new here."

Lucy was new to El Dorado, but like Special Agent Dawes, she'd met Ramon once and he'd made a strong enough impression to last a lifetime. Not only because he was sinfully handsome in the way of dashing, older men, but because his personality demanded and received center stage—even when he was trying to make amends to Daniel for never knowing he existed.

"I've only heard glowing reports about him from his clients," Lucy said.

Dawes snickered. "Yeah, well, most of his clients had dubious pasts themselves. Compared to them, he was probably a saint."

Lucy arched a brow to show that she was interested in hearing more. Nothing that Dawes was saying came as any surprise. Daniel had researched his father extensively, as he did with all his marks. His plan to steal the ring from Ramon predated the older man's death—and Daniel's arrest. The FBI agent wasn't exposing any deep, dark secrets by talking about her partner's father, but the conversation was building a rapport between Lucy and the agent—one that might come in handy later on.

"Are you saying these items are stolen?"

"Nah," Dawes said with a wave of her hand. "Michael'd pitch a fit if his father did anything illegal. But Ramon had a past. He'd gone legit by the time he married Michael's mother. I guess that's why Mikey turned out so upstanding and straitlaced."

Lucy glanced at the closed office door. "Like Alejandro."

"Unfortunately for the women of San Francisco, who are already lacking in available men," Dawes said, her voice suddenly low and lusty. "A real crying shame. If that Spaniard was a little looser, I might let him act the matador in my ring, if you get my drift."

Oh, Lucy got her drift all right. Over the past two months, Alejandro Aguilar had starred in several of Lucy's erotic dreams—and one had indeed included a twirling red cape and the impaling of a wild beast. Of course, she'd been the untamable animal in question and Alejandro had not been using a banderilla, but another long, stiff tool—one without colorful ribbons, but silky, hot and hard as steel.

This was all fantasy. She had no idea if Alejandro was skilled in the bedroom—but the whole Latin-lover stereotype had to come from somewhere, right?

"How do you know he's not adventurous at heart?" Lucy asked. "He might have all sorts of hidden talents neither one of us knows about."

Ruby licked her lips. "One can only hope and pray."

To cover her unbidden blush, Lucy retrieved the tray of

jewelry and returned it to the locked case. Her transformation into Alejandro's ideal woman by dyeing her hair and methodically selecting a wardrobe that was at once sharply professional and sinfully sexy had not, originally, been part of a scheme. She'd simply needed to make sure that he hired her over any applicants she hadn't scared off.

The unexpected recoil of her seductive teasing, however, was that every time he was anywhere near her, she became innately aware of everything about him. How his jaw tensed whenever she reached across his desk to retrieve a pen. How his shoulders locked whenever her arm not-so-inadvertently brushed his. How he followed her with his gaze when she left his office.

How she caught him staring at her whenever she stood with her back to him.

El Dorado possessed more mirrors than a fun house and none of them distorted anything about Alejandro. Not his lean body. Not his raven-black hair. Definitely not his intense jet eyes.

Suddenly, Dawes was in her face, scrutinizing her expression.

"You've got the hots for him," the agent accused.

Lucy waved her hand dismissively, but didn't deny it. Alejandro Aguilar was the pure embodiment of tall, dark and handsome. And he had an accent—one that required him to roll his *r*s so that the sound mimicked the vibration of a man's lips trailing up his naked lover's spine. Lucy was a talented actress when it came to cons and cops, but even she couldn't lie well enough about something so inevitable.

"He's an incredibly handsome man. But business and pleasure don't mix."

Dawes nodded. "Too true. Workplace romances are nothing but trouble."

"Speaking from experience?"

Special Agent Dawes laughed. "Honey, when I'm not married to a husband, I'm married to my job. I've learned to keep those two worlds completely separate."

Lucy nodded. The men she ran across in her own line of work weren't exactly dating material. Not because of superior morality on her part—thanks to her parents, her ideas about right and wrong were fairly fluid. But she'd learned early on that sleeping with some hot guy only to have him turn around and rip her off, wasn't good for her bank account, her reputation or her heart. The only man in her line of work that she trusted was Daniel—and he was family.

"How many times have you been married?" Lucy asked, glancing at the still-shut office door, then down at her watch. Alejandro was nothing if not efficient. Even if Michael had dropped by to discuss something life altering, Alejandro would make sure their meeting took place as scheduled.

"Three times," Dawes answered lazily, "but I'm considering a fourth if my latest is as good in bed as he is investing my portfolio."

"You're dating your broker?"

Special Agent Dawes winked. "I spend the majority of my waking hours either chasing down criminals or hanging out with g-men. Girls gotta grab any and every opportunity for some loving that comes her way."

Unbidden, Lucy's favorite fantasy of Alejandro surprising her in the warehouse basement and making passionate love to her atop a bed once owned by Rudolph Valentino skittered across her mind.

Technically, Alejandro was a mark, so dallying with him before she stole his ring wouldn't break her personal code. But for the moment, he was still her boss. She chafed at the idea of submitting to him so intimately when he was in a perceived position of power. Hell, he was in a real position of power. If he had any information about his father's ring, he had access to something she needed.

Of course, maybe he'd help her find the elusive treasure if she appealed to his tastes in bed as much as she seemed to as an employee.

Did she dare?

The door to the office jiggled, giving Lucy a split second to hurry to the ladies' room until she heard Michael and Special Agent Dawes exchange goodbyes with Alejandro.

Only seconds later, Alejandro called, "Lucienne?"

Leaning against the door, Lucy closed her eyes and let the sound of his deep, cadenced voice drift over her. Images of naked bodies in dusty, uncertain light curled in her imagination, spawning an electric tingle that danced down her spine and tweaked the tips of her breasts. She cursed herself for turning down the air-conditioning, because she was sweltering with need and nearly melting with lust.

And all he'd done was call her name.

"Lucienne?"

Alejandro's voice echoed again through the empty gallery. She flipped on the faucet, wet her hands and splashed her neck. The cool droplets sizzled on her overheated skin, but gave her the dose of reality she needed. She wasn't here to execute a seduction or fulfill her private fantasies. The auction was only a week away and her job at El Dorado was coming to an end. She needed to concentrate on finding and stealing the ring to save Daniel.

Once she accomplished that, Alejandro would want nothing to do with her.

"Just a moment," she called.

She checked herself in the mirror and groaned with

frustration. She really did look hot as a brunette. Lucienne Bonet was smart, sophisticated and sexy. Lucienne had degrees and professional bloodlines that had turned the head of a man who'd made a career out of exposing fakes and selling the most valuable originals for obscene amounts of money. Lucienne Bonet was the kind of woman who could seduce Alejandro Aguilar into her bed and steal his family heirloom while he was sucking her toes.

Lucy Burnett, on the other hand, had no such savvy. All she had was a sad childhood, a dubious past and a genuine longing to finish her mission and get the hell out before she made a terrible mistake—like falling for a guy who, the minute he figured out who she really was, would hate her forever.

3

LEANING PENSIVELY ON his fist, Alex alternated his gaze from the empty outer gallery to the ring on the desk. Despite his brother's cajoling, he still hadn't tried it on. But he hadn't locked the ring away in the floor safe again, either. Something compelled him to keep Ramon's treasure close to him—something he didn't want to examine too carefully. He wasn't sure he was ready to accept that thirty-six years should be sufficient time for him to finally forgive his father's sins.

He tilted the floating arm of his magnifying lamp closer and then flicked on the light. Underneath the concentrated lens, the ring looked no different larger than smaller. Except now, while alone, he could study it not as an expert, but as a son.

As an heir to the long and storied Murrieta legacy.

Old, battered and scratched, the gems grabbed the light and held it with fierce tenacity. The rare black opals sparkled with veins of electric green and turquoise against a backdrop of glossy jet. The rough-cut emerald, marred by what he now accepted to be a crude version of the letter Z, possessed the vibrant, enduring color of a stone mined long before anyone conceived of lab-created imitations. The back of the band had eroded to a smooth curve, but overall, the gold remained thick and sturdy, dulled only by age.

If this ring truly had survived over a century of daily wear, the condition was a marvel rather than a shame.

Alex scanned again through the documents Michael had presented to him—the ones Ramon had painstakingly gathered and hidden in the floor safe along with the ring. He hadn't wanted to read them, hadn't wanted to paw through pages from a past he'd never known belonged to him. But Michael hadn't given him a choice.

"What are these?" he'd asked his brother.

"Letters," Michael had answered calmly, as if the information he was about to impart to his brother wasn't utterly and completely remarkable, if not downright delusional. "Pages from journals. A few last wills and testaments. I think there's a note from a priest. Pop traced the lineage of the ring all the way back to its original source. To the first Murrieta who owned it."

Michael had then sifted through the papers and pulled out what looked like a Wanted poster.

Joaquin Murrieta.

"Why do I know that name?" Alex had asked.

Michael's smile had been small, but lit his eyes with a flash of something wicked that Alex never would have associated with a man who carried a badge along with a gun.

"Go to movies? Read books? Joaquin Murrieta was famous when he was alive, and then in the early nineteen hundreds when his story—under another name—was made into a silent film. Later there were serials, television shows, radio programs and countless short stories and novels. And not too long ago, a set of movies starring one of your countrymen."

Alex immediately made the connection. There weren't too many Spanish actors who'd made the leap into American cinema.

He'd turned to his brother, disbelieving.

Michael answered his unspoken question by tracing the Z on the inlaid box with his finger.

Alex had sat back in his chair, stunned. "You can't be serious."

"Ramon believed that if Joaquin hadn't won the ring from an infinitely more honorable Spanish nobleman, he would have spent the rest of his life as a bandit and a thug. Our father believed that the ring gave Joaquin something—a part of his soul that was missing. His sense of justice, to be precise. Unfortunately, Pop didn't realize what he'd been given when he found the ring in his own father's stuff after he'd been knifed in a fight. He was sixteen. He pawned the ring and didn't figure out what he'd done until much later, when he ran across documentation about the ring while in Spain. I think that may have been why he came back to the U.S. To find his family legacy. To reclaim the life he should have had. He came back and he found it. And it changed him."

Both then and now, Alex braced his hands on the edge of his desk. From the moment he'd first spoken to his brother on the phone, he'd found him levelheaded, reasonable and fair-minded. At the time, he'd been shocked that Ramon could have raised such an impressive son.

Now he realized that his brother had only been putting on an act. Obviously, he was *muy loco.*

"You want me to believe that Ramon turned his life around because of a ring?" he'd asked, incredulous.

Thankfully, Michael had shaken his head and rolled his

eyes, betraying the fact that he didn't believe the family legend any more than Alex.

"No, of course not. But he *believed* the ring changed his life. Pop wasn't a stupid man, Alex. He used his considerable research skills to hunt down this information about the ring's origins. He went all the way back to the man who'd commissioned the ring in the first place. According to this diary," he continued, pulling out a sealed plastic baggie containing a sheaf of paper, "Don Diego might have been bad at poker, but he had a strong sense of justice, an insatiable taste for adventure and—" he riffled the pages "—an irresistible talent with the *señoritas.* Once Joaquin had the ring, he possessed the same, when he hadn't had any of those traits before. It changed his life. He donned his black mask and raised his rapier to fight for the rights of the downtrodden and the abused. He romanced quite a few ladies and became the stuff of legend."

From this conversation, which had ended when Alex told Michael he'd heard enough and would discuss the matter with him later—preferably after Michael had regained his senses—Alex had come to three important conclusions.

First, the paperwork made it impossible for him to have any real doubts that he was indeed descended from Joaquin Murrieta, the infamous California bandit upon whom countless stories had been based.

Second, the father he'd heretofore believed to be conscienceless and cruel had actually abandoned his first family to pursue what had been no more than a legend.

And third, the fantasy had turned Ramon around.

He ran a cautious finger over the emerald, which he'd balanced atop the prongs inside the open box. Had the power of suggestion been powerful enough to save more than one Murrieta man from a wasted life?

As Michael had surmised, Alex needed no assistance from the bauble when it came to his sense of right and wrong. His strong moral core remained the roadmap for his life's straight and narrow course. And when it came to seduction—before his current dilemma of how to seduce Lucienne without putting their business relationship at risk—he'd had no trouble, either.

But even Alex had to admit that his sense of adventure was severely lacking. Unlike Michael, who risked his life pursuing criminals, Alex preferred to concentrate on his business and family responsibilities. He got his thrills, such as they were, from making a profitable sale or beating out a competitor for the right to market a fine collection of art.

But now that he'd traveled halfway across the earth to a city known for its history, beauty and excitement, what had he done? Gone out? Explored? Tasted the local food and wines and indulged in the world-famous nightlife? No, he'd sequestered himself inside the auction house to work until he could hardly see and then returned to his hotel for a solitary dinner and worse, solitary sleep…until he started all over again the next day.

What if the ring changed this? What if the gold, opals and emerald that had somehow altered the ne'er-do-well course of his father's life sparked something more in Alex as well? Something bold. Fearless. Daring.

By nature, Alex was suspicious. By training, he was a skeptic. While not exactly a man of science, he did have a strict policy about never appraising anything he had not held in his hands. Even beneath thin gloves, he could experience the textures of porcelain and learn when and where it had been crafted. He could scent the age of certain leathers and distinguish the lead content in crystal by the musical clink of his thumbnail against the rim.

So why didn't he just slip on Ramon's ring and see if the legend was true?

"Alejandro?"

Lucienne's voice rolled over him like the hands of a dozen masseurs. Instantly, his need for adventure gave way to a stronger desire. He scooped the ring into his pocket, closed the box and turned to the door.

"Yes?"

Her eyes darted to her watch, then to his desk and the beaten-down box in the center.

"Are we still meeting?"

"Of course," he said, standing.

She sidled into the room, her inner ear again tuned to some sensual music that he desperately wished he could hear. No matter her destination, Lucienne moved like a dancer. Her steps were graceful and minimal, and yet elicited a potent emotional effect—at least from him. The minute she drew near, her perfume—floral at the heart but with a top note of tart green apple—teased his senses. Only when she drifted just out of his reach again did he pick up on the warm base fragrances of vanilla and amber—spicy aromas that would linger long after she'd left.

Once in front of his desk, she gestured toward the box.

"May I?" she asked.

He hesitated, then nodded his consent. What did he care if she touched it? The thing wasn't his. He had nothing to hide.

Except the ring in his pocket.

She pulled on a pair of thin cotton gloves. He nearly told her not to bother, but why open the floor to unwanted questions?

"Beautiful construction," she said, her sensual intonation transforming every syllable into a song. "Spanish mahogany. Ivory and mother-of-pearl inlay, chipped here on the corner and oh!" She winced, and then turned the box to show him a large gouge in the other side. "That's unsightly."

Like the man who'd owned it last, the box was anything but pristine. But Alex said nothing, wanting her professional opinion. Not because he intended to sell the piece, but because he'd come to appreciate the unsurpassed depth of her knowledge—not to mention the slight lilt in her voice that reminded him of home.

"The pattern suggests late eighteenth or early nineteenth century," she went on.

She flipped the box over and examined the bottom. A frown curved her luscious mouth as she scanned the unmarked wood.

Her fingers hovered on the latch. "Do you mind if I peek inside?" she asked.

"Not at all," he replied.

She popped the brass clasp. Finding the container empty, she took a sniff.

"Cedar." She ran her protected fingers over the torn and frayed red lining. "And silk."

She leaned forward so that the box fell under the light of his desk lamp, though he hardly noticed thanks to the golden glow cast over her impressive décolletage.

Talk about priceless treasures.

She cut short his fantasy of buoying her breasts in his hands with an excited "Here!"

She folded back a corner of the lining to reveal a tiny stamp burned into the wood. "I'm not familiar with the maker, but by the uneven quality of the impression, it's hand-burned. From the size, I'd guess this was meant to hold jewelry, likely a single piece of great value to the owner. And although the box is in questionable condition, we might be able to fetch two hundred and fifty to five hundred dollars for it, based on the age and quality of the inlay. Bonus if the lock works."

With care, she flipped the top closed, then stabbed him with her dark, alluring gaze. "Was there anything inside?"

From his pocket, the ring seemed to pulse and vibrate. Alex fought the urge to slip his hand inside, and instead scooted closer to his desk.

"Two hundred and fifty to five hundred dollars and questionable condition is hardly worth our time," he concluded.

She set the box back down. "The entire collection is rather more impressive than this piece. In most cases, your father had exquisite, if somewhat eclectic taste."

Alex frowned, sparing a quick glare at his father's portrait. "Yes, we'll chalk this up to eclectic and return it to Michael at the first opportunity. Right now, I'd like to continue the conversation we were having earlier."

"Reviewing my report?" She slid into the chair so that he became instantly jealous of the plush velvet cushion. "I hope the estimation is higher than you anticipated."

Alex placed Lucienne's report atop the documents verifying the ring's history. "Your appraisals are precise and comprehensive. Your work has been impeccable and I cannot thank you enough for your unfailing dedication in preparing this collection for sale."

Lucienne sat forward and Alex spied a flash of temper behind her inky dark eyes—a flame of the precise color and temperature he'd been counting on.

"You sound like you're about to fire me," she said.

He so appreciated a woman who could cut to the chase. "That's because I am."

LUCY NEARLY CHOKED. This could not be happening. She opened her mouth to tell Alejandro Aguilar precisely what she thought of his decision when she realized that while Lucy Burnett might give a man a piece of her mind for making such a capricious announcement, Lucienne Bonet would not.

So instead, she narrowed her gaze and forced herself to relax into her chair. To stem the tide of adrenaline surging through her system, she concentrated on tugging off her cotton gloves. One finger at a time.

"You're sure this is the best decision?" she asked coolly.

He leaned forward, his hands tented in front of him.

"You don't sound upset," he said.

She chanced a saucy grin. "Will hysterics change your mind?"

He chuckled. "Are you capable of hysterics?"

She tossed the gloves aside, determined to appear calm even though her heart was slamming against her chest so hard, she was amazed he couldn't hear the beat. Up until his grand announcement, she'd thought she had at least another week to locate Ramon's ring—possibly two. Alejandro had contracted her not only to prepare for the auction, but also to see each and every sale through to completion. Since he'd dismissed Ramon's former staff, she'd assumed he meant to rely entirely on her.

Apparently not.

"I prefer to leave grand dramatics to women with more flair for it," she replied. "But we will both be better served if you tell me precisely what I've done to deserve this unexpected shortening of my contract."

Yeah, this was good. Stay calm. Make him explain. If he laid out his reasons, she could counter them. He'd at least have to dig deeper to justify his decision. She wasn't sure if she could change his mind, but she wouldn't know until she tried.

Unless Michael had recognized her and outed her to Alejandro?

That would certainly result in a quick and unceremonious canning.

But if that were the case, wouldn't Alejandro have confronted her with Michael by his side to provide testimony—or worse, proof—of her relationship to their jailbird brother?

Instead, he was looking at her as if she were a particularly juicy steak.

Surrendering to her deepest instincts, she crossed her legs, aware of how the move made her slim skirt ride up high on her thighs. With the desk between them, she wasn't entirely sure how much he could see...and then, his shoulders tensed.

Apparently, he could see enough.

"It's nothing you've done," he said, his voice a bit strangled. He stood, and then, almost as a second thought, picked up a stack of documents bound in a leather folder and gripped it tightly in his hands.

She slowly slid her hand down her leg and pretended to pick a speck of lint off her stockings.

When he finally dragged his gaze back up to her face, the look in his eyes was nothing short of incendiary.

God, she had made it much too hot in here.

He turned toward the bookshelf and she breathed a silent sigh of relief. She might not have come here to seduce him, but if Daniel's circumstances weren't so dire, she might have attempted just that. Impressively tall, lean and imposing, Alejandro Aguilar was the stuff of fantasies. He kept his dark hair styled close to his skull, but she knew that one run through with her fingers would set those dark curls free. His regal posture invoked images of a matador, and though his suit pants were tailored for loose elegance, she could see that his muscles were lean and powerful. Especially around the backside.

Before he turned around, she spared his father's portrait another comparative glance. She'd met Ramon once. His engaging, dark good looks were striking, but he didn't hold a candle to his firstborn son.

After Alejandro shelved the papers, he crossed to the front of his desk. She scooted her legs slightly to the left to avoid touching him, though judging by the heated simmer in his gaze, touching him might have been a cunning move.

From the first moment she'd sauntered into his office with a doctored résumé clutched between her quivering fingers, she'd sensed his interest in her even as she'd covered up her own. Until now, her seductive moves had only been a means to distract and manipulate him. He was Daniel's brother—a brother Daniel hated on principle. Danny only tolerated Michael because it didn't hurt for a thief like him to have an FBI agent in the family on the off chance he was ever arrested for a federal offense.

But the more time Lucy spent with Alejandro, the harder he was to resist. He appreciated her knowledge and hard work. Despite his habit of eyeing her bottom when he thought she wasn't looking, when he spoke to her, he looked her in the eyes—deeply and meaningfully. He didn't laugh easily, but when he did, the humor burbled from deep in his soul. He had impeccable manners and exquisite taste in everything from clothes to art to handcrafted weaponry.

And on top of all that, he was about a fourteen on the ten-point hotness scale.

But because of Daniel, she had to repress her own needs and focus on the task at hand. Alejandro didn't know her. He didn't know that she'd grown up with a mother who replaced her daughter on a yearly basis with younger, cuter foster-care models and a father so wrapped up in fundraising and curating for his museums that he never noticed his child had memorized the papers he'd written on the preservation of ancient Mesopotamian art in the Middle East or the secret trade of banned Medieval weapons during the early twentieth century. Alejandro might appreciate the depth of her knowledge, but he had no idea where she'd gotten it from—or why.

For Danny, she'd invented Lucienne Bonet—a woman she had nothing in common with beyond her extensive knowledge of antiquities. For Alejandro, she'd given Lucienne impeccable taste and impressive credentials. For him, she had also lengthened her hair with extensions and dyed it a sable color, and wore contact lenses that hid her mossy-green eyes behind discs of deep chocolate brown. She'd studied everything she could find about Alejandro's personal life before choosing her wardrobe, from the designer blouses to her spiky heels.

The transformation hadn't been easy to create or maintain. But for Danny, what choice did she have?

For her protection, Danny hadn't shared the exact details of the trouble he was in. She didn't know who was after him or why. But since he wasn't one to ever admit he had a problem that he couldn't handle on his own, the fact that he'd asked for her help meant that whatever hot water he was in was scalding.

Daniel had made some sort of deal that exchanged Ramon's ring for his continued good health while in jail. If Lucy could find the ring, they both might be free to finally move on.

If Alejandro fired her, she'd be out of options. She thought about coming clean to him, telling him about his second half brother in an appeal to his strong sense of family, but she dismissed the thought. Daniel had forbidden it, and Lucy knew Alejandro well enough to realize he wouldn't be sympathetic to his black-sheep brother's predicament. The man wore his lofty moral standards like a shield.

And despite her own questionable code of ethics, she found this infinitely fascinating.

"So," she challenged, flicking her gaze up to his. "Why don't you tell me more about what I haven't done to deserve dismissal? I've worked incredibly hard to prepare this collection for auction. I think I deserve the privilege of seeing it through to the end."

"Oh, you deserve that," he assured her, easing his backside against the front of the desk in a casual pose that belied everything she knew about him. Or thought she knew. "And so much more."

His stare took a leisurely stroll from the depth of her eyes to the exposed curves of her breasts and then down to her legs, encased in silk stockings that had cost her a fortune, but at the moment seemed worth every penny.

"Like?" she asked.

He cleared his throat, his gaze locked on her while he fished a crisp linen envelope out of the breast pocket of his tailored jacket. "Why don't we start with this?"

Half intrigued and half terrified that he somehow had proof she was really Lucy Burnett, she held out her hand. Maybe he had documentation about her ties to Daniel? Clippings about his recent arrest?

She flicked her fingers beneath the flap, her gaze trained on Alejandro, who gave nothing away. She slipped two sheets of paper out and scanned each one with confusion.

The first was a glowing letter of recommendation. The second, a certified check.

A check with a lot of zeroes.

Not enough zeroes to get Daniel out of trouble, but maybe enough to buy his safety until she found Ramon's ring.

"What is this?" she asked.

"Your commission. Or at least, an estimate based on your projections for the auction. Should we take in more, I'll make sure you get the adjusted amount."

"And if you make less?"

He shrugged nonchalantly, then braced his hands on the arms of her chair so that his cologne, a warm musk with a hint of tobacco and leather, sizzled through his crisp white shirt. "Our business always includes a certain amount of risk. It will be worth it if it means I'll have more time with you."

She tucked the check and the letter back into the envelope, trying to hide how her hands shook. "I thought you were firing me."

His dark irises simmered and his tongue slid slowly across his bottom lip. "Oh, I am. But only because I have a very strict policy against seducing my employees."

Once again, her heartbeat hammered within her chest, hampering her ability to breathe without gulping in air. Or worse, panting.

He grinned. "I've surprised you."

She opened her mouth to inhale, but the added awareness of his intoxicating scent only knocked her further into sensory overload.

When he moved even closer, she drew back and said, "No."

It was a quiet no. Barely audible. And yet, Alejandro had instantly complied.

He arched a brow, but moved no more than an inch in retreat. "Or perhaps you've surprised me."

She flicked her thumbnail on the corner of the envelope.

The clicking noise kept pace with her stuttering pulse. He was so close. A single breath separated his lips from hers. Until he'd breached the invisible boundary of her personal space, she hadn't realized just how long it had been since she'd kissed a man—any man, much less one she barely knew and who possessed the scruples to resist toying with an employee.

An employee whose ultimate goal was to rip him off.

She had to reach deep within her Lucienne persona for an adequate reply. "You didn't expect me to collapse instantly into your arms, did you?"

His eyes widened with even more surprise. "I believed our attraction to be mutual."

She smiled, glad when he backed up a bit, giving her room to inhale deeply. "Who says it isn't?"

"You're not exactly jumping at the chance to—"

"Fall into bed with you?"

The corner of his mouth quirked into a reluctant grin. "Even I'm not that presumptuous."

She quirked an eyebrow. "Then what else did you have in mind?"

"This is San Francisco," he replied, his voice a warm drizzle of rich, dark chocolate, "a bastion of fine dining and entertainment. Perhaps we could start with dinner or a concert. Maybe a stroll on the wharf. I haven't seen much beyond the walls of this auction house or the lobby of my hotel, but I'd like to. With you."

Again, his gaze swept over her with such potent scrutiny, she knew that what he truly wished to see more of was her body, preferably naked and supine beneath his. Instantaneously, her nipples pebbled and chafed against the transparent lace of her bra. Sweet pressure pulsed between her legs. He was interested in her—and vice versa.

Not because of Daniel.

Not because of the ring.

Because he was hot—and she was horny.

And yet, she had to continue to play her part.

"And you thought you should pay me for my time?" she asked, waving the envelope.

His dazzling smile against his dark skin nearly knocked her senseless. When he added a chuckle, she thought her insides might melt.

"You know that wasn't my intention," he said.

"You just wanted our relationship free and clear of business entanglements."

"If you hadn't been so perfectly qualified for this job, I might not have hired you in the first place just so I could have proceeded straight to a seduction. Instead, with a wealth of self-control and sacrifice, I put my own needs aside. Now, I have the collection expertly catalogued and you have your generous commission. On a professional level, we've both won. Where we go from here will be purely personal."

Bracing her hands on the arms of the chair, she stood. He gave no quarter, so that once she balanced on her spiked heels, they were nearly body to body. She couldn't speak for him, but she was primed for a hell of a lot more than a romantic meal in some candlelit bistro or a stroll through the Japanese Gardens at Golden Gate Park.

Glancing down, she saw how perfectly they'd fit if she took that final step and destroyed the last few empty inches between them. His hands were slung into his pockets, but with the right signal from her, she knew he'd grasp her hips, or even better, her ass. And if he tugged her against him, her breasts would nestle just underneath his impressive pecs. He'd definitely have to dip his head to press his lips to hers, but if not, she had perfect access to the spot on his throat that bobbed when he swallowed.

"How personal?" she asked.

His quick intake of breath sucked the air out of her lungs. "Let me show you."

4

"So did you tell him about Danny?"

Michael groaned. He hadn't even buckled the seatbelt of their government-issue sedan and already Ruby had cut to the chase. This was why he was glad to be on *her* side during interrogations.

"He patted me on the back on the way out, remember?"

"Right," she said, nodding sagely. "I expect that if he'd just found out he had a second brother he didn't know about, he would have kicked your ass out the door."

"Only because said brother is incarcerated with no bond, awaiting trial on grand theft and, if the security guard dies, second-degree murder. Alejandro's hardly ready to deal with me, much less Daniel. Hell, I'm not ready to deal with Daniel. Not that I have any choice."

Ruby flipped down the sun shield on the passenger side and looked in the vanity mirror. She seemed uncharacteristically interested in her earlobes.

"Leave it to Danny Boy to keep your life interesting," she said.

"*Interesting* is not the word I'd pick."

Michael shoved the key into the ignition. He'd only

told Alex half the story about the DNA discovered at the art theft crime scene—and clearly, telling him about the ring had distracted him from wondering whose blood had been on the frame if it hadn't belonged to either Alex or his father.

It had belonged to a third son—Daniel. One Ramon had tried to contact as soon as he'd learned of his existence. One who'd denied all of his father's overtures for reconciliation. The Bureau had dragged Danny in for interrogation, but he'd come up with a brilliant explanation that both explained his blood at the crime scene and provided him with an ironclad alibi. And when the painting was mysteriously returned to the original owners, the whole matter had been dropped and Michael's career had suffered only a momentary glitch in his rise to Special Agent.

But revealing Danny's existence to Alex wouldn't go so smoothly. Alex prided himself on being a good, upstanding, well-respected man who would never be involved in theft of any kind. It was hard enough for him to deal with the aftermath of his father's abandonment. Michael wasn't ready to heap on the baggage of another brother.

"He's going to find out about Danny sooner or later," Ruby insisted.

Instinctively, Michael scanned the street. The hill sloped up high just three doors down, so the view was only clear to the south. This district of the city, originally residential but zoned for business use over three decades ago, housed mostly art galleries, cozy restaurants, an occult shop, bric-a-brac boutiques and El Dorado auctions. With a cable car stop just a few blocks over, shoppers strolled down the street with glossy bags and disposable coffee cups. No one seemed to be in a hurry. No one looked out of place.

So why were his instincts on high alert?

"Later works for me just fine," Michael said, taking

his time as he drove down the street. He hadn't hung out in this neighborhood much since he was a kid. Would he even notice if someone or something didn't belong?

"Don't you think he's going to be pissed off that you took this long to tell him?"

"After what he's already learned about Ramon, if I tell him we have another brother who's currently awaiting a possible murder charge if that guard dies, Alex will go to Madrid before he sells so much as a toe ring."

"You don't care about the money," Ruby challenged.

"No, but my mother needs a nest egg. And if that serial kidnapping case goes in the direction I think it will, I'm not going to have time to handle the liquidation. And when he does leave, I'd like it to be on good terms."

"Speaking of rings," Ruby said, glancing again in the mirror. "That assistant of his seemed awfully interested in the emerald and opal your father used to wear."

Michael pulled up a little short at the stop sign.

"The appraisal expert?"

"Yeah, her."

"What was her name?"

"I didn't check her ID," Ruby said, slapping the sun shield back into place.

"No, but you asked her name."

"Lucienne," Ruby said in an exaggerated French accent. "Lucienne Bonet."

"She's from Paris?"

"New Orleans, or so she said."

"You don't believe her?"

Ruby shrugged. This was not a good sign. Of all the people he worked with in the San Francisco field office, Ruby was the best judge of character. She could look at a roomful of people and pick the liars and crooks out with hardly a second glance. Why she hadn't made it to the elite

Behavioral Analysis Unit was totally beyond him—except that she preferred northern California to Quantico, Virginia, and she valued having an actual life over moving up in her career.

"She might have been in New Orleans at one time or another, but I don't know if she was actually born there. There's something off in her accent."

"I never got a good look at her," Michael said, his brain only half engaged in driving while he tried to conjure a picture of his brother's assistant with any detail. He'd come to the auction house today with a mission to convince Alex to abide by their father's last request and wear the legendary ring. He hadn't given the assistant a second thought.

Until now.

"You think I should check her out?" he asked Ruby.

"All I said was that she was interested in your father's ring."

"And you don't think that's a coincidence?"

He hadn't told Ruby everything about the ring's legend, but he had confided about his father's dying wish that Alejandro be the next Murrieta to possess the family heirloom.

"She just asked if the ring was real or part of the mural."

"You don't think that's a strange question?"

Again, Ruby shrugged. "I think she just wanted to know more about your brother, to be honest. She definitely has the hots for him. I mean, who wouldn't?"

At this, Michael relaxed. This woman, Lucienne, had been working with his brother for weeks. Alex would not have left her to care for so many valuables if he hadn't done thorough checks into her qualifications and background. If she was interested in his brother romantically, then the guy had hit the jackpot. Michael hadn't seen much of her from the front—but from behind, she was quite the stunner.

"The Murrieta men have that effect on women," he said confidently.

Ruby snorted.

"What? We do," he said, thinking about the legend. There was something about a man in a mask—even a figurative one—that women found incredibly attractive.

"How the hell would you know?" Ruby asked. "When's the last time you went on a date?"

Michael opened his mouth to answer, but his brain stalled. It couldn't have been too long ago. He had been buried under with a cross-state custody kidnapping case, and before that, the money-laundering task force with members of the Secret Service. Now he was consulting on what appeared to be a serial kidnapping case that might have ties to the very legend he'd just discussed with his brother. In the midst of all of that, he'd buried the father he loved and tried to be a comfort to his mother. It had been a long time since he'd had the opportunity, energy or interest to pursue a social life.

Maybe too long.

"It's none of your business," he said.

She snorted again. "That's what I thought. Well, at least one Murrieta man has a shot at getting lucky, because if it's up to you or Daniel to live up to the family name, you guys are in trouble."

WHEN LUCIENNE LIFTED her fathomless eyes to his, Alex's control broke. He shrugged a hand out of his pocket, crooked a finger beneath her chin and touched his lips to hers. Instantly, he was struck by the twin sensations of satin over velvet—his smooth and cool to her warm and plush. A tiny moan from deep in the back of her throat goaded him to tease the edges of her mouth with his tongue and without hesitation, she responded. The full depth of the kiss lit him on fire.

He wanted to touch her—feel her—everywhere, but he restrained the impulse by clenching his hands inside his pockets, vaguely aware of a hardness there that didn't belong.

The ring.

He pulled back.

She gasped, her eyes wide and her mouth pale where her lipstick had transferred from her mouth to his.

"Lucienne, I—"

His words were cut short by a crash from the back of the auction house, followed by a piercing wail.

The security alarm.

Alex tugged her behind him. "Dial the police."

He dashed toward the door to the gallery, but a sharp crack and splinter of the doorframe stopped him short.

"Gun!" Lucienne screamed, and before he could react, she shoved him out of the line of fire and slammed the door shut, twisting the lock.

In a heartbeat, Alex regained his ability to think. At home in Madrid, the galleries, vaults and offices were protected by double-thick doors lined with steel and multiple computerized locks. Security guards stood sentry at entrances and exits, and took random sweeps through the premises at all times of the day and night.

Ramon took fewer safeguards. El Dorado had automatically locking doors at every entrance, a buzz-in system for entry, a monitored alarm and cameras, but no live security unless an auction was in progress.

And no challenging locks. One bullet to the deadbolt of the office door and he and Lucienne would be easy prey for whoever had staged such a bold daylight invasion.

The phone rang. Lucienne grabbed the receiver. From

the gallery, they heard the bangs and smashes of thieves at work.

"The intruders are armed. Send the police. Now!" Lucienne shouted into the phone.

Only Alex knew that *now* wouldn't be soon enough. He shoved a heavy credenza in front of the door, and then grunted as he stacked two lion statues cast in bronze on top.

This barrier might buy them a few more seconds—but to do what?

Ramon's office had no windows. No other doors. They had no means of escape.

Lucienne dashed to his side, her hands clutching his sleeve. "The police are on the way. And everything of value is out there," she reasoned. "They won't come in here."

"We don't know what they want or what they came here looking for," he countered. "And with the door shut, they don't know what we have in here."

"Then we need to leave."

Alex scanned the room for anything he could use as a weapon. Why, suddenly, was every sword, dagger, mace or pistol out in the main gallery with the intruders?

"There doesn't seem to be an emergency exit."

"Yes, there is."

She grabbed his wrist and pulled him to the far corner of the room.

"Help me," she said, pushing on a tall bookcase overflowing with rare first editions of the works of Edgar Allan Poe, Mary Shelley and Bram Stoker.

Alex had no idea what she meant to accomplish, but the chaos from the other room now included raised and angry voices. With one additional shove from him, the bookshelf slid a few inches forward—it weighed much more than it looked. Lucienne pounded on a loose block in the exposed brick behind it, and with a groan and a scrape, the wall opened.

"What the—?"

Lucienne squeezed into the confined space, grabbed him by the sleeve and tugged him beside her.

Once they were tucked inside, she reached up, yanked down on an old, rusty latch and the wall shifted into place behind them.

They were safe, but trapped.

"What is this?"

"Old-time version of a panic room, I think," she answered.

Ribbons of daylight streamed down from what looked like a grate high in the ceiling. At least they had fresh air. In fact, the cobwebbed, dusty closet-size space was cooler than his office had been.

And yet, with Lucienne pressed completely against him, he felt every bit as hot.

"How did you know this was here?" he asked, trying not to fully register how her belly was flush with his pelvis. So soft. So pliant. So insanely luscious. Like her lips. And her breasts, squashed upward against his chest.

"I found it when I was looking through the bookshelves," she explained.

"How exactly does one find a secret passage?"

Though muffled by the wall, they both jumped when gunfire blasted through the door from the gallery to the office. Obviously, the thieves weren't content to leave with the spoils from the outer room, which included several hundred thousand dollars' worth of jewels that Lucienne had pulled out to photograph for the catalogue. The rest were in the main vault, secure and locked in the basement. With the alarm still screaming and the police alerted, the invaders had little chance of breaching that barrier. Not without explosives, which would likely take down the whole house—Lucienne and Alex along with it.

Lucienne murmured something, but with the bass-drum beat of his heart and the echoes of the wailing alarm, he couldn't hear her.

"Perdóneme?"

"What are they looking for?" she whispered.

"Us?"

"Why?" she asked. "You're not in any kind of trouble, are you?"

He couldn't contain his laughter, though he did manage to keep his volume down. "I'm afraid it's more likely you're the one in trouble."

If there had been space for her to jump away from him, he was certain she would have. As it was, she stiffened… and unfortunately for her, the effect was not as icy as she might have imagined. In fact, the feel of her body going rigid against his only acted like a flame to very dry kindling.

"Why would you say that?" she asked, her voice quavering.

She shook all over. He supposed he should be terrified, too, but as he fisted one hand in his pocket and concentrated all his self-resistance on keeping the other one from caressing her backside, he realized he was completely cool. They were trapped, but safe. Even with the bookshelf out of place, he doubted the thieves would figure out precisely what brick to pound in order to open the secret door. For the next few minutes at least, he had her captured up against him, his body growing more and more accustomed to hers, the danger outside as fine a reason as any to revel in their forced and delicious proximity.

"Look at all the trouble you've caused me. Trying not

to stare too boldly when you were bent over a particularly fascinating necklace. Resisting the urge to touch you when your fingers were just inches from mine while we pored over authentication documents or bills of sale. Dreaming about having your body just like this—pressed hard and tight against mine. Though perhaps in less tense circumstances."

This elicited a sweet, yet incendiary smile.

From what seemed like a distance more miles than inches, Alex heard the thieves retreat from the office. The whine and wail of sirens taunted the edges of his awareness. But the only sound his brain acknowledged was Lucienne's satisfied moan when he wrapped his hands around her bottom and then kissed her with the full crush of his pent-up desire.

She tasted like mint and coffee. Her tongue tangled with his, skimming across his teeth and igniting nerve endings usually reserved only for the richest port wines. He reached down with both hands and bunched the tight hem of her skirt up her thighs so he could lift her against the wall.

Free from the constraints of her skirt, she opened her thighs and the fit of his body to hers sparked an explosion of sensations that launched them into a world where only they existed. The darkness, the tight quarters and Lucienne's hot and willing body had him dizzy with need. When she raked her hands through his hair and guided his face back to hers, he knew he had to have her. Not here. Not now.

But somewhere.

And soon.

5

SHORTLY AFTER HER fourteenth birthday, Lucy had started to run with a dangerous crowd. She'd gone on joyrides, played lookout for felonious friends and dallied with boys who even in their youth were too far gone for reformation.

And yet, none of these things seemed nearly as dangerous as kissing Alejandro Aguilar.

Pushing aside the myriad of secrets she kept from him—her true identity and purpose in coming to work for him—the man invaded her system like a drug. Their first kiss had rocked her to her core. This second round, even amid the passageway's collected grime and dirt and the possibility of harm from the assailants on the other side of the wall, nearly knocked her off her feet.

Or, more accurately, spirited her into a state of complete and utter hunger.

In the split second before lust disengaged her brain, she'd registered the fact that they were relatively safe in here—free to burn their pent-up adrenaline with a kiss that melted her insides to hot, bubbling goo. The lock operated from the inside. The invaders could press every stone from today until next Tuesday and the passageway wouldn't open. She'd found similar hiding spots in two other sections of the building, though each had been much more spacious than this one.

Not that she was complaining.

Then suddenly, her pleasured moans echoed off the compressed walls. The sound of Alejandro suckling her neck just above her pulse point thundered in her ears.

The security alarm had stopped.

The sirens were silent.

They could still hear voices, but they rang with calm authority rather than desperation.

Alejandro set her down, panting.

"La policía está aquí," he whispered.

She understood enough Spanish to realize the cavalry had finally ridden to the rescue.

Just in time? Or too damned soon?

"If we come out too quickly, they might shoot first and ask questions later," she said. "I don't know about you, but I'd rather not die today."

"I agree," he said, his voice ragged and torn with what she recognized as hard-won control. "But we can't stay here too long."

"Why is that?" she asked.

She tugged her skirt down and did the best she could to straighten her clothes, a task complicated by the feel of his rigid cock against the curve of her belly. The pressure tantalized her with promises she couldn't afford for him to keep. She'd entertained her fair share of naughty fantasies about making love to Alejandro here at the auction house, but none had included a dark, dirty passage with very little room to move.

"A man can only contain himself so long. You've pushed me to the limits and all I've kissed are your lips. All I've touched is your sweet, round bottom. I can't help but wonder what magic will happen when I am inside you."

The simmering thrum of her heartbeat accelerated and a tiny drop of moisture kissed the inside of her thigh. It was one thing for a man to talk dirty at a wholly inopportune moment. It was something else entirely when he did it with a thick Castilian accent.

"We barely escaped with our lives and you're thinking about sex?"

"You're thinking about something else?"

He brushed his mouth over hers, but denied her another kiss, intensifying the yearning ricocheting through her system.

"Not at the moment, no," she confessed.

His smile lit his eyes like fireworks. Hot, explosive, sky-illuminating fireworks.

But before she knew it, he'd reached above her head, disengaged the lock and latch until the hidden door creaked open and light poured into the dark crawl space, blinding them both.

The police acted much as Lucy expected. With guns drawn, they ordered Alejandro and Lucy out into the office with their hands clearly visible. Yet, in minutes, Alex had clarified their identities and the tension melted away. Lucy was shuttled to a chair with Alejandro's jacket draped over her shoulders, where she was left alone to mull over a different kind of tension—the kind she'd shared with Alejandro.

One that, until now, she hadn't known existed.

She'd had a fair amount of sex during her adulthood— even a couple of backseat explorations while still in her teens. She'd burned off her urges with a football player, a law school student, the guy she'd met when he came over to hook up her surround-sound and a neighbor in her condo building who worked as a professor at a small, local college. She'd even gone on a few dates with men she'd met at the market, while having coffee in the Embarcadero, or at the library doing research on some rare and priceless antiquity that Daniel had decided to steal and that she'd had to figure out how much to charge for on the black market.

Each and every one of her liaisons had started with a wild wave of lust. She'd always believed lust was just as good an emotion as any other for sparking a short-term affair. In fact, it was preferable. A hell of a lot better than anger or fear. Miles above sympathy or compassion.

Love hadn't even been in the running.

Love meant commitment. Complications. Heartbreak.

And her reliance on lust hadn't changed with Alejandro. A powerful, driving need had drawn them together even before they'd hidden in the secret passage and it would be a powerful, driving need that would fulfill the forbidden fantasies Lucy had entertained since she'd first met him. But with their desires so intertwined by the ring, Daniel, the auction, and now an attempted armed robbery, lust had no choice but to burn hot and die quickly.

But what a death it would be.

"Cómo estás, querida?"

"Me?" She looked up at Alejandro, who was flanked by a man in an off-the-rack suit. She assumed he was a police inspector. "Just shaken up, but I'll be fine. Do you need me yet? To help determine what's missing?"

Alejandro laid a protective hand on her shoulder. "Not yet. The police want to ask you a few questions first."

"Didn't you tell them what happened?"

Acid churned in her stomach—a bitter, corrosive blend of antagonism and hatred for law enforcement that had aged inside her belly since her father's arrest. Flashes of men in uniform dragging him away from the dinner table.

Her mother's screams. The flood of tears she'd shed for years and years, too young to understand that the cops weren't the bad guys, even if they had taken her father away.

"We'd like to hear it from you," the inspector explained. "Maybe you saw something or heard something that will lead us to the suspects."

"Have you checked the security cameras?" she countered. "They're placed at all the entrances and were fully functional when I came in this morning."

Since she'd meant to disable the system herself once she'd found the ring, Lucy had made it her business to know the complete workings of the security setup. Ramon hadn't installed the latest gadgets and wizardry, but his devices were solid and well-cared for—more than sufficient for day-to-day operations.

But what happened today wasn't normal. An armed attack? In broad daylight? Without cutting off the burglar alarms first?

Either these guys were desperate or they were amateurs. Either one meant danger.

"The police are reviewing the recordings," Alejandro replied, then turned to the detective and speared him with a look that was at once commanding and indisputable. "Make it quick, Inspector. I won't have Ms. Bonet subjected to more distress than she already has been."

The inspector inclined his head. "Of course."

Lucy stifled a tiny gasp. The cop had actually bowed to Alejandro.

Her lust spiked just enough to make her wriggle in her seat.

As promised, the police detective asked his questions quickly and efficiently. For once, the truth was on her side. Talking to law enforcement proved a lot easier when she wasn't trying to cover her or Danny's tracks. Only when the detective asked for her name did her heartbeat trip, but thanks to years of practice, her voice remained steady and certain.

"And you didn't see anyone?" the inspector asked, for the fifth time.

"No," she answered. "I slammed and locked the door and Señor Aguilar blocked it with the furniture. By the time the thieves made their way inside the office, we were already hiding in the secret passage."

"Lucky you found that," he said nonchalantly.

Lucy narrowed her gaze. Police inspectors asked no questions without an underlying purpose. Her instinct to insist that her job expectations had forced her to explore every nook and cranny of the auction house was hard to fight—but not impossible.

"Very lucky," she agreed.

After one more recounting of events, the detective left. She wandered into the gallery. Her chest ached at the destruction. Suits of armor lay defeated and disarmed on the polished wood floor. The remnants of a dozen different figurines and statuettes crunched under the feet of the crime scene technicians. The paintings that hadn't been tossed to the ground were hanging at skewed and uncertain angles. Her gaze then fell on the two trays of jewelry she'd taken out earlier to photograph. Everything was gone, even the opal and emerald earrings she'd shown to Special Agent Dawes.

"Did you call your brother?" she asked when Alejandro sidled up beside her, his hands shoved deep in his pockets and his mouth curved into a deep, intimidating frown.

"Not yet," he replied.

"Don't you think he might have some pull with the investigation?"

"The police seem to be taking this seriously without outside influence. This is Michael's legacy. His mother's financial future. I don't want to alarm him before we know precisely what is missing."

"Did they get the safe downstairs?"

"No," he replied. "But they tried."

Her brain whirred. It was an odd thing to be on the other side of a crime scene, but she might as well put some of her considerable knowledge to good use.

"Did they try a combination? Like maybe an old one we don't use anymore?"

With no live security guards on the premises and a cache of bitter former employees on the loose, Lucy had convinced Alejandro to change the vault and alarm codes. He might not have a lot of experience with thieves and lowlifes, but she did—and she wasn't about to let someone else beat her to the punch when she had the inside track.

His eyes narrowed. "I don't know. There are marks on the lock."

"What kind of marks?"

With the elevator occupied by crime scene investigators taking photographs and dusting for fingerprints, he gestured toward the stairwell that led downstairs. They reached the door, but had to wait for one of the detectives to clear them for entry.

As the safe had not been breached, the police had finished quickly with the area, though they asked Alejandro and Lucy to refrain from touching anything. So when Lucy leaned in to peer through the gray smudges of fingerprinting dust to examine the marks beside the small, wagon-wheel shaped locking mechanism, Alejandro cupped his hand on her shoulder to keep her from getting too close.

Even with his wool jacket still draped over her shoulder, the heat of his hand seared.

She glanced up at him. "I know what I'm doing," she said.

He countered with a wicked smile. "Perhaps, but when presented with an excuse to touch you, I couldn't very well allow it to pass."

"I hate men who make excuses," she said.

He slung his hands back into his pockets. "And I hate women who are insufferable teases, but we all have our crosses to bear."

"You're going to pay for that crack, Señor Aguilar."

"I do hope you're a woman of your word."

As Lucienne laughed, the warmth that spread through Alex's system was a magical combination of hot lust and sweet anticipation. Like a balm, her seductive chuckle lessened the guilt and self-recrimination that had racked him once he'd witnessed the full breadth of the thieves' destruction. On his watch, he'd lost part of his father's legacy—the part entrusted to him by a brother he hardly knew. But no matter his horror over the loss of necklaces, rings and baubles, he couldn't forget the crack and splinter of the bullet hitting the doorframe any more than he could erase the sensation of Lucienne's quaking body pressed hard and close against his in the hidden room.

But they were alive. They were together. And soon, they'd make good on the promises exchanged during hot, desperate kisses.

Alex stepped back, appreciating the curve of Lucienne's backside while she concentrated on the marks on the safe. She held up her hand to estimate the spacing of the scratches and nicks, then turned to face him, her sweet lips pursed in deep concentration.

"They tried to break the combination using an auto-dial device," she said, authority ringing in her voice.

"Qué?"

"It's a mechanism that safe-crackers use to break the combination of a target vault. They attach it to the computerized lock here." She indicated the area with her finger, though she didn't touch the steel. "It's usually a very model-specific device, meaning that the thief had to know what kind of safe Ramon owned in order to bring in the right apparatus. A generic auto-dial would take hours and this was clearly a smash-and-grab."

He'd known Lucienne was knowledgeable about a wide variety of periods in art and culture, but he'd never expected her to talk as if she'd recently graduated from the police academy.

"You know quite a bit about security," he said. Despite the dodgy backgrounds of most of Ramon's former employees, there had not been—to his knowledge—a single successful break-in while his father operated the business. If what Lucienne said was true, this might have been what the Americans called "an inside job."

"I've been in the auction business a long time," she said, turning quickly as if to examine the door again. "I expect you also know quite a bit about protecting your investments."

Alex watched her make her way down the corridor, touching nothing, but inspecting every inch of space between the stairwell and the storage rooms. God, he could spend an eternity watching the woman move. She had an otherworldly rhythm that entranced him, like starlight against a velvet black sky.

"My uncle is ex-military," he replied. "He handles all the security concerns for the House of Aguilar."

"Well, I expect you're about to take a crash course in the subject."

For some unexplainable reason, this thought made him

smile. "Maybe I should hire someone as a consultant. Not as an employee, per se, but more like a partner."

"A partner in crime?" she asked, chuckling at her own play of words.

"To a definition, *sí*," he said.

She arched a brow. "Have anyone in mind?"

"I believe you'd be the perfect woman for the job, if it gives you a reason to stay rather than run from this place, screaming for your life."

"I don't scream," she assured him.

He poked his tongue into his cheek to squelch a wholly inappropriate grin. "That remains to be seen, *querida*."

Despite his innuendo, she made quite the show out of shrugging with ennui even as she sauntered nearer to him and slid her hands up the front of his shirt. "I don't know. Thanks to that check you handed me earlier, I don't need the work."

He slipped his hands around her waist and tugged her close. Her perfume, enhanced by the heady scents of body heat and need, intoxicated him to the point of near-delirium.

"No, but a consulting position will give you a good reason to stay with me," he said.

"Do I need a *good* reason?"

"I want you," he whispered.

"That will do."

He might have surrendered again to the urge to kiss her, but a police inspector interrupted them with an embarrassed cough. They were needed upstairs to provide a rundown of precisely what was stolen.

Surprisingly, only the jewelry Lucienne had taken out for photographing was gone. It was a loss, to be sure, but fully insured. And thankfully—surprisingly—other valuables had been left behind.

"When can we start cleaning up?" Alex asked.

"Since there was a shooting involved, we need more time to process the crime scene," the inspector informed him. "We'll have units out here at least until morning. You're free to go. I will call you if we have any questions."

Alex provided his cell phone number, as well as Lucienne's. But when she went to retrieve her purse from her locked desk drawer, she realized that too was missing.

Someone had jimmied the lock and taken her personal items.

"They have my identification—my address, my keys," she said, her voice rising.

The inspector frowned. "Did anyone know that's where you kept your personal items?"

Lucienne shook her head. "I came on after Alejandro dismissed most of the staff. We've had a few clients stop by to view the collection. I suppose someone might have seen me put my purse in there. It's the logical place."

Alex asked the inspector for the list of dismissed employees that he'd already provided and added the last dates of their employment. "Only these people knew Lucienne. I suppose the warehouse staff might have known her as well."

"And any experts or clients I had in to evaluate the larger pieces," Lucienne added. Cooperating with the police wasn't her first instinct, but she didn't take kindly to having her stuff stolen or her life threatened.

"I have those names," the inspector said, holding up the sign-in sheet Alex had given him. "We'll check it out. But in the meantime, you shouldn't go home. It's not uncommon for thieves to hit secondary targets. I'll send uniforms by your place, but in the meantime, do you have anyone you can stay with until you've had time to change the locks?"

Alex met Lucienne's troubled gaze, then grinned. This wasn't exactly how he'd wanted to entice her to his hotel suite, but he wasn't the type to pass up a golden opportunity.

He slipped his hand around her waist. "It'll be my pleasure to look after her, Inspector."

And hers.

6

FOR A WOMAN who'd fantasized about having Alejandro Aguilar all to herself, Lucy was spending an inordinate amount of time trying to ditch him. Yes, she was freaked out about her stolen purse. She'd been careful to carry no incriminating information, but the thieves now had the keys to her apartment and her address. And while the contents of Lucienne Bonet's apartment included nothing of real value, with enough time and determination, they'd find evidence that proved she was not who she said she was.

And that could cost her everything.

"I should go by my place and pick up a few things," she said.

Alejandro shook his head, his attention focused on his smart phone. After they'd finished with the police, he'd called Michael. She'd waited patiently in the trashed gallery while he told his brother what had happened. With each word he spoke, his voice became harder. More clipped. Terse. He was angry, not at his brother, but at himself. She'd never seen a man take his responsibilities so personally.

Not that she knew many men who believed in responsibilities in the first place. Certainly not her father. Over the span of her childhood, he'd gone from being a respected museum curator to a criminal in the blink of her eye. And the only responsibility Danny ever took to heart was the promise he'd made to himself to steal as many pieces of art as he could without getting caught.

Though if he'd concentrated a bit more on the "without getting caught" part, she wouldn't be in this mess.

When Alejandro had ended his call and directed his driver to take them immediately to his hotel, she hadn't argued. The last thing she wanted to do was add to his troubles, which had gouged deep worry lines on either side of his otherwise delectable mouth. But the hairs on the back of her neck hadn't stopped pinching since she'd discovered that the smash-and-grab thieves had taken the time to break into her desk and steal her purse.

Too many things weren't right about this robbery. The brazen daytime attack. The guns. The missing items—a small cache of one-of-a-kind jewels and a Prada purse. The thieves had left valuable coins behind, along with two easily recognizable first edition books, the jeweled dagger and a jacket tagged as once belonging to Marlon Brando. Those were portable and easy to get rid of on the black market. Why were they left behind?

Were the invaders, like her, looking for something in particular? An item of jewelry, perhaps?

Maybe she was being paranoid. Or maybe someone was on to her con.

But who?

Had whoever was trying to leverage the ring from Daniel made a preemptive strike? Were they tired of waiting? And who could it be? Daniel was well liked in the cat burglar world, but thieves made a lot of enemies. The list of people who might want to thwart him was long and varied. If she were to figure out who might have nearly killed her and Alejandro in the break-in today, she'd have to talk to Danny...and that wasn't going to happen so long as his eldest brother had decided that her safety was his priority number one.

There was no way she could get to Danny now, anyway. Visiting hours at the jail were long over. And if the thieves broke into her apartment, they wouldn't find much. Yes, she'd stashed her real identification in an air vent, but she'd been careful not to have anything in her possession that connected her to Danny or her search for Ramon's ring. Very few people knew that she and Danny had grown up in the same household. Even the guards at the jail thought she was an ex-girlfriend.

She could only hope the robbers had just been after her credit cards, which she'd already cancelled. Yet, despite her precautions, she couldn't shake the suspicion that she'd forgotten something.

"Just let me pick up some clothes for tomorrow," she insisted. "We won't have to be there long. Five minutes, tops."

Alejandro did not look up from his text messaging. "Make a list of what you need and I'll have the hotel concierge take care of it."

The driver, who'd taken Alejandro's order to hurry with dead seriousness, drove over one of San Francisco's famous hills with a little more speed than was wise. When they reached the top, the bump caused Lucy to fly off the seat. She squealed in surprise and then fumed as Alejandro's lips tensed into a barely contained grin.

"This is ridiculous," she insisted. "I live only a few blocks from here."

"Unlike my chauffeur in Spain, this driver's job description does not include protecting us from bandits," he said calmly.

"Apparently, it doesn't include safe driving, either," she said, clutching a backseat handhold.

Alejandro chuckled and tucked his phone into his jacket. "Yes, well, he'll get us where we need to go, quickly, as I requested. I've had more than enough excitement for one day. I'd rather not confront either thieves or police at your apartment on account of fresh lingerie and a new dress. It's late and we're both exhausted. Whatever you need, I will provide."

She tried to ignore how his tone deepened, as if implying he'd give her more than clothing and toiletries. In fact, from the dark intensity of his gaze, he seemed to hint that to give her what she needed, she wouldn't require any clothes at all.

She crossed her arms over her chest, her mind spinning. Part of her wanted to surrender to those wicked possibilities, but the other part kept trying to figure out how to get back to her place and make sure she hadn't been found out as a liar and a con. She could wait until he was asleep, then sneak out and hail a taxi. Of course, she had no money. And while she'd already resolved to steal his father's ring if she ever found it, she had no desire to pick Alejandro's pocket for cab fare.

She considered calling Daniel's associates, but for all she knew, one of them could have been in on the robbery.

"You know, you're an incredibly bossy man for someone who isn't even my boss anymore," she groused, sounding entirely like a frustrated Lucy Burnett rather than calm and collected Lucienne Bonet. While she'd enjoyed slipping into the skin of someone with the kind of subtle sexuality men like Alex panted after, right now, she just wanted to cuss a blue streak.

"And you have a petulant quality that I find incredibly attractive," he said.

Suddenly, staying with Alejandro seemed nearly as risky as returning to her apartment.

For a split second, she wondered if he'd still want her if she tore out her extensions, removed her colored contact lenses, allowed her hair to fade back to her natural auburn and dropped her cultured accent. Would he still find her as intriguing? As desirable?

But where would that leave Danny?

Only as Lucienne Bonet did she have any chance of finding Ramon's ring. She had to keep up the ruse, if only for a little longer.

Despite her lies, the best place for her right now was with Alejandro. The police would contact him first if anything developed in the robbery. With him taking her under his protection, she'd have access to his hotel suite, where he might have stored the ring. Michael, the only other person who could possibly have Ramon's treasure, would stay in close contact, possibly opening up an opportunity for her to search his condo.

Until she could check in with Danny or come up with a new plan, she had no other recourse than to sit back, relax and enjoy Alejandro's protection.

And perhaps, much more.

Just as her brain began to open up to the possibilities, Alejandro's hand smoothed over her knee. She glanced up to find him staring at her, his eyes shadowed, but intense. He wasn't just looking at her—he was looking into her.

Or at least, attempting to.

"What?" she asked, rubbing her hand over her nose as if to remove a smudge. Now that she thought about it, she had no idea what she looked like since they'd taken sanctuary in the secret passage. For all she knew, she had spiderwebs in her hair.

"You are exhausted," he said.

She rolled her eyes, pretending his concern hadn't touched her. "You're a real sweet talker."

He proceeded to draw very tiny, tight circles with his finger on her skin, each spiraling a millimeter closer to the sensitive inner flesh of her thigh. "I would have preferred you rested. I had every intention of making love to you tonight."

God, the man was good. His worry was entirely self-centered and yet she appreciated his style. Alejandro Aguilar played no games; hid behind no pretenses. He stated what he wanted without the finesse of flowered words and honeyed promises, and still her insides liquefied.

And then there was that damned Spanish accent.

She blew a wayward strand of hair out of her face. "I suppose the dust and grime changed your mind?"

He scooted closer. Again, his driver took a dip with too much speed, and when she went airborne this time, Alejandro slid over to catch her on his lap.

He didn't give her a chance to squeal in surprise, but captured her mouth with his. The perfect thoroughness of his kiss blasted away all her thoughts about rings and thieves and secret identities. In her mind, nothing existed but desire. Need. Carnal cravings only he could sate.

By the time he broke away, she had her hands tangled in his hair and her knees parted, her center pulsing for his touch. But his hands never strayed any farther up than mid-thigh.

"When we make love," he whispered, "you will think of nothing but what I'm doing to your body. You'll feel only the pleasures I will invoke by touching you here." He slid his hand higher beneath her skirt, but stopped at an invisible barrier between his touch and her moist heat. "Or when I kiss you here."

He nuzzled her neck, brushing aside her hair with his nose and then sucking her pulse point until she nearly passed out with pleasure. The kiss was so simple, and yet so evocative. As he increased the gentle suction of his lips and tongue on her throat, she imagined other spots he might explore. Her breasts. Her nipples. Her belly button. Her sex. Instinctually, she shifted in his lap so that his fingertips met the lace of her panties.

The pressure was infinitesimal, but wonderful.

"Oh," she said.

He kissed a path to her ear, taking a second to curve his tongue around the inner shell even while his hand remained totally and frustratingly still.

"Do you want me to touch you?"

"Yes," she confessed.

"Oh, how I want to touch you," he replied. He teased his fingers along the edges of the lace and swept his lips across hers in a phantom kiss—enough for her to feel the heat, but insufficient to satisfy even the tiniest urge exploding inside her. "But if I feel your slick heat now, I won't be able to stop myself until I have you."

"Then have me," she begged.

Despite her request, he drew back. He blinked, clearing any shadow of need from his eyes even as his frown deepened. *"Lo siento, querida, pero no puedo,"* he said. "We're here."

THE SOUND OF THE ENGINE idling had alerted Alex that they'd arrived at the hotel. In a few seconds, the chauffeur would open the door and he had no desire to humiliate Lucienne by being caught *in flagrante delicto* in the main drive of the hotel.

After helping her straighten her clothes, he tucked a knuckle beneath her chin and lifted her eyes to meet his. "I will finish what we started soon, if that is what you desire."

The driver opened the door and Alex got out. He held out his hand to Lucienne, which she took, though her eyes never quite met his. Her sudden shyness intrigued him. He hadn't imagined that anything about Lucienne could pique his interests more, but he'd been mistaken. Even as he buttoned his jacket in an attempt to camouflage the hard evidence of his attraction, he inhaled the tangy scent of her perfume. The floral aftershocks sent his blood thrumming so loudly, he hardly understood when the concierge offered him a stack of documents sent from Spain and asked if there was anything else he could provide.

He invited Lucienne to give the concierge a list of items she would need for the next day. As he paced near the elevators in hopes that his erection would ease, he toyed with the idea of arranging for her to have a room of her own. If she asked, he'd provide it. It would be the honorable thing for him to do.

But he hoped she did not ask. He wanted her close. When he'd said that he intended to make love to her, it had not been a casual comment or seductive tactic. It had been the gut-wrenching truth.

Though Alex was known for his cool demeanor and calm control, he was not the kind of man who denied his emotions. Today alone, he'd felt lust, fear, anger and guilt—all in the span of a few hours. Of those, the only one he wanted to explore further was his need for Lucienne. But when she finally joined him by the elevator, the glaze of desire he'd seen in her eyes while in the car was now clouded by worry and exhaustion.

"They said they'd bring everything up to your room."

When she slid her hand in the crook of his arm, he released the pent-up breath he hadn't realized he'd been holding. "I'll order dinner while you take a shower."

"Am I that much of a wreck?"

"You're breathtaking. I just want an excuse to strip you naked."

She leaned slightly against his shoulder and laughed. Perhaps she thought he was joking, but he was not. Still, he'd let her set the pace. After the elevator doors shut behind them, he slid his keycard into the designated slot and pressed the button for his top floor suite.

When the doors opened onto a marbled foyer, she stepped out, took a few steps, then turned. "Wait, this is your room?"

He nodded.

"Wow." She wandered in a few more steps, stopping to inhale the sweet scent of the massive flower arrangement in the center of the entryway, this week featuring four dozen deep purple roses and clouds of stark white orchids edged with vibrant berries.

A shade of anxiety had been erased from her face. "You really know how to live."

He'd texted the hotel manager shortly after leaving the auction house, and the penthouse had been prepared for their arrival in ways he did not normally demand. The strum of soft Spanish guitars echoed against the candlelit walls. A fountain burbled in a corner. A plush cotton robe sized for her hung in his closet. Tomorrow, Lucienne might be able to return to her apartment. Tonight, he wanted her all to himself, engulfed in a seductive atmosphere.

He removed his jacket and folded it over his arm. "I know how to live in a hotel. My flat in Madrid isn't half as luxurious."

She tossed him a doubtful glance. "I don't believe you."

"The building I live in is four hundred years old. The ceilings are low, the hallways cramped and you don't even want to hear about the plumbing."

"But I expect it's filled with beautiful pieces of art."

"Just as this suite is, now that you're here."

She rolled her eyes in that particular way American women often did in the face of a grand compliment, but he caught the curve of her smile when she turned to explore the living room.

As he'd ordered, a fire crackled in the fireplace. His favorite brandy sat on the low table, along with two snifters. He laid his jacket over the back of the couch, and then gestured for her to join him.

"May I?" he asked, lifting the bottle of *Gran Duque de Alba Solera Gran Reserva.*

She looked at the bottle with yearning. "Oh, yes. But I think I should have that shower first."

"Of course," he said, setting the bottle down. "The bathroom is through here."

The suite was indeed spacious, with an open-air design and sleek, modern furnishings, but it had only one full bathroom. He walked her to the double doors leading to his bedroom and stopped, even though she continued inside.

After a few steps in, she turned. She was chewing her bottom lip with a keen anxiety he'd never seen in her before—not even when they were hiding from armed robbers.

"You don't want to join me?" she asked.

"Oh, I *want* to join you," he said. "But if I do, there's no telling how many hours will elapse until you get that brandy, and neither one of us will sleep for a long time."

She licked her lips and Alex felt his control slip a notch.

"Maybe I don't want to sleep," she said, her fingers artfully releasing the buttons of her blouse. She slipped the silky material off her shoulders, revealing a satiny bra that pushed her breasts up into the impressive curves that had driven him mad for weeks. His mouth watered as she twisted her hands behind her and worked the zipper of her skirt. "Maybe I want to forget this whole day ever happened. Maybe I'm the kind of woman who, with the right man, finds her second wind."

He didn't speak, but watched in reverent silence while she wiggled out of her skirt. Underneath, she wore silk stockings with tight garters and panties that were nothing more than a triangle of transparent material. Without another word, she turned toward the bathroom, leaving him reeling from the unhampered and mouthwatering view of her sweet, bare derriere.

Blood rushed through Alex's system, flooding his body with unbearable heat and heady, irrevocable desire. He tore at his collar and released his tie, nearly choking himself in his haste. His shirt would need the buttons replaced, but he didn't care. Only when he started to unbuckle his slacks did he pause. A weight slapped on his thigh from inside his pocket.

With a curse, he retrieved the ring.

Hell of a lot of good it had done him today when the thieves had broken into the auction house. Maybe if he'd worn the gaudy thing instead of stashing it out sight, he'd have thought of something more valiant to do than block the door with a heavy piece of furniture and follow Lucienne into a filthy hole in the wall.

At least he had looked for a weapon—which was an odd reaction for him, now that he thought about it. In his entire lifetime, he couldn't remember a situation where he'd ever needed to protect himself. Alex considered himself a lover, not a fighter. Yet when faced with gunfire and sirens, he'd been ready, willing and able to take up arms to protect Lucienne.

Had the ring brought out this unexpected side of him... or the woman?

From the bathroom, he heard the state-of-the-art, multi-head shower turn on and Lucienne's audible moan. She was naked now—the delectable lingerie abandoned, her flesh exposed beneath powerful jets that he knew from experience could pound out stress and inhibition with heated precision.

So why the hell was he still out here?

On impulse, he slipped the Murrieta ring onto his finger. For a few seconds, he waited—as if anticipating a change or sudden urge to don a black mask and cape and charge into the night to right the wrongs of humanity. And yet, the only thing he wanted to do was join Lucienne in the shower. So that's what he did.

Thanks to the dozen jets pulsing from the walls, ceiling and floor of the übermodern shower, the bathroom had already filled with steam. She'd draped her lacy underthings on a towel bar, and as he walked by, he brushed his fingers over the sexy silk.

Through the glass tiles, he spied her nude silhouette, her arms up as she soaked her hair, her back arched so that her buttocks rounded and the tips of her breasts jutted as if in offering. Despite the humidity in the room, his mouth dried. When he'd decided to release Lucienne from her contract so that they could pursue a personal relationship, he'd never imagined they'd come this far, this fast. He couldn't help but glance one last time at the ring. If making love to Lucienne wasn't the grandest adventure he'd ever undertaken, he didn't know what was.

On the surface, she was everything he desired in a woman. Beautiful, intelligent, educated and resourceful.

But now that the chains of her servitude to him—or more accurately, to the auction house—had been released, he'd picked up hints of an even more fascinating woman underneath her professional persona. She could be querulous and stubborn, seductive, yet shy. He'd spotted the seams of her true self and could not wait to peel aside the layers.

He removed the last of his clothes and paused outside the shower to adjust the computerized controls. She'd set the temperature to an intense 130 degrees and had employed all twelve showerheads, but she'd left the more imaginative features alone. With a couple of adjustments, the lighting in the shower transformed from warm gold to an intense cobalt blue. Then he engaged the sound system so that the lights pulsed to the music piped in from the other room.

Startled, she opened her eyes just as he came around the wall.

"Alejandro?"

"You did invite me," he said.

Her surprised expression melted to pure, undeniable pleasure. "And here I thought I was going to have to depend only on the water to satisfy my needs."

He closed the space between them until the spray from the showerheads dampened his skin. "I will give you everything you need, *mi tesoro.* My treasure. You only have to ask."

She slid her slick arms around his neck, and then tugged him fully beneath the water. "Then kiss me, Alejandro. Kiss me and make me forget this horrible day."

He complied, his cock thick against her body as she pulled up hard against him. He filled his hands with her luscious *culo* and lifted her a few inches so that her mouth met his without water streaming across their faces. The friction of her skin against his sex and the increasingly searing water pushed him past any thoughts of slow, measured seduction. His needs synched with the atmosphere in the shower: he wanted her hard, hot and from every direction imaginable.

He lifted her higher and she wrapped her legs around his waist. Their tongues clashed hungrily and he was hardly aware that he had pressed her against the far wall until she cried out in pleasure.

As much as he wanted to drive into her, he pulled back, untangling her hands from where she'd clutched the dripping strands of his hair and guided them around the showerhead directly above her head.

"Sí, sí," he encouraged before he slid his hands down over her hips and then up her sides, exploring her wet curves with the appreciation and expertise. "I want to see every inch of you. Taste every inch of you."

He kissed a path down her throat, loving the feel of her panting breaths beneath his lips. While he explored the tastes and textures of her collarbone, he cupped her breasts. Heavy and full, her flesh responded instantly to his touch.

When he brushed his thumbs over her nipples, she said, "Oh, yes, Alejandro. Yes."

At her urging, he took her into his mouth. With one flick of his tongue, she started to writhe, her body undulating against the tile with rhythmic, serpentine movements that brought to mind the most intuitive of dances—ritualistic and sexual. Torn between watching her move and spurring further expression of her pleasure, he continued to lave and tease her breasts until she'd dropped one hand from the showerhead and plunged it back into his hair, tugging at the strands and encouraging him to alternate his sucks and licks with nips and bites.

She was so responsive, so needy, so intensely hungry

for him that he couldn't deny her a single pleasure. He
dropped to his knees and adjusted the side showerheads
so that they splashed across her body while he explored
her navel with his tongue.

He kissed a scattered path down her pelvis, across to
her hips and thighs, then lifted her foot at the ankle and
paid homage to the back of her knee before slinging her leg
over his shoulder. He swiped water from his eyes, clearing
the misty steam from his view so he could drink in every
inch of her swollen pink flesh. Waxed clean and smooth,
she was a blank canvas on which he could ply his deft art.
With his fingers first and then his tongue, he explored
every visible crevice and fold, drinking in the moisture
that had nothing to do with the shower.

"Oh, Alejandro," she breathed. "Please."

She wanted release—and he wanted to give it to her. His
sex throbbed for the tightness her body promised. The friction. The heat. But he couldn't deny himself the pleasure
of tipping her over the edge with nothing but his tongue.

With his fingers, he parted her flesh and blew one cool
breath across her clitoris. On her gasp, he applied maximum pressure and suction until she pulled so hard on his
hair, it hurt. But he didn't care. He wanted to feel her come
undone, his mouth on the source, his fingers intensifying
every sensation until her screams echoed against the tile
only to be swallowed by the steam.

He continued his kisses until her quaking and quivering
subsided. Then he eased her foot back to the floor, careful
to bolster her with his hands on her hips as he blazed a path
up her body, stopping only when he reached her mouth.

"I can't...believe..."

"You were a feast for my senses, *querida*," he said,
unable to resist pressing against her so she could feel his

full, rigid length. "Your body is so fine-tuned. So sensitive to the touch."

"Your touch," she said between gasps.

His chest swelled even as she pulled his face to hers and kissed him with a desperation that belied her very recent orgasm.

"I want you, Alejandro. Inside me."

"I have no pro—"

"I don't care," she said, reaching between them to encircle his sex with her hand. Her grip, tight and insistent on his wet skin, detonated an explosive need that made his vision swim. He braced himself, allowing her to stroke and tug until he could hardly form a coherent thought.

He dug deep, beyond wanting, and pulled back enough so that he could gaze directly into her lusty gaze. "I care."

Her hold slackened, but she did not release him. "What?"

Tangled in her hair, the emerald stone on his right hand caught the hazy blue LED light and sparkled back in bold, vibrant turquoise. The ring couldn't make him a saint, but if it kept him from making a mistake, he was thankful.

He turned off the water, snatched the nearest towel, wrapped her in it and lifted her into his arms. "If we stop long enough to get protection, then I will have to make you hot for me all over again. Any objection?"

7

Lucy had entertained so many private fantasies about Alejandro, she'd figured reality could never top the dream. She'd been so, so wrong. As he lifted her into his arms—arms with much more muscle than she'd guessed would exist under his stiff, stark white shirts—she'd felt as light as air and as hot as molten gold.

With one free hand, he turned off the shower, and then set her down inside a patterned tile circle set just outside the stall. The combination of the dark blue lights and the languor of her orgasm made it hard to see precisely what he was doing when he tapped the computerized controls on the wall. Then a bright red column of light streamed down on her, blinding her with color and blazing her with warmth.

He helped her wrap her sopping hair in another towel and then proceeded to help the drying lamp along by dabbing her softly with a large, cotton bath sheet that was probably big enough to cover them both.

"Alejandro," she said, aware of the longing in her voice. She couldn't remember the last time such a glorious orgasm hadn't completely satisfied her, but instead left her wanting more. Truth was, she couldn't remember ever coming so hard. With the blue lights and the hot water, he'd given her a concentration of pleasure she'd never experienced, but took nothing for himself. Even now, when she was half ready to lie down on the cold tile so he could pump into her, he instead brushed the towel lightly over her shoulders and down her arms, humming his appreciation as if she were a sculpture by Michelangelo rather than a living, breathing woman who was on the verge of spontaneous combustion.

"Alejandro, please."

"Shh," he admonished. "I want to dry every inch of you before I get you wet again."

He smoothed the towel down her spine. The soft friction created a shivering sensation that had nothing to do with the cold. The orange-red glow from above had already amped up the temperature of her skin so that the damp towel felt like an icy respite from the intense heat.

When he dried her bum, he dropped to his knees and manipulated the towel over her flesh until she wanted to scream in frustration. If he just dipped the towel a little lower, if she just parted her legs a little farther, he might accidentally touch her where she most wanted it. Her heartbeat pounded between her legs, torturing her with pulses of need only he could assuage.

But instead, he dropped to his knees and kissed her, first high on her rump, then lower, until his lips adored the sensitive curve between her backside and her thigh.

"You're so perfect," he said, grasping her flesh possessively before he resumed his ministrations by swiping the towel in long, slow strokes up and down her legs.

"Not perfect," she argued, but without any force of will. At this moment, she imagined herself the most beautiful woman in the world, not because he told her—but because he showed her in the way he touched her, as if the sweet slowness was a kind of worship.

When he crawled around in front of her, she forced herself to look down. He'd said he'd do everything to her a second time. Was he serious?

The wicked look in his eyes made her body tighten from the center of her sex to the tips of her breasts. Tiny beads of sweat formed beneath her hair. She leaned over to disengage the heat lamp, and when she turned back to him, he made good on his promise, locking his mouth onto her and sucking her sex until her knees buckled.

She braced her hands on his shoulders, seriously afraid she might fall, though she suspected if she did, she wouldn't feel any pain. Primed from his slow and sensual drying, she embraced the feel of his tongue parting her labia, discovering her clit and then toggling it with swift, vibrating flicks. When he slipped a finger inside her, she lost all rational thought. She transformed into a creature of pure, undiluted need. With her hips, she matched the in-and-out rhythm of his hand and mouth until she reached the precipice between rapture and release. Without fear, she jumped, soaring with a cry that reverberated against the solid, tile walls.

"Oh, my," she said when he stood, catching her as she collapsed against him. "I can't—I can't breathe."

"I always make good on my promises, *querida*." He swept a kiss across her temple.

"Yes, you do. You really do."

Unable to focus her vision and only marginally able to speak in anything above a whisper, she surrendered to a swirl of colors as he lifted her into his arms again. This time, he carried her straight to bed.

While she nestled beneath the comforter and willed her nerve endings to return to a normal state, he disappeared then came back with an overnight bag that he tossed onto the nightstand. He padded through the suite, dousing all the lights until the shine from the city through the windows provided a sexy, uncertain glow. He dug into his bag and retrieved a trio of condoms.

She took a deep breath, and then tested her ability to speak.

"You came prepared," she said.

He slid into bed beside her. "A gentleman always comes prepared."

The minute he brought his body heat into the cool sheets, Lucy surrendered to the undeniable fact that when it came to lovemaking, Alejandro Aguilar knew what he was doing. From her first orgasm in the shower and the second after his sensual towel work all the way to his carrying her to bed and having protection ready and available, he hadn't missed a beat. In any other man, she would have questioned his motives—considered him too slick, too prepared...too much. But Alejandro donned the role of expert lover with elegance. She couldn't resist staring into his pitch-dark eyes and watching passion flame there while he ran his hand oh-so-lazily up her outer thigh.

"I could touch you all night," he whispered.

"No one's stopped you so far," she replied.

"The same is true for you."

His comment held just the right combination of challenge and chastisement to fuel her next move.

She'd been dying to fully explore his body, but so far, he'd made it impossible for her to think beyond her own needs. With his invitation, however, she drew a single finger around the shell of his ear, noticing how he flinched when she touched his earlobe.

What a wonderful place for him to have a sensitive spot.

She leaned forward and took the crescent of skin into her mouth, teasing him with her teeth and tongue while she smoothed her hand down his neck, across his muscular shoulders, down his chest, then across to his hip. His glutes were like stone. She couldn't resist the urge to grab hold and squeeze hard, particularly when he started nibbling her shoulder and her over-sensitized nipples scraped across his chest hairs.

"You have such a beautiful body," she said, curving her hand up his spine. Even his back was muscled. He wasn't bulky or stocky, but lean and hard. Like a runner. Like a lover's dream.

"Gracias," he said, closing his eyes as her hand skimmed across his abdomen and then followed the prickly trail from his navel to his cock. "How much would you appraise me for?"

She laughed as she explored, but nearly forgot the question when he cupped her breasts and softly traced the ring of her areola with his thumb. The sensation was lazy and unfocused—and deliciously intimate.

"I'm no expert in what men are going for these days."

She brushed her fingers lightly over his penis, which pulsed in response. He was thick and hard and long—the perfect size, in her estimation—with definitely an exquisite texture. His flesh felt like hot silk beneath her palm, his balls full, warm sacs that she fondled and caressed until his lids drifted closed in the beginnings of ecstasy.

With a ragged breath, he said, "Take a guess."

She grasped him tighter, encircling him with her thumb and forefinger. "I'll have to do a little more research."

"Do whatever you like."

The note of complete surrender emboldened her. She'd never been a shy lover, but she'd never invested much time or effort beyond the fulfilling of basic sexual needs. On the adventurous scale, she fell firmly into the lowest category possible. But with Alejandro, her place was yet to be determined. She wanted to try more with him—wanted to experience more. Wanted to give more. She didn't question why. She didn't question anything.

She pushed on his shoulder and climbed over him, her thighs on either side of his hips, his erection taunting her with its thick heat. Her eyelids fluttered as the sensations of his body beneath hers resulted in teardrops of liquid kissing his flesh and providing a warm lubrication.

She braced her hands on his chest and skimmed her body across him, the contact tentative, but torturously wonderful.

"So perfect," she murmured.

"Not quite."

He grasped her hips and set her down harder. He wasn't inside her yet—but he would be.

Soon.

Very, very soon.

Slick with need, her labia parted as she slid across him with a warm, moist friction. She'd never made love to a man with her body so primed, so ready, so on the edge of orgasm. Again. Until this moment, multiple climaxes, to her, had been a myth dreamed up by fashion magazines. But now she was learning. Orgasm required trust—and it was hard to trust men she barely knew.

And yet, she had no trouble surrendering her body, mind and soul to Alejandro. She'd only met him a couple of months ago. She'd been lying to him even before she'd first opened her mouth to introduce herself as Lucienne Bonet, the international art expert, rather than Lucy Burnett, a clever fence for stolen goods who happened to be best friends with the brother he didn't know he had.

But at this moment, she didn't care about her motives or her past, or that once he found out she was willing to snatch his family legacy, he'd want nothing to do with her. She didn't even care about the damned ring or saving Danny. She just wanted to feel Alejandro deep inside her. She wanted to ride him hard and milk every ounce of pleasure from his body.

"Alejandro, I—"

"*Por favor, mi tesora,* call me Alex."

She blinked and stopped moving. "What?"

He clutched her backside and restarted the sensual undulation of her body over his. "Alejandro sounds too formal. My friends call me Alex."

The little intimacy made her smile. "What do your lovers call you?"

He brushed his tongue over his lips and she could tell he was trying hard to contain what she suspected might be an arrogant grin. Then he slid his hands up her back, pulled himself into a sitting position and wrapped his lips around her right nipple.

"Insatiable," he murmured.

She slid across him, back and forth, while he suckled and nipped at her breasts. When the tip of his head came into contact with her clit, she nearly bucked out of her skin. In a maelstrom of mad fumbling, she retrieved the condom from the bedside table, tore open the package and unrolled it over him.

The brand he chose provided an extra layer of lubrication so that when she tilted her body, he slid into her with ease. In one thrust, he was inside her, full and long and oh-so-deliciously hard. She remained still for a long moment, waiting for her body to stretch and accommodate him even as she reveled in the sensations shooting through her like white-hot stars.

He continued to pleasure her breasts, alternating between gently twisting her nipples with his teeth and laving away the pleasurable pain with a stiff, darting tongue. Once she realized she could move without coming immediately, she raised herself up, then slowly inched down. The power was overwhelming. He crooned to her in lyrical Spanish. Though she had no desire to translate, even just in her head, she understood him perfectly when he clutched her hips and pressed her down harder and faster.

He dropped back onto the pillows, his eyes closed, his mouth curved in a shape that wasn't as much a smile as it was a sign of bliss. She braced her hands on his pecs, then tugged at the chest hair near his nipples until his eyes flew open and speared her with needs so intense, she nearly stopped moving.

Nearly. But she couldn't stop this train now. He tightened his grip on her waist, his fingers biting into her skin.

"Encantadora," he murmured.

"Kiss me," she pleaded, leaning down so that she could reach his mouth.

The new angle spawned shockwaves of fresh sensations. Alex growled as her mouth met his and in the span of a heartbeat, he was ravishing her lips and tongue even as he ground his hips so that his sex tunneled deeper into hers. Just as she reached the precipice of need, he flipped her onto her back and delivered the last few thrusts. She wrapped her legs around him, dug her heels into his ass and screamed in pure, unadulterated joy.

Moments into her orgasm, he joined her, pounding harder even as he kissed her hungrily. The pressure was overwhelming. He gave more than she thought she could take—and now, she wanted more. She tilted her hips, and with one last thrust, he ground out her name, shuddered and then collapsed beside her.

His skin was shiny with sweat. His hair, which he hadn't dried since the shower, rained cool droplets of water onto her sizzling skin. When he leaned up on his elbow, grinned, then kissed her again until she was lost in the pure pleasure of his mouth, she feared she might pass out from contentedness.

Was that even possible?

"So how much?" he asked, breathless.

"What?"

"How much am I worth?" he asked. "You've now experienced just about every part of me. Give me a, *cómo se dice,* ballpark estimate."

Lucy laughed. When it came to pillow talk, Alex won that contest, too. Hands down.

"Are you fishing for compliments?" she asked, rising to his comically naughty bait.

"Yes," he replied.

"My three orgasms weren't enough?"

"When it comes to orgasms, I find that three is never enough."

"On what planet?" she asked, shocked. "Most of the men I've been with don't even care if I have one. Now you seem determined to set a record."

"Don't speak of other men," he said, but his voice was gentle, almost pleading. "No one exists in this bed but you and me. You'll have as many orgasms as you can handle here—and perhaps one more, as you Americans say, for luck."

She snuggled into his chest, keenly aware that he was lax inside her. It might take some work on her part to rectify that situation before the night was through, but she was nothing if not industrious.

"If you mean all that, then you, sir, are priceless."

SENSING EYES ON THE BACK of his neck, Michael clicked twice on his computer keyboard so that his screen popped to the default FBI homepage. When he spun around on his swivel chair, Ruby stood behind him, grinning.

"Why are you sneaking up on me?" he asked.

She narrowed her dark eyes. "What are you doing that's making my sneaking up on you necessary?"

"Nothing," he lied, turning back toward his desk. To his left, he had a stack of ongoing investigation files that needed updating since he'd pushed them all aside to concentrate on a new primary case involving a string of adult female kidnappings, the first of which had happened in California, but now included four states. On his right, a second stack contained estimations, contracts and letters of intent to purchase, all associated with the upcoming auction that would liquidate his father's estate on his mother's behalf. In the center of his mind, however, was new concern for Alejandro.

The brother he'd never met, with one request from him, had abandoned his fruitful life in Spain and traveled halfway across the ocean to take care of family business. In the course of doing what was best for El Dorado, Alex had brought in a seemingly qualified appraiser who had, in two short months, earned not only Alex's professional trust, but his personal interest.

After the robbery, however, Michael realized that in trying to keep on top of his most important priorities, he'd allowed a lot of little things to fall by the wayside—including keeping an eye on people who were trying a little too hard to go unnoticed.

Like Lucienne Bonet.

Ruby shoved his case files aside and popped onto his desk, swinging her feet as if she were five years old.

"You're a big liar," she accused.

"Don't you have work to do?"

"The boss asked me to help you with your backlog. So here I am."

He grabbed the top five manila folders behind her and slapped them into her lap. "Have a party."

She took a disinterested glance through the files, then set them back on top of his stack. "I'd much rather know who you were just checking into before I walked up. Suspect on the kidnapping cases?"

Michael groaned, not sure why he bothered trying to keep anything from her. The woman was like a bulldog when she sniffed out the meaty scent of something secretive.

"It's a little closer to home," he admitted.

"You're checking out the chick from the auction house."

"Why would you think that?"

"Because I read the police report, too. A daytime robbery like that isn't random. Not with shots fired. Though I'd check out the fired employees first, I don't blame you for giving her background a look-see. She was hot."

"That's what worries me," Michael said. Under normal circumstances, he would never interfere in his adult brother's love life. But now that Alex had taken responsibility for the woman's safety—a fact he'd learned from Alex's call—he couldn't help but worry that by asking his brother to orchestrate El Dorado's last auction, Michael had invited danger into Alex's life. He'd already faced gunfire and armed robbery. What if Lucienne turned out to be even more dangerous?

"Her hotness worries you?" Ruby questioned. "Boy, you and I need to have a serious talk."

"This isn't about me, it's about Alex. He's sleeping with her."

Ruby's eyebrows sprang up. "Since when?"

Michael frowned. "Since tonight, if I'm reading the signals right. She's staying with him at his penthouse. Her purse, keys and wallet were taken in the robbery. The cops don't think it's safe for her to go home."

Ruby slid off his desk and into a chair she dragged over from the hall. Per usual, she changed from a thorn in his side to a serious crackerjack agent in the space of a heartbeat.

"And this woman didn't have anyone else she could stay with?"

"She's not from San Francisco," he said, clicking the computer back to the screen he'd banished when Ruby first walked up. "Says here she's from New Orleans originally, like she told you, but she hasn't stayed in one place for very long."

"Is that unusual, with her job?"

His scowl deepened. He didn't know what it was about Lucienne Bonet that had his hackles up, but he'd learned a long time ago to trust his instincts. Something wasn't right about her—which made her a danger not only to his brother, but to the auction house, too.

"Not according to my research, but I can't help thinking something's up. She talked to you, but she kind of went out of her way not to be around me for more than a few seconds—and not for the first time. She's been working for my brother for two months, but I've never really talked to her. Never really seen her. Why is that?"

Ruby shrugged. He didn't know the answer, either, but he would find out.

"I'm going to stop by the auction house later and pick up a copy of her résumé. I know Alex checked out her references, but I have a feeling he asked different questions than I would."

"And you think that she had something to do with the robbery?"

He shook his head. "If the robbers had inside knowledge from her, they wouldn't have tripped the security alarm and they wouldn't have failed to get into the main vault. But something about her makes me uneasy."

Ruby patted him on the shoulder, her calm attitude back in full force. "Maybe it's just that she's gorgeous and hot for your brother and you wouldn't know what to do with a babe like that."

She was four paces out of his cubicle before Michael smacked down his shock and shot back, "I'd know exactly what to do with her."

"Maybe on a theoretical level," she quipped, then sauntered back to her desk on the other side of the partition. "But in practice? Ha!"

Michael opened his mouth to counter her assertion, then decided against it. What proof did he have that he could handle a woman as gorgeous, sophisticated and mysterious as Lucienne Bonet? The last girl he'd dated with any regularity had been a barista at the coffee shop in the lobby of the FBI building. She'd been a little young, but sweet and a decent date for movies and dinner. But like most of his relationships, the whole thing had petered out rather quickly—probably because she expected more excitement from a federal agent than he could provide. His work was his love, his passion. At the end of the day, he had very little energy left for anything else. Or *anyone* else.

So maybe Ruby was right.

Michael hadn't inherited the Murrieta charm when it came to women. Although his father had, by all accounts, remained faithful to his mother during their marriage, he'd been quite the ladies' man before, as evidenced by the fact that he had not one, but two sons by two different women. The number of female mourners at Ramon's funeral had nearly required the funeral home to truck in an 18-wheeler full of tissues.

And in less than a couple of hours since Alejandro had announced his desire to seduce Lucienne, the woman had moved in with him. Clearly, his brother had inherited Ramon's charm. Even Daniel, who was a no-good, two-faced, lying sack of thievery, always had plenty of female names on his approved visitor's list at the jail.

Michael's chest constricted. With shaking fingers, he called up the file on Lucienne Bonet again, this time opening the photograph from her Louisiana state identification. He leaned close to his monitor, ignoring the color and cut of her hair and concentrating only on the shape of her face.

He'd seen those eyes before—though they'd been vibrant green at the time.

He remembered the angle of her cheekbones, the slope of her nose and the thickness of her lush lips.

He had seen her before—and not at the auction house.

"Ruby!" he shouted.

Ruby didn't appreciate summoning by this means and countered with an aggravated, "What?"

"I need you to look at something."

She clomped over. "If whatever you want to show me has anything to do with my crack about you not knowing what to do with a woman, I take it back. There are some things about my coworkers I don't want to know."

He jabbed his finger at the computer monitor. "I just remembered why Lucienne Bonet looks so familiar. I met her once—and not at the auction house."

"Where?"

"In lockup. With Daniel."

8

LUCY PEEKED ONE EYE OPEN, wondering how the hell sunrise had come so early. How long had she slept? An hour? Two?

She rolled over slowly, but her muscles protested and the sheets, tangled around her body, pulled tight into a constricting serpentine of thousand-thread Egyptian cotton. She vaguely remembered the comforter falling to the floor at some point during the night, along with her and Alex.

Rule to live by: when making love on the floor, it is preferable to do so in a luxury penthouse suite with four-inch pile carpet and the world's most amazing lover. For the rest of her life, she'd think of the rug burns as war wounds in the most pleasurable battle ever waged between man and woman.

As consciousness crept into her brain, she registered the scent of coffee. She inhaled deeply, and then battled the restraining sheet until she could sit up.

"Buenos dias."

Blinded by her bone-dry contacts, Lucy rubbed at her eyes and pried apart the clumps of mascara on her lashes. After yawning inelegantly, she blinked enough moisture into her eyes to see Alex sitting in a chair by an east-facing window. Sunlight streamed behind him, casting him in sexy silhouette. He was dressed in his typical sharp-creased slacks, crisp white shirt and expensive Italian loafers.

"How long have you been awake?" she asked, her voice raspy.

"An hour. I hope you don't mind that I've been watching you sleep."

She attempted to run her hand through her hair, which was a mass tangle of her dyed locks and expertly applied extensions. "I can't imagine why you would. I must look like hell."

"You look like a woman who's been thoroughly loved," he countered.

"Yeah, I've seen those women," she quipped. "And they look like hell."

While he chuckled, she tugged the sheet free from the knotted comforter and pillows on the floor and wrapped herself like a regifted present. She scuttled into the bathroom and shut the door, not giving a damn if she looked ridiculous. Over the course of the night, the man had seen her from just about every angle imaginable. She wasn't going to play shy now simply because the sun had risen.

But here in the dark bathroom, she thanked the hotel gods for dimmer switches. After unraveling herself from the sheet, she found the sink and scrubbed her face free of her leftover makeup, then took out her contacts. Once free of the color-changing lenses, she could see well enough to locate a basket of toiletries filled with the items she'd requested from the concierge. She dropped the contacts into a cleansing solution, brushed her teeth and peed, then headed to the shower and hoped that this time, Alex didn't follow her.

Last night's foray into the magical water jets had been

an amazing amalgamation of fantasy and reality, but she had no illusions that this affair would go beyond today. She had to get her head out of the clouds and back into the game she'd started when she'd agreed to help Danny steal the ring.

First on her priority list was finding a way to visit Danny in jail and figure out what he knew, if anything, about the robbery. Thanks to his less than sterling track record—which included a failure-to-appear five years ago in Phoenix—he had been denied bail before his trial on charges of grand theft. In addition to the missing jewels, an injured security guard had still not regained consciousness, leaving the prosecution open to file murder charges.

Lucy believed Danny when he told her he hadn't gotten anywhere near the guard and that he hadn't been armed. In his entire career, he'd never shot anyone and never carried a gun. Either he was being set up or someone else had shot the guard in a bid to steal the loot—a rare pink diamond—from the private collector, but Danny had beat him to the punch. Danny had insisted she not worry about his legal troubles. He'd needed her to focus solely on procuring the ring. Without it, he might not make it to his trial.

They'd had to plan this entire operation in the prison visitor's room, using code words and shoptalk they'd perfected over many years. But she supposed that someone could have overheard them.

If that was the case, some other con might have decided to take advantage of her presence in the auction house, hoping to score big and then pin the robbery on her. If so, the guy was an idiot. Yeah, they'd made off with several hundred thousand dollars' worth of jewels, but selling them was going to be tough.

No one knew about her association with Danny—at least, no one who was going to tell. She hadn't given the

police photographs and detailed descriptions of every item
taken so they could pass the information on to pawnshops.
And the first chance she got, she was going to contact her
main competitors and make it clear that if he or any other
of her associates moved a single piece from the El Dorado
heist, she'd make sure they paid—and dearly.

Not that she had any idea how to do that, but Danny
did—and Danny never made idle threats.

After inspecting the instructions on the shower stall a
little more carefully than she had last night, she selected a
single showerhead and set the temperature to a tepid 100
degrees. She grabbed shampoo, conditioner and a soothing
body wash and put them all to good use. When she rubbed
some of her more sore parts with soap, she was glad that
so far, Alex hadn't attempted to recreate last night's adventure.

She wasn't sure she could take another one of his show-
ers—either physically or emotionally. Not when she knew
that by the end of the day, she'd have to leave him.

For good.

No matter her promise to Danny or her simmering attraction to Alex, Lucy knew the time had come for Lucienne Bonet to disappear. She'd spent nearly two months
looking for the ring—and if she hadn't found it by now,
she was pretty certain she wasn't going to. She'd have
to figure out another way to make sure Danny survived
prison—one that didn't include lying and stealing from a
man she was beginning to care about.

As if summoned by her thought, Alex knocked on the
door.

She turned off the water. "I'm almost done."

"May I bring you a cup of coffee?" he asked. "I can
leave it on the counter."

A chill chased up her spine. Somehow, hearing tentativeness in his voice was wholly unnatural. She could only blame herself—her signals had been pretty clear since she rolled out of bed.

Stay away—a message she repeated when she said, "I can wait until I'm through."

"Of course," he replied. "But I'm needed downstairs. I shouldn't be too long."

She folded her lips together for a second, and then replied with forced brightness, "Take your time."

"I won't be long," he promised again, and then shut the door with a definitive click.

Once he was gone, Lucy relaxed against the wet tile, flooded by the contrasts Alex presented. On the job, he epitomized the confident commander. No-nonsense, pragmatic and entirely certain of his skills both as an art expert and a businessman, he'd came across as someone who wasn't to be trifled with. Even in bed, he'd demonstrated how accustomed he was to being in control—and she'd loved every single minute.

Yet at the same time, he'd been an unexpectedly giving lover. He'd focused on her pleasure above and beyond his own. Though she hadn't exactly left him wanting, either. Still, when morning dawned, he'd allowed her to sleep in, arranged everything she needed to be waiting for her in the bathroom and had even offered to fetch her coffee. She had a little trouble reconciling the man who had a chauffeur and a penthouse suite with someone doing something as simple and thoughtful as bringing a lover her first morning jolt of caffeine.

As she mulled over the dichotomy, she turned the water back on and finished her shower. She skipped the lamp drying and instead wrapped herself in a towel and sat in front of the vanity mirror with cosmetics, a blow dryer and hair straightener until she'd re-created Lucienne Bonet— possibly for the last time.

From her perfect smoky eyes to her long, luxurious hair, Lucienne embodied Alex's fantasy—but she was also the woman Lucy might have chosen to become if she'd known a different life. But with a father who'd used his position at museums to move stolen goods and a mother who had fooled an entire community, including the judicial system, into believing she took in foster kids out of her giving nature rather than to run scams, Lucy was a product of her upbringing.

Thanks to Danny, however, she'd ended up better than most. She wasn't a petty thief with a rap sheet a mile long, a drug addict or a troubled single mother fighting the demons of her past. He'd taught her to use her keen eye, extensive knowledge and crack negotiating skills to move the merchandise he appropriated. He'd schooled her on how to change her appearance, alter her accent and slide through society without getting noticed—until getting noticed was the means to an end. Together, they'd turned their rotten childhoods into financial security.

She owed him so much. Other than an expunged juvenile record, she'd never had any direct run-ins with the law. She'd parlayed her street smarts and excellent memory for details and facts into a fine career as a mover of stolen goods. And now that she'd had a taste of legitimate employment, she considered—not for the first time—that maybe once Danny was safe, she might try to find a way to go straight.

The clothes she'd asked to be brought over from her apartment weren't in the bathroom, so she pulled on the white robe and padded into the bedroom. Alex was still downstairs, but the coffee he'd promised was waiting for her in an insulated carafe.

She poured a cup and wandered into the living area, spying the empty snifters and expensive brandy they'd never gotten around to drinking the night before. Her stomach growled, reminding her that they hadn't wasted any time with food, either. She was scouting around for some fresh fruit or a granola bar when she heard the elevator ding.

"Alex?"

But it wasn't Alex who came around the corner—it was Michael.

Her heart jetted up her esophagus and lodged in the back of her throat.

"Lucienne, isn't it?"

She pulled the lapels of her robe tighter and gave the sash an extra tug.

"Alex isn't here," she said.

He smiled, but it was a small expression that didn't meet his eyes. "I know. He's downstairs, meeting with an insurance adjuster."

"That was fast," she commented.

"My father had as many friends on the right side of the law as the wrong one. And Alex, well, he's already proven himself to be a force to be reckoned with. I don't expect the holders of Ramon's policies will give him much of a hard time."

She sipped her steaming hot drink, but didn't reply. She recognized Michael's tactic. He was trying to intimidate her. Bully her a little. Had he remembered her as the woman he'd met at the jail or was he just playing bulldog to his brother's new lover?

Michael held out a gift bag emblazoned with the hotel's logo. "This is for you."

Her lack of clothing had given her a reason to keep her distance, but when she didn't move nearer, he held the bag out farther and gave it a little shake. He wanted a closer look at her—which might mean that he thought he recognized her, but wasn't sure.

If it was a game he wanted, she'd play. What choice did she have?

Forcing confidence into her step and a bright smile onto her lips, she crossed the room and took the bag, turning in what she hoped was a natural swirl while she peeked inside.

"Oh," she said, surprised. "The concierge here certainly goes above and beyond. He went all the way to my apartment to get my clothes."

"The concierge didn't," Michael said. "I did."

Again, her chest seized. It was one thing to know that thieves might have pawed through her belongings—it was something else to realize an FBI agent had.

"That was very sweet of you," she lied.

He shrugged. "That remains to be seen. I'm sorry if they're a little wrinkled. By the time I got there this morning, someone had already been through your stuff."

"The thieves?"

"More than likely."

"I thought the police were watching my place."

"They had a car patrolling the area, but the thieves had a key. They must have slipped in unnoticed."

She eyed the couch, but decided that if she remained standing, she could keep him from getting too close. She moved to the bright, east-facing windows and turned so her face was in shadow. "What kind of damage did they do?"

"They knocked over some stuff, dug through drawers," he said, moving closer. "They were definitely looking for something. Might have found it, too. Even the air vents were torn off. Why do you think they'd do that?"

She fought the instinct to give any outward sign that his information had caused nausea to roil through her stomach and make her thankful she hadn't eaten.

"How should I know?"

"Because my brother rarely hangs out with people who aren't somehow tied into his business. Even his lovers tend to be the kind of women a guy wouldn't turn his back on in case she decides to steal his wallet."

She straightened her spine, channeling the indignation she imagined Lucienne Bonet might feel, even though felonious Lucy Burnett wondered if the elevator was the only exit from the penthouse. "Alejandro's reputation is pristine. I can't imagine him ever consorting with anyone who'd stoop so low as to pick a pocket."

"I wasn't talking about Alejandro."

When Michael closed the distance between them, she couldn't resist taking a step backward until she bumped into the windowsill. Michael's sapphire stare, intense and focused, bored through her, but she held her ground, tilting up her chin and meeting his gaze with defiance.

"Then who are you talking about?"

"Daniel."

"Who?"

He cracked a smile, but again, nothing remotely like humor touched the piercing blue of his eyes.

"You're going to try to tell me you don't know Daniel."

He was fishing. He had no proof. If he did, he would have already presented it—if not to her, then to Alex.

"I'm not trying to convince you of anything," she said. "But I am going to insist that you take a few steps back."

He glanced down. She had a perfect shot at his balls with her knee. Recognizing his vulnerability, he complied.

"Thank you," she said sweetly. "Now that we've reestablished personal space, Special Agent Murrieta, I will volunteer that I don't think I know anyone named Daniel. I mean, I believe there was a man named Daniel who worked in the shipping department at the museum in Toronto I worked for several summers ago, but I doubt he's your brother…unless you have an Asian side to your family."

His gaze never wavered and though it required a lifetime's experience to remain unaffected, she retained the insulted look on her face until he finally turned away.

The worm had just dropped off the hook, so she decided to make sure the bait sank to the bottom, undigested.

"What is this about? Do you think I'm somehow involved in the robbery at the auction house?"

He slung his hands into his pockets and was just about to speak when Alejandro strode into the room and answered for him.

"Of course he doesn't."

The anger in Alex's voice crackled in the air like lightning. He locked his stare with Michael's, and for a split second, Lucy was nearly capsized by a wave of testosterone. Alex's presence always commanded respect and deference, but when Michael was riled, his charming blue eyes hardened and his chin abandoned its rugged charisma for a more implacable set.

For the first time, the men's blood relationship struck her hard. They were both strong. Both stubborn. Both fierce. Adding Danny to the mix in her mind, she realized that Ramon Murrieta had fathered sons who ran the gamut from smart to kind-hearted and loyal—but they were also hard-headed and immovable.

And when riled, downright scary.

With the shopping bag clutched against her chest, Lucy hurried across the room and laid a gentle hand on Alex's arm. "Is everything all right?"

His gaze didn't waver from Michael's.

"Fine," he said, his tone curt. After a moment, he glanced down at her, and in the instant that his dark eyes met hers, his mouth softened. He casually slipped his hands into his pockets, and when he spoke directly to her, his voice was every bit as indulgent and melodious as it had been last night when he'd spent a good ten minutes ruminating on how much he adored the way her ass fit in his hands.

She couldn't help but smile.

"You had coffee?"

"Not a lot, but enough to offset my grumpiness," she said. "I'm sorry if I was awful this morning."

"You were understandably exhausted. But now that you have something to wear, why don't you go get dressed while I finish talking to my brother?"

She spared Michael a glance, but decided not to argue. She had to act innocent, and since Alex had already risen to her defense, she was better off leaving her fate in the hands of someone who had no idea how guilty she truly was.

Besides, she hadn't stolen anything. And now that she'd started planning her exit strategy, she was fairly certain she never would.

She nodded and was two steps away from Alex when he grabbed her by the elbow and yanked her flush against his body. He swallowed her yelp of surprise with a deep, erotic kiss that counteracted her equilibrium so that when he swept one hand on the small of her back, he kept her from falling.

Lucy knew she should pull away. Michael was, after all, watching. She could feel his outraged stare burning through her thick terrycloth robe—or was that just her temperature rising in memory of all the delicious and decadent things Alex had done to her the night before? But no matter the perspiration gathering between her breasts, she couldn't seem to let him go.

This could be their last kiss.

She clutched her hands on either side of his face and twirled her tongue with his. She memorized his taste, his textures, his flavors. She tilted her pelvis to his so that his sex pressed against her, hardening in response. What wouldn't she do to have him inside her one last time?

The limitlessness of her answers frightened her to her core.

She winced, and instantly, Alex set her right. She fluttered her eyes open and nearly drowned in the liquid desire pooling in his obsidian irises. He held her fast, not releasing his grip on her until she'd taken a deep breath and found her balance.

His wicked grin immediately reminded her of Danny. Alex had not only kissed her because he wanted to—but to vex Michael.

"I'll dress quickly," she said, a little vexed herself. Well, if she could use him, she supposed he had every right to use her right back to get under his brother's skin.

Especially since Michael wasn't exactly lily white with innocence, either.

Everything she'd done so far had been for Danny—the brother Michael hadn't told Alex about yet. And though she couldn't imagine that her new lover would ever agree with her choices, if she read him right, he'd at least understand that sometimes family—even without shared blood—came first.

He skimmed his hand lovingly on her cheek. "Take your time, *querida.*"

She'd started toward the bedroom when a flash of emerald and gold sparked in her peripheral vision. Surreptitiously, she glanced over her shoulder to work out what she'd seen. Michael had his back to them, apparently disgusted by their public display of affection. Alex had also turned, but had hooked his hands behind his back as if anticipating a confrontation.

When Lucy spied his right hand, she nearly stumbled over her own feet. Instinctively, she quickened her pace until she was in the bedroom with the double doors shut tight. Her lungs seized, but when she closed her eyes in an attempt to will her body to remain calm, the picture of what she'd seen solidified in her mind's eye.

Alex was wearing Ramon's ring.

And now, after finally making love with him, she was in the perfect position to steal it.

9

AT THE SOUND OF THE bedroom door shutting, Michael turned, his disgusted expression heightening Alex's anger to a dangerous level. For Lucienne's sake, he'd made light of his brother's insinuations. Then, to distract her and to prove a point to his brother, he'd swept her into a kiss.

Only the kiss hadn't simply been about Michael's accusations—the kiss had been a claiming. She was his, and he'd be damned if his brother was going to get in the way.

As an expert in his field, Alex had learned to appreciate the finest creations of the world's most creative minds. He sometimes purchased objects that pleased him, but more often than not, items he admired stayed in his possession only long enough for him to sell them to someone else.

In many ways, his love life operated on the same principle. He admired women, he even kept them close for a short time, but sooner rather than later, they left him for men with more money, more time, a greater willingness to lavish them with attention and worship.

He'd never minded—until now.

With Lucienne, his entire world had been upturned. The flavor of her kiss, bittersweet from coffee, lingered on his palate. Her warm scent saturated his nostrils and he ached for another touch of her soft, pliant skin. But even as his body thrummed with desire, his brain fired with anger at his brother.

It was time to put Michael straight on a few important matters—not the least of which was his lover's innocence.

"So was that public display of affection supposed to impress me?" Michael asked.

Despite the fact that nothing about their circumstances was the least bit comical, Alex chuckled. "Don't be ridiculous."

He crossed the room and grabbed the carafe he'd left for Lucienne. Finding it nearly full, he poured a cup of coffee for his brother, added a teaspoon of sugar and then did the same for himself. He joined Michael by the window, which sported an impressive view of the Golden Gate Bridge, and pressed the drink into his hand.

"Then you regularly plant sloppy, wet kisses on your lover *du jour* in front of strangers?"

"Trust me, Michael, nothing about my kisses could ever be described as sloppy. And you're not a stranger, you're my brother. However, if you wish to interpret secondary meanings to my exchange with Lucienne, let it be this— before you accuse her of anything untoward, you'd better have solid proof."

With a snicker, Michael took a gulp of coffee. "If I had proof, I would have given it to you downstairs."

"So instead, you trapped me with a loquacious insurance estimator and then oh-so-helpfully volunteered to bring up Lucienne's clothes so you could interrogate her while she was alone and naked?"

Michael glanced sideways, but guilt darkened his eyes. "She was wearing a robe."

Alex sipped his hot drink, tamping down a rumbling

of intense possessiveness that had no place between brothers—especially siblings who were still establishing boundaries. Rationally, he knew that Michael would never interfere in his personal life unless he had a reason. But his law enforcement experiences probably made him see conspiracies and suspect double-crosses even when none existed.

"If only her lack of attire were the point," Alex muttered.

Michael set his cup down on the sill and stalked across the room. Alex was starting to recognize a pattern. When Michael had news he did not want to deliver or a subject that would prove difficult to discuss, he paced. Alex had noticed a worn tread in the carpet at the auction house. Had their father shared the habit?

When Michael finally spoke, his volume was low and his tone measured. "There's something about her that isn't right, Alex."

"Her credentials are impeccable," Alex replied, controlling his temper.

"And you checked those references? Personally?"

"Perhaps not as diligently as I might have for someone less attractive, but I made a few calls. And I'm an excellent judge of character. Moreover, I'm more than satisfied with her work. She's proven her expertise. She completed the daunting job of preparing the El Dorado holdings for auction one week earlier than I'd asked, and thanks to her contacts with Ramon's clientele, we already have pre-bidding interest on a majority of the pieces. In the absence of any concrete proof to the contrary, I have no reason to believe that Lucienne is in any way a liar, thief or fraud."

Michael cursed. "Good cons don't get to be good unless they've honed their craft. Doing her job well could have been just another way to gain your trust."

"That's ridiculous," Alex scoffed. "I'd know."

"If she's a pro, then even a smart guy like you could be fooled. I've seen it."

Alex crossed his arms over his chest, mostly to keep from punching his brother in the face. He'd never been a violent man, but Michael had insulted Lucienne, and now Alex himself. He might not have Michael's background in law enforcement, but he wasn't naive. No industry, save gambling, attracted more liars, cheats and thieves than the world of expensive art. And up until now, he'd yet to be scammed.

"You go too far, *Miguel,*" Alex said, emphasizing his brother's given name. "You have no documentation to bolster such an attack on Lucienne's character. I was under the impression that *innocent until proven guilty* was the basis of your legal system."

"I'm not a judge or a lawyer," Michael snapped. "In my business, sometimes we have to act on gut instincts."

"Well, in my business, I've learned that instincts, while valuable, mean nothing unless there is proof. I can *feel* that a work is a Monet because of color depth and brushstrokes, but unless I can prove it to the most skeptical buyer, no one will pay a penny for it."

"If I had paperwork to back me up, I'd show it to you," Michael shot back. He took a deep breath and continued his pacing. "That's the problem. I can't find anything concrete." He spun and speared his finger toward Alex. "But I will."

Alejandro bit back his retort. Yesterday, he and Michael had argued over their father. Today, they were raising their voices over Lucienne. This wasn't how he'd imagined his relationship with his only sibling would develop.

They shared so much beyond DNA and the father named on their birth certificates. They both held themselves to high standards of behavior that contradicted the man Ramon had been. Like Michael, Alex prided himself on doing the right thing in any and all situations. For this reason, he knew his brother hadn't come here on a whim. Though he trusted Lucienne and had no reason to believe she had anything to do with the robbery, he had to admit that beyond an intimate knowledge of what she enjoyed in bed, he didn't know very much about her.

But that would change—in time.

"Lucienne was a victim of this robbery herself, Michael. And she knows the combinations to all the safes, as well as the security alarm codes. If she'd been involved, the auction house would have lost more than a half-million dollars' worth of jewelry."

Michael grunted in response.

"Not able to get around that hurdle of proof, I see," Alex assessed. "Then I advise you to drop this insanity. The insurance agent assured me that Ramon's policy is up-to-date. He only had a few minor claims over a decade ago, all settled without incident. If the police don't recover the stolen items, you and your mother will be compensated for them, and the auction of the remaining inventory, which is considerable, will go on as planned."

"This isn't about money."

"Then what is it about?"

Michael's stare met his only briefly. If Alex hadn't believed his brother incapable of lying, he might have suspected him of keeping a secret.

A very important secret.

Michael moved toward the door. "Just keep your guard up, okay? The thieves already hit her place and took whatever they wanted, so once she gets her locks changed and maybe invests in a big, scary dog, there's no reason why she can't return to her apartment. In the meantime, I'll do what I can to help the police investigation."

Alex nodded. "As will both Lucienne and I."

The moment the elevator doors slid closed with Michael on the other side, Lucienne emerged from the bedroom.

"Is it safe to come out or is Michael going to arrest me on charges of upsetting his gut?"

Alex extended his hand to her, a smile tugging at the corners of his mouth. "How much did you hear?"

She glided over to him, dressed with simple sophistication in a short, fitted gray skirt and a pale green sleeveless sweater that scooped modestly across her collarbone, then draped dramatically low in the back. Her makeup was effortless—a smoky gray on her eyelids, a light dusting of pink powder on her cheeks and a glossy shell color on her lips that enhanced their utterly natural kissability.

She was the picture of casual elegance, and yet, when he took her hand, she was shaking. He reeled her against him, determined to hold her until the shivers subsided, but if anything, the close contact made her quiver even more violently.

"You know I don't believe you had anything to do with the break-in," Alex said, gazing intently into her eyes. Tiny red capillaries spiraled toward her dark irises, testifying to her need for more sleep—something that wouldn't happen if he gave in to his instinct to carry her to bed and show her how much he trusted her.

"I know you believe in me," she said, her voice sad. "But that doesn't mean you should. Especially if I'm causing bad blood between you and your brother. Family is important. I'm not worth it."

He wrapped his arms completely around her and marveled at how perfectly she tucked into his body. He'd made love to many women, but couldn't remember once offering comfort to a lover—or engaging in an issue as intimate as trust.

With his paramours, he discussed art, politics, religion and business. He wasted idle hours on gossip and industry speculation. But to broach the topic of personal trust, one first had to attain a level of intimacy. And lovemaking aside, he'd never quite managed to dig that deep into a lover's heart before. Or vice versa.

Why now? Why with Lucienne?

Despite the pressure from his family to marry and produce heirs who, like him, would bear the name Aguilar, Alex had never sought out a serious relationship. He'd graduated at the top of his class at Oxford, procured highly sought-after apprenticeships with both Sotheby's and Christie's, and had earned his family's respect through the business he generated for the auction house and the expertise with which he did his job.

His relationships had all started much as the one with Lucienne—attraction leading to sex, and then…nothing. Once the lusts had been sated, the liaisons ended. Sometimes with hurt feelings, he supposed, but never any grand heartbreaks.

Not for him, anyway.

For years, he'd rationalized that he was too busy building his professional reputation to give any woman excessive emotional attention. He knew firsthand the hurt that an inattentive husband could wreak on a wife. Instead, he opted to be only a short-term lover.

But with Lucienne, the need to protect her, shield her, support her, was undeniable. Her strength and intelligence aside, he spied vulnerability deep in her dark eyes that stabbed him like a grappling hook and wouldn't let go.

"You're worth more than you give yourself credit for,"

he said, brushing a kiss over her forehead, then down to her temple, her cheek, her nose.

He was just about to press his mouth to hers when she wound her way out of his embrace.

"I'm not," she said, her voice shockingly small and tremulous.

She wandered to the windows that overlooked the city, standing nearly in the same spot where Michael had wrestled with his unsubstantiated suspicions. At night, San Francisco sparkled with sexy mystery and lascivious intentions. But in the daylight, the possibilities in a sun-drenched city poised on a sparkling bay seemed endless.

He couldn't resist edging up behind her and winding his arms around her waist. For a split second, she tensed, but with a defeated sigh, she melted against him. Her shampoo-scented hair teased his nostrils and he couldn't help but bury his nose in the thick, dark strands and inhale until he was nearly dizzy with desire.

But he didn't want to go back to bed. The day was too perfect to remain indoors, no matter how delightful the activities could be. The police had not yet released the "crime scene" at the auction house, so returning to the office was out of the question. He'd handled all he could with the insurance adjustors. A beautiful day with a beautiful woman stretched out in front of him. He had no responsibilities, no obligations that would keep him from doing anything except enjoying time with Lucienne—not as business associates, but as lovers.

"How about if we order breakfast and then head out for some sight-seeing?" he suggested.

"I can't," she said.

"You have to be starving. I am." He tried to keep the sensual double-entendre out of his voice, but by her weary look, he'd failed miserably.

"I heard your brother say I could return to my apartment now. I'm sorry, Alejandro, but I have to go."

And without another word, she headed back to the bedroom. She didn't shut the door behind her, but she'd erected a barrier just the same—and he wasn't sure why. He'd defended her to Michael and had proven that he trusted her, even if she didn't think she deserved it.

Confused, he stalked into the bedroom to find her stuffing the clothes she'd worn yesterday into the glossy gift bag stamped with the hotel's regal crest.

"What are you doing?" he asked.

"Leaving."

"*Por favor, querida.* I do not wish for you to leave."

"You should."

"Why? Because of my brother's ridiculous suspicions about you? I've told you. I don't believe you were involved in the robbery."

She hooked the bag over her arm. Like oil on canvas by a Renaissance master, she was slick, bold strokes—from her dark brunette hair to her flashing dark eyes. But her expression, so uncertain and confused, reduced her to a post-Impressionist portrait by a master like Serrault. Only from a distance could he fully appreciate the whole painting. Once close up, she'd dissolve into diaphanous dots of color.

Michael's accusations had broken Lucienne into a woman of two parts: the art expert who could properly identify a medieval scabbard, with keen expertise and a lost little girl about to venture into the big, bad world with nothing to her name but the clothes she'd stuffed into a borrowed bag.

"I appreciate that you believe in me, Alejandro." Her voice brimmed again with strength and certainty, but her eyes gave away her fear. "But I need to regroup and I have to do that alone. I hope you can understand."

He opened his mouth to argue, but stopped. She wasn't his to order around any more than she was his to pamper and spoil, no matter how much he would like to do both. He wanted to demand she stay. He wanted to strip her bare and feed her breakfast from the center of their large, rumpled bed.

"Of course," he said, forcing an understanding smile onto his face. "But I insist that you call a locksmith first and have your apartment properly secured before you return there."

She shook her head. "I'm sure whoever broke in took what they wanted last night. They have no reason to come back."

"You don't know that," he countered. "Maybe what they want is you—and if so, I can understand how they feel."

He arched a brow and she rewarded his suggestive quip with a half smile.

"Well, if you're going to make me wait for a locksmith, then I'm going to have to take you up on the offer of food."

"Good," he said, surprised by how much her agreeing to a meal invigorated him. "I'll call room service."

She captured her bottom lip with her teeth and chewed for a second, her eyes darting between the tangled sheets on the bed and the glorious sunlight on the other side of the windows.

"Or we could go out," he offered.

"Great. I know this place that has amazing, fresh sea-food." She headed toward the door, her bag still in her hands.

Delay or not, she still intended to leave him. Unless, of course, he came up with a better reason for her to stay.

The minute she pressed the elevator button, it chimed

and the doors slid open. Before climbing into the lift beside her, he checked his pocket for his wallet and phone. As he did so, the weight of his father's ring dragged on his hand.

Was this the best he could do with his family's infamous sense of adventure? Take a beautiful woman he'd just made love to out for seafood on a Friday afternoon? Since he'd ordinarily spend the day sequestered at the auction house, he supposed this was a vast improvement.

And yet, for the first time in forever, Alex wanted more. More than he'd ever imagined—more than she'd ever expect.

Maybe with the ring, he'd get both.

10

LUCY HAD LOST HER MIND. The minute Michael had shown up in Alex's suite, spouting off his suspicions about her, she should have taken off. Instead, she'd stuck around to hear exactly what Michael knew—which thankfully, wasn't much.

However, Danny had told her a long time ago that Michael was a dogged do-gooder. The youngest Murrieta brother wouldn't rest until he had solid evidence to back up what his damned gut instincts were telling him—that the woman who was now sharing his eldest brother's bed was a liar, a would-be thief and a fraud.

And he was one hundred percent right.

What Michael didn't realize, however, was that her worst crime had yet to be committed. Even if she never stole their father's ring—even if Alex never discovered her duplicity and dishonorable intentions—she'd still hurt him more than he deserved. Sooner or later, she was going to have to walk away from the man who'd defended her to the brother who was trying his best to protect him.

In other words, she'd messed everything up.

Sleeping with Alex had been a lark—an adventure—a

chance to milk the Lucienne Bonet persona for everything it was worth. Lucy had not created the name for Alex—she'd used it countless times over the years. But until Alex, that's all Lucienne had been. A false name.

Now she was a living, breathing woman with needs only he could fulfill—desires only he could satisfy. Before Alex, Lucienne had simply been an übereducated, sophisticated *nom de plume* she could hide behind until the heat from some heist cooled and she could return to San Francisco as Lucy Burnett.

But now, Lucienne belonged to Alex and Alex alone. No matter what trouble Lucy got into from this point forward, she'd never take that name again.

Alex had not only awakened the long-ignored libido of her secret self, he'd burned away all pretense until he'd reached her very core. His Prince Charming's kiss on her dormant conscience woke her up to all she was risking—all she would lose.

The worst she'd done until now was misrepresent her name and reason for taking the job at El Dorado. But no matter her previous agenda, she'd completed the task he'd paid her for—and in less time than he'd allotted. If not for yesterday's smash-and-grab, the auction would have gone off without a hitch and Lucienne Bonet would have helped him achieve a grand success without ever taking anything that did not belong to her.

Except, perhaps, a tiny piece of Alex's heart. But since she'd be leaving him with a bit of her own, she figured it was an even trade. No harm, no foul. Pleasure for pleasure.

But now, Alex had the ring.

Damn him.

Where had it come from? Why was he suddenly wearing it? Had he had it on last night in the shower, when the combination of uncertain lighting and their erotic activities had kept her from noticing it?

Then she remembered the old box he'd had on his desk. Its time period and origin matched what little she knew about the ring. How could she have been so blind?

The glitter of emerald, opal and gold drew her attention no matter how hard she tried to ignore it. She salivated for a closer look, both as someone who appreciated the fine craftsmanship of the antique piece and as the woman who'd relentlessly pursued it for six weeks. Since Alex was on the phone, arranging for a locksmith to meet them at her apartment in a few hours, he didn't seem to notice her staring.

But as they neared the lobby exit, she ripped her gaze away. What if her sudden interest in the ring gave credence to Michael's accusations? Alex had come to her defense, but Michael's suspicions might have planted seeds of doubt. If Michael had remembered precisely where he'd first met her, he'd eventually find proof of her real identity, though she had gone to visit Danny under another false name. But once he made the connections, Alex would have no choice but to accept that she could not be trusted.

Michael was his brother. Michael would have proof. She was just some woman he'd taken to bed.

A sudden fear seized her. What if Michael already knew where he'd first made her acquaintance, but simply lacked proof that she was the woman who'd signed in to see Danny?

"Wait!" she said, tugging on Alex's arm as he started through the hotel's revolving glass door.

"Hold one minute, please," Alex said to the person on the phone, then pressed it to his chest. "What's wrong?"

"I forgot something upstairs."

He eyed her quizzically, but turned to go back to the elevator.

"No need for you to go up, too," she said, forcing calm into her voice. "Finish your call. I'll just run up, if I may have the key?"

Without a moment's hesitation, Alex extracted the key card, which he handed her as he continued his discussion in rapid-fire Spanish.

As she hurried back to the suite, she tried not to think about the fact he hardly knew her, and yet trusted her so easily. She also tried not to imagine the bitter depth of darkness she'd see in his fathomless eyes once he realized she'd lied to him. When was the last time anyone had looked her at like Alex did—without a single hint of suspicion that eventually she would rip him off?

Her entire life, she'd associated with cheats and liars and thieves—her parents first and foremost. Even Danny hadn't trusted her enough to tell her exactly how a ring that wasn't worth more than a couple of thousand dollars could save his life.

He'd said his silence was for her own good—the less she knew, the less she could reveal if caught or interrogated. But what if he was lying, too?

Everyone in this scenario was lying about something—even Michael, who hadn't told Alex about the third Murrieta son. Everyone except Alex, who possessed no instinct as strong as his need to be honorable.

When the elevator doors slid open in the penthouse, she filed away her worries about everyone's lies but her own. Right now, she had to make sure that she hadn't left anything behind that Michael could use against her.

She darted into the living room and searched for the coffee cup she'd had in her hands when Michael had come up for his impromptu interrogation. She wouldn't put it past him to return to his brother's suite and retrieve the mug so he could run her fingerprints. As an adult, she'd never been arrested, so she *shouldn't* be in the system.

But she had a juvenile record. What if the court had never sealed it? Or worse, what if the FBI had the power to crack it open?

Luckily, none of the cups were missing. She dug underneath the sink in the wet bar for liquid cleanser and gave them each a good scrub. She then darted into the bedroom and wiped down the surfaces she'd touched—the vanity, the mirror, the handle of the blow dryer, the bedside table. If Michael came back while she and Alex were out, he'd find nothing to use against her.

Before she left, she collected the things she'd left in the basket from the concierge—including a toothbrush, hairbrush and lip gloss. With no purse, she dropped them all into the bag with her clothes. Before she called the elevator for her return trip downstairs, she rummaged through the pockets of her pencil skirt and found the check Alex had given her.

She'd cash it at the first opportunity, but for now, she kept it safe by tucking it in her bra. Maybe the cash could buy Danny more time.

No matter what secrets he might be keeping from her, she couldn't let him down. If Danny suffered because she'd been too blinded by sex or guilt to finish what she'd started, she'd never forgive herself. Danny had never been a brother to Alex or Michael—but he'd always been one to her.

When she reappeared downstairs, Alex was not in the lobby or in his car. On the off-chance Michael was lurking around, she refused the chauffeur's offer to take her bags. She doubled back into the hotel and spotted Alex inside a boutique, admiring a brown leather messenger bag—as well as a coordinating purse and wallet.

"The hotel is arranging for a new cell phone for you," he said when she entered. "My driver will collect it while we have lunch. I won't feel safe leaving you until I know you have a way to contact me. In the meantime, you can put your belongings in here."

She stared at the gifts with openmouthed awe. She wanted to refuse his generosity, but she couldn't manage more than, "I'll reimburse you as soon as I get to a bank."

He waved her offer aside. "No need."

She grabbed his arm and impaled him with her stare. "I appreciate your giving nature, Alex, I honestly do. But thanks to you, I can afford beautiful things like this."

The battle between his gallant nature and his desire to please her played out on his face. God, he was the most amazing man. Handsome beyond imagination, strong beyond measure and yet smart enough to know when to back down.

"Of course," he said. "But in the meantime, you'll allow me to pay for these purchases until we can get to your bank?"

"Thank you," she said.

Alex touched the spot on his face where her lips had met his skin. She thought maybe she'd left behind some of her lip gloss, but there was no trace of the pale pink color.

He leaned forward and whispered, *"De nada, mi tesoro,"* and then returned the gesture by brushing his lips across her temple.

Chaste as the kiss was, she flushed. And this time, her trembling wasn't from fear, as it had been upstairs, but from a build-up of emotion that would have to burn through her skin in order to escape.

In what seemed like a single spike in body temperature, Lucy had transformed from a woman hell bent on grand theft to one consumed by need and desire. Her mind swirled with the heated memories of the night before. Her body quaked with the hunger to relive every sensation, every convergence, every glorious release.

In the dark and in his bed, she'd been neither Lucienne Bonet nor Lucy Burnett. With Alex touching her, arousing her, driving inside her, she'd morphed into a new and foreign being—a woman who took her pleasures because they were offered freely and because they felt amazing. She hadn't worried about the consequences. Not to Alex or herself.

But now, in the daylight and under his intense gaze, the weight of her regrets nearly crushed her. Nothing she'd ever done in the past had haunted her as intensely as what she was going to do to Alex.

As he took care of signing the bill of sale, Lucy concentrated on regaining her equilibrium. She'd never experienced so many emotions at once: attraction, desperation, gratitude, resentment, guilt. They swamped her with their conflicting depths and shallows. Before Alex, sailing through life had been so much simpler.

And so much colder.

But there was no "before Alex" anymore. For the rest of her life, no matter what happened to Daniel or the ring, she'd judge her every happiness or failure against the time she'd spent with the man she might have loved—and who might have loved her—if only she hadn't lied.

11

DURING THE ENTIRE silent ride from the hotel, Alex watched Lucienne silently toy with the strap of the leather messenger bag. She alternated between gazing at the simple tote with a secret smile on her lips and staring sightlessly out the window, the corners of her mouth on the brink of a heartbreaking frown. No matter what demons she was fighting in the privacy of her thoughts, she never let go of his gift.

And this unconscious gesture made up his mind.

She was the woman for him.

Like his father's ring on his hand, the realization weighed on him with both heaviness and warmth. Though the ring had once belonged to another man—actually, a long line of men—the circle of gold and gems fit his finger like an extra layer of skin. In much the same way, Lucienne had become a part of him.

In keeping with the ring's legend, he supposed he should have swept her away on a parasailing excursion across the rough waters of the bay or taken her rappelling in nearby caverns. Instead, he'd arranged for them to enjoy a simple day on Fisherman's Wharf. He craved the sunshine, the energy of the city in all its kitschy glory. And he wanted to learn more about Lucienne, beyond her erogenous zones or her knowledge of art and antiques. For a man who rarely knew more about his lovers beyond their full names and what they did for a living, this was the truest adventure he'd ever embarked on.

In the first ten minutes after his driver dropped them off, he learned that since moving to San Francisco, she'd only come to the Wharf once. While they ate Dungeness crab fresh from the ocean and gently steamed in a pot perched on a street vendor's single burner, he discovered that she adored seafood despite a very bad reaction to her mother's first and only attempt at *ceviche.*

"My mother's *ceviche* is passable," he said, "but my grandmother's? It sings."

"So your grandparents are still alive?" she asked.

He nodded. "*Mi abuela* is eighty-three and *mi abuelo,* eighty."

Lucienne raised her eyebrows. "She married a younger man. I like her already."

"She'd like you." He had no basis for this statement. He'd never officially introduced a single one of his paramours to his family. His grandfather and mother had met a few at various charity functions or social events, but neither voiced an opinion—probably because they knew not to bother. None of the women lasted for very long.

"Well, I'm sure I'd like her, if she had a hand in raising you. Are you still close to them? I mean, do you see them often?"

"Every Sunday, when I'm in Madrid, or *mi abuela* would have my head. After my father left, my mother moved back into her parents' estate. We had our own private wing, but I rarely stayed there except to sleep. My cousins were always at the house and my grandfather, when he wasn't at the auction house, spent every free moment teaching us chess or taking us to museums or introducing us to his artist friends or celebrities. We were never bored or idle."

"Sounds like an idyllic childhood."

The longing in her voice grabbed him—and the faraway look in her eyes tugged at his chest until it hurt. He had absolutely no idea what kind of life she'd led in her youth, but he had no doubt it lacked the unconditional love he'd experienced on a daily basis. He may not have had a father, but maybe he'd had something better?

"As far as childhoods go," he said, brushing a soft kiss along her temple, "I have little to complain about."

"And yet, you still hated your father for a very long time."

He glanced down at her, surprised. Had he discussed his feelings toward Ramon with her? As far as he knew, he'd kept his resentments to himself, except for Michael.

"How do you know that?"

Guilt flashed across her wide dark eyes. "You don't look at his portrait. And when someone comments on the physical similarities between the two of you, you flinch."

He straightened, knowing she spoke the truth, even though he'd hoped he'd been a little less transparent. "Yes, well, that's where things weren't quite so idyllic."

He'd considered turning the conversation to her own childhood, but the set of her forced smile convinced him otherwise. Pressing her for self-revelation—particularly if her memories were painful—was completely counterintuitive to his plan to enjoy the day in a relaxed and buoyant atmosphere. Instead, he took her hand, and after consulting a large map painted on a weatherworn marquee, headed leisurely toward Pier 39.

In a million years, Alex never would have figured himself for the kind of man who'd laugh over pithy sayings on T-shirts hanging in tourist shop windows or toss a large bill into the overturned cap of a man playing guitar on the sidewalk outside a bar. But the shirts were funny and the musical strains, strummed with a rhythm born on the cobbled streets of Madrid, reminded him of home.

After he exchanged greetings in Spanish with the musician—clearly down on his luck if the holes in his shoes were any indication—Lucienne whistled in surprise.

"You object to my giving him money?" he asked.

"Give all you want, but don't be surprised if we soon have a half-dozen vagrants trying to explain how we can use the cable car system or find Ghirardelli Square. For a fee, of course."

Alex eyed her warily. She suddenly didn't sound like someone who had only come to the tourist area of her new city once.

"I'm from Spain, not Mars. I understand about...*cómo se dice*...street smarts."

"Right," she said.

Without warning she tugged her hand out of his. She made a show of reaching toward the bags and purses hanging from a vendor's lopsided cart, but Alex wasn't fooled.

Lucienne had inadvertently given something away. Had she lied about her familiarity with this area of San Francisco? And if so, why?

And could she be lying about other things as well?

Alex met her forced smile with one he hoped was more natural. He refused to believe that Michael's instincts about Lucienne had any merit, though he had to admit—at least to himself—that his brother's unsubstantiated claims had planted a seed of doubt. Maybe he'd misconstrued her innocent observation. She had traveled widely and the rules of engagement with panhandlers did not vary much from city to city.

But it wasn't so much the comment that set off his warning bells; it was the way she suddenly did not meet his eyes.

"Is everything all right, Lucienne?"

"What?" she said, and this time, her surprise seemed entirely genuine. "I'm having a wonderful time."

He took her hand and reeled her in close so that her knuckles brushed his cheek. "Then why are you shaking?"

Her eyes flashed with something so reminiscent of fear, he thought for a moment that she might run. To keep her still, he smoothed the back of her hand over his cheek, and then kissed the spot on her wrist where her pulse thrummed against her flesh. In moments, the tension building up within her released on a sigh.

"You're too good to me, Alejandro."

Her mouth curved into a tentative smile. Now he thought he understood. He was unaccustomed to treating a woman with gentle care and consideration and she was unused to accepting it.

"I've only begun to be good to you, Lucienne. That is a promise."

LUCY BIT THE INSIDE of her mouth and silently cursed herself for the slip.

It was a small mistake. Barely noticeable. But to a man poisoned by his brother's suspicions, one minor error could cost her everything.

Alex might not be a native, but he was no rube. Next to Danny, he was the smartest man she'd ever met. Actually, he was smarter than Danny, as evidenced by the fact that to date, Alex had never spent a single second inside a jail cell.

Maybe it was the soft, salt-scented breeze. Maybe it was

the warmth of her hand in his or the lazy tempo of their steps, but she was forgetting who she was—or, more accurately, who she was supposed to be. He spoke about his childhood and his family with such aplomb, she couldn't help but envy him. Alex might have been abandoned by his father, but he'd turned out fine. Damned fine.

She, on the other hand, had grown up in a seemingly perfect nuclear family and had ended up using her considerable brain power and eye for art to support an illegal trade in stolen goods.

She wasn't sure if this qualified as ironic, but it was close.

When Alex had made love to her wrist with a single, tender kiss, she knew she was safe with him—but not for long. The more time she spent with him, the greater his chances of figuring out her scheme. And yet, she couldn't muster quite enough fear to bolt. She was feeling too safe, too comfortable with her arm hooked in his and his shoulder the perfect pillow for her cheek as they strolled.

"You're one surprise after another," she said as they crossed from the sidewalk onto the busy, noisy pier.

"Why? Because we are taking time to enjoy our afternoon instead of setting up a mobile office at the hotel and working?"

She laughed.

He stretched his hand out in front of him—the one with the ring. He seemed to be observing the scratched stone from several different angles before he caught her looking and tucked his fingers in his pocket.

He tightened his arm around her waist. "It's a beautiful day."

"Every day since you arrived in San Francisco has been beautiful," she argued. "I was starting to wonder if you'd ordered up Chamber of Commerce weather along with your room service."

"If only I had that power. No, I believe today exceeds all others. I am, after all, with you. Everything is different now. Everything is better."

Man, oh, man. Lucy couldn't resist snuggling close and inhaling the scent of the bay as it mingled with the fine wool blend of his jacket.

"I think you're the one who has changed everything," she murmured, but from his gentle squeeze of her waist, she knew he'd heard.

"Someone certainly has," he replied, then he laughed. "My grandfather still takes long, leisurely strolls like this every afternoon before siesta. He claims it keeps him young. But I fell out of the habit years ago. If not for the robbery, I would have been sequestered at the office today, shut up with reports and paperwork. Instead, I'm walking with a beautiful woman in the crisp, fresh air and enjoying the simple pleasure of holding her hand."

And on that note, Lucy fell hard.

Never in her life had a man revealed himself so willingly, all the while shattering nearly every pre-conceived notion she'd had about him since before they'd met. A man devoted only to urbane pursuits would not have laughed so genuinely at the preschoolers barking and clapping with the sea lions lazing on the end of the pier. A man obsessed with only the most sophisticated pursuits would not have hailed a cab so they could backtrack to Ghirardelli Square and stand in line for a brownie nut sundae that melted down the sides and dripped pure, gooey heaven onto their fingers.

A man raised on entitled expectations would not have licked the fudgy sauce off her hand. Not, at least, in public. But even amid the crowds of tourists jostling past them

he feel of his tongue flicking into the crevices between
her fingers invoked an intimacy she couldn't deny. He was
reawakening yearnings and desires she'd tried to contain
all morning—needs he would willingly fulfill, if only she
gave him the chance.

But there was no more time. She'd had her fun last
night, and this afternoon was simply a long and luxurious
goodbye. Once their driver retrieved them and returned
her to her apartment, she'd shed the Lucienne Bonet persona for good. She couldn't risk hurting Alex by stealing
his father's ring. Not even for Danny. She'd help him some
other way.

But more than that, she couldn't risk hurting herself.

He spotted his car and gave the driver a curt wave to ac-
knowledge his presence. For that split second, the starched,
straight-backed Alejandro Aguilar made a return appearance, though he instantly disappeared the minute he turned
his openly hungry gaze back to her.

The man brimmed with passion. She couldn't imagine
how she'd ever viewed him as cool and unaffected, though
that had been Danny's assessment, not hers. But now, she
looked at Alejandro with eyes opened by a night of hot sex
and a lazy day in the crisp sunlight. What else might she
learn about him, if only she had time?

Time.

She had about as much of that as she had cash on hand.
He'd already slid his palm to the small of her back to guide
her toward the car. In less than a half hour, he'd deposit
her in front of the apartment, and thirty minutes after that,
she should have shed her hair extensions, popped out her
colored contacts, swapped her sleek business attire for
jeans and a sweatshirt and disappeared into the rolling
San Francisco fog.

In the time it took most women to get ready for work

in the morning, Lucy would say goodbye to the woma
who'd snared the world's most intriguing and sensual ma
then let him slip away.

Thanks to traffic, the drive took twice as long as she
expected. Although the city of San Francisco was onl
about thirty-five square miles, steep hills and windin
roads impeded easy travel. Usually, she relied on publi
transit. If not for the occasional quick getaway or visit t
Danny in jail, Lucy would not have needed her car, whic
she kept far from her apartment in a Financial Distri
parking lot easily accessible by streetcar or bus.

Concentrating on how she could get to her vehicle an
hit the bank to cash her check before the close of the bus
ness day, she hadn't noticed the fixed direction of her ga
until Alex moved his hand across her knee.

Lost in thought, she'd been staring at the ring.

"I'm surprised you haven't asked me about it," he sai

"I'm sorry?"

He tilted his hand toward her, so that she got her fir
full-on look at the piece of jewelry that had turned her li
upside down.

"My father's ring." He twisted and turned his hand
that late afternoon light caused the center emerald to spa
kle like deep, Caribbean waters. "Michael brought it to n
yesterday. I wasn't going to wear it, but…"

As much as she wanted to ignore this final temptatio
the art dealer in her would not let her off so easy.

"It's remarkably unusual," she said, taking his hand in
hers. Noticing the center stone, she winced. The unsight
scratch almost looked like a rudimentary number *2…*
was it, perhaps, a *Z?*

Though the black opals on either side were pristine, tl
emerald was clearly damaged and the gold worn. How
earth could an old ring like this save Danny's life?

"Is this what was in the box you had on your desk yesterday?"

It was a natural question, she thought. Now that he'd introduced the topic, she had no reason to hide her curiosity. He'd expect as much from Lucienne Bonet, a fact that threw her fully back into character for the first time since morning.

He nodded. "Apparently, it's been in my family for generations. It even comes with a legend, though I'm reluctant to believe a word of it."

She glanced up into his eyes. In the dark depths of his gaze, she saw longing and, if she wasn't mistaken, pride. But most telling was what was missing. Up until this moment, every word he uttered from declaring the time to ruminating on the weather held the power of conviction.

Not now. She heard uncertainty in his words. And maybe, hope.

"Tell me," she encouraged.

He removed his hand from hers and waved away her request.

"Es tonto," he said. "A childish story. A fairy tale."

She scooted closer and slid her hand up his leg, enchanted by his denial. She wanted to hear this story—and not because it might explain the ring's value to Danny. His father's legacy clearly meant something to Alex and she wanted to know why.

"Please," she begged. "I love fairy tales."

"Even the kind *without* happy endings?"

A sad smile welled up from deep inside her. "I've learned not to worry too much about endings anymore, Alex. In my world, it's the endings that cause all the trouble."

12

ALEX SWALLOWED DEEPLY, disoriented by a sudden wave of uncertainty.

He'd already revealed so much to Lucienne. He'd told her things he'd never shared with any other lover—insights into his childhood and upbringing that he rarely thought about, much less spoke out loud. But somehow, telling her about his father's crazy belief that he was the direct descendant of a legendary lover and hero pushed him beyond his comfort zone.

But then, wasn't that what the ring was all about?

"It belonged to a man named Joaquin Murrieta," he said.

Her expression was quizzical. "Murrieta? Like your father?"

He nodded.

"Is that why the name sounds so familiar?"

"Probably, unless you've done extensive research into the history of colonial California."

She frowned. "That's not exactly my area of expertise. But the name still rings a bell. I think…there was a book about him on the shelf in your office."

"There was?"

She nodded. "Right below your father's portrait. First edition, actually. I listed it in the holdings of the auction house, but I didn't see any reason to move it. I figured that if your father kept it so close, it must have been a personal favorite."

How had Alex not noticed? Probably because he spent so much time trying to avoid looking at the mural.

"Who was he?" she asked.

"From all accounts, a notorious *bandito*."

"*Bandito?* Like who, Zorro?"

If he continued, he'd sound like an idiot at worst and a man caught up in delusions of grandeur at best. Neither circumstance would be particularly appealing, but he'd come this far. He might as well dive into the deep end. He didn't reply, but pierced her with a potent stare.

She took a second to absorb his meaning.

"You're joking, right?"

He shook his head. She pulled his hand into the light and up to her face.

"That's a *Z*?"

"Reportedly."

"It could have been etched by anyone," she said, with an odd note of desperation. "Maybe to increase the value of the piece by attaching it to a romantic myth?"

Alex might have considered that as well, if not for the fact that he'd examined the documentation himself. "If that were the plan, it failed miserably. The last time the ring changed owners through a sale, it fetched thirty-five dollars at a Los Angeles pawnshop."

She grasped his hand tighter. "The black opals alone are worth ten times that amount. They're huge."

He couldn't contain a wry smile, which, if her blush was

any indication, she interpreted precisely as he'd mean
her to.

"A similarity between you and the ring?" she asked
saucily.

"You must be the judge."

She cleared her throat and glanced toward the driver
whose head was turned dutifully toward the road.

Still, they were in a sedan, not a stretch limo.

"That's a conversation for another time and place," she
said.

"If you insist," he teased.

She sat up straight, shifting focus. "Do you have paper
to support the ring's legacy?"

"Ramon put together an impressive collection of letter
and journal entries that trace directly back to the man wh
commissioned the ring and then lost it to my notorious an
cestor in a game of chance."

"Where?"

"Here, in California, I believe."

"No, I mean, where are the papers?"

It took Alex a split second to remember, and when h
did, he leaned forward and grabbed his driver's shoulde
"Take us to El Dorado Auction House. And hurry."

"What's wrong?"

"The documentation for the ring," he said. "I did no
lock up the portfolio before the thieves broke into the auc
tion house. I'd only just received them from Michael an
did not think to look for them before we left."

"Why would anyone steal papers? They're not wort
anything. I mean, not on the open market."

"No, but they are worth something to me."

The driver diverted to the auction house. The police
done with their investigation, had released the building a
hour ago, according to the text message that Alex had ig

nored in favor of enjoying ice cream with Lucienne. Now, he could barely get the key into the door or remember the alarm codes in his charge to reach the office. He found the leather portfolio shoved between two books with faded titles on the spine, precisely where he'd left it.

"The ring must mean a lot to you."

Lucienne's tremulous voice barely broke through the rapid pounding of his heart.

"Excuse me?"

She gestured at the way he clutched the history of the ring's progression to his chest as if it were a priceless first edition rather than a dusty collection of old papers. He relaxed his hold, but the damage was done.

"May I?" she asked.

She must think him a crazed lunatic. He instantly held the package out to her. With a smile, she accepted his offering between flattened palms.

With only a brief glance over her shoulder, she made her way across the mess on the floor to his desk, sat down and spread out the papers in front of her. She flipped on the magnified lamp and used it to scan the harder-to-read pages. She lingered quite a while on the journal entry from the *señorita* who'd witnessed firsthand the change in Joaquin's prowess once he'd won the ring. Of all the documentation Ramon had gathered, this had been the most convincing evidence—at least, to him.

And the most provocative.

"Do you need help with the translation?" he offered.

His attempt to keep his tone even wavered. Barely a day ago, he could have cared less about his father or the ring. Now, so much had changed.

Was it because of the ring…or because of Lucienne?

She did not answer immediately, but clutched the paper tightly, her mouth moving wordlessly as she read. Her eyes widened a bit, but he didn't know if this was because of her struggle with Spanish or the document's racy content.

When she turned to face him, her expression revealed nothing.

"Yes, a translation would help." She smiled slyly as he held out the page, encased in slick, crinkly plastic.

She turned the chair to face him.

Strolling through the city, he hadn't realized just how short her skirt was—or just how curvy her breasts looked in her silky, backless blouse. With a deep breath that he hoped would stave off his instinct to seduce her, he knelt beside her and lowered the light so that he could see the faded ink.

"It was written by a woman," he explained.

"I got that much," Lucienne replied, running her fingers lazily up his arm.

He shifted and tried to ignore the heat low in his groin. "She says here that she was Joaquin's betrothed, promised to him because her father owed the bandit a debt."

"Sucked to be a woman back then." She reversed the direction of her hand so that her touch slid down his arm.

Her fingernail scraped across his knuckles. The vibrations of her touch reverberated against the gold of his ring, which suddenly felt hot and heavy.

"Sí." He shifted so that his eyes were level with her breasts and her legs were tucked against his side. "Luckily, things have improved."

He looked away from the paper and watched her lick her lips. "They have, haven't they? What was her name?"

He flipped the paper over. "Maria Rosa."

"I love when you roll your *r*s," she said, breathless.

He leaned in closer and thought about pressing his lips against the hollow of her throat when he repeated the name.

"Maria Rosa," he continued, grinning when she sighed,

"was not a total stranger to the ways of men and women. In fact, prior to his winning the ring, Joaquin took his future bride for a test drive, so to speak."

Lucienne leaned in close. "And I bet he was a magnificent lover," she said, her lips brushing against his cheek.

"Actually, no. That's why she wrote this letter to her more knowledgeable married sister. Apparently, before the ring, he'd barely lasted five minutes and didn't even remove his boots."

"Barbarian," she murmured, spawning a trill of awareness through his veins.

"Once he had the ring, however, he developed a sudden interest in taking his time."

"How like a Murrieta man."

She slipped the letter out of his grasp and scanned the pages until she found the passage. She read aloud—in perfect Spanish.

"But he came to me again last night a different man. He climbed in through my window, and with a whispered plea promised that if I didn't shout out, he'd convince me to marry him because I wanted to and not because of his bargain with papa. He had me sit on the bed and watch him undress, slowly. He told me how heavy his guns were on his hips. He showed me the scars on his shoulder and chest. He invited me to touch the puckered skin. I was afraid to go near him, but he asked so kindly, I took my candle and did as he said. Then he removed his boots and pants. He asked me to watch him while he washed the dust and grime of the street from his body. Then he invited me to dry him with the blanket from my bed. I am almost shamed to admit that I did.

"Is that where you got the idea?"

The break in her recitation caught him unaware and his obvious shock sparked her explanation. Her pronunciation was not perfect, but her lilting voice had conveyed the sheer innocence and wonder of Maria Rosa's discovery of her lover's naked form. He'd been smooth, Joaquin, to try and undo the damage of his first tryst with his future bride.

"He asked her to dry him off, like you did for me," she continued. "Is this where you got the idea?"

He shook his head. "You alone inspired me, *querida*. I haven't read this letter before, not with care. I just skimmed it for the general idea."

"It's pretty hot stuff, considering the source," she said.

"I thought you needed a translation," he chided.

She smiled. "No, I just wanted you closer. I've done some work for a group of Colombian collectors, so it helped to pick up the language. My Spanish isn't as perfect as yours—"

"You speak beautifully," he assured her, trying to ignore the spike of hope this fact inspired.

Since he'd met Lucienne, he'd known he wanted to sleep with her. Making love to her had been a fantasy come to life, but he'd never considered that perhaps he did not have to leave her once his time in the United States was over. If she spoke his native tongue, maybe she'd want to learn a bit about the culture.

Firsthand.

"She was shocked by the sudden change in Joaquin." Lucienne leaned forward, turning her body so he could see the text she was pointing to. "She says here that he convinced her to touch him and watch how her fingers transformed him. That must have been heady stuff to a girl who had no say in whom she married or who crept into her room in the middle of the night."

Their shoulders pressed together and Alex inhaled her sweet perfume, tinged by the scents of the bay and the aroma of chocolate that lingered around her lips.

"Is it heady to you?"

His voice was raspy with pent-up passion. His skin, even beneath his clothes, sparked with needfulness. When she slid her hand down his chest and expertly released his belt, the rush of blood to his groin made him waver on his knees.

She scooted forward and pressed her hand between the waistband of his briefs and his bare flesh, encircling his cock completely. She constricted her fingers and the exquisite pressure nearly squeezed him out of his skin. To counter his impending loss of control, he nuzzled her breasts and blazed a matching trail up her legs with his hands.

"Oh, yes," she said.

Under her skilled ministrations, he grew harder than an uncut diamond. She tugged and taunted, teasing his head with her thumb, sending shockwaves of fire throughout his system.

Though his lips were mere inches from hers, he could not tear his gaze away from her pupils. Even when he pressed her legs apart and reached beneath her skirt to find her panties damp with need, her eyes remained a steady and unwavering brown.

His brain tripped, but the sudden sense that something was wrong disappeared under the power of her mouth on his. She kissed him hard, thrusting her tongue deep while she stroked him. In seconds, he could think of nothing but matching her need by unleashing his.

He removed her panties and his slacks. While she cleared away the detritus from his desk with one swipe of her arm, he ripped into his pocket and retrieved a condom. Without a single thought to slow, measured seduction, he snapped the latex over his engorged flesh, lifted her onto the polished mahogany and pushed into her.

"Alex," she said. "Yes, Alex. God, yes."

He lifted her blouse, tore aside the cups of her bra and took the whole of her areola into his mouth, biting and nipping and suckling her until she cried out again, this time her words nonsensical. He drove deep and hard into her warm, tight wetness, his balls slapping painfully against the edge of the desk.

But he didn't care. He simply scooted her forward so that her amazing ass cushioned the blows.

"Dios mio, Lucienne. Me vuelves loco."

And then he told her, in the coarsest language he knew, how he would not stop until she screamed in pleasure.

She replied with another long litany of "Yes, yes, yes."

He buoyed her hips with his hands, adjusting his thrusts until the pitch of her cries peaked. He increased the tempo and depth, and with one last, long stroke set off an explosion of sensation that rocked him to his core.

When he was certain he wouldn't pass out from lack of air, he kissed her again, still inside her, still wanting her, even though they were both sweaty and spent.

He withdrew from her long enough to dispense with the condom in the adjacent washroom and return with a damp towel, which he used to smooth the perspiration from her body, starting with the swollen pink flesh between her thighs.

For a long instant, she allowed him this intimacy—long enough for him to realize that he wanted to be with Lucienne, not just for one night or even a succession of nights, but for the full breadth of a relationship. He did not know how long they would last. That hardly mattered. But he didn't think he could live with himself if he didn't take this chance to explore every intimacy, every conversation, every experience a man and a woman could share together.

And that could take a very long time.

Alex slid the towel up her bare thighs, across her middle and then around her red, freshly bitten breasts. He bent forward so that he could use his tongue to soothe the tiny welts he'd put there with his teeth, but she braced her hands firmly on his shoulders and pushed him back.

"Alex, don't," she said.

He obeyed, watching in confusion as she rolled off the desk and attempted to straighten her top.

"Lucienne?"

She nearly tripped over him in her haste to retrieve her panties and skirt. "We have to go."

He dressed quickly, but not without keeping his gaze locked on Lucienne as she lingered in the doorway, swatting at her hair to tame the tangled locks, but not looking in the mirror that was only a few steps away.

Once he was dressed, he locked the portfolio documenting the ring's origins inside the floor safe and then joined her in the doorway. He attempted to cup her elbow, but her infinitesimal movement away from him was effective.

"Lucienne," he started, then stopped. He knew he should apologize, but he couldn't quite wrap his tongue around the words. He was not sorry. She'd initiated this unplanned tryst and he could not regret that he'd succumbed. The experience had been fast and furious—but no less amazing than last night's slow seduction.

She pressed her hand to his chest and looked up at him. Her gaze only met his for an instant before she engaged in a fruitless attempt to smooth the wrinkles out of his shirt. "I'm sorry, Alex. I mean, I'm not sorry we made love again. I've fantasized about a hundred different ways we would make love inside this auction house, and on top of your desk was at the top of the list."

"But?" Taking her hand into his, he kissed the center of her palm.

She made a tiny squeak of protestation before pulling completely out of his grasp.

"My apartment. We've probably missed the locksmith."

He shook his head. "When I called, I offered him his daily rate by the hour if he waited for us. I have no doubt he's stayed."

"Oh," she said. "Great… I mean, that's so generous."

She was backing up in the gallery and stumbled over an upturned column. He hurried forward to catch her, but she waved him off.

"I need space, Alex," she insisted. "Time to think."

"Think about what? I want to be with you, Lucienne. Don't you want the same?"

Though she shook her head, she couldn't seem to push out any more words with which to bolster her weak denial. He could not argue that things were progressing rapidly. In any other circumstances, he might have been the one grasping for an excuse to put some distance between them, especially with a woman who challenged everything he'd ever believed about relationships and sex.

But with Lucienne, he had no fear, no desire to retreat. He did not know whether he should blame the ring's legend or the power of his undeniable chemical connection to Lucienne. Or was his longing for her a progression from the man he'd been before she sauntered into his life and the man he was becoming now that he'd put his resentments aside?

In the short time since he and Lucienne had become lovers, Alex felt transformed. He was no longer the person he'd been when he left Spain—obsessed with work and honor and appearances of success. He no longer hated the father who'd abandoned him as a child. In fact, he felt a slight pang of gratitude. If not for Ramon's wandering ways, Alex never would have had a brother, never would have come to San Francisco. Never would have met Lucienne.

The revelation rocked him back on his heels. Maybe they did need some time apart.

He straightened, first his spine, and then his clothes. "Perhaps you are right. Distance could serve us both."

For good measure, he slipped off his father's ring. He scanned the desk for the inlaid box, which had been knocked unceremoniously to the ground. He shoved the ring inside and reopened the floor safe.

"You're not going to leave it there, are you?" she asked. "That kind of safe could be cracked by an amateur."

He glanced up into her shocked expression. "If the amateur knows it is here, I suppose. They showed no interest in it yesterday and I have no reason to suspect they'll come back."

She dropped to her knees beside him and locked her hand around his. This time, when their eyes met, she did not look away.

"Don't leave the ring behind, Alex. Please. It's worth too much."

She had no idea how true her appraisal was. The ring was priceless, not only because it connected him to his family, but because it would forever tether him to Lucienne.

For that reason alone, he knew he'd never part with it.

"The first time I wore this ring was when we made love," he explained, retrieving it from the box and slipping it back onto his hand. "It connects us, Lucienne. It always will, whether you like it or not."

13

THE TROUBLE WAS, Lucienne did like it. Very much.

After convincing Alex to keep the ring with him, they'd returned to the car. If he sensed her continued wariness, he had no clue to the true root cause. His confession about his connection to her and the ring had cut her deeper than any double-edged blade. How could he know that the piece of jewelry that he thought bound them together was actually the wedge that would drive them apart?

Not because she was going to take it, though she now understood why a collector might risk a daylight robbery to get it. With the documentation Ramon had amassed, the ring's value had increased beyond the sum of its parts. Lucy's mind whirred, trying to connect the many collectors she'd done business with over the years—the collectors Danny had worked with—who'd go to such lengths to procure such a treasure, but no one came immediately to mind.

Danny needed to know the truth about the ring, and he needed to tell Lucy everything he knew about who wanted it from him and why. Before Alex had shared the ring's history with her, she'd been able to delude herself that the robbery could have been random. Now, she knew better. She did not believe in coincidences. The thieves had specifically targeted jewelry. They'd stolen her purse, but left perfectly sellable items behind, like the jeweled dagger. Somehow, someone other than Danny knew that she was working for the auction house—and until she found out otherwise, she had to operate on the assumption that they were after the ring, too.

Her life, and Alex's, had been put in danger. She had to get to Danny right away, before either one of them got hurt. She believed in her heart that if Danny had known his brother—truly knew Alex's heart the way Lucy did now—he never would have asked her to steal their family legacy or put his brother in harm's way.

Danny wasn't exactly scrupulous, but he wasn't cruel. More than anyone, she knew his innate kindness and loyalty. And she had Alex's check. With it, she hoped to buy off whoever had decided to trade Danny's safety for the ring. Or at least, buy them some time.

But none of this changed her predicament with Alex. She'd still deceived him about who she was. And she'd continued to lie long after trust had cemented their bond. When he'd stood up to Michael on her behalf. When they'd made love—not once, but twice.

She'd had chance after chance to tell him why she'd really come to work for him.

But she couldn't run from the truth anymore. As soon as they returned to her apartment, she had to come clean. Alex deserved to know the whole story, so he could protect himself. So he could protect the ring. So he could despise her the way she deserved.

The minute she made the decision, the trip to the apartment building seemed to happen in a flash. Oblivious to her dread, Alex asked the driver to pull up next to the locksmith, who was, as he'd assured her, waiting patiently in his van, drinking a latte. Together, they went into the lobby and met the building super—a young, artistic, twenty-something known as Dice, who always dressed either in all black or all white, save for one dot of the opposite color. Today, he looked like the Good Humor man who'd sat in a pool of ink.

He smacked the air near Lucy's cheek with a kiss.

"Damned cretins," he said, his voice lilting with outrage. "None of the neighbors heard a thing. Did they get anything irreplaceable?"

"I'm not sure," she said, trying not to think about the one stolen item she'd never get back—Alex's trust. "I haven't been inside since the break-in."

Dice gave Alejandro and the locksmith a cold appraisal, though his gaze heated when he returned to Alex for a second stare.

She slipped her hand into Alex's arm. She hadn't meant to be territorial, but her time with him was growing shorter. Dice gave her a sassy smile and whacked her lightly on the shoulder.

"Well, you seem to have everything under control now. Give me a buzz if you need anything repaired. I'd have changed your locks myself, but that's the one craft I've never mastered. I can install security cameras and alarms, though, so let me know."

After he left and they started up to her third-floor apartment, Alex said, "Friend of yours?"

"I wish," she said honestly. What she wouldn't have given for a real friend right now, one with no ties to illegal activity or Danny or her past. Someone who'd let her cry on their shoulder over all she was about to lose.

Alex arched an eyebrow.

"I haven't had much time to make friends with anyone

here, but Dice has been sweet," she replied. "I only moved in here a week before I started at El Dorado, and in case you haven't noticed, the boss there is a real taskmaster and doesn't leave a lot of time for socializing."

"So I've heard."

Despite the lack of belongings inside her apartment, it was still a shock to see the place in disarray. She had only Michael's word that the scattering of her clothes and up-ending of her dresser drawers had been done by thieves rather than a rogue FBI agent on a mission. Of course, if he'd been the one to discover her hiding place in the air vent, he would have revealed what he'd found. With her real driver's license and credit cards, he could have proved to Alex that his appraiser—and now lover—was not who she said she was.

A fact she'd reveal to Alex once the locks were changed and they were alone.

"Did they take much?" Alex asked, exploring the apartment while the locksmith got to work removing the destroyed doorknob.

From a pile on the floor, she picked up a sweet pink nightie she'd brought with her from home. For a split second, she imagined what Alex might think of her in it—especially after she'd returned her hair to its natural reddish brown and wore her favorite plum eyeliner to coax out the full depth of her green eyes.

For the first time in forever, she yearned to embrace her true self—the woman she'd become thanks to her roller-coaster ride of a childhood, topsy-turvy love life and fun-house career choice. Without her past, she would not have been able to pull off the impersonation of Lucienne Bonet. Without her past, she would never have met and started to fall in love with Alex.

Because that's what was happening, she realized, as

her heart and throat constricted even as her fingers tightened on the diaphanous shell-pink baby doll. Who would have thought that the one time that she opened herself up enough to fall in love would be the one time she was pretending to be someone else?

Suddenly, his dark-skinned hand appeared beneath hers, cupping her fingers along with the lingerie.

"Mmm," he said, leaning in close so that the locksmith wouldn't hear what he was saying, "I think I'd like to see a little more of your secret wardrobe."

She chuckled humorlessly. "This is the only one."

"We should remedy that," he declared.

She looked up and met his gaze straight on. Okay, enough was enough. She needed to rip the bandage from the wound.

"Alex, we have to talk."

He pulled his hand away. "*Querida,* I didn't mean—"

She mustered the last of her resolve and touched his cheek. She couldn't do this. Not yet. Not when they weren't alone. "Why don't you go back to the auction house while I start cleaning up this mess?"

And what a mess it was.

"I can help."

She shook her head. "You should call Michael, go back to work and start putting the gallery back together. I'll meet you there soon, I promise."

"You shouldn't make promises you can't keep."

Alex and Lucy looked up. Standing in the doorway between the living room and bedroom was a man holding a gun.

A man Lucy had seen before.

Instinctively, Alex shoved her behind him. "Who are you? What do you want?"

"Ask Lucy," the man said. "She knows me, don't cha,

Luce? I liked you better as a fiery redhead, but I guess a girl's gotta do what a girl's gotta do to get the job done, right?"

Alex cast a quick glance over his shoulder. "Lucienne? Do you know this man?"

She started to shake her head, but stopped. Both denial and confession caught in her throat.

She'd never wanted Alex to learn the truth about her. She'd wanted to walk away. Disappear. Leave him with a mysterious, evocative memory of a woman who, for a brief moment in time, loved him with all her heart and soul.

Unfortunately, she'd never been that woman. Yes, she cared about him. Yes, with time, she might have truly fallen helplessly and hopelessly in love with him. But forever and always, she'd only be a woman who'd lied to him and who, in this moment, caused him to lose the one and only piece of his father he'd ever possessed.

"I remember you," she admitted to the gunman, pushing aside her regrets and focusing only on saving their lives. "You weaseled a referral out of one of my regular clients three years ago. Baxter. Boxer. Braxton." She knew his name was unusual, not the sort of moniker normally associated with a two-bit hood. "You needed me to move merchandise from a foreclosed house. Easy pickings. Slim, too. My commission barely bought me a manicure."

The man's sneer twisted his face into a grotesque mask, but Lucy didn't flinch. Now wasn't the time to show weakness—or worry about what Alex thought about her. Right now, she had to concentrate on keeping them out of the morgue.

"I've moved on to bigger and better things now," the gunman said.

"That business transaction was our first and last," she said.

"Yeah, well, this time, you ain't getting a piece of the action."

A few feet away, the locksmith's drill continued to whine and whir. Either the guy was in on this, or he'd been knocked out with his tools still running, which had the added effect of masking any shouts for help—or perhaps even gunfire.

"What do you want?" Lucy asked, knowing the answer even as the question left her lips.

"What do you think?" The man tilted the gun toward Alex's hand, which he'd held out in front of Lucy as if his ancestor's ring could somehow protect her from a bullet.

"My ring?" Alex asked. "It's not worth anything to you. I have cash in my wallet that exceeds its worth on the open market."

The man held out his free hand, palm up. "Yeah? Well, I don't sell my loot on no open markets. I'm going to get top dollar for that piece. Hand it over."

Alex started to remove the ring, but Lucy grabbed his arm. "No, Alex, don't."

"Shut up, bitch," the gunman shouted. "Let the man do the noble thing."

God, what had Danny gotten them into?

"You expect us to believe that if he hands over the ring you'll take it and just turn around and leave?" she challenged. "Who sent you?"

"Lucienne, *¡cállate!*" Alex whispered.

She ignored him. "Did you hit the auction house, too? Is this what you were after? Who wants the ring? And why?"

The man chuckled. "Like I'd tell you. Look, I'm not interested in shooting the shit with some two-bit fence and her latest fuck buddy. I just want what I came for. Hand over the swag and no one'll get hurt."

Again, Alex prepared to take off the ring, and though

Lucy couldn't fight the instinct to grab his arm and hold on tight, she didn't make a second attempt to stop him. The ring meant a lot to him—and now, to her—but not more than his life.

The trouble was, the guy ripping them off hadn't bothered to wear a mask. She might not remember his exact name, but she and Alex could both provide a detailed description of his shock of brown hair, close-set hazel eyes and acne pockmarks that heavily scarred his cheeks and throat. Was he counting on her to keep Alex from calling the police or was he going to shoot them both to cover up his crime?

Alex held the ring toward the gunman.

"Good, now toss it on the ground!"

"No!" she shouted, staying Alex's hand. "Those opals are delicate. If they hit this tile floor, they'll crack and the emerald might shatter. Didn't whoever sent you tell you what this ring is worth?"

The man hesitated, his expression losing some of its menace to uncertainty. This gave Alex and Lucy a split second to exchange glances.

Lucy's blood froze. In Alex's fathomless black eyes, she'd expected to see fear, anger or confusion.

Instead, she saw determination.

Confidence.

And if she wasn't mistaken, a plan.

"Fine," the gunman said. "Give her the ring. She can bring it to me."

Lucy reached for the ring, but Alex did not move.

"She's not going anywhere near you," he said, turning to face the thief, straight-spined and regal. Even Lucy couldn't resist taking a half step back.

"Then we have a problem," the man said, raising his weapon higher.

Alex pierced the gunman with a determined stare. "If you'd come here to kill us, you would have by now. Theft is one thing, but murder is quite another. I'll give you the ring, but you'll leave Lucienne out of this dirty business."

The man's laughter was a bark of derision. "Don't you know who she is? She's been in this dirty business longer than me."

If the gunman had meant the revelation to chip at Alex's cool self-assurance, he had miscalculated.

Alex quirked a smile and took a step forward, his arms outstretched in seeming surrender. "You let me worry about who she is and you worry about getting what you came for and then getting the hell out of here."

The man stretched out his hand to accept the ring and his gun hand lowered infinitesimally. Alex stole the advantage and grabbed the man's hand and twisted until the crack of bones popped loud enough to be heard over the droning drill. The gunman fell, howling over his broken fingers. Alex kicked the weapon across the floor, where it slid underneath the bed.

They dashed into the living room, only to be blocked by another man holding the locksmith's drill. The workman lay unconscious on the floor.

"Going somewhere?"

This guy, Lucy recognized. On the streets, he was called Jimmy the Rim because he specialized in jacking expensive cars and selling the parts for exorbitant prices on the black market, specifically to high-end collectors.

She and Danny had catered to this crowd. They were wealthy. They were ruthless.

And unfortunately, they were legion.

Lucy chanced a glance over her shoulder. The thief Alex had attacked had slid across the floor, cradling his hand as he tried to jam his large body beneath her bed to retrieve his weapon.

When she turned back to Alex, he'd retrieved the rickety old hat stand that had come with the apartment and used it to yank the drill's cord from the outlet. Swinging the pole around, he knocked Jimmy hard under the chin. The hat stand split and shattered. The guy fell, flailing like an overturned turtle, his considerable girth blocking their only path to freedom.

Alex turned, prepared to fight off the gunman with the piece of the hat stand still in his hand.

"Lucienne, get out of here!" he commanded.

"Not without you," she said.

They weren't going to die over a stupid piece of jewelry. Lucy ran to the coffee table and grabbed a heavy glass orb she'd bought to give the place a little bit of color. When Jimmy finally made it onto his hands and knees, she bashed him on the back of the head until he fell, unconscious, to the ground.

She dashed to the locksmith. He was coming to. Before she could speak to him, tell him to get out before he was hurt worse, Alex dragged the man by his shoulders until they were out in the hall.

Alex grabbed her hand and tugged her down the hall. They took the stairs, Alex still wielding the hat stand in front of him like a knight with a lance.

Or a bandit with a sword.

At the second floor, they spilled out into the hall.

"We can't go to the lobby," she said, breathless. "They… might…have…"

"Accomplices," he finished. "I agree. Do you know anyone on this floor?"

She shook her head. Even in her own apartment building across town, she'd never taken the time to get to know the neighbors.

Alex tossed the splintered hat stand into a corner, straightened his clothes and shoved the ring onto his finger.

"Then let's hope the ring helps elevate my charm. We're going to need it."

14

WHEN THE WOMAN WHO answered the door turned out to be an attractive blonde wearing nothing but a sports bra and tight running shorts, Alex became a complete believer in the power of the ring. With only a few flirtatious words from him, she let them inside. Lucienne remained near the door, listening to see if anyone had followed.

"You sure you're not the bad guys?" the woman asked, clutching her cell phone to her buxom chest.

"Do we look like bad guys?" Lucienne snapped.

The neighbor mirrored Lucienne's incredulous stare. "Actually, honey, you look like hell. You can hole up here for a few minutes, but I'm calling the cops."

"No," Alex said.

His denial surprised even him, but the look of fear on Lucienne's face at the mention of the police convinced him that he needed to keep her away from law enforcement—at least until he sorted through all he'd heard in her apartment. He'd suspected Lucienne was a woman with secrets, but he'd never expected they involved consorting with lowlife scum like men with guns.

"My brother is an FBI agent," he explained to the woman

as he dug into his wallet to retrieve one of Michael's cards. "Please, call him. It's the safest course of action…for all of us."

The woman took the number and immediately dialed while Lucienne clutched the doorknob even tighter.

"Alejandro," she started, but he shook his head.

"Not here," he chided, casting a glance at their unwitting hostess. "My only concern right now is keeping you safe."

She turned away from him, but not before he caught the sparkle of moisture in her eyes. His chest constricted as he tried to imagine what circumstances might have caused her to lie to him. But the possible scenarios were too wild for him to contemplate.

For the moment, he followed his instinct to protect her. And the ring. His legacy from his father was a family matter. He would not discuss the situation in front of a stranger.

By the time Michael arrived, the men who'd attacked them were gone. The unconscious locksmith had come around. Between his description of the assailants, visible blood and car tracks, the police had a trail to follow. Michael called the local cops, then shuttled Alex and Lucienne into his vehicle.

He arranged for Ruby to collect descriptions of the assailants and then pulled strings so that the victims of the assault—Alex and Lucienne—went into his protective custody.

Ruby waited beside the car, her hand on the bulge in her jacket.

"Local LEOs put out a BOLO on your perps," Ruby said, her shoulders tense. "With both of them injured, we might get lucky."

Michael nodded, but didn't say a word. None of them did. What was there to say? Now that they were safe, Alex felt numb. Lucienne had lied to him, that much he knew. The extent of her lies was yet to be determined. But he wasn't a stupid man. He'd begun to care for her, and once she finally confessed her ugly truth, he would be destroyed.

And yet, he couldn't help but suspect that the truth might be just as devastating for her. In the backseat, he watched her fold into herself, leaning so close to the door, he feared she might fall out—or run. Michael seemed to sense the same risk because he clicked the locks shut. In the rearview mirror, he met Alex's questioning stare with an expression utterly devoid of any emotion except anger. His brother, it seemed, had quite the temper, but was able to keep it under control.

Another thing they had in common—the ability to shut down when needed.

But he wanted to know the truth—and he wanted to know it now. Demands died on his lips. Lucienne had shut down. Turned off. He had to take another tack.

He slid across the seat and attempted to clasp her hand.

"Don't," she begged, her voice barely audible.

The broken sound tore through him, ripping straight into his chest. "What secrets are you keeping, Lucienne?"

Glossed with tears, her eyes, deep and rich and brown, had an unnatural rim around the irises. She was wearing colored contacts.

She shook her head. "Too many secrets, Alejandro. Too many to count."

He moved away from her, buckling his seatbelt with a loud snap. Lucienne Bonet was indeed someone he did not truly know. She consorted with criminals. She'd lied about her identity, even to the man she'd shared her body with, if not glimpses of her soul.

When Michael stopped the SUV, Alex was surprised that he'd brought them to the auction house rather than the hotel. Ruby took up a protective position beside the vehicle while Michael went inside and scoped out the building before waving him and Lucienne inside.

Alex walked directly to his office, but Lucienne stopped at her desk in the gallery. Michael remained near the door.

When Lucienne spoke, her eyes darted to Michael.

"Are you going to tell him or shall I?"

Michael's stare bored into her, but she raised her chin an inch and held her ground.

"Tell him your real name," Michael ordered.

Lucienne narrowed her gaze and then complied. When she looked at Alex, her stare was so sharp, it sliced straight through his heart.

"Lucy," she said, her voice no longer melodious and cultured, but flat with a twang that was decidedly American. "My name is Lucy Burnett. Lucienne Bonet is a fake identity I've assumed off and on for years."

Years?

"I checked your references," Alex insisted.

Honestly, this was the least of his concerns, but it was the first thing that popped into his mind. He'd expected her to have secrets, but only now did he realize that her lies had been meant specifically for him.

"My references were real. I'm a fence. I move the stolen art and jewels that other people steal. When a job went bad or heat from the cops got too out of control here in San Francisco, I used the Lucienne Bonet name to find work in museums, auction houses or for private collectors. I am an art expert. I didn't lie about that."

"But you lied about everything else?" he demanded.

Her gaze dropped to the floor.

"She's not the only one," Michael said.

He strode across the gallery, taking a position near one of the tables that had held the jewelry collection. The three of them created a strange and confusing triangle of connections that Alex did not understand. Lucienne had told him next to nothing about herself. He'd hoped that the more time they spent together, the more she would open up. The more she would trust.

Now he learned that the little she had told him had been a lie. Yet, how could he still feel that he knew her as well as he knew himself?

"Don't tell me that whole story about Joaquin Murrieta was some ruse to catch me up in the history and romance of the thing," Alex said to his brother.

"No, that's all true, every word. Mine is more of a lie of omission. And I think you should sit down."

The last thing Alex wanted to do was relax into news so disturbing that his brother had waited months to tell him. Instead, he crossed his arms over his chest.

"I never told you what happened after both you and Ramon were cleared of that art theft. What became of the DNA sample taken from the blood on the frame."

Alex blinked. He'd been hit with so much information during Michael's revelations just the day before, he had not thought the circumstances all the way through. Until now. If the blood had not belonged to Michael or Ramon or him…

He nearly gave in to Michael's initial request that he sit. But instead, he locked his knees and stared directly into his brother's guilty gaze. "What are you trying to tell me, Miguel?"

"His name is Daniel," Michael answered. "Daniel Burnett. And he's our brother."

Lucienne snickered. "He shares your genes, but he's not your brother. If he was, he wouldn't be sitting in a jail cell for a crime he didn't commit."

A curse exploded from Michael and bounced off the suddenly hollow walls of the auction house. Somewhere in the distance, his voice and Lucienne's rose in a heated argument over the innocence or guilt of someone named Daniel Burnett—someone connected to Lucienne in a way Alex could not currently comprehend. His stomach lurched with the suspicion that he might have made love to a woman who was related to him by blood, but a blast of angry words broke through the white noise filling his ears when Michael shouted, "Your family adopted him. No wonder he turned out to be a crook."

"Daniel made the best of what life gave him," Lucienne argued back. "Gave both of us. Maybe if your father hadn't abandoned him, he wouldn't have needed my father to teach him how to survive. Maybe then he would have turned out more like you. But he didn't have Ramon, did he? He didn't have anyone, except for me."

"Our father didn't even know about him!" Michael shot back.

"So *he* said," Lucienne replied, her voice dripping with disdain. "Danny's mother was a meth addict who died when he was four. He went to ten different foster homes in seven years before he landed in my house. And even after all that misery, he was the first kid who ever came into our place who could make me laugh. We've been inseparable since—like real siblings."

"And both criminals," Michael spat.

"Maybe," Lucienne said. "But that doesn't mean he deserves the death sentence if the security guard dies. He didn't shoot him, Michael. You know his M.O. You know he's never once, in all his cons, used a weapon. He was set up."

"That's for the court to decide," Michael muttered, but he was losing his steam.

"Right," she said. "And if the case ever goes to trial, maybe he'll luck out and be acquitted. But in the meantime, he's under another kind of death warrant—one I had to try and help him escape. Even if it meant lying to you."

She turned her desperate face toward Alex. Up until this point, he'd felt entirely disconnected from the situation, the sounds of their heated exchange bouncing around the inside of his brain like jai alai *pelota*. But when her eyes met his, the defiance that she'd shown to Michael melted off her face. A face he knew. A face that had captured him. Enraptured him.

A face that belonged to a woman he did not know at all.

"I came here, Alex," she explained, "because Danny is in serious trouble. I don't know all the details—he said it was better if I didn't. All he told me was that he needed the ring. Someone wanted it and if they didn't get it, they'd kill him before his case ever went to trial."

Alex glanced down at his hand. He should have suspected the thing was cursed. It was one thing to have thieves threaten his body with bullets—it was something even more painful to have a beautiful woman toy with his heart.

He took an unguarded step toward her. "Michael had the ring. Why didn't...Danny ask him for help?"

Lucienne sneered. "Michael's known about Danny for years. The only time he contacts him is to gloat when Danny's in custody."

"That's not—" Michael objected, but Lucienne cut him to silence with a single glare.

Alex chanced moving another few inches closer to her. He couldn't help himself, despite her devastating secrets and lies. "Then why didn't he just ask me for help? Why did you lie and scheme?"

At this, the fake colored eyes on her equally counterfeit face glossed with moisture again. Neither armed robbery, gunfire or the threat of death had elicited a single tear from her, and yet her cheeks were suddenly streaked over questions that amounted to nothing less than common sense.

"Danny didn't want you to know anything about him. He spent his whole life as a phantom, a ghost who slipped in through cracks in the walls, took what he needed and left without a trace. That was his specialty, in business and in life."

"That's not business," Alex insisted. "That's thievery."

She nodded, but he didn't think the agreement was for him. "And that's why he didn't want you to know about him. He knew you'd think he was only getting what he deserved."

"He didn't know anything about me!"

Only inches separated them now, inches that only hours ago might have turned into hot, punishing kisses or unbridled, animalistic sex. Now Alex's passion turned into rage. How dare she betray him. Lie to him. Mislead him. And how much of what she'd said—how much of what she'd done since they'd been together had been a sham?

All of it? Every kiss? Every touch? Every pleasured cry?

"If he knew he was my brother, he should have come to me," Alex insisted. "Not when he was in trouble, but before. Long before."

A teardrop splashed off her chin, and despite the fact that they were not touching, he could feel her trembling.

"He did." She swallowed and brushed the tears off her face with an angry swipe. "When he found out about Ramon, he did research. He found out about you. He went to Spain to meet you."

Alex shook his head emphatically. "He never approached me."

"He never told you who he was, but he met you. He went to your gallery, and according to him, you treated him like something foul you might have stepped in while walking across the sidewalk. He left without telling you who he was. Who could blame him?"

"I could," Alex retorted. "How dare he judge me based on one test I didn't even know I was taking? And you weren't there—you have no idea how he presented himself to me. More than likely, I recognized him as a con and a thief and had him removed from the House of Aguilar, as I would have done with anyone who I sensed was there on false pretenses. I used to be able to spot such imposters—an ability I've apparently lost."

His jab hit its mark because she turned away.

"Where is this Daniel now?" Alex asked Michael.

"County jail, awaiting trial."

"I want to see him."

"Not a good idea," Michael said, shaking his head.

"Why the hell not? He's our brother. How dare you keep this from me? You're as bad as she is."

"Alex," Michael said, his voice pleading.

Alex didn't care. Not only did Ramon's unscrupulous blood run through the veins of both of his siblings, but it had infected the people around them, too. Perhaps if this Daniel hadn't been accepted so readily into her household, Lucienne—née, Lucy Burnett—might have grown up to be a woman who valued honesty and honor and morals. But she had not. And now he had two brothers who wouldn't know the truth if it slapped them in the face and a lover who'd done nothing but lie to him since they'd first met.

He'd had enough. He retrieved his cell phone and called for his driver, instructing him to meet him a couple of blocks away. He needed to walk. He needed air.

But mostly, he needed to get away.

15

"WHERE CAN I TAKE YOU?"

Lucy jumped, having forgotten that Michael was still in the room. She couldn't tear her gaze away from the door Alex had slammed on his way out. Had that been moments before, or hours? Her body had nearly become accustomed to the pain slicing through her. She'd taken a man who'd built himself up on a foundation of truth and honor and torn him down with lie after lie after lie.

"Don't worry about me." She glanced down at her desk as if to gather her things, but nothing here was hers. Nothing here was real. She started toward the door, but as she passed Michael, he grabbed her arm.

His grip was gentle, but firm. Still, she freed herself with one definitive tug.

"Why didn't you tell him you and Daniel were lovers?" Michael asked.

"Because we're not," she answered.

"You told the jail you were his girlfriend," he argued.

"I also told the jail my name was Sienna Bruce. Danny didn't want people to know we were related."

"You're not related," Michael insisted.

"Maybe not by blood, but that doesn't seem to mean all that much in your family anyway, does it?"

He took a step backward. "Why should I believe anything you say?"

She shrugged. "I don't give a damn if you believe me. Now that you know who I really am and why I came here, you also have to realize that I've had easy access to your father's ring. I could have taken it from Alex and disappeared and saved Danny and you never would have known. I don't have a record, Special Agent Murrieta, and there's a reason for that—Danny's always protected me. And illegal or not, I'm good at what I do. So before you expend all your righteous indignation on me, remember that I did not steal your father's ring, not even to save the brother I love. Why don't you chew on that for a while and figure out what it means?"

She stalked out of the auction house and immediately turned left. Two blocks downhill would take her to a busy street where she could jump on a cable car or trolley. But she spotted Alex moving in the same direction, so she turned right and trudged up the steep slope that would lead to another major thoroughfare, albeit one that was farther away.

"Hey!"

She turned to see Special Agent Dawes jogging toward her.

"Where you going?" she asked, not the least bit winded by the run.

"I have no idea," Lucy said. "I suppose you don't want me to leave town."

"I don't give a shit where you go," Dawes replied. "I'm off the clock. And as far as I know, other than bashing some asshole over the head, you haven't committed any crime."

"But I meant to," Lucy argued. "I think that's all that matters to Alex. And to your partner."

"Yeah, well, I've been *meaning to* knock Michael on his ass for stealing my last slice of cheesecake out of the break room, but no one's arrested me for that just yet, either."

Lucy nearly laughed. Under any other circumstances, she might have found a friend in Special Agent Ruby Dawes. She was everything Lucy wasn't—genuine and honest and strong. Before Daniel had sent her on this fool's errand, Lucy had thought she was all those things, too. Well, maybe not the honest part. But always genuine. And always strong.

But now, she was none of those things. Somehow, in finding Alex, she'd lost herself. Or maybe he'd simply forced her to see that she'd never truly known her own identity. And as for strength, she'd had the power to cream a bad guy in order to save her life, but she wasn't entirely sure she had the power to walk up the hill and find her way home.

"Let me give you a ride," Ruby said, cupping her hand over Lucy's shoulder in such a gesture of caring that Lucy nearly dissolved.

"I don't think Michael will be too happy about that," she replied.

"Yeah, well, I've got the keys. And besides, you might still have bad guys after you. No one's caught up with Jimmy the Rim yet, or his partner, whose name, by the way, is Baxter Jones. But the locals have leads. Guys like them can't stay hidden for long, but they also have mean friends who might come looking for the woman who bashed them on the head. Let us help you."

Lucy glanced up the steep incline. She'd been on her feet all day. The thought of climbing to the top of the hill and then taking a side street to the main road exacerbated the burning in her arches. She couldn't help but scan downhill again. She could no longer see Alex. Trying not to think that her final memory of him might be the sight of his retreating back, she swallowed the tears burning down her throat and nodded her silent consent.

As anticipated, Michael's displeasure at playing bodyguard to Lucy wasn't hard to miss. He sat beside her in the backseat, anger radiating off his skin. As much as Lucy wanted to lose herself in the flashing streaks of neon as they cruised through a neighborhood packed with restaurants and clubs on the way to her apartment, she forced herself to turn and meet Michael's eyes. By the time he finally spoke, her own were dry and burning.

"Did you care about him? About Alex, I mean."

"I fell in love with him," she replied.

"You've only been together for two days," he argued.

From the front seat, Ruby snorted.

"Actually, we've been together for almost two months. We've worked side by side organizing an auction that is going to make you and your mother a lot of money. And in that time, we got to know each other pretty well."

"Actually, you got to know him," Michael said. "The woman he knows doesn't even exist."

"Yeah," she said. "Maybe."

Until she'd met Alex and tailored the Lucienne Bonet persona to entice him, the name had been nothing more to her than a disguise—a safe personality she could slip into until the heat died down. Knowing it was only a matter of time before Danny called her back to be Lucy Burnett again, she'd never embraced the life of a woman who actually loved her job, enjoyed her coworkers and was respected for her skill and knowledge by people who appreciated art enough not to steal it.

Now she didn't know who she was. She couldn't be

Lucy again—at least, not the Lucy she'd been in the past. Because of Alex, she fully understood Lucy's loneliness and lack of moral center. And she couldn't be Lucienne. Like Michael said, the woman had never truly existed.

"I don't have answers, Michael. Not about who I am. But I swear to you that I never meant to hurt Alex. Once I knew him…once I understood what the ring meant to him, I couldn't take it. I couldn't steal the only…the only piece of his father he had left."

Her voice caught and Michael cleared his throat.

"What were you going to do about Danny?"

"I didn't know," she wailed, throwing up her arms in frustration. "I wanted to get away from Alex and talk to Danny and try to work something out, but then we were attacked at my apartment and Alex learned the truth. Wait… Alex! Michael, if someone still wants the ring and he's out there all alone, they could grab him! You have to—"

"Already covered," Michael insisted. "I called in a favor and a pal of mine has been watching him since we left the auction house. After we drop you off, I'll take over his protection myself. I've arranged a short leave of absence until this matter is cleared up. Once he goes back to Spain, I'm not too worried."

This time, Lucy couldn't help but look away. Deep in her heart, she knew that returning to his homeland was the best thing for Alex. What did he have left here that she hadn't destroyed? Even his relationship with Michael needed rebuilding, thanks to her and Danny.

Unfortunately, six thousand miles would not be enough to sever the connection they'd made—at least, not for her.

"You're not safe, either," Michael continued.

"I've never done business from my home," she said. "Unless we're being followed, no one knows where I live.

When someone had product for me to move, I went to them."

"What about the IDs that were stolen during the robbery?"

"The Lucienne Bonet IDs were fake, but that's how they found my rental. The Lucy Burnett IDs have the address of a cabin my family owns up north, but no one has been there in years. My apartment is leased to a dummy company that Danny set up years ago to protect us from situations exactly like this. I'll be fine."

"Will you?"

This time, his question held no accusation or disdain.

She could only shake her head.

"Look," he said, reaching across the seat and placing his hand on top of hers in a gesture so tentative and sweet, she thought she might lose her mind. "I've visited Danny a lot in jail. Clearly more than he's told you. I keep trying to reach out, but he's a block of stone."

"Must be a family trait," Lucy said.

"Hey, I'm not that stubborn."

Again, Ruby snorted in the front seat.

"Hey," he chided.

She started singing along to Lady GaGa on the radio.

"I guess the Murrieta men can be fairly pigheaded," he confessed.

"Yeah, they can," she agreed. "I asked Danny to go to you as soon as he was arrested. Danny is a lot of things, Michael, but he's not a killer. He never takes jobs where there's a risk that someone other than himself might get hurt. Someone set him up—maybe the same someone who's trying to get their hands on the ring. Jimmy the Rim and Baxter Jones are two-bit hoods. They'll work for anyone if the money is untraceable. I told Danny myself that you might be able to help, but he wouldn't listen. I begged him to let me tell Alex the truth from the start, but he wouldn't hear it. It was his choice. I guess I should have gone against his wishes, but I never have. I'm not sure I know how."

Michael's hand curled around hers, lifting it up so he could look at their entwined hands in the glare from the oncoming headlights. She realized that all this was hard for him, too—that he didn't trust any more easily than his brothers. She supposed that was the risk of having Ramon Murrieta for their father. Michael's childhood had differed from Alex's and Danny's, but in the end, all three of them carried the sins of their father, whether they'd realized it or not.

"As much as I tried to reach out to Danny, I never accepted him for who he was or what he went through as a kid," Michael admitted. "I condemned him too much for him to think I'd ever help him out of a jam like this."

"He doesn't trust easily," she said. "In fact, except for me, he doesn't trust anyone."

"But he didn't tell you anything more about who wanted the ring?"

"I don't know if he knew, to be honest. He just said the less I knew, the better. Once I had the ring, he was going to make the arrangements. And Michael, that's the most disturbing part. Danny doesn't scare easily. He's been through a lot. Whatever they're holding over his head is big."

"Maybe they were threatening to hurt you if he didn't turn over the ring. Maybe he thought that if you transformed into the personality that had kept you safe so many times in the past, he was somehow protecting you."

She raked her hands through her hair, more anxious than ever to remove the extensions, pop out her contact lenses and, at the very least, look like herself again. When she'd become Lucienne Bonet in the past, she'd never altered her appearance so drastically. She would cut her hair or wear it up, maybe throw in a temporary dark wash to tone down the auburn and add a pair of funky glasses, but otherwise, she looked relatively the same.

This transformation had been for Alex alone, and if he didn't want her, then she saw no reason to continue the charade.

"Maybe," she said.

"Well, we won't know until we talk to Danny."

"He won't talk to you."

"We're all going to see him. I'll arrange it. It's time we had a family meeting and worked this all out. Together."

"I'm not a part of your family," she insisted.

"You're part of Danny's. For now, that's enough."

MICHAEL CALLED Lucy the morning after he and Ruby had dropped her off at her apartment and told her that he'd arranged to have Danny moved to a more secure area in the jail. He was working with Danny's attorney to set up a meeting for the whole family—something she still had trouble wrapping her mind around.

She'd have to see Alex again. When she did, she wanted to look like herself again. For once, Lucy Burnett would be the persona who protected her. Or at least, that's what she hoped.

Until the conference could be arranged, Michael insisted that she lie low and contact no one. He even sent Ruby over to make sure Lucy had everything she needed. She had no idea why he was being so nice to her, but she decided it probably had more to do with his own guilt about misjudging Danny and lying to Alex than anything else. But since she didn't want any more run-ins with men with guns, she did as he asked.

The daughter of a hairstylist, Ruby helped her take out

her extensions and then they made an afternoon out of
dying her hair back to its original color and boiling up a
pot of delicious gumbo that would keep her fed until she
could resume her life in the open. By the time the sun went
down two days after her world imploded, they'd finished
three bowls of spicy stew and had downed half a six-pack
each of Ruby's favorite beer.

"How are you holding up?" Ruby lounged beside her
on the couch, watching a DVD of *The Big Easy* with the
volume turned down low. Ruby was big on theme nights.

Lucy lifted her beer bottle and swallowed the last of the
cold, yeasty brew. "Bored, mostly. Except today. Thanks
for spending so much time with me, Ruby. Honest to God,
I don't know why you and Michael are looking out for me
after all I've done."

"As you pointed out to Michael a couple of nights ago,
you didn't do anything but lie about who you are," she answered. "And as I'm thinking you don't really know who
you are, it's an understandable mistruth."

Lucy looked to the left. Her reflection bounced back
at her from the window. Funny how her face and hair and
eyes seemed familiar again, but she still didn't know the
woman in the mirror. She'd been alone with her thoughts
for a long time. Over and over, she'd reviewed every single
mistake she'd made, not only with Alex, but her whole life.
And so far, she'd come up with only one life lesson she
could take away from all the hurt and pain she'd caused:
she needed to learn how to be herself.

Trouble was, she didn't know who that "self" was. And
she wasn't sure how she could find out.

"Maybe there's no such thing as an *understandable mistruth*," Lucy said. "Maybe a lie is just a lie."

Ruby lined her empty beer bottle up with the other five
on the table. "In my line of work, lying is part of the job.

Catching bad guys requires it. You lied to catch a good guy. Who the hell am I to judge?"

Ruby's cell phone trilled, but when she answered, the call was for Lucy. Michael confirmed that the meeting with Danny would happen the next morning.

"And Alex is going to be there?" she asked, her voice so shaky, she could feel her cheeks reddening with embarrassment.

"Absolutely," Michael replied. "He's anxious to bring all of this to a close."

"I bet he is," she said, and hung up.

After Ruby left, Lucy went through her normal routine of checking the locks on all windows and doors. She engaged the security alarm, and despite all the beer, she wasn't tired enough for sleep. Instead, she drew a bath. A long shower would have brought up memories she didn't want to deal with—not when she was going to see Alex in the morning.

Once the water had started to fill with frothy suds, she scooped her shoulder-length auburn hair into a loose knot on top of her head and lowered herself into the bubbles while the tub continued to fill. The white noise of the rushing water, coupled with the hot temperature and the soothing lavender scent, blocked out all but her deepest thoughts. What was Alex doing right now? Only three days remained until the auction. Ruby had told her that Michael had been helping Alex put the auction house back together, and that as far as she knew, everything was on schedule. But Alex must be working long days. She supposed that was better than sitting around an empty penthouse suite thinking about how much he hated her.

Her attempt at relaxation effectively thwarted, she rinsed, dried off and put on a short nightie not unlike the little pink one she'd left behind at Lucienne's apartment—the one that Alex had intimated he'd like to see her in before he'd nearly been shot. This one was a deep, dark purple. As she sat in front of her vanity mirror and brushed out her hair, she couldn't help but fantasize about how Alex might have reacted to her if they'd met under different circumstances.

"Tu eres tan hermosa."

Lucy leaped from her chair, her hairbrush thrust in front of her like a weapon—a weapon that tumbled out of her hand the moment her brain registered that it was Alex standing in her doorway.

16

IF NOTHING HAD CONVINCED Alex of the ring's special powers before tonight, the fact that he'd effectively broken into Lucienne's apartment without alerting her, her neighbors or the police sealed his belief that Joaquin Murrieta's bandit blood ran strong and hot through his veins. Yes, he'd had some help from Michael with the alarm code and he'd learned about picking locks from the unlikeliest source of all—Daniel—but his need to toss aside all his hurt and anger in order to pursue the woman he loved came from a deep well of emotion he hadn't realized existed until she came into his life.

"What are you doing here?" she asked. "How'd you get inside?"

Fear and surprise stole her breath so that she panted, causing her breasts to rise and fall in ways that tightened his groin.

"A few tricks I learned from my brothers."

"Brothers?" She straightened from her instinctive crouch. "Plural? You've spoken with Danny?"

"At length," he replied.

"I thought his lawyer wouldn't let us see him."

"Yes, well, I can be rather convincing when I put my mind to it," he assured her.

"What did you do, fire his lawyer?"

Alex grinned. "I merely offered him a much better one, one who arranged for private meetings. Michael helped. Apparently, having a federal agent in the family goes a long way in your judicial system."

Her lips quivered, as if she wanted to smile, but couldn't quite manage. Instead, she busied her hands with rearranging the lotions and perfumes on her vanity until she relaxed enough to exhale and then turn to face him.

She wore a torturously short confection of purple silk that swirled around her upper thighs, drawing his gaze to her smooth legs, then back up to her generous breasts and slim shoulders. His mouth watered with want, but he gulped down his desire with a dry, painful swallow. He hadn't come here tonight for seduction.

Had he?

When she finally looked up at him, he was nearly tossed backwards by the keen purpose in her jade-green eyes.

"If you're bankrolling his new mouthpiece, then why haven't we been able to see Danny?"

"He and I had some things to work out first," he told her.

She clenched her jaw and crossed her arms over her chest. "That's real nice for you, but what about those of us who have been his family for more than a couple of days? I've been worried sick about him."

"I'm sorry," he said. "He knows you want to see him, but he's afraid for you."

"I can take care of myself. And he knows it."

Alex nodded. "That's not the issue. Danny appreciates all you've risked for him. He doesn't want you involved anymore. He's just trying to protect you. From what I gather, that's his style when it comes to you."

Sensing a break in the tension, he moved to step into the room. Instinctively, she retreated, rattling the knick-knacks on the table behind her.

"Don't be afraid of me."

"I'm not," she replied, but her voice trembled enough that she cleared her throat and repeated her claim, a little louder and with more conviction. "Maybe it's just your outfit. Black pants. Black, open-collared shirt. If you added a cape and a mask, you'd look like your famous ancestor."

"I confess, that was part of the appeal."

A tiny smile edged her lips. "The last thing we need between us is masks and costumes."

"Verdad," he said, reaching up to unbutton his shirt.

Her eyes widened. "What are you doing?"

"Stripping away my costume. You've already removed yours."

She did not move away as he approached, but she did reach behind to brace herself. By the time he was standing directly in front of her, his shirt hung loose and open. He wanted more than anything for her to reach up and stop his forward movement with her flat hand on his bare chest—if only to feel the warmth of her skin on his again.

"Have you lost your mind?"

"Sí, completamente."

He started to unbuckle his belt, but she stayed his hand. A spark of electricity flared from her flesh to his, causing her to instantly draw back.

"Don't be afraid to touch me," he said.

"I'm not," she confessed, her gaze locked on his waist until she asked, "Why are you here?"

"Because I couldn't get you out of my mind."

"You mean you couldn't get Lucienne out of your mind.

She doesn't exist, Alex. She's just a fake name I adopt whenever I'm in trouble."

"But she's a part of you. Are Lucienne Bonet and Lucy Burnett so different?"

She groaned and spun away. "My God! Two women couldn't be more different! Lucienne would never steal from you! She'd never lie to you. She has morals and a conscience and fears the consequences of her actions. Lucy Burnett will do whatever it takes to keep her head above water."

"And she'd put her life and liberty at risk for my brother."

"He's *my* brother," she insisted, her arms flailing with indignation. "I grew up with him. He chased off the bullies and distracted me from the fact that my mother lost interest in me once I was no longer a cute little moppet who lived and breathed to please her. He was my lifeline, Alex. My best friend. In all his exploits and schemes, I never once feared for his life. He was invincible. Even when he did get picked up by the cops, he rarely spent more than a couple of months in jail. But he's in deep trouble this time. I'm scared for him. And for me. If something happens to Danny, I'll have no one."

He wanted to tell her she would not be alone—that he would not allow such a tragedy, but he held back. He had a lot to apologize for, not the least of which was turning his back on her shortly after she'd told him the truth.

"I'm not heartless, *querida.* I was angry, I confess. I felt betrayed and fooled. But I realized that despite those difficult emotions, I still care for you. I still love you."

"You can't," she insisted.

"And yet, I do. I love you, Lucienne."

"My name isn't Lucienne," she argued, her voice cracking even as her eyes glossed with barely checked emotion.

"Your name is whatever you want it to be. If Lucy Burnett is associated in your mind with a sad childhood and a life of crime, then toss the name aside. Be Lucienne. Be someone else. Be whoever you wish to be—but be her with me."

As he'd hoped, as he'd prayed, as he'd gambled before he'd tossed away the last scrap of his pride in order to find Lucienne and win her back, she fell into his arms and wept. She told him things he already knew, thanks to Daniel. About her mother's neglect, about how she revered her father, only to learn that he'd supplemented his income for years by illegally selling items from the museums where he was curator. But mostly, she told him about her love for his brother—an abandoned boy who'd never known love in any other form his entire life.

While she unburdened her soul, he smoothed his hand over her hair, loving the light, silky texture and the crimson color more than he had anticipated. He reveled in the fact that though the color and length had changed drastically, the scent and texture remained hauntingly familiar.

"I don't understand how you can forgive me so easily," she said in the end, her voice hitching.

"Easily? No, not easily. But inevitably. Before I learned the truth about why you came to El Dorado, I was already half in love with you. We spoke the same language, shared the same interests, saw the world through the same eyes. When I realized that you'd risked so much to help my brother, my fate was cast. I wish he'd listened to you when you asked him to tell me the truth. I wish that you would have trusted me enough to defy him—but I understand why you didn't. So much was at stake. You didn't want to take the chance."

He caressed her cheek, and when she placed her palm over his fingers, she realized what was not there.

"The ring? Where is it?"

"With Michael," he said. "The ring is safest with him, but in truth, I no longer need it. I've had my adventure, and it was finding you, whoever you are."

He swallowed her laughter with his kiss, and her flavors sent his blood pressure soaring so that he could barely remain inside his skin. Luckily, she tore away his shirt and unzipped his pants while he backed them up against the vanity, buoying her glorious backside in his hands long enough to lift her onto the table. The clinking of toppling glass, followed by the sudden, powerful scent of perfume, alerted him that perhaps he'd been a bit more careless than necessary.

And yet, he didn't care. He wanted this woman with a primal need that demanded satiation. She speared her hands into his hair, tugging at the longer strands at the back as if holding on for her life.

"*Te amo,* Alejandro," she murmured as he bathed her neck in kisses. "I never thought I'd fall so hard for anyone. Never."

He kissed her for what seemed like forever, and with a sense of renewed curiosity, she explored his body, running her hands over and across his shoulders, down his arms, then up his abs. She clutched at his chest hair and pulled, as if her desperation came straight from the depths of her soul.

Then she scooted off the table.

"I can't do this."

"Can't…what?"

She grabbed him by the cheeks and planted a long, luxurious kiss on his lips. But the moment he slipped his hands beneath the short hem of her nightie, she pulled away again.

"I want you to call out my name when you come, Alex.

I want you buried deep inside me, knowing who I am. I don't want to be Lucy anymore, but she's a part of me. I can't be Lucienne anymore, but I can't let her go. She's the woman you fell in love with. She's the woman you want."

"I want you, *querida*."

He lured her back to him with outstretched hands, which she took, then positioned her in front of the mirror of her vanity.

"Mira," he said, drawing her gaze to his through the reflection. He buried his nose in her hair and inhaled, then ran the strands through his fingers as if they were silk. "Who do you feel like at this moment?"

He kissed her shoulders, slowly drawing down the thin straps until the nightgown slipped, revealing the full curve of her breasts. He traced his fingers along the edges, causing her nipples to peak beneath the lacy edges.

She relaxed into his body, her backside cradling the hard ridge of his sex, her head resting just below his collarbone.

"Lucienne," she replied. "She's the woman who seduced you."

"And was likewise seduced," he said with a smile.

She matched his grin, and even when he tugged her lingerie to her hips and cupped her breasts with both hands, she did not break eye contact.

"And who do you want to be from this moment on?" he asked, his thumbs toying with her stiff nipples, causing her to coo with pleasure.

"The woman who loves you," she said.

"What about the woman who loves herself? Is that Lucienne or Lucy?"

He turned her around and lifted her onto the vanity again. He could resist no longer and took one nipple into his mouth while pleasuring the other with his thumb.

"Lucienne," she said, her voice hoarse with need.

"Sí," he agreed, and then breathed into the hollow between her breasts. "Lucienne. My Lucienne. Always my Lucienne."

When he'd come here tonight, he'd had no preference either way. She had to make her own choices. But if she'd opted to return to her life as Lucy Burnett, a thief's accomplice, he knew this coupling would be their final goodbye. Alex knew his own conscience too well. If she chose to be Lucy, they could have no future together.

Did she know it? Was that why she'd made the choice to be Lucienne?

He broke away from her, grasped her cheeks on both sides and gazed deep into her green eyes, a color that had unexpectedly become his new favorite shade.

"Are you sure?"

"Yes," she said. "She's the woman I've always wanted to be, who I might have been if I hadn't let my life derail me. You might not have meant to, and it may have happened for all the wrong reasons, but you showed me the woman I want to be—sophisticated and educated and resourceful. Not just for you, but for me, too. You showed me the life I could have if I just had the courage to take it. Now I want it. And I want you."

"Then you shall have both."

As much as he adored how the silk of her lingerie hugged her sweet curves, he needed to see her, all of her, from every angle. He tugged the material down the rest of the way, dragging her panties off with it, and then carried her to the bed and settled her among the cushions. He took his time adoring her mouth, neck, breasts and stomach. When he dipped his tongue into her sex, he knew he'd crave these flavors for the rest of his life.

She lifted her knees to give him fuller access. He

splayed his hands beneath her backside and allowed the fullness of her fleshy bottom to fill his palms.

"I love your ass," he confessed.

"I love that you love my ass," she replied with a feminine giggle.

"Then let me truly love it," he said, "and let me love you."

He eased her onto her belly, grabbing pillows from the headboard to press underneath her so that her sweet bottom lifted in offering to a very appreciative man. He plied his mouth to every plump curve, growling out words of appreciation in Spanish and English that had her squirming in delight.

When she spread her legs as if in invitation, exposing the sweet, swollen flesh of her labia, he groaned with insatiable need.

"You're torturing me," he confessed, sitting back onto his knees.

She drew herself onto her elbows and cast a desperate glance over her shoulder. "God, Alex, if you don't do me right now, I'll never forgive you."

He gave himself a moment to savor the moment and then shifted the pillows to pose her at the perfect angle. The penetration of his sex into hers while his hands splayed over her glorious backside led him into a state of pure bliss.

"Oh, Alex," she cooed.

He drew back, then slowly slid into her again, this time a little deeper.

She cried out his name again, and like a red cape waved at a raging bull, he answered the charge. She turned her head so he could see the ecstasy on her face—the rapture as she abandoned her body to his.

He took her, cherished her, aroused and impaled her until she panted with unbridled need.

"Please, ohmygod, please," she begged, raising herself on her elbows and adjusting her position until they found the path to paradise.

When they climaxed, Alex curved his body completely over hers, his chest slick against her spine. He slipped his arms underneath her and just when she thought it was over, he slid his hand through her dark curls and found her clitoris.

"Alex, no, I can't—"

"*Sí, sí, querida.* One more, Lucienne," he begged. "One more, for luck."

She squealed in needful pleasure, unable to form words as the orgasm overtook her body. In mere moments, with his cock still inside her, she came again.

By the time he finally found the strength to pull away from her, they could do no more than shift the pillows off the bed and collapse beneath the covers. He was vaguely aware of her leaving the bed, but she wasn't gone long, and when she returned, the lights in the apartment were off, the alarm system reset and her body, cooled by her absence, sent shivers through his system.

"Don't leave again," he said.

"Not until morning."

He pulled her closer. "Don't leave in the morning."

She laughed. "We have to. We have an appointment at the jail, remember?"

"Oh, right. My errant brother."

"He's a good man, Alejandro. He has a naughty streak, but obviously, that runs in the family."

He tweaked her on the backside in punishment for comparing him to his brother.

"And you're sure you were never in love with him?"

"Are you jealous?" she teased.

"Yes," he answered.

She lifted his hands to her lips and trailed a string of kisses across his knuckles. "Don't be. I've never loved Danny that way. But he has a good heart, even if he doesn't forgive and forget easily."

"I know," he said, and meant it. When he'd shown up at the jail the day after Lucienne's lies had come to light, Daniel had not welcomed him with open arms. But with persistence and the show of faith he'd made by calling in a powerful criminal attorney, he'd gained headway.

His brother. The realization still boggled his mind. To find one sibling, Michael, had been an unexpected surprise. To find a second stunned him to his core.

"Dios mio," he said, realizing that he and Lucienne had just made love without protection. "What if you're pregnant?"

"What?" she asked, then laughed. "I'm a big girl, Alex. I know all about birth control."

"Good," he said, only half relieved. "But…what if you're pregnant…someday?"

There was so much he didn't know about Lucienne. Likely, there was much she'd yet to discover about herself. His good sense told him he should go slowly and resist the urge to push her. But then, with Lucienne, his good sense rarely won over his gut instinct.

She took his hand and splayed it over her flat belly. "I've never in my life thought about having children. How could I, when my parents did such a shitty job? But you know, if I did get pregnant, you'd be a fabulous father."

"Ramon wasn't."

"He was to Michael. And anyway, you're not Ramon. You're Alejandro Aguilar of the House of Aguilar," she said, sounding entirely respectful, impressed and, if he wasn't mistaken, a little turned on.

If he hadn't been satiated and exhausted, he might have puffed up a little.

"And, in the American tradition, you will be Lucienne Aguilar," he said.

Part of him expected her to object, but instead, she scooted even closer and wrapped his arms tighter around her middle.

"That's a name I think I can live with," she said with a sigh.

"Forever?" he asked.

She twisted until they were body to body, their arms and legs entwined, her breasts pressed tight against his chest. "If you're game, for the rest of our lives."

He kissed her until they were both out of breath, then he took her right hand in his and circled her finger with his tongue while he imagined the precise size and shape of the diamond he intended to put there at the first opportunity.

"To the ultimate adventure. You and me, together."

Epilogue

MICHAEL TRIED not to be annoyed, but it was damned hard to fight his gag reflex while Lucienne and Alex sat so close together in the interrogation room that they might as well have been sitting on the same damned chair.

He glanced down at his father's ring and smirked. When he was selling his brother on the legend, he hadn't believed all the nonsense. He'd only been thankful for whatever inspiration had caused his dad to transform from a notorious conman to a devoted husband and father. When Ramon had professed his belief that his ancestor's ring could change a man for the better, Michael had humored him.

But he hadn't really believed it.

However, looking at Alex got him to wondering.

The overeducated, pampered prince of an influential Spanish family had not only successfully broken into Lucienne's secured apartment without alerting the police he'd had watching the place, he'd also escaped two direct threats on his life. And he'd won the girl. And since the girl had spent the majority of her life selling illegally acquired artifacts to some of the most ruthless collectors in the black market, she was a danger in and of herself.

And yet Alex had her giggling like a high school cheer-leader.

"Sickening, huh?"

Since he hadn't wanted to be cooped up with the love-birds on his own until Danny arrived, he'd asked Ruby to tag along. She would wait outside once his incarcerated brother showed up, but for now, she was having a good time taunting him about Alex and Lucienne's new rela-tionship.

"Hey, if they found their bliss, more power to them," Michael said, struggling to be sincere.

"So I guess the ring's magic worked."

He shoved his hand into his pocket. "The ring isn't magical."

"So you say," Ruby argued. "Looks like it did a number on them. I wonder what it'll do for you."

"I'm only wearing it to keep it safe."

"You could lock it up in a bank vault," she said.

"Pop didn't want it locked up. Least I can do is wear it myself, now that Alex claims threats of robbery are cramp-ing his style."

The two men who had attacked Lucienne and Alex at her apartment had been apprehended. But neither Jimmy the Rim nor Baxter Jones seemed to know precisely who'd hired them to retrieve the ring from Lucienne. Until they mined their way through the twisted connections of the criminal underworld, the danger of another attack re-mained.

"You have a death wish," Ruby said.

"I just want to protect what's mine. Nothing wrong with that."

Ruby eyed him carefully, and for a moment, it was as if she was looking at him for the first time.

"What?" he challenged.

But before she could answer, the locked door buzzed open and Danny came in, flanked by his new lawyer and a guard who released the prisoner's shackles. Ruby left and the attorney, after a nod from Alex, exited as well.

Danny stood just inside the doorway, rubbing his wrists warily until Lucienne threw her arms around his neck and squeezed him so hard he nearly lost his balance.

"Easy, Luce. You're going to squeeze the life out of me."

When she stepped back, her expression was fierce. "Better me than someone else. What the hell is going on, Danny? I want the whole story this time."

She jammed her hands onto her hips. With a chastised look that shaved a layer of toughness off Danny's face, he glanced at Michael as if for help.

"Don't look at me," Michael said. "I want to know everything, too."

Alex came up behind his new lover and eased his hands around her waist. "I've found, *mi hermano,* that it's best not to argue with a woman like Lucienne."

"Lucienne is it now?" Danny said, a brow arched.

"Yes," she shot back. "You have a problem with that?"

"Luce, you can be whoever you want to be. Maybe it's better if you run off to Spain with Alejandro until all this is settled."

"We're not going anywhere," Alejandro said. "Not until you are free from this place."

Danny shifted from foot to foot, then nodded toward the metal table in the center of the room. They each took a seat, and for an instant, Michael wondered what it might feel like to share a meal with these people—his family.

Danny's face was battered, but still good-looking. Like Ramon and Alejandro, he had a dark, olive complexion and jet-black hair. Like Michael, who'd inherited his blue eyes from his mother, Danny's irises were light, albeit green. He looked thinner than the last time Michael had seen him, but healthier, especially since the bruises he'd been accumulating had finally started to fade.

"Alex's lawyer is top-notch," Danny announced. "He's already found out that some of the evidence used to get me locked up is missing. The district attorney's office is flailing. And the security guard woke up two days ago. They think he's going to recover."

"So there's a good chance you'll be out soon?" Lucienne asked hopefully.

Danny shrugged. He probably didn't want to get his hopes up, but Michael knew this was good news. If the attorney could break down the DA's case prior to trial and the murder charges were off the table, they might drop the matter altogether.

"That's all fine, but it doesn't explain how you got into this mess in the first place," Michael said.

Danny leaned forward. Alex, Lucienne and Michael all followed suit. The room was secure, but none of them wanted to take any chances. "A couple of months ago, I had a collector contact me, wanted me to procure a certain item for him."

"What kind of item?" Michael asked.

"A statue. Gold. Heavy as hell, though it wasn't big. Seven inches in height, about four inches at the widest part." He gestured with his hands to describe the piece.

"Who owned it?"

"Private collection in one of those old Hollywood mansions. There wasn't even supposed to be a security guard there. I'd cased the joint for two weeks."

"You think someone tipped off the owners?"

Danny shook his head. "I don't know, but I'm telling you this much—I didn't get within five feet of the statue before the cops swarmed the place. When the lights came up, the guard was unconscious on the floor and he was holding the statue. The police took it as evidence."

"Why was it so valuable?" Lucienne asked.

"No idea. The guy needed me to lift it quick, so I didn't do much research beyond figuring out how to get in and out. After my arrest, my cell mate got swapped out for some big dude with a message for me. The collector was pissed I'd screwed up with the statue. It was locked up in an evidence locker and he wanted his money's worth. He wanted Ramon's ring instead."

Lucienne sat back, her face twisted in confusion. "A statue made of solid gold, of the size and shape you described, would be worth a lot more than the ring, even if the ring's history was common knowledge—which it's not, right?"

Michael ran his hand through his hair. "No way. Pop was supersecretive about the ring's history. I knew. My mother knew, but she'd never tell anyone. He didn't want anyone but family to know."

"But this collector," Alex asked. "He knew the ring's story?"

"He never said," Danny answered. "I didn't even know the story until Alex told me. Load of crap as far as I'm concerned, but it might explain why someone thinks it's so valuable."

Lucienne entwined her arm with Alex's and leaned her head on his shoulder. Michael watched Danny for any sign that he did not approve of this romance between his adopted sister with his newly found brother, but he saw nothing but a warm smile his brother tried—very unsuccessfully—to hide.

"We got the name of the collector from the stooges he sent after Alex," Michael said. "But the guy doesn't exist."

Danny chuckled. "Of course he doesn't. I don't think he

ever wanted that statue. He was setting me up so I'd send someone after the ring. Probably figured that as long as an FBI agent had it, he couldn't get near it. Not unless he had an inside track through a family member."

"So you're acknowledging that we're family now?" Michael asked, surprised.

"Are you?" Danny shot back.

"Neither one of you have a choice," Alex declared, and for the first time, Michael understood what it meant to have an older brother whose word was law.

Michael didn't want to argue the point anyway. He disapproved of Danny's choices, but little by little, he was starting to understand what had pushed him down this road. He hadn't had a family to keep him out of trouble.

Until now.

"I'll see what I can do about finding this collector," Michael said.

"No," Danny insisted. "This is my fight. When I'm out, I'll deal with him myself."

"Or he'll deal with you," Lucienne countered. "Maybe with a single gunshot to the head?"

"He doesn't want me dead," Danny argued. "He wants the ring. My lawyer thinks he'll have me sprung in no time. So you'll just have to keep it safe and watch your back until I'm out of this joint."

Michael chuckled and tried not to imagine the trouble his brother might get into if he played vigilante. "You're a thief, not an enforcer. Looks like I'm heading out to Louisiana soon for a case. When I get back, we'll work together to find out who's after Pop's legacy."

"Our legacy," Alejandro corrected.

He reached across the table and slapped his hand over Michael's. With a girlish laugh, Lucienne slipped her hand atop his, then eyed Danny pointedly. With a groan, he joined the pile-on, but only for a split second before he tore away from the table and pounded on the door so his lawyer and the guard would return.

"Take good care of my sister," he said to Alex while the guard reattached his handcuffs.

"Sister-in-law," their older brother amended. "Soon, at any rate."

"Yeah, well, wait until I'm out to marry her, okay? Someone's gotta walk her down the aisle."

In his lifetime, Michael never would have imagined that Danny was so sentimental. But then, he never would have imagined that less than a year after his father's untimely death, he'd have more brothers than he knew what to do with and soon a sister-in-law to boot.

Their lives were changing—irrevocably and with lightning speed. And as he looked down at his father's ring, he couldn't help but wonder if the bandit's influence had something to do with it.

* * * * *

EXPOSED

1

"HEY, SWEET THING. Wanna lift?"

Ariana Karas swung her pack securely over her shoulder, ducking her head so the tube of architectural plans shoved inside didn't knock off her lucky hat. She secured the Greek fisherman's cap by pressing the brim firmly over her dark bangs and stepped onto the Powell-Hyde cable car for her ride back to the restaurant. She flashed a weary grin at Benny, the sixty-something brakeman who flirted with her on a nightly basis, just enough to make her smile—even tonight.

"Sweet thing?" she asked, eyebrow cocked. "I should be offended, Benny." She produced her transit slip.

Benny rubbed his bearded jowl and laughed. He released the lever and tweaked the bell, setting the car—empty except for her in the front and a group of chilled tourists riding inside—in motion up Powell Street toward Fisherman's Wharf.

"Heaven help me if I ever offend you, Miss Karas. That tube you've been carting from the restaurant to Market Street for the past few months would end up whacked upside my head."

Ariana laughed silently, wondering how Benny and everyone else in the world could ever get the idea that she was so tough. Sure, she talked a good game to keep her rowdy bar patrons in line or to ward off the aggressive transients that sometimes hung around in front of the restaurant, but on nights like tonight, Ariana relived all the uncertainty she'd felt when she'd left home, young and starved for independence. Against the wishes of her entire family—grandparents, father, mother, two brothers and two sisters—she'd packed up and moved across the country from Tarpon Springs, Florida, to San Francisco, California. She'd had a degree in accounting from the local junior college and little knowledge of the world outside her tight-knit Greek community.

But she'd also had dreams taller and wider than the Golden Gate Bridge. She'd wanted to be her own woman, make her own dreams come true—on her terms and with few debts owed to anyone when her lifetime of fantasies became reality.

Eight years had passed. And tonight, three years of marriage, one divorce and five years of fourteen-hour days later, she was one week away from seeing her dream begin. Starting tomorrow afternoon, the restaurant she operated would be closed for business for the first time since her uncle had turned management duties over to her. When the remodeling was done and she reopened, she'd have a large, airy, modern space to serve locals and tourists alike. Customers would line up to taste her eclectic blend of hearty Greek and Italian foods and sip original libations in her signature bar.

She'd call it Ari's Oasis.

She'd worked so long, so hard to compete with the other operations on the Wharf, some of which had been serving food to San Francisco since the turn of the century. Her uncle inherited the building from her aunt Sonia's family, fishermen who used to sell their catch from make-shift carts. The permanent structure had evolved over the years, but the crisp, white-paneled walls, quaint fishing nets strung from the ceiling and red checkerboard table-cloths, while homey, were showing their age. Even Uncle Stefano knew the time for change had come. But he enjoyed sipping strong Turkish coffee in the mornings and ouzo in the evenings with customers more than supervising the menu or balancing the books.

Ariana had left home specifically to work for Stefano and Sonia, in hopes of inheriting the business from her childless relatives. Marriage to Rick got in the way. But soon after Ariana found herself divorced and jobless, she'd accepted Stefano's offer to take over. In record time, she'd put the restaurant in the black and on the map, and had secured financing for much-needed renovations. She'd even approved every blue pencil mark on the prints she carried in her pack.

Now she had seven days—the contractors wouldn't arrive until a week from Monday—to clear out the place before they started knocking down walls. Since Uncle Stefano insisted that he supervise the moving of the equipment and furniture into storage, he ordered Ariana to take the week off—her first real vacation since she moved to California—to rejuvenate before her life descended into complete turmoil.

And who was she to argue? Stefano had a way of making his rare commands sound like sweet talk—a skill he'd developed to deal with his loving but willful wife. A woman Ari reminded him of, judging by the times he called her Sonia, particularly during a disagreement. Ari swallowed a bittersweet smile.

Sonia's death and Ari's divorce had been strong catalysts to her single-minded pursuit of success for the restaurant. She'd worked tirelessly for five years. But now she really needed a break. For herself. For her sanity.

The cable car rattled and shook as it moved uphill, a familiar buzzing hum beneath her feet and a crisp San Francisco night chilling her cheeks. The fog was rolling in late tonight. Fingers of smoky moisture twirled toward them from the Bay. But over her shoulder the scene was clear—the glittering, neon and historic charm that was San Francisco.

The cable car paused between the intersections at Geary and Powell, then shrugged forward when no one jumped aboard at Union Square. The main cable car traffic at this time of night was on the return trip, from the Wharf to the hotels at Market Street and stops along the way. At least, that's what she'd heard.

On most Friday nights, and Saturday through Thursday as well, she was helping her hostess find seats for customers, checking on orders with her chef or serving her specialty drinks in the bar. She knew little to nothing about the charming, diverse, anything-goes city she called home. Her explorations were limited to the nightspots her former husband once played with his band and the blocks around Chinatown where she lived in a rent-controlled apartment above Madame Li's Herb Shop.

But she had one week to see the city, every inch of it if she could, before she immersed herself in supervising the contractors who would turn her quaint dockside eatery into a restaurant of international reputation.

Before she could contemplate what her father would

think of her bold, risky move from storefront eatery to full-fledged culinary powerhouse, a flutter of glossy pages caught her eye from farther down the bench. She slid over and plucked the magazine from the seat, recognizing it as one of the hip women's periodicals her landlady bought for her shop so the older patrons who stopped by for her delicious blend of tea and gossip could laugh at their younger counterparts and their silly ideas of womanhood.

She might have agreed with them about some of the magazine's topics, but this issue's feature caught Ari's eye. *Sexy City Nights: San Francisco Style.*

Sex. Now *there* was an interesting activity Ari barely remembered. She fanned the pages until she found the large color spread featuring a couple leaning against the bright orange railing of the Golden Gate. Darkness and a fine mist of fog shadowed the models' bodies, but their faces were angled into the photographer's light just enough to capture expressions. Wanton desire on the man's. Sheer ecstasy in the eyes of the woman.

Whatever he was doing to her, she was enjoying it.

A lot.

The cable car rattled along, slowing beneath a bright street lamp long enough for Ariana to see that the man's left hand had disappeared somewhere beneath the woman's incredibly short and fluttering skirt.

Ari swallowed, briefly marveling at the bold sensuality of this mainstream magazine. But soon her intimacy-starved imagination superimposed her own face, equally enraptured, equally pleasured, over the model in the photograph. A pressure, not unlike the sensation of a man's fingers, slipped between her thighs and stirred a throbbing loneliness she usually felt only late at night after a hot shower or early in the morning after a restless battle with erotic dreams.

How thrilling, how inviting—to be in a public place while a man touched you privately—with only the night and the thin misty remnants of fog to shield the sensations from prying eyes. For a woman to risk such discovery, the desire for a man's touch and utter need for intimacy would have to override every ounce of good sense, every inkling of decent behavior.

Ari sighed. Once upon a time, she'd been caught up in a man enough to leave her logic at the door. Unfortunately, though the sex hadn't been bad, her ex-husband, Rick, had been more concerned with his own pleasure than hers. And she, barely into her twenties and wholly inexperienced, hadn't known better.

On the bumpy road to now, she'd learned about her needs. But by the time she knew what she wanted from a man, Rick had packed his bags for a gig in Seattle, leaving behind the divorce papers, their apartment lease and an ocean of emotions she'd only just emerged from.

But now she had a whole week off and a magazine detailing a city full of possibilities.

Benny leaned over the wooden bench to peek over her shoulder. "So, what are you planning to do when Athens closes?"

Ari turned the page of the magazine, intrigued by another sultry photo shot in a cell at Alcatraz. *Talk about bondage.*

She glanced up to see if Benny had noticed, but his eyes were back on the line, his hands working the brake and bell with practiced grace.

"We'll be closed for over a month, but I only have a

week for vacation. I'm not letting those contractors tear out one nail unless I'm watching."

Benny shook his head and clucked his tongue. "You can't be there all the time. Girl as young and pretty as you shouldn't be cooped up in that restaurant as much as you are. You need to get out. See the city. Enjoy being young while you can."

Ariana folded the next page over, her breath catching at the image of nude lovers immersed in the mineral baths in nearby Napa Valley. She'd never been to Napa. Not once. And by the looks of the photo, she was missing a lot more than wine.

"Sounds like a plan," she answered. "I've got one week to experience San Francisco. Think that's enough?"

Benny laughed heartily, the booming sound coming from even his belly. The straining cables beneath the street, the heartline of old San Francisco seemed to chuckle right along with him.

"With the right man, a woman can experience the world in one night."

Ariana laughed in response, but privately mulled his words over, allowing her romantic side to believe Benny knew what he was talking about—that there was a man out there for her. One completely enamored with her. One who would put her pleasure, her satisfaction, before his needs. No, her pleasure and satisfaction would *be* his needs.

She wanted a sexy, uninhibited, confident man who would show her the soul of the city and the depths of her desires. And then, at the end of the week, he would fade away as if he'd never existed, leaving her with a lifetime of scorching memories to heat her through the cool San Francisco nights.

Without warning, the quixotic fantasy was slapped out

of her head. Her hat tumbled onto her lap and she scrambled to catch it and the magazine before they flew off the car. Adjusting her backpack, she grinned wryly at the long tube that had just hit her—and at her own fanciful interlude. Such a dream lover didn't exist...in her experience. She had no men at all in her life except for Ray, the restaurant's day manager, who was happily married and treated her like a sister; her uncle, Stefano; the majority of her waitstaff; and, of course, her customers.

Customers.

One in particular.

Benny slowed the cable car to pick up a trio of laughing coeds, then made the turn at Jackson Street for the brief ascent to Hyde, up toward the fancy houses on Russian Hill. Toward the place where she'd heard *he* lived. *He* being one Maxwell Forrester. A customer.

But not just any customer. The customer she lusted after. The customer who'd shown up in one too many of her fantasies as of late, even though they'd exchanged no more than twenty-five words in the past year, not including, "Would you like lime in your club soda?" or "The crab pasta is particularly good today." He'd become a regular at Athens by the Bay, though one she'd wisely kept a distance from.

He possessed too much potent male power for a woman like her, at first reeling from a divorce and then determined to make her own way without any distraction from her goals. And Maxwell Forrester most definitely distracted her.

He jogged into the restaurant every morning for coffee before finishing his run to his office somewhere in the Embarcadero. Luckily, since she usually came in around two o'clock to handle the afternoon and evening crowds, she'd only seen him in the mornings on rare occasions. His sleepy, bedroom eyes and barely combed-through hair did a number on her senses each and every time. Not that seeing him after a long day at work was any better. He often jogged back from his office, in sweatpants and a jacket that were just ratty enough to mold to his broad shoulders and lean thighs, and just designer enough to remind her that he was out of her league.

She didn't know much about him—he was wealthy, did something in the real estate business and lived in Russian Hill. Ordinarily, she wouldn't even see him again until the restaurant reopened sometime at the end of next month.

Ordinarily.

Except that if fate was on her side... She checked her watch, shifting the magazine so she could activate the blue light. He might still be at the restaurant. The private party, a wedding-rehearsal dinner, had been booked at Athens by the Bay by Maxwell Forrester's friend, Charlie—another regular customer, but one she'd gotten to know a bit better. Charlie had worked with her to plan tonight's dinner, using their one-on-one meetings to casually drop the information that Max would be his best man at his upcoming wedding.

Charlie Burrows had all the subtlety of a barge. The groom-to-be made no secret that he thought Max and Ari should get to know each other better. Until she and Charlie had met yesterday to finalize the plans, Ari interpreted Max's cool friendliness toward her as a hint that he'd also heard Charlie's matchmaking arguments and wasn't interested.

But during their last meeting, Charlie had claimed that her assumption wasn't true. He'd never encourage Max to date anyone since his pal hated fix-ups. Unfortunately,

Charlie was a horrible liar and Ariana sensed that there was something in his claim that didn't ring true.

But completely focused on her goals, Ariana had waved away Charlie's suggestion. She didn't need a date with anyone but her architect and her loan officer, and those were strictly business.

Of course, now all the blueprints were authorized and the financing was signed, sealed and delivered. She had to face the fact that she had a whole empty week ahead of her, a fascinating city all around her and an ignored libido driving her crazy.

Suddenly, crazy didn't seem so bad—and it definitely wasn't out of place in San Francisco. She fanned through the article, witnessing once again what this amazing, charming, insane city had to offer—with the right man and the right attitude.

MAXWELL FORRESTER SHOVED his platinum credit card back into his eelskin wallet and shrugged over the cost of his and Madelyn's wedding-rehearsal dinner. He had more than enough money to cover the expense, but growing up poor had saddled him with a frugal nature he constantly battled. A day didn't pass when he didn't remember going to bed hungry, knowing the food stamps had all been used, all too aware even at the age of ten that if he wanted so much as an extra peanut butter sandwich, he'd have to go out and earn it himself.

As expected of a man in his current financial position, he'd told Charlie, his best man, to spend whatever was necessary to make the evening elegant for Max's future bride, their families and wedding party. He should have known better than to hope Charlie, Madelyn's favorite cousin and Max's best friend, would even think of capping his spending.

"You ready to go?"

"It's early yet," Charlie scoffed. "You've got one more night of freedom and you want to call it quits at—" he pulled his sleeve back to read his watch "—midnight?"

Charlie's argument lost some of its punch when even he realized that it was indeed late, what with the wedding less than twelve hours away.

Eleven hours, to be exact, Max realized. Not twelve. Not a minute more than eleven. Once he said, "I do," he'd be stuck with his decision to marry Madelyn. He shrugged away the thought. He wouldn't be any more stuck tomorrow than he was today. Max had already made a promise to Madelyn that was just as binding as a wedding vow. And though he considered himself an arrogant, driven son of a bitch who sought financial gain over just about anything else, he'd never break a promise to a friend.

"Marriage to Madelyn isn't a threat to my freedom," Max grumbled. He wasn't lying. Madelyn couldn't be a threat to his freedom when he'd really never had any in the first place. Max was a prisoner of his ambitions—he'd accepted that fact before he turned sixteen. But tonight the reality really rankled, partly because he was tired of this conversation with Charlie, and partly because as he scanned the crowd in the barroom off to the left, he saw no sign of a Greek fisherman's cap bobbing behind the bar—or more specifically, the exotic dark-haired beauty who wore it.

"That's only because you don't know what freedom feels like, tastes like." Charlie grabbed his jacket from behind the chair, but slung it over his shoulder instead of putting it on, a sure sign that he wasn't ready to go. "You

should leave that office of yours every once in a while—
and not to jog through a city you don't see or to show a
property you don't appreciate as anything but a potential
sale. Heck, you and Maddie barely even dated each other!"

Max attempted to tear his gaze out of the bar before
Charlie noticed, but he wasn't quick enough. Charlie's grin
annoyed him all the more.

"I don't want to hear this, Charlie. Madelyn is your
cousin. You should be supportive of our marriage. It's
what she wants."

Charlie grabbed Max's arm and tugged him into the bar.
"Maddie is not just my cousin. She's my *favorite* cousin.
She's the one person in the whole snooty family who didn't
write me off when I flunked out of Wharton or when I decided to try my hand at acting before I moved back home.
I owe her." He forced Max onto a bar stool and waved at
the carrot-topped, college-age kid tending the bar. "She
introduced me to you, didn't she? Got you to give me a try
selling real estate. And who was your top agent last year?
For the third time? Who's helping you become a millionaire more than any of the Yalies or finishing-school love-
lies who show your listings?"

Max glanced back at the door, knowing he should
leave. He needed sleep. At least when he was sleeping,
he wasn't thinking. And tonight, he didn't want to think.
He'd promised Madelyn Burrows that he'd become her
husband. They'd been friends since college. She'd helped
him take the coarser edge off his Oakland habits, teaching him about designer clothes and fine wine and which
fork to use at the country-club dinner. He'd repaid the debt
by giving her a shoulder to cry on when she broke her engagement to P. Howell Matthews, her parents' handpicked
son-in-law. She'd wept, not because she'd loved the guy,

but because her parents had treated her like a mass murderer rather than a woman scared to death of choosing the wrong man.

So instead, she chose a friend, her best friend. He and Madelyn shared a love for jogging and naturalistic art, and they both appreciated old buildings—she saved them, he sold them. They also had a mutual desire to marry for reasons other than love.

Max had nothing against love. In fact, he admired the emotion. Revered it, even. His parents loved each other, and they loved his footloose brother, Ford, and Max unconditionally and with all their hearts. But love hadn't paid the rent on their tired Oakland apartment. Love hadn't kept his father from working twenty-hour days driving a cab. Love had only marginally helped his mother endure the frustrations of teaching six-year-olds how to read and write when most of them were more concerned with getting their one state-subsidized lunch, usually their only decent meal all day.

Love hadn't been enough to keep his family together when his father was shot on the job. Unable to work, John and Rhonda Forrester had shuttled their sons from resentful relative to resentful relative. Eventually, the family had reunited, but the result was Max's single-minded pursuit of wealth and, over time, power, which had led him directly to the eve of a marriage that had nothing to do with love at all.

And he wouldn't even go into the havoc the emotion caused his brother. Ford was the most easygoing, likable man on the face of the planet, but he fell in and out of love quicker than Max unloaded a waterfront foreclosure. His younger brother had absolutely no idea what real love was about, and this was one lesson his big brother wasn't qualified to teach.

He was certain of only one immutable fact—love was fine and good for people willing to sacrifice and suffer for it, but Max preferred to pursue success and financial satisfaction. Romance was a distraction. Until he'd met Maddie in college, he'd considered dating an unnecessary expense. Then she'd introduced him to her friends, girls with rich fathers and boundless connections. He'd dated the ones he liked, but drew the line at emotional involvement. So after graduate school, when Madelyn had suggested they "date" to keep her parents from fixing her up with another son of the country-club set like P. Howell Matthews, Max agreed. The ruse was born and had lasted all these years.

Madelyn was a pal. She understood his desire to make all of San Francisco forget that he was once a poor kid from Oakland—that now he was a force to be reckoned with in the lucrative business of buying and selling the most valuable properties in northern California. The marriage thing was more than he had bargained for, but Madelyn insisted the deal would work out for both of them.

Married to a Burrows, Max would have every door in San Francisco opened wide to him. Her father, her grandfather and her great-grandfather before him had all been prominent bankers with ties to every section of the diverse San Francisco community.

For Madelyn, the trade-off wasn't so clear—at least, not to Max. She claimed that marrying him would not only appease her parents, but the union would give her more clout with the wealthy matrons who financed her building restorations. Personally, he thought Madelyn deserved better—a man who loved her like a wife and would give her the passion she deserved. And he'd told her so on more than one occasion. But he owed her so much, cared about her so much, that when she begged him not to worry and to trust her decision, he'd gone along.

Like Charlie, he wasn't so sure he was doing the right thing. But he'd made his choice and he couldn't betray Madelyn now because of a bout of uncertainty.

"You're a real pal, Charlie, but Madelyn and I have discussed this over and over. I won't back out."

Charlie ordered two beers and shook his head. "You and Maddie are so blind. Neither one of you knows what you're missing. Lust, passion, desire. Marrying a friend is all well and good, but without the fire..." Charlie's words trailed off, his blue eyes glazed over.

Recently wed in Las Vegas to a woman he'd met in a suspicious jogging accident at Pier 39, Charlie was still high on the thrill of pure passion and uninhibited lust. Max paid the young bartender when he slid the beers in front of them, shaking his head at his friend, then glanced over his shoulder to see if anyone had overheard this unusual prewedding conversation.

That's when he saw her.

She entered through the front door between a departing party of four, stopping to shake hands with satisfied customers while Stefano Karas, the host for the evening, grabbed her backpack, shoved it at a nearby waiter and then ushered her into the bar.

Max turned aside. The last woman he needed to see tonight was Ariana Karas, with all her long, jet hair, ebony eyes and curves even her slimming black turtleneck, jeans and boots couldn't hide. She was exotic sensuality and alluring confidence all molded and sculpted into a compact package that made him fantasize about endless nights of sex. Nights that turned into days. And weeks. Maybe months.

Nothing but sex. No work, no money. No troubles.

He downed half his beer without taking a breath.

"Sex isn't everything, Charlie."

Charlie took a generous slurp of amber brew. "Oh, yeah? Says who? And I'm not just talking about sex, anyway. I'm talking about true love."

He sang the last two words as if he was joking, but Max knew Charlie well enough to realize his friend was a hopeless romantic. He was a free spirit who'd finally found some level ground with a job he was damn good at and a woman who obviously adored him, and vice versa.

"Yeah, well, if marrying your true love is so highly rated, what the hell are you doing here with me?" Max asked. "You should be home in bed with Sheri, not keeping me out till dawn."

Charlie chuckled, then quieted when Ariana grabbed a black apron from the coatrack behind the bar.

"Sheri could use a little time to herself and you need me to talk some sense into you."

Max barely heard Charlie's explanation, more intrigued with watching Ariana flip the apron over her head before freeing her dark hair from beneath the pretied knot around her neck and fanning the luxurious length of it over her back. While wrapping the tie around her slim waist, she instructed the young guy who'd served their beer to cover the tables while she took over behind the bar. She tilted her hat at that jaunty angle that grabbed Max right at the center of his groin, and before he could look away, she captured his stare with a questioning glance.

"Something I can get you?" she asked.

Max sipped his beer, trying not to wince when the brew suddenly tasted strangely flat. "I'm fine, thanks."

She smiled, then made her way from one end of the bar to the other, checking on her customers, making small talk, replacing empty glasses and refilling snack bowls—all done with a quiet animation that made her both friendly and mysterious at the same time.

Max decided then and there that he was an idiot. He knew all about the lust Charlie lectured about. He'd been feeling the pull with growing intensity ever since he jogged into Athens by the Bay a little over two years ago and caught sight of the owner's niece helping a crew unload boxes from a delivery truck.

If he'd simply flirted with her and gotten to know her, he'd probably be long over this intense interest. Instead, he'd played cool, ignored the attraction, turned away from her not-quite-shy, not-quite-inviting smiles that haunted him long after he'd run from the restaurant to the office, showered and parked himself behind his desk.

Now he was less than a day away from marriage, and the woman of his dreams was only an arm's length away.

"Hey, Ari," Charlie called, "how 'bout one of your specialty drinks for the road?"

"You driving?" she asked, grabbing a cone-shaped glass from beneath the bar.

Charlie grinned sheepishly. "Yeah, guess I am. Then how about making one for my old friend here?" He slapped Max on the shoulder. "He needs it more than I do, anyway."

Ariana didn't laugh as Max expected, or as perhaps Charlie expected as well. Instead, she grabbed a collection of exotic liqueurs, one blue, one green, one amber, pouring the jewel-toned liquids into the glass on the edge of a knife, skillfully layering them with a clear, unidentified libation, so the colors barely mixed. After floating a layer of ruby-red grenadine on top, she moved toward them.

With confident grace, she lifted the drink in one hand and a bottle of ouzo in the other. She set the glass down in front of Max and without a word, swirled the ouzo over the grenadine. Focused on the glass, Ariana shielded her eyes from Max behind thick lashes, pressing the lips of her generous mouth into a pout that was focused and sexy as hell. When she finally looked up, meeting his thirsty stare straight on, he caught the glimmer of a smile twinkling in her night-black eyes.

He slid his hand forward, brushing his fingers over the base of the glass. She crooked her finger around the stem. "Not so fast," she instructed, her voice breathy and low, but compelling all the same.

He questioned her with raised eyebrows.

She stepped up on the lower shelf behind the bar so she could lean forward and keep their exchange private. Max wanted to glance aside to see if Charlie or anyone else was watching, but he was slowly, surely, losing himself in the depths of her fathomless eyes. To hell with everyone else. She was just offering him a drink, not her body.

"This is my most special specialty." She skimmed her finger on the top layer of ouzo, careful not to disturb the rainbow of liqueurs underneath, then dampened the rim of the glass—precisely where his mouth would be when he took a drink. "I don't make it for just anyone."

Max's mouth dried. He moistened his lips with a thickening tongue. "I'm flattered."

"You should be. But you have to do your part, too." She dampened her finger again, but this time she touched the taste of ouzo to her lips. "This drink is called a Flaming Eros. Just like good loving, it takes two to make it hot."

Hot? Oh, yeah. Max was learning about heat very, very quickly. His collar grew tight around his neck. His body dampened with sweat. The perfectly starched shirt beneath his perfectly pressed jacket was starting to buckle.

"Makes sense," he managed to say.

Her fingers dipped into the pocket of her apron, then she slid her hand toward his, something small hidden beneath her palm.

Her phone number maybe? The key to her apartment?

He glanced down. A box of matches?

"So," she said, slightly louder, but still in a voice meant entirely for him, "care to light my fire?"

2

ARIANA SWALLOWED, savoring the ouzo she'd boldly stolen from his drink. She didn't know where the seductive move had come from; she wasn't exactly experienced with this sort of thing. But she'd spent enough time tending bar to watch some real pros work the room. Judging by the way Max Forrester's pupils expanded and darkened his eyes from pale jade to pine green, she wasn't doing half bad.

One week of freedom was all she had and, dammit, she wanted to spend at least one night with the man she'd lusted for since the first time she'd seen him. She'd never had an indiscriminate affair and, quite honestly, she wasn't starting now. Hell, since her divorce, she'd become the most discriminating woman in San Francisco. But Max Forrester exceeded even her high standards. He was gorgeous, had not just a steady job, but a full-fledged career and, according to Charlie, wasn't in the market for a wife.

She'd made the mistake of marrying her first lover and ended up waylaying her own goals and dreams in favor of his. Charlie claimed Max was a man of strong ethics, but he wasn't interested in long-term entanglements. And according to her own personal observation, he was potently sexy, inherently classy and, most important, he was undeniably interested.

Max took the box of matches from her, fumbling slightly while sliding it open, and extracted a single match without spilling the others. She couldn't help but be impressed. She, being incredibly clumsy, had long ago taken to inviting her customers to remove a match rather than risk her sending them flying across the polished teak countertop. But she'd never made the offer with such a libidinous double entendre as "Care to light my fire?" Or if she had, the second meaning simply hadn't occurred to her before. That invitation to fire her personal hot spot belonged to Max and Max alone.

He shut the box, then poised the red-tipped end of the match against the flint. "My mother told me never to play with matches."

She leaned forward a little closer, unable to stop herself. Once she'd made the decision to seduce Charlie's best man, she wouldn't back down. Couldn't. The tide tugging her toward Max Forrester was more treacherous than the waves outside Alcatraz, and just as invigorating.

"She told you that when you were a little boy, right? Well, you're not a little boy anymore. Are you?"

He struck the match, inflaming the head, emitting a burst of smoke and sulfur that tickled her nose. She listed closer to him like a boat following the command of the waves. Amid the wispy scent of fire, she caught wind of his cologne. A musky blend of spices and citrus flared her nostrils and rocked her equilibrium.

He held the match toward her and she blinked, knowing she'd better get a hold of herself before she lit her Flaming Eros. She was already hot enough without adding third-degree burns.

She skimmed her fingers beneath his, brushing his hand

briefly as she took the match away. The warmth of his skin was soothing. The look in his eyes was not.

She slid the glass back and skimmed the fire over the alcohol until the drink ignited in an impressive blue and orange flame. The bar erupted in applause and Stefano shouted last call. Ariana couldn't wait around to watch Max drink her concoction. She immediately had orders for three more. After sliding a small plate from beneath the bar to help him extinguish the flame and instructing him to do so before the fire burned through the grenadine, she grabbed his half-empty beer and her bottle of ouzo and moved farther down the bar.

She needed space. She'd probably only imagined the increase in her body heat the moment he'd stroked the match against the box, but she hadn't imagined the look of utter fascination in his eyes. How long had it been since a man looked at her that way? Since she'd *let* a man look at her that way without extinguishing his interest with a sharp phrase or quip?

Since her marriage? If she took the time, she could count it down to the minute. But she wouldn't. For the life of her, she was going to make sure that her marriage and divorce would cease to be a milestone in her life. Tonight would be the turning point.

She mixed the three flaming aperitifs, each more quickly than the last, letting the customer remove the match, but doing so much more silently and efficiently than she had with Max.

Care to light my fire? she'd asked. Trouble was, he'd done that a hell of a long time ago without even trying— simply by coming into her tiny wharfside restaurant one evening, ordering his beer with cool politeness and leaving a big tip—and then disappearing into the night. But he'd come back, nearly every weeknight. Never saying more than a few words, but speaking to her nonetheless—in sidelong glances, clandestine stares. Perhaps saying things she wasn't ready to hear.

Until tonight.

Little by little, the crowd thinned. The dining rooms were emptied, vacuumed and reset for the final breakfast crowd. Uncle Stefano stuffed the night's receipts into a vinyl bag then disappeared in the office to secure them in the safe so Ari could tally them later. In couples and trios, the customers went home. Waiters called good-night after scooping their tips from their pockets and tossing their aprons into the laundry basket by the kitchen.

But Max Forrester didn't move.

Ariana stuffed dirty glasses in the dishwasher, replaced all the bottles she'd used, stacked the mixers in the small refrigerator and wiped down the bar—all the while aware that Max hadn't left. Charlie had, sometime when Ariana hadn't noticed, and he'd done so without saying goodbye or thanking her for her help with his rehearsal dinner, which she thought odd but not surprising. The man *was* getting married in the morning. She was more than likely the last thing he had on his mind.

But obviously she was of interest to Max. Never before had he stayed late. Why else but for her? She was flattered. Terrified. Excited. He'd never flirted with her in the past, never so much as attempted to strike up a conversation beyond the day's specials. At the same time, he'd never been cold or dismissive. Just standoffish, controlled. As if he chose to ignore their mutual attraction just as she did.

And yet, he'd lagged behind tonight. That had to mean something.

Ariana poured ouzo into a short shot glass and downed the fiery liqueur in one gulp. The licorice-tasting essence of anise coated her mouth, burned her eyes and her throat, but she needed the fortification. If Max hadn't left, it was, perhaps, because he'd read the subtle invitation in her eyes earlier, understood the hidden meaning in her question. Possibly she was about to be granted the wish she'd made while riding that cable car down Russian Hill, the bright moon shining just over the Bay Bridge, casting a hypnotic glow over the dark waters of San Francisco Bay.

She wanted to have an affair. This week and this week only. With Max Forrester and Max Forrester only.

She smoothed her damp cloth closer and closer to him at the bar. He didn't turn toward her. He sat, staring straight ahead, his gaze lost in the rows of bottles behind the bar. His Flaming Eros had barely been touched.

She glanced at the collection of whiskeys and bourbons and vodkas, wondering what held his attention so raptly.

"Hey, Max? You all right?"

Cautiously, she walked directly in his line of vision. There was a distinct pause before his eyes focused on her.

"Yeah. I'm great."

He blinked once, then twice. She saw him sway on his bar stool.

She shot forward and grabbed his hand. "No, you're not."

She glanced down at his drink again. He'd sipped maybe a quarter of the concoction and though her mixture was potent, she'd never seen anyone get drunk on just one. Maybe a little silly, but not ready to pass out.

"What did you drink tonight?"

She remembered clearing away a half-empty beer, but she had no idea what he'd had before she returned from her appointment with the architect.

She waited for him to answer and when he didn't, she asked again.

"What? Oh." He glanced down at his drink. "You made me this."

"No, I mean before. At dinner?"

He squinted as he thought. Remembering took more effort than it should have. He was drunk. Ariana rolled her eyes. *Great. Just great! I finally decide to have an affair with a guy and he's three sheets to the wind.* She recalled the distinctly forgettable experience of making love to her husband when he'd had more than his share of tequila after a gig in the Castro. Not an experience she'd *ever* want to repeat.

"Max, what did you drink at dinner?" she asked once more, losing her patience with the same speed as her attraction.

"Tea," he answered finally, nodding as the memory apparently became clearer and clearer. "We had tea."

"Long Island Iced Teas?"

Ariana hated that drink. She'd seen more than her share of inexperienced drinkers get sloshed thanks to the innocent-sounding name. Too bad there wasn't a drop of tea in the thing. Just vodka, gin, tequila, rum, Collins mix and an ounce of cola for color.

"Great, just…"

"No, iced tea. Unsweetened. With lemon."

As the truth of his claim registered, she stepped up on the lower shelf behind the bar again to look directly into his eyes. His pupils were huge—and passion had nothing to do with it. He was sweating more than he should have been. His jaw was slightly lax.

"You're sure? You've had nothing to drink but iced tea, half a beer and a few sips of my Flaming Eros?"

For a moment she thought she'd given him way too much to think about, but he managed to nod. "I feel kind of weird," he admitted. "I think I should…"

He pushed off his stool slowly, his hands firmly gripping the bar. If she hadn't been watching so closely, she might not even have seen him waver when his feet were firmly on the floor.

"You're not going anywhere."

Ariana scurried around the bar and caught him before he'd taken a single step toward the door.

"I can walk home," he reminded her, though he didn't pull away from the supportive brace of her shoulder beneath his arm.

"Oh, really? You make it to the door without my help and maybe, just maybe, I'll let you go." She had absolutely no intention of allowing him to go anywhere by himself, though her idea of seducing him was a great big bust. "You're not drunk, Max. Someone…someone in *my* establishment," she added with increasing anger, "slipped you a Mickey."

"A Mickey?"

She ignored his question, knowing that after a brief time delay, he'd understand. Someone had drugged him and it certainly hadn't been her. However, since the event had happened in her place, she could only imagine the trouble that could come just as she was about to break into the international restaurant scene. She'd heard about people using such deception at college parties. She'd read about the practice at raves and in dance clubs. But in a family-style restaurant? A neighborhood bar?

"Why?" he finally asked.

She shifted beneath his weight and guided him toward the door. "I have no idea." She called to the kitchen, which she suddenly noticed was quiet. She shouted twice more, than leaned Max against the hostess stand and ordered him not to move.

"Uncle Stefano? Paulie?"

The kitchen was empty. The floors were damp and the dishwashers steamed, but no one was around and the back door was bolted tight. She checked the office. Empty. Uncle Stefano and her chef, Paulie, never left without saying goodbye and making sure she had a ride home. It was nearly one o'clock and the last cable car left the turn-around at 12:59 a.m.

As she grabbed her backpack from behind her desk, removing the architectural plans and placing them atop the file cabinet, she wondered if Uncle Stefano had seen Max lingering in the bar and assumed she had plans for the night. She didn't know why he'd make such a ridiculous assumption except that, this time, he might have been right. And he had been hounding her about dating again, even agreeing with Charlie that Max made a good potential suitor. Perhaps Stefano thought she'd finally taken him up on his advice.

"Looks like it's up to me to take you home." She closed the office light and grabbed the keys.

Max shook his head, staggered then steadied himself to catch his balance. "Just call me a cab."

Ariana glanced at the phone, frowning. Yeah, a cab could get him home—he supposedly lived only a few blocks away. But what would happen in the morning when Maxwell Forrester, San Francisco real estate and power broker, woke up with a severe headache, possible memory loss and other unpleasant side effects? What would happen when he realized that she could be held culpable for his condition, even if no one who worked for her was involved? She didn't know how mad he'd be, but she imagined herself in his place and didn't like the picture that came into focus.

Negative word of mouth would be the least of her worries. He could call the press, file a lawsuit. If she lost her liquor license, even for the briefest time during an investigation, her business would be dead in the water. She'd invested in the reopening every asset she and her uncle held. She couldn't risk what had happened to Max—though through no fault of her own—jeopardizing her future.

She'd planned to take Max home tonight. No sense in changing the blueprint of her original plan this late in the construction.

"If we hurry, we can make the last cable car. Your place is…"

She moved to slip her arms beneath his again, but this time he caught her off guard. With one hand balanced on the hostess stand, he used the other to brush a strand of hair from her cheek. The friction of his fingernail against her skin was not unlike the lighting of the match. Heat flared where he'd touched her, so gently, so softly and yet with a pyrotechnic flash of instantaneous desire.

"Ariana," was all he said, four syllables on a deep-throated breath scented with anise, teasing her skin, fanning the flame she'd not so effectively tamped down just moments before. "I don't think I've ever said your name before," he said, curling the strand behind her ear, skimming her suddenly sensitive flesh as he thread his fingers into her hair.

She blinked, wondering if the mystery drug was the reason for his sudden interest, and if it was, wondering if she cared.

"I like the way you say it," she admitted, liking also the feel of his hand bracing her neck, his chest pressing closer and closer to hers so that the edge of his tie skimmed across her nipples. Her breasts tingled. Her breath caught. His arousal pressed through his slacks, taunting her. In the morning, he might not remember ever wanting her.

And again, she wondered if she cared.

"You're incredibly beautiful, Ariana. I've wanted to tell you that for a long time."

"Why didn't you?" she asked instantly, wincing when she realized that she might not want to know the answer.

His smile was crooked, tilted slightly higher on the left side. Still, the grin lacked the sardonic effect such an uneven slant might have on anyone else. Her insides clenched in a futile attempt to rein in her response—a cross between a magnetic pull and a bone-deep hunger for a man who was, in reality, a stranger.

Only he didn't *feel* like a stranger anymore, and he hadn't for a long while.

"Union Street," he answered.

"What?"

He hadn't answered her question, wasn't making sense.

He pushed away from her slightly. "You asked where I lived. On Union."

She nodded. Right. Get him home and to bed—though not at all in the way she'd originally intended.

"THIS IS INCREDIBLE!"

Max heard his voice echo beneath the clanging grind of the cable car, not certain he'd intended to share such an exuberant sentiment aloud. Yet when Ariana glanced over her shoulder and rewarded him with a smile that crinkled the corners of her eyes and flashed the whiteness of her teeth, he was glad he had.

"Haven't you ever ridden a cable car before?"

Max couldn't remember. He must have, but never like this. Against Ariana's wishes, he stood on the side step, one hand gripping the polished brass pole, the other aching to wrap around her slim waist and tug her close, back against him. So she could feel his hard-on. And know he wanted her.

And God, he wanted her.

So what was stopping him? He was sure there had been some reason at some time, but he couldn't remember and he certainly didn't care. The crisp San Francisco night air, clouded with a late-night fog, trailed through her nearly waist-length hair and fluttered the glossy strands toward him. The tendrils teased him with a scent part exotic floral, part crisp ocean—and all woman.

Without thought, he did as he desired, slipping his hand around her waist and stepping against her full and flush.

She stiffened slightly and nearly pulled away.

"I want to hold you," he said, beginning to accept that simple thoughts and simple explanations were all he could manage while intoxicated by whatever she'd said someone had put in his drink. He doubted her claim anyway. She had drugged him all right, but no pharmaceutical agent was involved.

She didn't protest when he curled his right arm completely around her waist, careful to remember that he had to hang on to the cable car with his left. His brain was fuddled, but his heightened senses compensated for his total lack of control.

He fanned his fingers across her midsection. The texture of her ribbed shirt felt like trembling flesh. When he brushed his fingertips beneath the swell of her breasts, her back firmed, then relaxed, then pressed closer against him.

He dipped his head to whisper in her ear, "I want to touch you."

The cable car rocked and shimmied to a brief halt. A clanging bell blocked her reply, if she'd made one, but when the car moved again, she turned around and traded her handhold on the brass pole for a firm grip around his waist.

"Where?" she asked.

She'd pulled her cap low and tight, so the dark brim pushed her bangs down to frame her large eyes. She bent her neck back to see his face, exposing an inviting curve of skin from the tip of her chin to the sensual arc of her throat.

His mouth felt cottony, but the desire in her eyes spurred a moisture that made him swallow deep. He ran his slick tongue over his lips and when she mirrored the move herself, his blood surged.

"Where will you touch me?" she asked again.

He blinked, a thousand thoughts racing through a brain too thick to harness them. The mantra "location, location, location" played silently in his mind then drifted away. Every single place he wanted to touch her—her lips, her throat, her shoulders, her breasts, her belly and beyond—seemed too intimate, too private to speak aloud.

He'd just have to show her.

He shook his head, grinning when his dizziness sent him swaying. She gripped him even tighter, giving him an excuse to dip his hold lower, over the swell of her backside, another place he most desperately wanted to touch with his hands and lips and tongue.

Max decided then and there that he had to accept his current limitations. As he had his entire life, he had to work with his immediate circumstances and the most basic skills at his disposal. His ability to speak was severely hampered. Forming a complex thought was out of the question. But he still had his instincts—natural, unguarded responses to basic, inherent needs. Hers and his.

"I'm going to touch you wherever you want me to."

Her smile was tentative, a little surprised and entirely fascinating—as if he'd said something that shocked her.

"What if that doesn't mean what you think it does?"

He shook his head. Processing that puzzle of a comment

was impossible in his condition. He didn't even consider trying.

"Whatever that means, I'm game. I'm in no condition to be in charge tonight. You're going to have to tell me what to do."

She chuckled. The sound was warm and deep and soothing like the liqueurs she'd poured in his drink, like the passions he'd kept in check for way too long.

"You may regret that," she quipped.

Somehow, he doubted he'd regret anything about tonight, especially when the cable car slowed at Union Street and she jumped off the car and crooked her finger into his waistband to tug him to follow. So what if someone had supposedly doctored his drink, making his mind so fuzzy he had a hell of a time remembering his address? So what if some crucial reason, currently out of reach, existed why he shouldn't let this incredibly sensuous woman take him home?

But no thought, no logic, no amount of reason could override the surge of power he felt even as she fairly dragged him up the sidewalk. He was going to make love to this mysterious woman with the sassy black hat.

Just as soon as he remembered where the hell he lived.

3

ARIANA SLID HER HAT off her head. Her backpack came down off her shoulder with it, but she held tight to the strap so it didn't touch the polished marble floor. She wasn't exactly a rube from some hick town, but standing in Maxwell Forrester's living room certainly made her feel like one. She'd expected wealth, not sheer opulence.

Everything was white. Pure white. The carpet, the furniture, the walls. Do-not-step-on-or-touch-me white. Glass cases of crystal sculpture reflected sparkling rainbow prisms, but the color was icy, precise. Only Max, a mass of gray and brown and flesh tone who shuffled in front of her before he flopped on the couch, shedding shoes and jacket and tie along the way, warmed the room with subtle invitation.

"Could you dim the lights? I had no idea I'd installed three-hundred-watt bulbs in my living room."

Ariana grinned. Filthy-stinking-rich or not, Max was in bad shape and needed her help. They'd walked nearly three blocks to his house and, with each step, the playfulness he'd enticed her with on the cable car had begrudgingly faded away. Right now he was in no condition to tell her where the light switch was, never mind detailing how and where he was going to seduce her. Maybe things were working out for the best. She would dim the lights, make sure he was comfortable and get the heck out of Dodge before she made a huge mistake.

But first she had to find the light switch. She searched fruitlessly, soon realizing that when they'd first come in, Max hadn't flipped any switches. He'd opened the door, they'd walked in and, snap, the lights had flared to life.

Oh, great. A house that was smarter than she was.

She backed up in the foyer and reluctantly laid her ratty leather backpack in the corner closest to the door and propped her hat on top, running her fingers through her windblown hair while she scanned the wall for a control panel that simply had to exist.

"Ariana? Are you still here?"

His voice was a mere whisper, but the sound still stopped her, warmed her—frightened the hell out of her. There was no mistaking the sound of hope mingling with the possibility of utter disappointment if she didn't answer, if she'd abandoned him in his glittering marble palace.

She found the switches behind a thick drape and slid the controls until the recessed lights shone like subtle moonlight rather than like the outfield at Candlestick Park.

"I'm here. Is that better?"

He'd removed his arm from across his eyes, then slid his elbows along his sides and propped himself up. "Now I can't see you."

She remained in the foyer, her boots firmly planted. "What's to see?"

The only thing coming in clear to her was the fact that she couldn't seduce Max Forrester. Not tonight. Maybe not ever. And she couldn't let him seduce her. Could she? She must have lost her ever-lovin' mind. She obviously didn't belong here—with him—even temporarily. She was just a middle-class Greek chick trying to make a name for herself in the big city. He lived in a world she didn't understand and, therefore, couldn't control.

This was all a very big mistake.

"I said I'd get you home safe and sound. I should—"

"Don't leave."

For a man muddled by an unknown substance, he could issue a command with all the authority of a mogul, yet all the vulnerability of a man lost in a foreign land. She couldn't leave him—not, at least, until she was certain he'd be okay.

Somewhere between leaving the restaurant and sprinting to catch the last cable car, the desire that had deserted her when she thought he was merely drunk had crept back under her skin. The mystery substance made him dizzy, yes, but it also loosened his tongue and his inhibitions. The way he teased her on the ride, touched her, innocently and yet with utter skill, fired her senses and fed her fantasies.

If she forgot about the million-dollar town house, the imported sculptures, the computer-controlled light switches and focused only on the man, the possibility of making love to him didn't seem so impossible. Just… simple. Elemental. A fact of life in the wild, sexy city they called home.

Still, she held back, even while her mind said, *This is it.* Her chance of all chances to step onto the snowy carpet, shed her own jacket and make her fantasies come true. Heck, Max was already in a semireclined position. He'd already detailed several delightful means to "get to know each other better." How hard could a seduction be at this point?

But even if he wasn't drunk, he was, technically "under the influence." If and when she and Max explored their mutual attraction, she wanted no regrets—from either of them.

"You don't know me, Max."

His grin lit his face, contrasting against the shadows all around him. "I'd like to remedy that."

His smile wavered at the same time as his balance. He slid his arms down, plopping back onto the cushions of the long couch and letting out a deep-throated groan. "Just my luck. I have the most beautiful woman in San Francisco standing in my doorway and I'm too dizzy to seduce her."

She laughed at the wry turn in his voice—until his words actually sunk in. Those drugs sure were powerful. The most beautiful woman in San Francisco?

She crossed her arms over her chest. Doubt and hope clashed in a war that resulted in her usual sarcasm. "You don't get out much, do you?"

He turned his head on the leather cushion. "Ariana, come closer. I'm in no condition to attack you, if that's what you're afraid of."

"I'm not afraid," she insisted, straightening her backbone, crossing her arms tighter and nearly stamping her foot on the tile. She wasn't afraid of anything, or anyone. Except, perhaps, of herself…with Max.

He shook his head and chuckled. The sound, like warm molasses, sweetened her indignation into humor, despite her preference to remain offended and aloof. Safe.

"I've seen you toss men twice my size out of your bar when they've gotten obnoxious. I didn't think you'd be afraid of me, particularly not when I'm seeing two of you."

She tugged on her lower lip with her teeth and released her arms to her sides. Just as Charlie had told her, just as

she suspected from her own observations and brief interactions, Max was a man she could trust. Trouble was, she
didn't trust herself.

She hadn't factored in his natural charm and instinctive
warmth when she flipped through the pages of that magazine and imagined Max making love to her in all those
exotic locales in the city. What if, after a night of hot sex,
she wanted more? What if sating this particular hunger
only whet her appetite? Would she be able to walk away?
Would she have the chance? The courage?

"Can you see the Golden Gate from here?" she asked,
pointing at the bank of clear-glass windows in Max's
dining room facing the bay, delaying her decision if only
a moment more.

Glancing over her shoulder at her backpack, she thought
about the magazine. She hadn't read the whole article, but
she remembered one of the romantic settings was an incredibly posh hotel suite overlooking the bay. The view of
the Golden Gate glittered to the northwest, the Bay Bridge
gleamed somewhere farther southeast and the lighthouse
at Alcatraz flashed at the center. The couple made love
against a wall of windows with an unhampered view of
the city.

"The best view is from the third floor, my balcony. I
would show you…"

She lifted her foot to step onto the carpet, then sat instead and unzipped and removed her boots.

"You're not in any condition to climb stairs. Maybe I
should make you some coffee." She lined up her shoes by
the door. "Point me in the direction of the kitchen and I'll
brew a pot."

"I think I've had enough of your libations," he answered.

"I could just leave—" she teased.

He hoisted an arm in the air from where he lay stretched full length on the sofa and pointed to her right. "Through the archway and up the stairs. I'm not sure where the coffeemaker is."

She stepped onto the carpet, sinking nearly an inch, the plush softness of the flooring cushioning her stockinged feet as she walked. "I know my way around a kitchen."

"What about bedrooms?"

She stopped beneath the archway. Damn, but anything the man said sounded like a come-on, with that deep, raspy voice of his. She was suddenly glad they hadn't exchanged more than a few dozen words over the past two years or she'd have ended up in his bed a long time ago.

Nevertheless, so long as he was asking about bedrooms, she might as well find out exactly what he had in mind. She stepped slowly to the edge of the couch. Leaning forward, she braced her hands on the armrest on either side of his bare feet.

"What do you want to know about bedrooms?"

A lock of her hair fell forward, brushing over his toes. His lips opened as if to answer, but no words came out.

"Max?"

"Sweats. I could use a pair of sweats."

She nodded and smiled, then headed back toward the kitchen. "I'll see what I can do."

Again, the room lit up the moment she entered, and like the living room, the light gleamed off polished white surfaces. She searched first for the coffee and a pot to brew it in. Then she'd think about his bedroom.

His bedroom. Dangerous territory.

She had no idea if his request for sweatpants had been what he'd originally intended to ask for, but she didn't doubt that he'd chosen a safer topic by requesting the change of clothes. He had no way of knowing that her knowledge of bedrooms was essentially limited to the art of sleeping in one. Her sexual experiences from her marriage—more specifically, the first few weeks of her marriage—seemed a lifetime ago rather than just a few years. She vaguely remembered the sex between her and her husband to be wild in the beginning, but even then she hadn't had much of a reference from which to draw comparisons.

She'd married as a virgin, sheltered by a family and community who clung to strict codes of feminine conduct—codes she'd wanted to rebel against for a very long time, but hadn't had the courage until her nineteenth birthday. She'd packed her bags and bought her plane ticket without telling a soul. Only after she was securely on her way to live with Uncle Stefano in San Francisco did she call her parents from her layover in Atlanta. She hadn't wanted a big scene. She just wanted to experience life on her own, with her own rules.

Her first goal had been to meet some gloriously sexy man and have a whirlwind affair. And she'd actually met Rick while waiting for a cab at the airport. A musician with his guitar slung over his shoulder, shaggy blond hair and kind eyes, Rick had captured her sensual imagination with his first smile. He'd offered to share the cab, and on the twenty-minute ride to the Wharf, they'd chatted and laughed and flirted and fallen in love.

But it was the wrong kind of love. The kind of love that didn't last. The kind of love exchanged by people who had little in common but lust. The kind of love that destroyed her second goal—the restaurant she finally now had just within her reach.

She'd learned the difference between lust and love the

hard way, even if she'd never really experienced the latter emotion firsthand. Working with Stefano and Sonia, even intermittently before her aunt's death, taught her that what she'd had with Rick wasn't even close to what she deserved. She'd confused lust and love once. She certainly wouldn't do so again.

After her divorce, she realized that maybe if she'd just slept with Rick a few times before the quick wedding ceremony at the courthouse, the magic might have worn off long enough for her to see that they weren't in the least compatible. His goals included fame, fortune and, ultimately, a move to Nashville where he now lived and performed. At the time, her only goal had been independence, complete freedom from her family and the chance to run her own business. Marriage pretty much canceled both out. She'd inadvertently traded one controlling force for another. Once Rick was completely out of her life, she'd realigned her goals, recaptured her dream of being in charge.

But her personal goals? Her private wants? Until tonight, until she'd glanced through that magazine, she hadn't allowed herself the luxury of those. Such an unattainable, dangerous dream could spin her in the wrong direction yet again. So she limited her fantasies to when she was sleeping, or when the romance and rattle of the cable cars worked a sly magic on her tired, lonely heart.

Until tonight, she hadn't had time for a lover, even a temporary one. She worked twelve to sixteen hours at the restaurant every day of the week. Her one indulgence to pampering herself was practicing tai chi with Mrs. Li, her landlady, and sharing an occasional tea and conversation with the women who gathered in the shop below her apartment.

If she'd learned one thing about men in the past eight

years—heck, in her whole life—it was that they demanded attention. Men like Max Forrester needed either a dutiful, socially acceptable wife to cater to his every need, or taffy-like arm candy—sweet and pliable to his slightest whim. She couldn't allow herself to be either. She'd end up investing herself in her lover rather than in her own future. She'd done it before and damned if she'd do so again.

She found and set up the coffeemaker, impressed at the organization she found in the cabinets and drawers. Either Max was completely anal-retentive or he had an incredibly efficient housekeeper. Probably a combination of both.

While the coffee perked and popped, emitting an enticing aroma that reminded her that she'd had nothing to eat since lunchtime, she decided to search his bedroom for the clothes he wanted. The staircase she'd taken to the kitchen continued upward and she figured the master suite more than likely took up the greater portion of the top and final floor.

The house reacted to her entrance by engaging the lights again, but this time the glow was slight from a single lamp at the bedside. The lampshade's geometrically cut, stained-glass design reflected hues of gold and amber, with a touch of ruby red that reminded her of fire. Where the bottom floor reflected cold class and wealth, his bedroom was all male heat and casual comfort, though the lingering smell of money still teased her nostrils like aged wine or hand-rolled tobacco.

The walls were paneled with rich wood—not the cheap stuff her father had in his den back home, but thick, carved planks of teak that reminded her of the opulence of a castle—the sort of room a knight or duke might entice his lover to. The paintings, from what she could make out with the individual lights above them unlit, captured outdoor scenes—listing cutters with fluttering sails on an angry ocean, a majestic lake surrounded by snowcapped mountains, a single aquamarine wave rolling in on a honey beach.

And the bed—the California king, with a simple sleigh headboard and footboard—was huge and, most likely, custom-made. The fluffy comforter, half-dozen pillows and coordinating shams picked up the blues and greens from the paintings and swirled them with just enough gold to brighten the dark space to a subtle warmth. A pair of gray sweatpants had been tossed across the perfectly made and arranged linens. This was Max's room. The real Max. The Max she had wanted to seduce.

Truth be told, the Max she *still* wanted.

She grabbed the sweatpants, then thought to bring him a T-shirt as well. With a shrug, she carefully opened the drawers in his dresser, smirking when the top drawer yielded an interesting collection of party favors he'd obviously gotten from Charlie's bachelor blowout: a package of cheap cigars shaped like penises, chocolate lollipops sculpted like breasts, several foils of condoms with doomsday sayings about marriage printed on the packages.

She hadn't exactly planned and prepared for this evening's possible seduction, so in the interest of safe sex, she grabbed the square with the least offensive message and tossed it on the bed before resuming her search for a shirt. After grabbing one with Stanford emblazoned on the front, she moved to return to the kitchen, but stopped when she noticed the wall of heavy drapes facing the bay. Curious after remembering his comment about the best view being from the third floor, she fumbled behind the thrice-lined curtains until she found the right button. One click and the window treatments slid aside, a mechanical hum accompanying her awed gasp.

The entire wall was a window—sliding glass doors, to be exact. Beyond was a tiled balcony almost entirely enshrouded in thick San Francisco fog. She couldn't resist a closer look. Tossing Max's clothes back onto the bed, she worked the locks with ease, then stepped into the mist as if entering a dream.

The air stirred with the breath of the Bay. An instant chill surrounded her, penetrating her clothing and dampening her hair. Her clothes drank in the moisture, making the cotton cool and clingy. Her nipples puckered beneath her turtleneck, rasping tight against her satin bra. She thought of Max, nearly passed out in the living room. Dizzy. Flirtatious. Sexy and charming and more potent than 120-proof rum.

Too bad he wasn't here when she needed him, when she just might be tempted to surrender to desire.

Tiny red lights blinked to the west, indicating the span of the Golden Gate. She strolled through the wispy fog until she approached the wall, surprisingly low—maybe three feet tall—that enclosed the patio. She kept a safe distance from the edge and closed her eyes, remembering the image in the magazine of the lovers on the bridge, right up against the railing. She superimposed her face on the woman again. And this time she did the same to the man, giving him Max's thick, dark hair, rugged square chin and gentle, probing fingers.

She saw them clearly. A man—*Max*. A woman—*her*. An undeniable desire, hidden by just a touch of fog. Tonight's mist was particularly thick for such a late hour— San Francisco fog usually rolled over the city around four o'clock and dissipated by midnight.

Yet nothing about this night was usual. Definitely not her. Not her uncontrollable desire for Max. Not the circumstances that brought her here or the consequences she'd face in the morning if she stayed.

She pursed her lips, realizing the consequences—a little embarrassment, perhaps a dose of discomfort in the morning light—were more than worth the price of living her fantasy, grabbing her dream with both hands and saying, "Yes! Now!" That strategy had paid off once when she'd taken over the operations at the restaurant. Had she not succumbed to her youth and married the first man she met at the airport, she might have been able to say the same about the day she bought her ticket to San Francisco and left her loving, but stifling, family behind.

"Yes. Now," she repeated aloud, trying the words on for size.

"Just tell me what you want."

His voice rolled over the tiles and through the thick fog like a warm blast of summer air. The contrast spawned a ripple of gooseflesh up the back of Ariana's neck, then crept beneath her turtleneck and played havoc with her skin.

She squeezed her eyelids tighter as the sensations rocked her balance, nearly unraveling her completely when Max's breath mixed with the fog and whispered into her ear.

"Tell me what you want. Anything, Ariana. Anything goes."

4

"IS THAT A FACT?"

Her tone was saucy, despite the whimper begging to erupt from the back of her throat. She tamped down the sound of surrender with a thick-throated swallow and willed herself to remain in control. Acquiescence to the night—the passion, the mood, the man—should be resisted. She had to keep her wits. But she couldn't deny that this liaison would be more than a fantasy come true, more than a living dream.

The night. The fog. The man. The desire. Ariana knew without a doubt that what swirled around her at the ledge of the balcony was a gift, a once-in-a-lifetime twist of fate that she'd be a damn fool to refuse. If only he was thinking clearly!

Max stepped around, taking her hand and leading her to the ledge. His bare arm brushed against hers as he reached for the round, brass railing that edged the thigh-high brick wall enclosing his patio. Tan skin stretched tight over powerful arms and sinuous shoulders.

He'd removed his shirt. The sprinkle of tawny hair over his arms and across his chest prickled in the cool air. When the fog shifted, she realized he'd shed his pants on the way upstairs as well. He wore nothing but a thin pair of midnight-blue boxers, damp from the mist.

She tried not to allow her gaze to linger, but found her quest impossible. The shape of his erection, swathed in silk and taut with want, ignited a throbbing heat between her legs. A thrill skittered straight to the center of her chest.

She swallowed and rubbed her arms to ward off a shiver that had little to with the temperature. "Aren't you cold?"

He inhaled deeply, his chest expanding impressively. His muscles were distinct and smooth, honed from running and perhaps some weight lifting or rowing—the kinds of exercise a rich man used to mold his body for the torture of women like her.

"I like the cold. It's invigorating." He turned and sat on the low railing, his legs stretched leisurely outward. Plucking her sleeve with his fingers, he snapped the clingy material against her skin. "You should experience it for yourself."

A zing of awareness shot through her arm, but she found it hard to enjoy with him poised so precariously on the ledge. Her stomach clenched. A threatening whirl of dizziness danced at the edges of her eyes. God, she hated heights!

"That railing is awfully low, you should be…"

Max smiled and leaned completely backward. Ariana screamed and shot forward, grabbing both his arms and fully expecting both of them to tumble over. But a wall of clear, thick Plexiglas caught him before he rolled them off the three-story building. The shield vibrated from their combined weight.

The wall of his chest caught her, vibrations of a sensual kind rocked her to her core.

"Cool feature, huh? Lower wall, better view," he explained, slipping his arms around her waist and pulling her between his thighs and onto his lap. He was hard beneath her, hard all around her. Hard and male and dangerous. "But still completely safe."

Ariana decided then and there that men like Max Forrester shouldn't be allowed to use the word *safe* in any form. She shivered from the cold, from the pure, unadulterated lust coursing through her bloodstream and firing her every nerve ending. She panted to catch her breath.

"That was a cruel trick," she answered, forcing herself to look him in the eye.

His grin faded. "The cruel trick is you coming out here without me and leaving one of these on my bed for me to find when I came looking for you." He held the foil packet aloft. "An invitation?"

She arched an eyebrow. "A friendly reminder."

"I do remember that I promised to show you this view myself." He tugged her closer. The scent of sandalwood, enhanced by his body heat and diffused into the fog, assailed her. The result was a light-headed euphoria that made her hold him tight.

"And I promised to touch you wherever you wanted me to. Put those two promises together," he said, grinning at her impassioned grip on his arm, "and the experience will be absolutely unforgettable."

He swallowed deeply, and Ariana watched the bobbing of his Adam's apple and the undulation of his throat, fascinated.

"You say that now. But that drug can alter your memory."

"I don't feel drugged by anything but you."

Her chest tightened in response to his declaration. She

couldn't see clearly in the dim lighting on the balcony, but Max certainly seemed to have control of his balance now, something he hadn't had earlier. Maybe the Mickey had lost some of its effect.

Anticipation warred with her uncertainties—sexual excitement battled with a lifetime's worth of repression and regret. She had every reason to believe that Max's desire was honest—true in a way that was elemental to a man and ideal for a woman like her. She could have him tonight, love him tonight, knowing they were both sating a desire born long ago and hidden for reasons that, right now, simply didn't matter.

What did matter was that in the morning she'd have an adventure to remember, a sensual liaison that would erase the erotic pictures from the magazine with images of delight so much more personal and real.

She grazed her hands upward from his elbows to his shoulders, kneading the thick sinew as she worked inward to his neck. For a man who reportedly wielded great power during the day, his muscles were now completely relaxed and pliant to her touch. His eyes, half shut as she threaded her fingers into his hair, were focused entirely on her, seeming to see something fascinating, something no other man ever had.

She moved forward to kiss him, but his hands snaked from her waist to her elbows and stopped her.

"Wait," he ordered.

Confused, she instinctively pulled back from his grip. He released her, but stood and stepped immediately back into her personal space. She gasped and retreated. He shadowed her move.

"Don't bolt, Ariana."

"Why'd you stop me? This isn't a good idea."

"You were going to kiss me," he answered simply.

She bit her lower lip before replying. "And?"

"And you were touching me." He did as she did earlier, sliding his hands from her elbows to her shoulders, then massaging inward to her neck until his thumb teased the lobes of her ears.

"You didn't like it?" she murmured. She couldn't imagine how he wouldn't have. She was having a damn hard time keeping her eyes open and her moan of pleasure contained in her throat.

"I loved it, but that's not what tonight is going to be about."

"Huh?"

If a more intelligent response existed, Ariana couldn't summon it. Not with his scent, hot and male and potent, assailing her nostrils and his body heat defeating the night's chill like fire against ice.

"My brain has defogged. My balance is back. And if I remember correctly, I promised that if you stayed, tonight would be about you. Me pleasing you. Not necessarily the other way around."

She barely had time to register that he had just voiced her ultimate fantasy, when he lowered his head and brushed her lips with a teasing sweep. The sensation unleashed that imprisoned whimper, then several more as the kiss deepened, mouths opened, tongues danced. Before she realized it, Max untucked her shirt from her jeans and skimmed her belly with a light, exploratory touch.

Electric need surged through her. She jumped, startled and thrilled and excited, then grabbed his cheeks and pressed closer to force herself past her panic. Max wouldn't hurt her. Max would stop if she asked.

And she definitely didn't want to stop.

His lips stretched tight as he grinned beneath the kiss. He unbuttoned her jeans and released the zipper, barely touching her in the process, which only stoked her hunger for more. She broke the kiss long enough to whip off her turtleneck, tossing it aside to disappear in the soupy mist swirling around them, then kissed him again. He led her backward until her calves bumped against an outdoor chaise lounge.

Pressing his hands on her shoulders, he guided her into the chair, following her down so that he knelt beside her. With intimate slowness, he eased her fully against the cushion, altering his kisses from bold and insistent to soft and scattered, touching her nose, her eyelids, her cheeks, her chin, lulling her into an anticipatory state where she held her breath and waited for his next touch.

When she finally opened her eyes, his grin was pure sin.

"Do you feel it?" he asked, his green eyes twinkling with some untold secret.

"Feel what? You stopped."

"Oh, honey—" he smiled as he removed her jeans, the denim rasping over the sensitive skin of her legs, leaving her wispy panties askew "—I've only just started. I meant the anticipation. Do you feel that?"

She nodded, rubbing her tongue-dampened lips together tightly. The fog kissed her bare legs. The chill made her shiver, but the sensation was nothing compared to the waves of want rocking her from the inside out.

"It'll only get better, I promise."

He tugged the denim off her ankles, then straddled the chair so he could attend to her bare feet. He massaged her arches and toes with a strong pressure that at first made her wince, then he kneaded softly until she sighed. She hadn't realized how tired her feet were. But with each press and swirl, his hands erased the ache of the workday and enhanced the bittersweet torment of unsatisfied need.

He inched upward, lifting her left leg and placing an anklet of wet-tongued kisses on her skin, followed by a seam of laving up her calf and behind her knee. She started to slip down the fog-slickened cushion. The plunging sensation made her grab the arms of the chair.

"Relax, Ariana. I won't hurt you."

"It's not that. I feel like I'm falling."

"You are. You're falling for me."

She shook her head, smiling at his sweet sentiment, but not surprised that he didn't understand.

"I'm afraid of heights," she admitted.

"Heights of passion?" His teasing tone and sparkling eyes drew her into his double entendre. He scooted forward another few inches, then draped her knee over his shoulder. She held her breath, watching, fascinated and vulnerable and thrilled, as he smoothed his hand from beneath her lifted thigh, down to her nearly bare bottom. Wordlessly, he grabbed an elongated cushion from a nearby chair and placed it behind her hips, securing her in the semi-lifted position. She grabbed the neck roll and slid it behind her head, assisting him as he arranged her body for his full view and complete attention.

"I wouldn't know about the heights of passion, Max," she admitted. She'd avoided them the same way she'd avoided climbing Coit Tower or walking the span of the Golden Gate. The possibility of plunging down, losing herself, was a real one she'd always meant to avoid. "Never really climbed them."

He shook his head. "A damn shame, beautiful woman

like you." He tilted his head and kissed her knee. "That will change. I promise."

With a glance half skeptical, half intrigued, she surveyed the unusual position he'd sculpted her body into. Her knee remained draped over his shoulder and, with the pillows beneath her hips, he could see all of her, touch all of her while hardly moving.

"I can see that," she quipped.

He chuckled appreciatively, raking his fingers down the inside of her thigh. "This is San Francisco. We don't do things the conventional way here."

Ariana took a deep breath, swallowed the last of her ingrained apprehension and folded her arms behind her head. She concentrated on the sensuous trail Max blazed with his hands, up and down her leg, touching her but not touching her—promising intimacy with a wicked tease.

"So far, you're all talk," she said, biting her lip the moment her provocation lit his eyes with a fire she doubted she could contain.

"Talk can be good," he answered.

"Talk can be cheap."

One dark eyebrow tilted, along with the corner of his incredible mouth. "I don't buy cheap."

"You're not buying me," she answered, still grappling with the incongruity between her standard operating modes and this incredible dalliance with a stranger. The sensations, the heat emanating from his body to hers dulled reality, but couldn't erase it entirely, no matter how she tried.

He kissed her knee again and slid it down his arm so that she straddled his thighs. Scooting forward, he ran both hands up her legs and hips, spanning his fingers inward across her stomach then upward, lightly over her breasts to her neck. He unhooked her hands and pulled her forward until they sat, entwined, his mouth to her ear.

"There are some highs that can't be bought, even by men like me."

She gasped as he skimmed his fingers down her back and unhooked the back of her bra. The satin loosened as he drew the straps aside, one at a time, releasing her, revealing her. He tossed the lingerie aside, pressing his hands hotly against her shoulder blades so she arched toward him and he could look his fill.

"Care to borrow a little ecstasy with me?" he asked. His grin was part irreverent, part hopeful.

She could only nod.

He skimmed his hands up her sides and cupped her breasts.

"Tell me what you want," he said.

She licked her lips. "This."

Tracing a lazy circle with his thumbs, he skimmed the full circumference of her breasts, spiraling inward until he reached but didn't touch her nipples. Round and round and round he traced tight, grazing rings that never made contact with the sensitive centers, but eased them into a taut, hungry pucker that made her coo.

"Now what?"

"Kiss me."

"Your breasts?"

"Yes."

He glanced up and captured her gaze from her half-closed eyelids.

"Offer them to me," he said.

She blinked, uncertain. He took her hands and guided them up her own rib cage, until she cupped herself.

He met her stare with sweet challenge. "Offer them to me," he repeated.

She smiled and did as he commanded, lifting her breasts high and arching her back. She closed her eyes tight in anticipation, dizzy from the sensation of taking control of her own pleasure.

He didn't disappoint. Splaying his hands beneath her bottom, he lifted her the last inch he needed to take her fully into his mouth. His lips were cool from the breeze, his tongue hot, alternating between soft and stiff as he pleasured her with a sweet attendance to detail.

Max the stranger became Max her lover with each and every intimate kiss.

He cupped her with his hands, flicking his thumbs over her moistened flesh while his kiss wandered across her collarbone and up her neck. Their lips clashed in a hot, breathless battle. She touched him everywhere, down his back, up his arms. Fingers crashed through his hair, dipped into his boxers. Learned him as he learned her.

He lifted her as he stood, letting her feet touch the ground long enough to remove the last scraps of clothing between them, then he wrapped her legs around his waist as he carried her to the ledge.

Max set her down and turned her so her half-closed eyes could see the glorious view of the bridge and the bay drifting in and out of the fog. Lights twinkled in the distance as he pressed against her back and enveloped her with his heat. The flashing lights appeared behind her heavy eyelids when he slid his hand down her belly through her dark curls to test her need.

He nestled his cheek to hers, stroking her gently with one hand, caressing a breast softly with the other. "Open your eyes, Ari. I promised to show you the view."

Swallowing deep, she managed to form a coherent sentence as her mind drifted in and out of utter ecstasy. "Don't wanna see. Mmm. Just feel."

He tugged her earlobe with his teeth. "Do both. Don't settle for less when you can have it all."

Have it all. Ariana grinned and forced her eyes open. Swirls of whitish gray fog shifted and drifted on the other side of the Plexiglas wall, allowing her glimpses of the city she hardly knew but loved anyway. The irony didn't escape her. She felt eerily the same about Max, a stranger who touched her with such tenderness, and who was slowly becoming her most intimate lover.

"Are you watching?" he asked.

The question may have been meant to distract her from the fact that he'd stepped away to put on the condom, but she felt his absence so deeply, she grew chilled.

When he returned, his first order of business was reigniting her warmth.

"I'm looking," she said, bracing her hands on the brass railing as he kissed and caressed her, rubbing her arms, nuzzling her neck, grinding his stiff sex against her bottom. "I'm not seeing much with this fog."

"Look closer," he whispered, touching her ear with his tongue.

She blinked and refocused, noticing with a gasp that with the light bouncing out from the bedroom behind them and with the thick fog, their images were reflecting back from the Plexiglas like a bathroom mirror steamed from a hot shower. She could see his hands easing from her hips to her belly to her breasts. She watched, enthralled, as he plucked and stroked her. Electric sensations drew her lids down with a magnetic pull.

"I see you touching me. Feel you…"

Her voice drifted into the fog and disappeared as images, opaque and erotic, rode across her vision. He pressed closer, slipping his sheathed sex between her legs, teasing her with a gentle friction, while his hands tilted and guided her.

"Tell me what you want," he said again, and she couldn't imagine why.

"Make love to me," she answered.

"That's what I'm doing, sweetheart." His fingers dipped low. Jolts shook her.

"I'm going to come. Too soon."

Fighting the sensation was fruitless. Fruitless and senseless and entirely out of her control when his hands still stroked her, played her, building the madness to an unbearable peak.

"Not too soon. Don't fight me. Let me."

With the hand that wasn't driving her wild, he swept her hair over her shoulder so he could suckle her from the tip of her shoulder to the pulse at the base of her neck. His fingers probed deeper, stroked harder until the image she saw in the misty glass was a woman driven completely wild. She bucked, but he held her fast. She screamed, and he cheered her lack of inhibitions, demanded she hide none of her rapture.

Just when she started on the downward side of ecstasy, he pushed inside her, stretching her with one, slow thrust.

She gripped the handrail so tight, her fingers ached. She couldn't. Not again.

But when he smoothed his palms over her hips in lazy, gentle circles, she knew he would wait. And the wait would be worth her while.

"Max," she started, nearly breathless, completely unsure what she had to say to convince him that she'd never experienced something so incredible, something she most certainly wouldn't experience again until after a good night's sleep.

He caressed her softly, teasingly, up her sides, beneath her arms, then guided her arms upward, placing her hands firmly on the Plexiglas. She stared into her own diaphanous reflection. Even amid a cloud, the undiluted satisfaction in her eyes was impossible to miss.

"That's one way to enjoy the view," he whispered, wrapping his arms around her so he could love her breasts again. "Wanna try another?"

Ariana swallowed, forcing herself to inhale and exhale, forcing herself to accept that her body, her mind, her soul wanted this man inside her—wanted to share the incredible fantasy again and again and again in every way imaginable. The feel of him, slick and hard, taut and silky, penetrated her, enveloped her in a heat that was inherently pure, amazingly simple. Like a beating heart. Like a breathing soul.

"I trust you, Max," she admitted, not meaning to say it aloud, but glad when she did.

He stopped his sensual assault long enough to give her the sweetest, softest embrace, topped with a touch of a kiss on her cheek.

"I won't let you down."

5

"DID YOU GET IT?"

Jangling the change in his pocket, Leo Glass hooked the receiver of the pay phone beneath his chin. "Not exactly."

"What do you mean *not exactly?* Photographs are photographs. What did you do, put your thumb on the lens?"

Leo bit back the urge to tell the jerk on the other end of the line exactly what he could do with his condescending attitude. But he needed the cash the man was supplying. And the revenge wasn't so bad, either. "I'm not that stupid."

"Remains to be seen."

"I heard that!"

"I wasn't exactly whispering, was I? There's only an hour left. Did you get pictures of them or not?"

"I got 'em. But the damn fog…"

"They were outside? How disgusting." After a pause, the man snickered. "But interesting, for my purpose."

"Might have been, if you could *see* anything."

"So you didn't get the photograph?"

"I wouldn't say that. You can't exactly tell who's who,

but the two figures in the shot are definitely doing something interesting on that balcony."

The next pause nearly drove him insane. Leo shook his pockets again, annoyed at the sound of four quarters, two dimes and three pennies swirling around with nothing green to keep them company—at least, not yet.

Finally, the bastard with the cash to make his future easy gave him the answer he wanted.

"Bring them in, with the negatives. With the right spin, we might be able to use them to our advantage."

I TRUST YOU, MAX.

The voice, soft and feminine, was familiar, stirring a misty memory Max struggled to stay asleep to relive. The tone was deep, sultry, exotic. Impressions fleeted by. Abandon. Rapture. Release.

Freedom.

I trust you.

"Max?"

His eyelids snapped open at the crisp sound of his name, this time as real and strong as the sunlight streaming into his bedroom. Who left the drapes open? He never left the drapes open.

"Who?"

A figure stepped over to the window and pressed the button that drew the drapes closed with painful slowness. In the meantime, he fell back onto his pillow and laid his arm across his eyes until the sickening swirls of oranges and reds and purples dancing in his eyelids faded away.

"Are you okay? Max?"

"My head is pounding. My mouth feels like I swallowed a sheep," he answered to whoever the hell was asking the question. A woman. A woman he highly suspected he should know.

A woman with a sultry, exotic voice.

Her laugh was light and might have annoyed him under other circumstances. He pressed his hands against his temples, surprised to discover he *wasn't* wearing a football helmet that was two sizes too tight. Actually, he realized, drawing his arm aside, if her laugh didn't piss him off in his current misery, which it didn't, the buoyant sound probably never would.

The room was a cloud of shadows, but he felt her weight when she sat on the bed beside him.

"If you sit up, you can drink my special blend. It may not make you feel a whole lot better, but it most definitely won't make you feel worse."

Sit up. She may as well have asked him to shoot up the steepest part of Lombard Street on in-line skates.

"I can't move."

"What a shame. Your moves last night were incredible."

It may have been a while since he'd heard the distinctive purr of a woman just recently satiated and satisfied, but the molasses-sweet and sun-warmed sound was impossible to forget. He pushed his physical discomfort aside long enough to prop himself up on his pillows.

His eyes adjusted. The skylight in his bathroom threw just enough glow into his room to let him see what he was certain was a dream.

Ariana Karas? Offering him coffee? In his bedroom? Wearing his Stanford T-shirt?

She placed the hot mug in his hands, then curled her legs up onto the bed.

Bare legs. Bare to the thigh. Bare beyond the thigh.

"You going to drink that, or is there something else you'd like better?"

He took a long, deep swallow of coffee. The liquid scalded his tongue and throat, but he didn't flinch.

Ariana Karas was sitting half naked in his bed, her dark eyes and soft mouth plush with the warmth of a woman well loved and he had absolutely no idea why.

"Thanks," he said after his throat cooled.

"Right back at you." She scooted off the bed and shuffled toward the drapes, testing the thick folds for the opening. "You might want to turn away from the light, but I have some things on the balcony I need before I can leave."

"Leave?"

She let out a soft "Aha!" when she found the opening, twisting her body through so that the sunlight didn't flash his sensitive eyes. He took another sip of coffee—prepared just the way he liked it with one sugar and a heavy dose of cream—and wondered what in the hell she'd left outside. He didn't remember going outside. Hell, he didn't remember coming home.

He squeezed his eyes shut. A few vague images answered his desperate summons, but most placed him at Athens by the Bay. A match. He remembered something about…lighting a fire?

When Ariana reentered wearing a pair of unzipped and unbuttoned black jeans beneath his T-shirt, his hold on the recovered memories slipped away. A bra and panties, pink and satiny, dangled from her hand alongside a long-sleeved turtleneck.

"Ariana?"

She looked up at him expectantly and he realized he hadn't really said her name for any other reason than to reassure himself that she really was in his room.

"Max?"

The staring game that followed lasted several seconds. Max watched the expression on Ariana's amazing face progress from boldly flirtatious to slightly shocked.

"You don't remember last night, do you?"

He'd never heard a question he wanted to answer less. "Not yet," he admitted, hoping that once the two-ton fog lifted from his brain, maybe after more coffee and a hot shower, he'd regain whatever he'd lost.

And from the look in her eyes, he'd lost a great deal.

She shook her head. "I didn't think…you seemed all right by the time we…" She huffed in frustration, but until she completed a sentence with information he could use, Max was sure he had the market on confusion.

"Memory loss is a side effect," she finished.

"Side effect of…?"

Ariana folded her undergarments into the turtleneck and rolled them into a ball she twisted tight between her hands. She shuffled uncomfortably for a moment, then strode boldly forward and sat on the bed again, this time at a greater distance than before and without the fluid grace and sensuality she'd shown him when he'd first awakened. She was all business.

"You were at my restaurant last night for dinner and, afterward, you and Charlie came into the bar for drinks. Do you remember any of that?"

Max closed his eyes. Images warred with the pounding pressure squeezing his skull. He remembered a crowd cheering. A flaming swirl of colors captured in a tall glass. Ariana touching her finger to her luscious, moist mouth.

"Vaguely," he said. He downed another big swallow of coffee. He'd known Ariana for two years, since he moved into his Russian Hill home and started jogging to the office, stopping at her restaurant in the mornings for coffee and in the afternoons for a beer. Never in that time had she ever, ever been cold, but her natural friendliness and warmth had never extended into flirting or come-ons.

Yet here she was, wearing his shirt and sitting on his mattress after gathering her underwear from the balcony outside his bedroom.

"I didn't make it to the restaurant until just before closing," she explained. "But sometime during the evening, someone added something to your drink."

"A drug?"

She shrugged. "I suspect. Something that made it hard for you to focus, it loosened your inhibitions and, obviously, affected your memory."

There was a great deal of information to process in what she'd said, but the phrase "loosened your inhibitions" begged to be dealt with first.

Max arched an eyebrow in amusement. "I didn't know I had any inhibitions that needed loosening."

Ariana pressed her lips together, fighting a smile and losing horribly. "Maybe inhibitions isn't the right word," she amended, pretending to scratch her nose when she was really trying to hide her grin.

He sat up straighter and finished the coffee. His memory was still a fuzzy blur, but the jackhammer in his head seemed to have moved a few yards down the block. Her battle with laughter fueled his ire enough to jolt him with energy.

"Then what is the right word?"

She stood up and stepped toward the door. "I think goodbye would work. Someone was probably just playing a joke on you. A harmless one, really, since you're obviously fine and your memory will come back. Little by little, I'll bet."

"You brought me home?"

She inched toward the door, hooking her hand on the knob. "Seemed like the right thing to do at the time. I wanted to make sure you were okay. Whatever happened, happened in my restaurant, but I didn't have anything to do with it and I'm certain none of my employees did, either."

Max rubbed his chin, wincing at the thick growth itching his skin. He leaned across the bed and tugged his alarm clock, which was dangling over the bedstand by the cord.

Eleven forty-five.

Eleven forty-five! He *never* slept that late, even on a Saturday.

That thought gave him pause.

"Today is Saturday, right?" he asked.

She nodded.

Panic clutched his heart as his gaze drifted back to the glowing blue numbers on his alarm clock.

"Saturday the twenty-sixth?"

"Uh-huh."

"Holy…" He followed the oath with an expletive that made Ariana jump even before he vaulted out of the bed and scrambled down the stairs to the kitchen. He paused long enough to get his bearings, then shot toward the two-by-two bulletin board tucked into a corner of his custom-made cabinets. There, beside the note from his housekeeper with the dates of her vacation and a neatly penned grocery list that he was supposed to fax to his delivery service, was an embossed square of thick ivory parchment with elegant gold lettering. He snatched the invitation off the board.

Saturday, the twenty-sixth day of May, the year of our Lord…

He read back until he found the time.

Twelve noon.

And to make sure he punished himself, he jumped to the third line from the top.

...the marriage of their daughter, Madelyn Josephine Burrows, to Mr. Maxwell Forrester.

He swore again, suddenly realizing that he was standing near the window wearing nothing but a stricken expression. Ariana stared from the doorway, undoubtedly wondering if he'd lost his mind.

"Are you okay?" she asked for the second time this morning. Or was it the third?

"I'm late for the wedding."

She echoed his curse. "Charlie's going to kill me. You're his best man!" She rushed to him and grabbed the invitation. "What time is it at?"

But she obviously didn't find the noon notation first. Her eyes enlarged into big black saucers. Her jaw dropped with an audible gasp. Slowly, those ebony saucers hovered upward to focus on him.

"*You're* getting married today? Charlie told me *he* was the groom!"

Max glanced down at his bare stomach, somewhat surprised that the punched-in-the-gut sensation came from his own guilt rather than her fist to his midsection. He sure deserved it. He was getting married today and, loveless marriage or not, he'd just cheated on his fiancée. The fact that Maddie would understand wasn't the point. Max prefaced his answer with a string of self-deprecating curses. Some for Maddie, whom he'd betrayed. And some for Ariana, who didn't deserve to be used and deceived.

"Charlie lied. But I shouldn't have...we shouldn't..." It was his turn to leave a phrase unfinished. He shouldn't have what? Allowed someone to slip something in his drink? Agreed to a marriage of convenience? Denied the desire he'd had for Ariana over the past two years simply because a woman like her would undeniably complicate his life?

Ariana looked at the invitation again, then back at Max, then back at the invitation. "I knew Charlie was lying about something, but never about this!" She swallowed hard, then closed her eyes and took a deep breath. "Get dressed. You have fifteen minutes. I'll find your car keys."

ARIANA FOUND THE KEYS in the ignition of a current-model Porsche convertible parked in a pristine garage. With no idea how to disengage the security alarm blinking red and ominous on the garage door, she plopped into the driver's seat. It had been a while since she'd been behind the wheel of a car. Studying the instrumentation, she forced herself to focus on reacquainting herself with the process, when all she really wanted to do was scream bloody murder.

She'd spent the night with the groom! Not the best man. The groom! Why had Charlie lied to her? She couldn't really be mad at Max. She had been convinced last night and still was today that his condition had not been faked— though she had believed that he was clear and fully aware of his actions once he'd joined her on the balcony. But *she* should have been thinking clearly all night. She had made the choice to go through with the seduction in the fog… then in the bedroom—oh, and the shower. She couldn't forget the shower.

Oh, God! Only her second lover in her entire lifetime and she'd descended from virtual virgin to certified slut in one night? She'd made love with a man on the eve of his wedding to someone else. The fact that she didn't know he was getting married was no excuse, right? That was Charlie's fault. When she got her hands on that liar, she was going to make him pay.

Max slammed into the garage, denying her time to pile on more thoughts of revenge. Right now, all she could do was help him set things right. Unshaven and uncombed, but at least now dressed in pants and a shirt, a bow tie and tuxedo jacket clutched in his left hand, Max punched in the security code and activated the garage opener. Ariana turned the key on the ignition as he yanked open the passenger door and folded himself inside. Whoever had ridden with him last had not been tall.

Probably the bride, "Madelyn Josephine Burrows." Damn her.

"Do you know where St. Armand's Church is?" he asked.

"Unless it's Greek Orthodox, nope."

Max took a deep breath and closed his eyes. "Take a right out the driveway. And step on it." He flipped the tie around his neck and dropped the sun visor to use the vanity mirror.

"Max, about last night…" she said, revving the engine. Now, if she only knew what to say next.

Max stopped fiddling with his tie and laid his hand over hers. "Ari, do what I did. For now, just forget last night."

She pursed her lips as she tested the give-and-take of the clutch. "Easy for you to say. You had pharmaceutical help."

He squeezed her knuckles, then covered her hand completely, enveloping her fingers in his warmth. Ariana focused on the shape and size of his hand, instantaneously remembering the gentle skill that hand had practiced on every inch of her body. Her palms grew slick and her stomach turned.

She'd made love, freely and wildly, with a man who would, as soon as she shoved the car into drive and found the church, marry someone else.

She shook his hand away and manipulated the stick shift into first gear. "I'll be fine. You finish dressing and do the navigating thing. We have a wedding to get to."

THE PARKING LOT was virtually empty. Ari leaned over and checked the clock on the dashboard. It was only quarter past noon. Surely they'd wait fifteen minutes.

Ariana pulled into a space beside the single occupant of the lot, a shiny Honda Accord with several religious stickers on the bumper. "You sure this is the right place?"

Max dug into his pocket for the invitation.

"St. Armand's," he read, then gestured to the marble sign below the statue in the courtyard. "This is where we were last night for the rehearsal."

Ariana hadn't intended to get out of the car. She'd wanted to stop at the restaurant two blocks away and let Max drive the rest of the way alone while she called her uncle to pick her up. She didn't want anyone getting the wrong impression—which, technically, was the right impression if they thought Max had arrived at his wedding with the woman he'd picked up at a bar and slept with the night before his marriage.

But Max, still struggling with his damn tie while she ruined his clutch, begged her to stay with him until they'd reached the church, though he hadn't said why, not even when she'd asked.

"Is there another parking lot?" she ventured, trying to work a reasonable explanation out of a puzzling situation.

"Not that I know of. This is the pastor's car," he said, clicking open his door. "Come on."

Turning off the ignition, she exited the car and tossed him the keys. "Come on? I'm not going anywhere near that church! I have a particularly strong aversion to lightning smiting me dead."

His frown was incorrigible, and so damn cute. "You're a friend getting me to my wedding when I was too hungover to drive. No one is going to assume anything else. Not from Maxwell Forrester. Trust me on that."

His self-deprecating tone intrigued her. "What are you, some kind of Goody Two-shoes?"

He shrugged into his jacket, engaged the car alarm and pocketed the keys. "Something like that," he answered, motioning her to follow when he started up the stone walkway.

Ariana dug her hands into her pockets beneath the hem of her untucked turtleneck. Her curiosity was on overdrive. She simply didn't know what she wanted to learn more—where all the guests were or what this Madelyn Josephine Burrows looked like.

She stepped around the car and skipped up onto the sidewalk, drawing the brim of her lucky cap slightly downward while she matched her steps to Max's. "What the hell? Maybe I can find a confessional while I'm here."

Max didn't answer and judging by the way he scanned the church for anyone, much less someone familiar, she realized he had much more on his mind than the eternal damnation of her soul. The one time, *the one time,* she decided to throw caution to the wind and have a glorious adventure, she'd wrecked a man's future.

They entered the church through a side door and found the pastor, dressed casually in black pants and a short-sleeved white shirt, fiddling with the position of a glorious bouquet of satiny white tulips in front of the altar.

"Reverend?" Max asked quietly, stopping at the bottom step of the dais.

"Mr. Forrester? What on earth are you doing here?"

Max stared at the man for a long minute, then glanced over his shoulder for Ariana's help. She had paused halfway down the aisle behind him, her expression purposefully blank. She had no more idea than he did about what the heck was going on.

"What am I doing here? Well, I thought I was getting married."

The reverend, barely pushing forty, with streaks of gray at his temples and a spry, slender physique, placed his hands on his hips and gave Max a half scolding, half amused smile. "Well, so did I until Mrs. Burrows called this morning to tell me that you and Miss Madelyn had eloped in the dead of night."

The cleric squinted at Ari, who smiled and gave him a little wave. "You're not Miss Madelyn."

Ariana smiled. No, she wasn't. But she wasn't saying a word.

"She's a friend. She drove me here." The explanation rushed out before he stopped and nearly shouted, "Eloped?"

"I take it Mrs. Burrows wasn't telling the whole truth?"

"Eloped?" he repeated.

Max backed up until his legs hit a chair festooned with tulle and bows and he plopped into it. Ari took a step forward, then stopped. This was none of her business. She shouldn't be here. But, good Lord, did Max just get left at the altar?

Why would any woman leave this man at the altar?

Ariana slapped her hand over her mouth to contain a gasp. She and Max had made love outside! What if someone saw? What if Madelyn saw? *Oh, God.* What if Max's poor innocent bride had stumbled onto them sometime during the night or morning and, heartbroken, had her mother lie to the priest and all the guests? Ari slid into a pew and buried her face in her hands. She was going to hell for sure.

The pastor's voice carried across the empty church. "I take it Mrs. Burrows' explanation for the cancellation of the wedding wasn't true."

Ariana looked up in time to see Max shake his head. "If Madelyn eloped, it wasn't with me."

The pastor stepped down and sat beside Max, laying his hand across his shoulder. "Did the two of you have a fight?"

"I haven't spoken with Maddie since the rehearsal dinner. She left before I settled the bill."

The pastor glanced over his shoulder, his eyes sweeping over Ariana quickly, but with clear suspicion in his gaze. "And you haven't done anything that might have prompted Miss Madelyn's change of heart?"

What? Did she have the word *homewrecker* tattooed on her forehead? Ariana stood, pursing her lips. Dammit, she didn't know Max was getting married! She'd been deliberately deceived by Charlie Burrows. If anyone was going to pay, it was going to be him, and Ariana wasn't going to depend on divine intervention for that retribution.

Charlie had lied to her about who was the groom. Then the bride's mother lied to the priest about Max eloping. Why was this family acting so despicably? Was Charlie really Max's friend? For all she knew, he could have been the one to doctor Max's drink. But why?

Max stood, holding up his hand to stall Ariana from

bolting, which she fully planned to do. "I need to find Madelyn."

The pastor nodded, his expression grave. "A wise course of action. Let me know if you need my assistance."

The men shook hands and before Ariana knew it, she and Max were marching back to his car, their footsteps tapping loudly on the stones—in time, in sync, as if the rhythm of their bodies were composed by the same master musician.

Just like last night.

"Max," Ariana spoke when they reached the car, pausing as he clicked off the alarm and opened the passenger door for her.

"I'm okay to drive," he assured her. "I *need* to drive."

She shook her head. That wasn't what she was going to say. "You can drop me off at the corner," she answered. "I'll get a ride home."

"No way. Didn't you say that Charlie told you *he* was the one getting married?"

Nodding, she watched with wonder as the rage built in his eyes, turning them from warm sea green to cold pinpoints of emerald fire. "We planned the rehearsal dinner for weeks," she told him. "He kept encouraging me to flirt with you, talking you up and saying how perfect..."

Her voice trailed off. She sounded like an idiot, trying to justify her own stupidity and blind lust. She hated being duped, the pawn in some grand design of someone else's making.

"Get in, Ariana. We've both been screwed, and—"

She didn't mean to laugh, but couldn't help herself.

He touched her arm then, jolting the humor out of her with a shock of awareness that had no right to exist between them but did.

"Bad word choice. I'm sorry."

"I'm the one who should apologize. I just want you to know I don't ever, *ever* sleep with men I hardly know. Last night was...never mind. You don't remember and maybe it's better that you don't. I should leave well enough alone."

His grin was halfhearted, and she thought—hoped— she saw regret in his eyes. "This is 'well enough'? I just got jilted."

"Maybe someone saw us together."

That erased the half smile from his mouth.

"Maybe. But we won't know until we ask some questions. Charlie owes *both* of us an explanation." He stepped back and opened the car door farther. "I'll try to get one out of him before I wring his neck."

Ariana couldn't disagree. She wanted to find Charlie as soon as possible and she had no way of knowing how to do that without Max. She also wanted to wring Charlie's neck first, but she'd argue for that right after they found him.

"Aren't you going to call Madelyn?" she asked, sliding into the car.

Max didn't answer. He slammed her door shut and walked around to the driver's side, got in, turned the key and backed up with perfect grace. He'd undoubtedly left all vestiges of his hangover in the church vestibule.

"Max, why don't you let me deal with Charlie and you go see Madelyn?"

He shook his head as he maneuvered out of the parking lot. "Maddie can wait until I find out the details."

Men! He'd been duped and drugged, and he proba- bly suspected Charlie had something to do with that. She couldn't blame him. Charlie was suspect number one in her eyes, too. But she was perfectly capable of torturing the truth out of Charlie on her own. Max had something more important to do.

"Max, you need to see Maddie. She could be crying her eyes out because the man she loves cheated on her the night before their wedding. She's probably humiliated!"

At the stoplight, he twisted into his seat belt then motioned for Ariana to do the same. Cool and calm didn't begin to describe the precision of his movements, the controlled expression on his face. So this was how a man made millions, Ariana decided. Little by little, Max had reined in his emotions, tucking them away so she could see nothing but concentration on his face.

"I'll take care of Maddie. I promised to do that. I don't break promises."

Ariana sat back into the seat, silenced. He'd pledged last night to pleasure her beyond her wildest fantasies, to touch her precisely where she wanted to be touched and show her a few places she hadn't known would lead her to complete ecstasy. A thrumming heat suffused her veins as each caress, each kiss, replayed in her mind. Their interlude had been about abandon, exploration, unhindered freedom. She hadn't imagined or intended that they'd hurt anyone in the process.

She'd learned things about herself, about her body, about her needs, that she'd treasure forever. How many women would be so lucky? She knew then that if Max said he'd take care of Maddie, she would believe him.

Max Forrester was most definitely a man of his word.

6

"CHARLIE, OPEN THIS DAMN DOOR!"

Max pounded and jabbed the doorbell until he was certain that if anyone was inside Charlie and Sheri's North Beach walk-up, they were either dead or scared shitless to answer. He growled, knowing his best friend, conniving son of a bitch that he was, would never cower or hide. He'd face the music, no matter how loud or how ugly. It was one of the reasons he loved Charlie, bastard that he was.

"I don't think anyone's home, Max."

Ariana leaned on the front end of his Porsche, looking remarkably like one of those calendar models his mechanic had all over his shop. Except that her clothes covered nearly every inch of her skin, from her jaunty cap to her long-sleeved shirt, snug jeans and boots. He jabbed his fingers through his hair before he attacked the door again. To add to his frustration, he had very little trouble imagining her in nothing but those pink satin underthings she'd dangled from her fingers earlier. Too little trouble. He rightfully felt like a lying, cheating bastard, and women like Ariana Karas—and Maddie—deserved a hell of a lot better.

Giving up at the door, he jogged to the car, parked halfway on the curb and grabbed his Daytimer from the back seat. Ripping out a page, he carved a note with his felt-tip pen, then flashed it at Ariana so she could see he was serious.

Call me or you're fired. Max.

"What? No death threat?" she asked.

"Charlie just got married a few months ago. Sheri has expensive tastes. Threatening his life won't be nearly as effective as promising to cut off his income."

"Funny," Ari quipped. "I was planning on cutting off something else that Charlie's wife values."

Max raised an eyebrow, but Ariana didn't crack a smile or give him any indication that she wasn't dead serious.

Note to self: Don't piss this woman off.

Max pinned the paper beneath the door knocker and then slid back into the car as Ari did the same. He started the engine and pulled onto Greenwich Street before he realized he didn't know where to go next.

"If you can't find Charlie, shouldn't you call Madelyn?"

Ariana's concern for Maddie made Max feel even worse, not that he didn't care about Maddie himself. Nothing could be further from the truth. But he did know without a doubt that Maddie was not and never had been in love with him. No matter what happened to cause her to call off the wedding, Maddie wasn't experiencing the level of betrayal Ariana undoubtedly imagined.

They were just friends working out a mutually beneficial deal. Weren't they? All of a sudden, Max wasn't so sure. He had, technically, cheated. The act alone, drug-induced or not, denoted a lack of loyalty that tasted bitter in his mouth. Maddie didn't deserve such treachery.

And Ariana? What could she possibly be thinking, knowing she'd been lied to and deceived? For the moment, she focused on Maddie's feelings, but sooner or later she'd have her own to deal with, just as he'd have his. However, her apparent concern over his fiancée rather than herself only proved yet again that Ariana Karas was too good for the likes of him.

"It really bothers you that she might have gotten hurt, doesn't it?"

"*Might have gotten hurt?* She called off her wedding, Max. She made up an elaborate story about you eloping. Why else would she do that unless she saw us together last night? We weren't exactly practicing the depth of discretion."

He remained silent, but made a choice. He'd find Maddie soon enough and explain everything until she understood and forgave him. He'd take care of her, just as he'd promised. But right now he couldn't fight the urge to sustain whatever connection he'd formed with Ariana.

He'd dreamed about her for so long, cast her in countless forbidden fantasies. He couldn't waste this chance to fix what had gone so horribly wrong. The reverberation in her voice told him she blamed herself for last night's liaison.

If only she knew how he'd spent quite a few nights staring from his empty bed out to the view he'd paid way too much money for, wishing he could share the skyline with someone as intrinsically drawn to the hypnotic vista as he was.

He'd shown the view to Maddie once—and not from the vantage of the bed—but when she looked out onto any part of San Francisco, all she saw were the sights that needed to be changed. The beaches suffering corrosion. The neighborhoods overrun with liquor stores and strip clubs. The houses being renovated with no respect for the architect's original intentions or the character of the building or street.

He loved Maddie, in the way good friends should, but she wasn't the woman for him any more than he was the man for her. He'd never once fantasized about stripping her bare on a clear, cool night, then making love to her outside, with the stars and the city as witness to their passion.

But he'd imagined it with Ariana Karas, more times than he cared to count.

"I'll take you home first and then I'll call Maddie. I'm sure she's fine."

"Shouldn't you go *find* Maddie?"

Max shook his head, then shrugged. Honestly, he didn't know what to do. His anger subsided long enough for him to realize that his head was pounding like a bass drum. As much as he'd like to think he knew Maddie better than anyone, he couldn't be certain about how she would react if she had somehow stumbled onto him and Ariana last night. They'd never pretended to love one another *that* way. They hadn't even talked about how they'd handle sex during their marriage.

Up until last night, he hadn't put much value or importance on sex. His priority had been achieving his business goals and establishing himself as an independent, successful powerbroker in the world of San Francisco real estate. And so far as he knew, Maddie felt the same way.

But judging by the stricken expression shadowing Ariana's face, he needed to explain his arrangement with

Maddie before she traded her tight turtleneck for a hair shirt.

"Look, Ari, I know you feel guilty about Madelyn. But we didn't have that kind of relationship."

Ariana glanced at him sideways and puckered her lips while she considered what he meant. Spending his adult years in San Francisco had taught him never to let uncertainties linger. There were too many deviations available in the city, too many possibilities for why he and Maddie's marriage would have been purely platonic. And dammit, he didn't want Ari thinking he swung the other way.

"That didn't sound right," he said.

"No, it didn't. If you've been thinking all these years that you were gay, I hate to be the one to break it to you..."

"I don't think I'm gay," he insisted.

She smacked her lips. "That makes two of us."

Part of him was pleased. Part of him was frustrated beyond frustration that he had no memory of why she'd be so smugly certain.

"Good."

"So..." she sang, obviously wanting—and deserving—more explanation than he'd given her.

"Maddie and I have been friends a long time, since college."

"That's sweet," she injected, clear by her tone that she was only half sincere. "You marrying a woman you weren't sleeping with and had no intention of sleeping with? That's what you're trying to tell me, right? Why?"

She was too damn smart for her own good. And for his. "We had a mutually beneficial arrangement planned."

Boy, that sounded cold when he said it out loud.

"You were using each other," she clarified.

"No! I mean, well, not exactly."

"Using is using whether it's friendly or spiteful. She wanted something from you, you wanted something from her, all the cards are laid out on the table and everyone's happy. So why then did she call off the wedding and tell everyone the two of you eloped? Do you think she was seeing someone?"

"Maddie?"

Ariana's expression told him she heard the fury in his outburst. His tone surprised him as well.

He turned north onto Grant Avenue, for no other reason than because he had wanted to feel as if he was going somewhere. Somewhere other than down the road where he learned he'd taken Maddie for granted.

"If Maddie had found someone, she would have told me. I've encouraged her for years to look for someone who would love her, but she wasn't interested in having her heart broken."

Ariana nodded silently, as if she commiserated with Maddie on a personal level he didn't want to contemplate. He didn't want to think about some man hurting Ariana any more than he wanted to think about hurting Maddie. The idea introduced a hint of rage more potentially harmful than the murderous intentions he planned to wreak on Charlie whenever he got his hands on him.

Of course, at the moment, the man who could potentially hurt Ariana most of all was him, unless he did something to avert the inevitable. Right here. Right now.

"If Maddie did see us together and did call off the wedding," he said, hoping to ease Ariana's persistent guilt, "I'm pretty sure she'd do it because she thought it would make me happy, not because she felt betrayed or angry."

"Pretty sure isn't the same as certain."

"No, it's not. But I'll find out." Without thinking, he reached across and laid his hand over hers. "Trust me."

A grin bloomed, despite her apparent effort to tamp it down. "I've already done that."

"Any regrets?"

She turned her hand over so her palm nestled with his. "Just that you don't remember."

"There's no way in hell you regret that more than I do."

They sat silently at a traffic light, hand in hand, warmth to warmth. In the close quarters of his compact car, her scent, citrusy and fresh like a beach breeze, drifted in the air-conditioned space, teasing him, taunting him. Max shut his eyes against the bright sun, willing his brain to conjure a single clear image from the night before. Something wonderful. Something sweet. Something he could hold on to during the mess he was about to endure with Maddie, his parents, her parents and the entire social elite of San Francisco.

He got nothing but a dusky fog.

When he turned left at Bay Street, Ariana realized he was wandering and gave him directions to double back to her apartment in Chinatown. He released her hand to shift the gears and she busied herself with looking over the instrumentation of the car, asking him about the features as if she was honestly interested.

"Is this a car phone?" She pointed to the console.

"Yes. It's hands-free, for safety. There's a headset hidden in this panel if I need privacy."

"What's this blinking red light?"

Max glanced away from the road long enough to catch a ruby glimmer in the corner of his eye.

"A message."

He turned at Mason Street, glad when a cable car stopped in front of him so he could take a closer look.

"But no one calls me on this number. No one except…" He jabbed the playback button and tensed as the mechanical voice announced he had one message—from Maddie.

"Do you want the headset?" Ariana asked.

Before he could reply, Madelyn's cultured voice, soft and sad, echoed over the clanging of the cable car and the rumble of his engine. "Hi, Max. It's Maddie. I feel like such a coward. I should be telling you goodbye in person, but I've got to get away while I can. I'm sorry if I've embarrassed you, if I've ruined everything. But I've got to do this. I'll call you once I figure out where I'm going. Don't worry. For once, I'm going to be okay on my own. You might want to lay low for a couple of days, pretend we really are in Hawaii. I love you."

Max pulled over onto the first driveway he saw and worked the buttons until the message replayed. Ariana didn't say a word, but stared at him with confused eyes.

"I don't understand what she means," he admitted. "Why is she apologizing to me?"

"Play it again."

He did. The third time was not the charm. He still had no idea what Maddie was talking about, but he did catch the automatic announcement of when the call was received—just before midnight the evening before.

"What time did we leave the restaurant?" he asked.

"Just before one o'clock, clearly after she called."

They both sighed in relief, but Ariana couldn't shake the feeling that something more was wrong with Madelyn. She didn't know the woman—she shouldn't care. But she did.

"She may not have known anything about us when she

made this call," Ariana said, "but something is going on with her. How does she sound to you?"

Max replayed the message, this time listening for the emotions in Maddie's voice. She was slightly nervous, but clear. A sound of intense determination deepened her tone, despite her apologetic words.

"She sounds like a woman with a plan, which for Maddie is somewhat normal."

"She sounded a little scared to me," Ariana added.

Max nodded. He did hear anxiety in Maddie's tone, but nothing that got his hackles up or engaged his protective instincts. He and Maddie had known each other for so long, he felt confident he'd know when and if to be worried.

And he wasn't worried. Maddie may have finally come to her senses and realized that their marriage would have been a huge mistake for her. He'd tried to tell her that she shouldn't work so hard at living up to the expectations of others at the expense of her own wants and needs, but it was an empty argument coming from him. Wasn't he guilty of the same crime? Maddie needed time and space and, like the clever minx she was, she'd probably cooked up the elopement ruse to cover her escape.

He couldn't help but grin. When push came to shove, she'd always been the more courageous of the two of them. Looked as if he needed to take a lesson from his best bud once again.

"She sounds a little scared, but a whole lot more determined." He shifted the car back onto the main road, nodding quietly as they progressed, proud of Madelyn for making a stand, even in this roundabout way. "I think Maddie has gone off to find herself and used the elopement as a smoke screen."

Ariana sat back in the leather bucket seat and chewed

her bottom lip as she processed all the information he'd given her, asking questions at intermittent moments between giving directions to her home, clarifying her understanding and filling in the gaps.

"So, Maddie was marrying you because…"

"She was tired of the pressure from her parents to get married. And the women she worked with in her building-restoration efforts were older, very conservative—they had an elemental distrust of a female over twenty-one who wasn't properly wed to a man of power and prestige."

"And now you think she ran away to get her priorities straight and told everyone the two of you eloped?"

He shrugged. "Well, either Maddie cooked that one up or her parents did when they realized she was AWOL. They wouldn't stand for something so humiliating as a runaway daughter, even if she is nearly thirty years old."

"And you don't think you should go look for her? Make certain she's okay?"

He shook his head. "Definitely not. Maddie knows exactly how to contact me if she needs to."

Ariana accepted his claim with a nod. "Pull into that alley. You can park behind the shop. There aren't any deliveries on Saturday."

Max concentrated as he made the sharp right turn into a narrow alley between the blocks of Pacific and Powell. Driving in wasn't so hard, but the thought of them opening the doors to get out caused the imaginary sound of metal scraping brick to echo in his head. Still, what was a little scratched paint when he had the chance to see where Ariana Karas lived?

"Is the car safe here?" he asked, eyeing the deserted alley with the skeptical glare of a man who rarely ventured into Chinatown except to take some out-of-town client for dim sum.

"Well, there's always an off chance that Mr. Ping's rooster will take a liking to your convertible top."

"Mr. Ping's rooster lives in the alley?"

"No, the rooster lives in his guest bathroom, but he comes out here for fresh air."

"Are you teasing me?"

She winked before she flipped open the door with just enough speed to make him wince and enough alacrity not to scrape the door on the wall. "If you had any memory of last night, you'd know I'm not a tease."

Grabbing her backpack from the tiny space behind her seat, she shut the door with due care and slipped around to his side.

"You coming in?" she asked through the glass, her thumb hooked toward the dingy metal door neatly hand-painted with "Madame Li's Herb Shop. Deliveries here," first in Chinese, then in English.

He took the key out of the ignition and opened his door just wide enough to bend out of the car.

"I'm invited?"

"Well, let's see." She slung the backpack over one shoulder, where it promptly hit the wall, then she ticked off her reasons on her fingers. "Your fiancée just jilted you for parts unknown so she could go find herself. She or her family has told everyone that's important to you that you've eloped. I assume you've already arranged for a week off from work and I doubt anyone would dare to contact a newlywed on his honeymoon. And since the only person either you or I feel compelled to contact is probably going to make himself scarce today, can you think of anything else you need to do? Other than come upstairs with me?"

Her smile was reserved, but no less filled with possibilities.

"So you're saying I should come with you because I have nothing else to do?"

She frowned, just as he'd expected, just as he'd hoped. He didn't remember anything solid from last night's encounter, but if he was going to start over, nurturing this connection between them—at least for the week she had pointed out he now had free and clear—he wouldn't let her think she was anything but his first choice.

Because even before they'd made love, she had been his first choice. His only choice.

"Ouch," she said. "That's not what I meant at all."

He slammed the car door shut and clicked on the alarm. Two quick beeps told him the automobile was shielded from thieves, though he wasn't entirely sure about Chinese roosters.

"I didn't think it was. That's why I pointed it out."

She smiled and nodded, obviously appreciating his pragmatic reasoning. "So, if you're not coming up because you have nothing else to do, why are you?" she asked.

He edged around the side mirror, stepping into the inches separating Ariana from the hood of his car. She straightened against the wall, her backpack further padding them close. With his tuxedo jacket and tie tossed unceremoniously in the trunk and his shirt unbuttoned, he could feel her breasts mold softly—bralessly—against his chest. The effect was an instantaneous hardening of his sex.

"Think Madame Li has something to alleviate my headache?" Seconds ticked by before she looked up at him, then down at his obvious erection, then back up with a slanted glance that was half saucy bravado and half blatant interest.

"If she doesn't, I think I may have something to ease your discomfort."

MADAME LIN LI WAS a tall woman, statuesque in every sense of the word. Her great-great-grandmother had been the concubine of a Norwegian prince, so her nearly six-foot height and pale blue eyes were attributed to his genetic influence. But otherwise, she was Chinese in every sense of the word. Proud of her ancient heritage, Madame Li wore her sleek, embroidered satin dress with all the beauty of an Oriental princess, her jet-black hair twisted and secured with enamel chopsticks festooned with tiny red ribbons.

Her shrewd eyes and keen business sense, however, were decidedly American. The minute Ariana and Max passed from the alley into her kitchen, the private room she used to brew her specialty teas for her customers, her pencil-thin eyebrows shot up over wide eyes.

Ariana gave her a respectful bow. "Good morning, Madame Li. This is Maxwell Forrester. He's a friend."

Madame Li gracefully lifted a copper teakettle from her gas-burning stove and doused the blue flame. She nodded at Max while she poured the hot water into a porcelain pot etched with fine blue Chinese symbols.

"A new friend, Mr. Forrester? I've never heard Ariana speak of you."

He bowed respectfully, all the while stretching his hands in his pockets so Mrs. Li didn't see the most pressing reason for his interest in her boarder.

"We've known each other for a few years."

She hummed her suppositions, but kept her obvious skepticism to herself.

"I was hoping you could brew a tea for Max," Ariana said. "He has a terrible headache. Someone put something into his drink at the restaurant last night."

"On purpose?" Mrs. Li asked.

Max shook his head, but Ariana shrugged. She knew he didn't believe the drug was put in his drink accidentally. He suspected Charlie just as much as she did. Apparently, he didn't want to discuss the matter with a stranger. She couldn't blame him. Ariana had invited Max into her home, something she hadn't done for any other man since she'd been married. She was taking another chance based on the two things they had in common: a betrayal by Charlie Burrows and a rather hot attraction. They absolutely had to deal with the first one. With regards to the second, well, that remained to be seen.

Ariana knew what she wanted, but whether or not grabbing the brass ring for a second time was prudent, she wasn't entirely sure. But she sure as heck wouldn't know the answer if she just sent Max on his merry way, now, would she?

"What happened, exactly?" Mrs. Li asked.

Ariana looked askance and Max pressed his lips together.

The Asian matron chuckled. "Okay, forget I said 'exactly.' Just give me a list of your symptoms, Mr. Forrester."

"I was drowsy and disoriented at first, then…"

Ariana filled in the blanks in the most delicate way she could. "He was very…relaxed."

Madame Li busied herself placing several teacups and saucers on a tray beside the brewing pot. "And this morning?"

Max shook his head, as if to clear the cobwebs. "I can't remember much, if anything, about last night. And there's the headache."

Mrs. Li lifted the tray and placed it on an ornate, carved teacart without jangling one cup. "I have four ladies waiting for tea, but I'll mix something up and bring it to you."

"I can come down," Ariana insisted. She admired Mrs. Li a great deal and already felt as if she was taking advantage of her hospitality by bringing Max in through her back door. She felt like a teenager trying to sneak a boyfriend into her bedroom. Not that Ariana knew what that felt like. But Madame Li had been her landlady for going on eight years, renting first to Rick and then subbing the lease to Ariana after he took off. If Ariana didn't spend so much time at the restaurant and so little time at home, they might have developed a mother-daughter relationship.

As it was, they were friends. Friends who shared a few secrets—including Ariana's reluctance to let a man into her life again. And yet, here she was, ushering one upstairs into her room.

Mrs. Li shooed Ariana and Max toward the back stairs. "You have other matters to tend to. I'll bring the tea. Now, out of my kitchen."

Ariana thanked Mrs. Li again and led Max by the hand behind the silk curtain that led to a narrow stairwell. They climbed two flights, emerging on the third floor just outside her apartment. She fished her key out of the front pocket of her backpack, silently aware that Max remained just inside the archway from the stairs.

She opened the door and her window sheers cast a glow like fire into the hall. She saw Max's eyes narrow as he peered around her. He'd see nothing but scarlet until he came in—even after, for that matter.

"I've done some rather interesting decorating," she said by way of enticement. "Care to see?"

She disappeared into the yards of red silk she'd draped across the archway leading into her rooms. She dropped the backpack atop her black enamel treasure chest and tossed her hat onto the head of a five-foot-long ceramic dragon.

Walking into her apartment always made her feel as if she'd entered a different world—a luxurious, exotic world with ancient secrets and erotic promise. And when the door shut behind Max, she felt as if her world wasn't just bolts of secondhand fabric and rescued treasures from Madame Li's attic.

Max's presence made her home the stuff of fantasies. And if Ariana knew one thing about Max, she knew he was a man who could make all sorts of fantasies come true.

7

"SO? WHAT DO YOU THINK?"

In all his fantasies about Ariana Karas, never once had he imagined what sort of place she lived in. If he had, he most definitely wouldn't have dreamed up this decor. Not that he didn't like it. What man wouldn't like a room that was a cross between a harem den and a Buddhist temple?

"It's red." Going for the obvious seemed like the smartest move, particularly when his real reaction bordered on obscene. Okay, not obscene, but depraved. No, not that, either. Not with Ariana. Memory loss or not, he guessed that making love with her had been nothing short of glorious. In a setting like this, he might not ever want to leave her bed.

Or more factually, he'd never want to leave the endless collection of thick, embroidered throw pillows scattered on her shiny hardwood floors and over the plush carpets.

"I like red," she said with pride. She moved across the room to a black enamel table and lit a thin reed of incense. The scent snaked toward him, teasing his nostrils with a potent spice he couldn't identify. Not as sweet as cinnamon or as pungent as frankincense, the odor brought his senses alive, then seeped into his lungs and relaxed him from the inside out.

"In the morning, this room is very cheery." She touched a long match to a row of candles and then opened windows and switched on lamps capped with paper-thin shades. "In the evenings, it's soothing."

And in the afternoon, it's erotic as hell.

"Make yourself comfortable." She gestured toward the mound of pillows he realized was actually a couch. "Do you want the phone? I'm going to take a shower, if you don't mind."

I wouldn't mind taking a shower with you.

"Phone would be good. I'm going to see if Charlie is hiding out at the office."

She grabbed a portable phone from around a doorway he assumed was an entrance to her kitchen, but a reluctant pause accompanied her handing it to him.

"What?" he asked.

"Just be careful who you call."

"Why?"

She bit her lower lip, hooking her fingers into her belt loops again while she rocked on her heels. "You have a unique opportunity here. Too many phone calls could ruin it."

God, her eyes were fathomless. Black as the finish on her furniture, yet as soulful as the ancient accoutrements she'd placed around her home. Ariana Karas was a mystery, no less fascinating or arousing as a foreign land to an explorer. The opportunity she spoke of wasn't lost on him. She was ever so sweetly making him an offer he'd be a fool to refuse.

"You mean my chance to have one week of pure freedom? With no one expecting me to be around? No one looking for me?"

She grinned and backed away. "A once-in-a-lifetime opportunity. Just like my week off." Slinging her backpack over her shoulder, she moved quickly across the living room to an archway shielded with dark, glossy beads and another layer of silk. "Help yourself to whatever. Look around. I don't have any secrets."

She disappeared through the strands of ebony beads, her departure accompanied by a musical tinkle that reminded him of wind chimes. This small space, no more than three hundred square feet, if his instincts were right, exuded relaxation and escape. She worked long hours at the restaurant; he knew that for a fact. Every restaurant owner he knew pushed twelve hours a day. But while he'd hired a decorator to give his home the proper signs of the wealth he slaved for all day, Ariana had created her very own mystical haven to escape to after the hustle and bustle of her busy workday.

No secrets, huh? Max seriously doubted that. In fact, he knew she had secrets—mainly, the mystery of what really happened between them the night before. He took the phone over to the couch, sighing as the velvet cushions swallowed the aches in his body. He kicked off his shoes and shed his socks, then tucked the polished loafers out of the way.

Stretching his legs, he scanned the room. He had entered a different world. A world where color and texture and scents mixed to create a sensual experience like no other.

An experience he could enjoy for an entire week, if he took a wild chance.

Seven days. No responsibilities. No expectations. Because of the wedding, he'd made certain to close all his major deals last week. He'd signed off on several hundred thousand dollars' worth of real estate transactions that little by little, were making him a very wealthy man. He'd left only one deal open—the big one—the stage of development too early to close off. It killed him to let the purchase of the old Pier sit for an entire week. Still, he'd talked his partners into putting off any progress until he could give the project his full attention.

Max punched the number to Maddie's parents' house into the phone, calculating his words carefully before the butler answered the call and informed him that the Burrowses were at the reception hall with the rest of the wedding guests, who were celebrating Miss Madelyn's marriage without the bride and groom.

Max grinned. Randolph Burrows wasn't a man to waste money and Barbara Burrows wasn't a woman to miss throwing the social event of the season. Bride and groom? Obviously, unnecessary. He hung up and redialed Randolph's cell phone.

Barbara answered. "Maxwell? Why are you calling from your honeymoon? Is Madelyn all right?"

That answered his original and most pressing question. The elopement was Maddie's lie, not her family's. Madelyn had crafted a tension-free escape, and laid the groundwork for him to enjoy one of his own.

"Yes, ma'am," he answered. "She's fine."

She was away from their influence and away from him. Madelyn was more than fine.

"I just wanted to apologize for our…spontaneity."

"Just as long as you aren't calling about business. I confiscated this phone from Randolph so he'd have a good time."

Max laughed. "No, no business. I know you put a great deal of time and effort into the wedding."

"Not an ounce of which is being wasted, I assure you. You kids have a great time. And don't you worry about that deal you and Randolph have been working on, either. Every one of your investors is here, slurping champagne as if the world will end tomorrow. None of them will be in any condition to think about business for a couple of days at least."

Max thanked his former would-be mother-in-law and disconnected the call. For an instant, he allowed himself to wonder how Barbara and Randolph would react once they realized that both he and Maddie had lied about their marriage. Of course, if Max managed to make Randolph a millionaire yet again, he was certain he'd be forgiven. Maddie would have to sculpt her own redemption with her parents, if she even wanted their approval anymore. Naturally, he'd help her, but she'd wasted so much of her life seeking the respect of her family, he hoped she'd wait until she was truly ready to make a stand.

Max realized for the first time since he was eight that he had an entire seven days with absolutely no responsibilities, no expectations, nothing. Whether he liked it or not, his big deal was on hold. His office staff had clear instructions to handle all emergencies as if he were dead and even his housekeeper was on vacation. He had nothing to take care of—nothing but a sexy woman showering in the adjoining room…a woman who had the same number of days to escape from everyday life. With him.

The shower stopped running at the same time as a light rap echoed on the door. He set the phone on the cushions and answered the knock. Mrs. Li stood on the other side, greeted him with a slight bow and handed him a laden tray.

"This tea will help you, I think."

Though probably near fifty years of age, Mrs. Lin Li was an exceptionally attractive woman, partly because of her classic Asian features—almond-shaped eyes, glossy hair and fine skin—and partly because she broke the mold in unexpected ways—her height, light irises and steely carriage. A woman like her commanded respect and Max immediately gave it.

"I appreciate your hospitality, Mrs. Li. I'm sure your tea will work wonders."

"It is not my hospitality you should value. Take care with my boarder, Mr. Forrester. She isn't as worldly as her decor or behavior might indicate."

Mrs. Li wordlessly disappeared down the hall, but her warning was clear. Max promised himself he'd heed it. He set the tray carefully on a low table in front of the couch. Fact was, he didn't know very much about Ariana Karas. About what she knew or didn't know. About what she wanted or didn't want.

But he had an entire week to find out.

ARIANA PROPPED OPEN the bathroom door, spilling a billow of steam into her small, messy bedroom. Damp and aware of Max's presence in the adjoining room, she couldn't tamp down the memory of making love with him in the fog. Seeing and yet not seeing. Using touch to guide touch. Exploring the full breadth of sensual pleasure.

Too bad Max didn't remember a thing.

With a grunt, Ariana twirled her hair into a towel, then dried herself briskly with another. She tried not to think about where Max had run his hands or mouth last night or how wonderful it would be to invite him into her room right now to help her remove the moisture from her skin while he evoked a separate wetness deep inside.

She wondered if he'd accept her invitation until she recalled the hard evidence of his desire that had been more than apparent downstairs when he'd pinned her against the wall.

But even if he didn't remember what happened last night, they had just survived a tense morning-after. They'd done okay, too. He'd made no lame excuses for his questionable judgment with Madelyn, but had given Ari the facts to decipher as she saw fit. And she wanted to believe that Max was incredibly kind, but equally misguided. Marriage, in her experience, was *never* a convenience.

She knew that truth firsthand. Watching her aunt and uncle, whose marriage was even healthier than her parents' thirty-five-year union, had taught her that making a lifetime commitment required more than friendship or mutual goals. Those characteristics helped, but without passion—without love—the union was destined for disaster.

For Max and Madelyn's sake, Ariana was glad they'd learned their lesson before they'd taken their vows. She didn't wish the heartbreak of divorce on anyone. And now that her hot shower seemed to have cleansed away any lingering and unnecessary guilt over her night with Max, Ariana knew she couldn't let this opportunity pass. Max was a free agent. And most important, his interest in her matched the fascination she harbored for him.

Time to grab the fantasy while she could.

Living in Chinatown gave her the advantage of owning one of the most complete collections of silk clothing of any non-Asian woman she knew. She swept through her assortment of silky robes and satin pajamas until she found her favorite: a thick, pink satin robe piped in red and sporting a glorious gold dragon on the back. With care, she laid the robe across her pillows, collected the assortment of discarded clothes and socks and underthings her hectic schedule kept her from gathering throughout the week and tossed them into an overflowing hamper in the corner.

She tidied and straightened wearing nothing but the towel on her head, stopping dead when she heard Max's voice from the other side of the thin curtain. His shoulder or hand must have rustled the beads, because they tinkled in the silence, adding a musical accompaniment to the thrill of hearing him so close while she was so exposed.

"Mrs. Li brought the tea," he announced. She silently inched to the opening, marveling at the subtle change in the atmosphere as she neared him—the way her body reacted instinctively with a pulsing thrum. The man was potent. Potent and dangerous. Just what she needed for a weeklong fling.

"I'll be right there," she whispered, swallowing when the curtain rolled with his movement, brushing inward as he shifted his weight.

They stood silently, mere inches away. One of them had to move away first. But neither did, for a long, torturous minute. Then the ebony glass she'd strung from the archway chimed ever so slightly and the air lost a degree of thickness. She heard Max sigh as he settled back into the cushions of her couch.

She towel-dried her hair, unwilling to waste fifteen minutes with a blow-dryer, combed it out and twisted it up into a loose chignon secured with chopsticks. She applied a dusting of powder and blush to her face, along with a light application of liner and mascara. She used a heavier hand with her lipstick, choosing a brick color that brought out the lush shape of her lips and hinted, however subtly, of the ancient tradition of the Chinese concubine or Japanese geisha.

After spritzing her body with jasmine-scented cologne, she donned the robe and tied the sash with a snug but easily undoable knot. One glance in the mirror reminded her she was an attractive, alluring woman. And attractive, alluring women deserved to live out a fantasy or two, even if only for a week.

And to that end, she unzipped her backpack and retrieved the magazine. The photographs gave her a delicious idea, an inspired plan. And she suspected she wouldn't need much to convince Max to join her.

When she emerged from her bedroom, Max was moving the tray from the credenza to the coffee table. With a shake and rattle, he dropped the tea the last inch.

"Wow."

She twirled around, pausing with her back to him to model the dragon.

"You like?"

Her final half spin swirled the hem of the robe against her bare legs. She watched him swallow thickly and couldn't believe that she'd once considered him standoffish. Uninterested in a woman like her. Untouchable and somewhat remote. The man now wore his desire with the same rumpled charm and sexy innuendo as his half-discarded tuxedo. She forced her triumphant grin into an understated smile, more than willing to take some of the credit for Max's new attitude.

"What's not to like?" he asked.

Snagging her bottom lip in her teeth, she bounced onto the cushions beside the couch with a barely checked energy—a revved mixture of sexual excitement and daring spirit. She slipped the magazine beneath a cushion. First things first.

"Well, let's see. I seduced you on the night before your wedding. That might make a man a little annoyed."

He slung his hands into his pockets and eyed her with an irresistible mix of amusement and disbelief. "I may not remember the details of last night, but I think it's safe to assume we each did a fair and equal amount of seducing."

"Yes," she conceded, "but I was completely sober."

He squatted so they were eye level. "That gives you the advantage of knowing precisely how great we were together. Of course, I'm assuming we were great together or you wouldn't have invited me to your apartment and offered me tea."

She grabbed the edge of the tray and pulled it forward, sliding onto the cushions that had fallen from the couch to the floor beside the table. "That's a fair assumption. Does it bother you that you still can't remember?"

With a tentative touch, he laid his hand over hers while she lined up the cups and saucers.

"Bothered isn't the right word. It's more like torture. You may not know this, but I've been attracted to you for a very long time. Since the first time I saw you."

His hand disappeared beneath the gape in her sleeve, his fingers inching up and down her arm slowly, erotically.

"Really?" she asked with a gulp. "You never flirted or came on to me."

He closed his eyes and grunted in frustration. "No, I didn't. Just proves once again that when it comes to women, I'm a full-fledged idiot. In hindsight, that drug in my drink may have been the best thing that's ever happened to me."

She laughed. "Even with the headache?"

He snorted. "That's the least of my discomfort, Ariana."

She pressed her lips together. The silken wet texture of her lipstick, coupled with the image of her smearing the brazen color on his mouth, emboldened her to the point of no return. "I have an idea that might alleviate your pain."

From the way his emerald eyes darkened, enhancing the flecks of gold she hadn't noticed until right this moment, she gathered he had a few ideas of his own.

He turned her hand palm up and swirled an erotic shape in the center with his fingertip. "I was thinking we drink our tea, relax, then go back to my house and wait until to-night. You could reconstruct the evening for me. Kiss by kiss."

"I like the way you think," she admitted, somewhat breathless at the suggestion. But while his idea brimmed with sensual promise, hers bordered on outrageous. Sin-fully outrageous.

"But we didn't kiss that much," she finished.

"We didn't?"

She shook her head and licked her lips, shocked that her mouth fairly vibrated with anticipation of his kisses.

"See? I obviously wasn't myself. I've spent more hours than I'd care to admit fantasizing about doing nothing more than kiss you."

The flattery pushed her further. "Nothing more?" she challenged, certain that a grown man like Max would never settle for just kissing. And why should he, when touching and caressing and exploring and mating were so incred-ible?

"Well, maybe a little more. But only after a lot of kiss-ing."

She nodded and poured the tea into one tiny cup, then the other. The spiced scents of ginger and clove flared her nostrils instantly. This was Madame Li's most potent tea, a mixture of herbs and spices and secrets handed down from generation to generation.

"Smells strong," he commented as she slid the cup over to him. He settled more comfortably into the cushions, folding his legs to his side rather than attempt to squash them beneath the low table.

"Oh, it is. She brewed this tea for me once, a long time ago. It'll clear your head."

He started to lift the cup, but she stopped him by laying her hand on his wrist.

"Don't rush."

Chuckling, he removed his fingers from the cup. "What? Is there a tea ceremony for alleviating hangovers?"

She plucked the top off a small china pot, allowing a stream of amber honey to drizzle from the imbedded spoon. When the rivulet thinned to a golden thread, she flicked her finger across, breaking the string momentarily.

She slipped her finger into her mouth and sucked away the sweetness. "We could make up our own ceremony."

Ariana dipped the top back into the pot, then lifted the honeycomb-shaped end again, dripping sweetener into his tea.

"A little sweetness and a little spice?" she offered.

He hummed, then silently watched as she added honey to her own tea. She removed the cups from the tray and slid it out of the way, positioning his tea in front of him and drawing hers closer. Folding her legs completely beneath her, she pulled up on her knees. He mirrored her position, directly across from her.

"Close your eyes," she instructed.

He did so without hesitation.

Her heart swelled. *Gotta love a man who takes orders.*

"Now, lift your cup to your mouth, but don't drink."

He peeked long enough to make sure he didn't spill the piping-hot contents and brought the porcelain to his lips. The cup was so white against his tanned, rugged skin. So delicate in hands that Ariana knew could be demanding and rough in the most wonderful ways.

"Take a deep breath."

His chest lifted as he complied then stilled while he held the scent of the tea in his lungs for a long instant.

"The smell alone can clear the brain," he said.

"Wait until you taste it."

He interpreted her comment as an invitation to drink, but she stopped him again with a gentle, "Not yet. Put your tea down."

His eyes remained closed, but he followed her directions, this time without peeking. He adeptly set the cup on its saucer. The corners of his mouth twitched. He wanted to smile, but was valiantly fighting the urge, causing Ariana to grin from ear to ear.

"Lean forward."

He did so as she drank from her own teacup. When the liquid had heated her mouth, she leaned forward to meet him halfway across the table, swallowing when their lips touched, then parted. The taste of the tea flowed from her tongue to his, filling their kiss with the delicious flavor of exotic desire.

When his hands touched her sleeves, she broke the kiss but didn't back away. Their noses brushed as his eyes sprung open.

"Can't I touch you?"

"Kiss me first."

"Can't I do both?"

"You could, but that would be rather…ordinary. Expected. Don't you think?"

He inched back just far enough to study her face. The taste of the tea and the heat of his mouth filled her with the courage to see her fantasy through. She had one week of freedom, as he did. Why fill it with an ordinary affair when they could have a sensual and special liaison? A touch of imagination? A dose of risk? Like in the magazine. Like in the dozens of daring ideas dancing in her head whenever she thought of Max.

"You want the unexpected?" he asked.

"Think about it, Max. When's the last time you really let yourself go? Grabbed the excitement of life and didn't worry about how your adventures would affect your work or responsibilities?"

He shook his head, tilting his face downward so she nearly missed the regretful look that twisted his features.

"That sounds like my brother, not me. Ford is a drifter. He goes where the excitement is, whenever the mood takes him."

"You say that with envy in your voice."

"You think?"

"I'm calling it like I see it. You and I have a bit in common. Both of us have a very clear picture of what we want from life."

"Crystal," he added with emphasis.

"And we've both sacrificed a lot, from a very early age, to get where we want to be. I mean, I left my family on the other side of the country and I work long hard hours every day of the week, but I'm this close—" she pinched her fingers together "—to reopening Athens by the Bay and making it a real force in the restaurant world. That's what I want—a business that's mine, that people talk about, that they travel to San Francisco just to visit."

"That's a big dream," he said, but not a single syllable suggested that he thought she couldn't make her dream come true.

"Yeah," she said proudly, "but I almost have it. And you know what? It's not always enough."

Max's tongue still tingled from the united tastes of spiced tea and Ariana, and his mind reeled as she made admissions that seemed to come straight from his own heart—from the part he routinely ignored so he wouldn't have to face how empty and predictable his life had become.

"Not always," he agreed.

"Well—" she scooted forward, cradling the teacup in her hands "—imagine we both had a chance to grab some excitement, really drink life. And in the end, there'd be no consequences, no repercussions except a collection of amazing memories."

"Sounds too good to be true."

"I don't think so. I think it sounds too good to pass up. Come on, Max. Have an adventure with me. What do you say?"

8

GOT 'EM.

Leo swung past the dingy narrow alleyway a second time, this time slowing enough to read the license plate. This was too easy. He'd nearly lost them when Forrester doubled back to Chinatown, but despite his employer's low opinion of him, he wasn't stupid enough to blow a second chance at a rather hefty amount of untraceable cash.

Hell, he'd pocketed a cool five hundred just for some misty photos of assorted body parts flailing in the fog. He clucked his tongue as he scanned for a parking place, wondering what the hell the old man was going to do with such screwed-up pictures. But what did he care? He had a wad of twenties in his pocket and a chance to make a hell of a lot more.

He waited for a carload of tourists to pull away from the curb and took their spot. With binoculars, he surveyed the uneven row of old buildings across the street and half a block down. A gift shop. A tea shop. T-shirts. Two restaurants. Cameras for sale.

Luckily, he already knew where Ariana Karas lived. Trading his binoculars for his camera, complete with a telephoto lens, he trained his view to the third floor above Mrs. Lin Li's establishment and snickered. Madame Li might be selling rare herbs and unique tea blends out the front door, but upstairs? Her boarder was selling something entirely more choice. He only wished he'd have a chance at some. But he'd made that offer only to crash and burn. He'd have to settle for the cash.

Red curtains fluttered from open windows.

They were there, all right. And he was going to get them. Mr. Thien Wong owned the porcelain shop across from Mrs. Li. And upstairs, Wong also rented rooms. He hadn't had any vacancies for a long time, but luckily for Leo, his young nephew, Ty, who lived in the room facing the street, facing *her* apartment, loved easy money just as much as he did.

And it wasn't hard to share when more was on the way.

"I SAY, YEAH."

Judging by the widening of her fathomless black eyes and a grin that ever so slowly bowed those luscious lips of hers into a burgundy smile, Max had answered her proposal faster than she expected. The dark lipstick did wondrously erotic things to her mouth, but he still could hardly wait to kiss off all that color.

"Really?" she asked.

"You seem surprised."

"No. Well, yeah, I guess I am. A little."

He shook his head, wondering how the hell she hadn't known how attracted, how enthralled he'd been with her from the first moment they'd met. Max had no idea his self-control and cool demeanor were so effective. Well, he'd certainly need neither of them over the next seven days.

"Good," he said with a grin. "It's not often that I surprise people, except in business. I'm a fairly predictable guy outside the office." He slid the honeypot to his side of the table, lifting the top to slowly swirl the golden contents. He had lots of unpredictable, incredibly surprising ideas about where he'd like to spread the sweet, sticky substance. Places he'd like to lick for the long spans of time required to remove the honey from her sweet skin. "But surprises are good, right? That's what you meant? One week of..."

"...Anything goes?" She reached across the table and dipped her finger in the pot, extracting a stream of honey that drew a thin path across the table leading to her. She dipped her fingertip in her hot tea briefly, then sucked the melting sweetness away, flashing him a devilish grin.

"Anything goes...I like that," he answered.

Her smile bloomed with some secret meaning. He questioned her with a curious glance.

"You said those exact words to me last night," she explained, untangling the long silk robe from around her legs. She fanned the material behind her, exposing her bare knees and thighs.

The warm scents of clove and ginger wafted from the teapot, calming him so he could tap into his practiced restraint. The honey would be good. Later. Mrs. Li had mixed a potent blend he longed to taste, especially when served in the warmth of Ari's kiss. "I said that? Doesn't sound like me."

"Maybe you *do* have inhibitions that need loosening," she suggested, drawing from an earlier conversation he did recall.

"I know I do. I'm all the things you said I am, Ari. Driven. Single-minded." The smile dropped away from his mouth when he admitted, "I can't make any promises to you beyond this week." He had to be sure she understood. Now that Maddie was on her own, the last thing he wanted to do was drag another woman into the craziness that was his life. Max knew he could afford only a brief respite from who he really was—a man who refused to forget what it felt like to be poor and helpless. Or from what he really wanted—the stability only an overflowing bank account and the respect and trust of his colleagues could ensure. Like Maddie, Ariana didn't deserve to be weighted or dragged down by his pursuit of true success.

She didn't deserve his late-night meetings, long phone calls or Sundays at the office. Women like her deserved pampering, attention and damn good loving. At least for the week, he could give her that—and receive the same in return.

She nodded. "I can't make any promises, either. I let my love life stand in the way of my dream once. I won't again. No matter how tempted I might be. But for this week, we can both have it all."

Max wanted to know more about her past, but now wasn't the time to ask, especially since he wasn't sure he was prepared to reciprocate. But they had all week to exchange secrets, to coax out the shadows and triumphs of their lives and loves, to dream and suppose about challenges yet to come. He'd never shared with a woman before—except Maddie. And he had a distinct impression that sharing with Ariana would be vastly different.

His passion for her stirred from a place higher than his groin, and deeper—from his heart. Ariana Karas was a kindred spirit, if one existed for him. How he ever deserved such a twist of fate, he didn't know. And he didn't care. He was grabbing this moment, dammit. This whole week. He suspected he'd never come across such an opportunity again.

"So…you still interested in showing me how this tea will cure my headache?"

His headache seemed to have completely disappeared, though he wasn't about to tell her. Not when showing her would be so much more fun.

Her eyes caught the glimmer of the streaming red curtains billowing from the afternoon breeze. "Oh, yeah. Most definitely."

In sync, they both took long sips of tea, then leaned forward, meeting halfway, mouth to mouth and heat to heat. Flavors mingled on their tongues. Spice. Sweet. Want. Need.

Max gripped the edge of the table, remembering that Ariana had wanted only his kiss before. He judged, by the tension in her arms as she held tight to the table, that she wanted to go slowly—as slowly as two people could go when they impose a time limit on their affair.

The idea was completely foreign, completely outrageous…completely thrilling. Why not? He had nothing to lose. She had nothing to lose. But they both had a world of experiences to gain.

He focused all his attention on learning her mouth. Her teeth were straight and slick. Her tongue bold yet pliant. Her skin was scented with jasmine, and the floral essence mingled with the spiced tea to create a heady combination that surged through his blood. He couldn't stand not touching her. Without breaking the kiss, he slid around on the pillows and pushed the table aside, rattling the teacups.

Ariana broke away, panting but smiling. They were on their knees, nearly thigh-to-thigh. She pressed her palms briefly against his chest and closed her eyes, as if willing both their hearts and passions to slow. Max waited. His gaze followed the bright red piping on her blush-pink robe, around her neck, down her chest, where the edging crossed at a shadowed curve of cleavage, rising and falling with each of her deep breaths. He ached to explore her, pleasure her. Know her.

She smoothed her hands down his arms, as if willing him to keep his raging passion checked for just a moment more. Leisurely releasing the remaining buttons on his shirt, top to bottom, she pulled the material toward her so her hands didn't accidentally brush his chest. She used the sleeve to guide his wrist toward her so she could undo the cuffs—again without allowing even a finger to graze his skin. Once all the closures were undone, she removed his shirt entirely in a quick billow of white. His flesh pulsed with the absence of her touch.

He swallowed. His tongue was thick, his mouth dry. She'd turned to retrieve her teacup, which she cradled with both hands. Swirling the golden liquid, she inhaled the steaming scent, warming her palms on the heated porcelain. After taking a long draught, she set the cup down and shared the heat on her hands with his chest, placing her palms flat so that his nipples touched their hot centers.

The sensation burned like a roaring fire on an icy day. Desire spiked when her lips, equally flamed by the tea, touched the pulse point at the base of his neck. Her tongue flicked a fiery trail across his shoulder, cooling along the way, but stoking his need to touch her, explore her, learn all the things he'd probably learned last night but couldn't remember.

When she started to nibble his earlobe, he'd had enough of remaining still. One hand was clenching the fringe of the nearest pillow; the other was nearly splintering the wood on her table.

"Can I touch you yet or I am I still limited to just kissing?"

She looked up at him with a flash of obsidian fire.

"I'm tempted to say no limits, but…"

"But what?"

Grinning, she reached down and undid the knot of her robe with one quick tug, then clenched the satin together so the material didn't spill open.

"We have all week." She loosened the robe, allowing him a peek of breast, a flash of belly. "And unless you have a condom tucked in your wallet…"

He didn't. He'd never tucked a condom in his wallet his whole life, though his mother had been known to do so when he'd come home from college on the weekends. If not for the freebies he'd gotten at his bachelor party, he probably wouldn't have had any in his apartment last night—assuming they'd used one. Wait, hadn't he gotten nearly half a dozen at the party?

"I have some at my place," he suggested.

She bit her lip. "Uh, no, you don't. Not anymore."

His eyes widened. "We used them all?"

Her laugh, a light sound somewhere between a giggle and a chuckle, inspired the same humor in him. She leaned forward, resting her forehead on his chest and the scent of her hair and the warmth of her skin nearly knocked the hilarity right out of him.

"So we can't make love," he concluded. "Not right this minute." He ran his hands down her satin sleeves. The friction was slick, liquid. Cool, yet hot. He hardened to the point of pain.

She pressed her cheek to his chest, then bestowed a

single kiss just above where his heart pounded hard against his ribs. "Like I said, we have all week."

And there are lots of different ways to make love. She didn't say the words, but he could see the possibilities dancing in her eyes, tugging her lips into a smile, loosening her grip on that robe. And even if the alternatives hadn't occurred to her, they did to him. In erotic detail.

She dug into the couch cushions and extracted a wrinkled magazine.

"What's that?"

"An idea. A fantasy."

"I have plenty of ideas and fantasies, thanks to you. I'm pretty sure I don't need pornography to get me hot with you around."

She laughed as she flipped the pages. "I'm flattered… I think…but this isn't porno." She found the page she wanted, but pressed the open magazine against her to hide the pages from him. "How well do you know the city?"

Max closed his eyes, knowing he wouldn't be able to think very clearly while the only thing separating him from a clear view of her naked body was a scrap of satin and a very tearable magazine.

"I've lived in the Bay Area all my life."

Her eyebrows lifted over disbelieving eyes. She flipped the magazine over so he could see the two-page photo spread. "Have you ever done this?"

Max briefly scanned the photo of a couple making love on the bridge. She flipped a page, then another, then another, flashing images of San Francisco and adventurous lovers at him with rapid speed. She moved to turn the page again, but he stopped her, drawn to a photo in a location he didn't recognize. The scenery, somewhat blurred by a photo effect, didn't grasp him as much as the expressions on the faces of the models.

What did he see there? Excitement? Oh, yeah. Daring? Most definitely. But something more. Something elusive.

"What is this?" he asked.

"I found it on the cable car last night." She tilted the magazine so she could glimpse the picture herself, though he wondered if her wistful expression meant she'd memorized every detail. "It's called Sexy City Nights and it kind of gave me an idea of all I've been missing, all I could discover, if I had the chance. In the city. In my personal life."

He grinned, wondering what that admission cost her, fascinated by how Ariana spoke as if they'd known each other forever—and by how he wanted to return the favor. He wanted to know her. He wanted to live her fantasy. Be her fantasy.

"You're amazing." He tossed the magazine aside, then cradled her cheeks with both hands. "I've never met anyone who can make pure determination sound like spontaneity."

Ariana tried to shake her head, but he held her steady with a soft kiss. She'd admitted a great deal to him—told him a secret about herself that she'd never shared with anyone—partly because she hadn't realized until just last night how much she missed a man's touch. She'd kept herself so busy, thrown herself into her job and her goal so deeply, she didn't have to face the emotional and physical emptiness that haunted her heart.

But being with Max, loving Max, even temporarily, forced her to confront her needs.

"I'm not that complicated," she finally whispered, brushing her lips down the tip of his chin, missing the softness of his mouth at the same time that she relished the roughened feel of his unshaven skin. "I just know what I want. For the first time in years."

"Want to know what I want?" he asked, unable to swallow the laugh that followed, and moving to slide the robe down her shoulders.

"I know what you want," she answered, scooting back, not because she didn't want him just as desperately, but because the front curtain had flown open a little too wide for her comfort. She'd caught her neighbor across the street peering out his window and straight into hers on more than one occasion. Usually, she wasn't doing anything the least bit titillating. Drying her hair. Watching television. Meditating in a roomful of candles.

But this afternoon? In the daylight? Exhibitionism was just fine and dandy for the magazine and under the cover of fog, but she was going to have to ease into that fetish just a little more slowly.

She pulled the robe around her, not bothering with the sash. She wasn't going to be gone that long.

"You're awfully confident," he teased, leaning back into the couch cushions while she made her way around the table.

"That's because I want you, too."

Before tending to the window, she lit another stick of incense and clicked on her CD player. The tune was soft, the volume low and easily drowned out by the sounds emanating from the busy streets below. Holding her robe tightly, she leaned out to catch her wayward curtain and pull it inside so she could shut the old casement windows that opened out over the street.

The minute she grabbed the silk, she felt Max's hand snake around her ankle. Startled, she spun, landing on the

windowsill with her back against the center sash to brace
her backward tumble.

"What are you doing?" she asked, breathless.

He adjusted the pillows she'd thrown by the window for
the nights she liked to read the newspaper and listen to the
crowds below. Holding her foot possessively, he settled in
comfortably beneath her, kneeling more than sitting as he
caressed her arch.

"You have incredibly small ankles."

She was tempted to pull her foot away, but he was doing
amazing things to her instep with his hands. Incredible
things to her toes with his mouth.

She whimpered. "Shouldn't I come away from the window?"

His green eyes lit with mischief. "No one can see me
from outside."

"They can see me."

"Just your back and your hair. Not your face." He kissed
a path up her calf, stretching her leg outward so he could
suckle the sensitive spot behind her knee—the spot he'd
found last night.

She captured her bottom lip with her teeth and bit down,
hard, to keep from whimpering again like some forlorn
puppy. Like some sex-starved female with a week's worth
of pleasure nibbling her flesh.

Clutching the sill to keep from tumbling back, she
closed her eyes and willed herself to enjoy the sensation.
Max Forrester might not be aware of his fetish, but he
flirted with exhibitionism more dangerously than he flirted
with her. Not that anyone could see him tugging her belt
until it fell away, or inching his way up until his kisses
reached her thighs.

Threading her fingers into his hair, she buried her

embarrassment in the soft feel of his mouth on her skin. She wanted this. She wanted to break the mold of a conventional affair, create a new, exciting liaison that would belong only to Max and her. She allowed him to coax her legs apart, to touch her, taste her. He parted her pulsing flesh with his tongue and found the center of her need quickly, but alternated his attentions—higher, lower, side to side—so she could no longer anticipate the thrill.

Each lick was a surprise. Each kiss a revelation of need and want and self. The sensation that she was falling had absolutely nothing to do with her precarious perch on the windowsill or her long-held fear of heights. His mouth, his fingers, his groans of utter delight pushed her toward a precipice she desperately wanted to jump from.

So she did. She pulled him closer, throwing her knees wider, taking what he so willingly gave. Below, on the street, the noise of business and tourism and trade muted her enraptured cries of sweet release.

The moment her passion spiraled, Max guided her to the floor, rolling her beneath him on the pillows where he kissed her climax into submission. She shuddered in his arms, shivering as if cold when all she felt was the most intense heat imaginable.

Once she'd regained her ability to form a coherent thought, she asked, "Making love in public turns you on, doesn't it?"

"Never thought about it before." He nuzzled her neck, reminding her that this release had been decidedly one-sided. He was hard against her hip. The thick sign of his desire renewed the pulsing want he'd only just satisfied.

"Well, you need to think about it," she said.

"I will, after we find a drugstore."

She rolled away, grasping her robe together at the same

time she gasped for air. This man was potent, nearly over-whelming. She needed to replenish her energy before attempting to return his passionate favor.

And she would. Very, very soon.

The Cheshire-cat grin on his face belied his unsatisfied state. By the twinkle in his lethal green eyes, she imagined he'd been the one to experience the glorious orgasm. "Dress comfortably before we go out."

Walking backward, she disturbed the beaded drape to her bedroom, the musical tinkle adding magic to the sparkle between them. "Comfortably? Do you have a plan, Max Forrester?"

He leaned on one elbow, his cheek cradled in his palm. "Oh, yeah. Thanks to you." He relaxed into the pillows and folded his hands behind his head. "We're going to have a sex city night, Ariana. Just like in the magazine. Only with a Forrester spin."

9

As Ariana accepted his hand, Max swallowed a decidedly appreciative, decidedly male sigh. Men didn't sigh, he reminded himself. They groaned. So he did, loudly, the moment her flesh met his. A breeze from the bay stirred the scents of the Wharf—a pungent mixture of sea, salt and sunbaked sails—then swirled around this alluring woman who wore a crisp perfume that beat the bitter smells into submission. She stepped out of his car, her long bare legs on stiletto heels appearing first, and challenged him a wink.

"I asked you to dress comfortably," he reminded her, not the least bit disappointed that she'd blatantly disobeyed.

"I'm comfortable. Aren't you?" She smoothed her hands down her skintight skirt, a long swath of black silk with a slit up the thigh that might have showed her panties had she been wearing any.

Her tone had been innocent. Her glance had been innocent. Even her fluttering eyelashes contrasted with her tight red sweater and come-hither smile.

"You're going to be cold," he answered, sure that she knew how...uncomfortable she was making him.

She threaded her arms into his jacket, her hands skimming beneath the hem of his sweatshirt. "You'll have to warm me up. I told you I needed to know where we were going in order to dress appropriately."

Max leaned in and grabbed her leather coat, helped her shrug into it, then slammed her door shut and engaged the alarm without breaking from her touch. He'd have to let her go in a minute, but right now he was enjoying the sensations entirely too much.

The entire day had been a feast for the senses. First, they'd dressed and toured Chinatown. Ariana introduced him around, showed him the sights few people except those who lived there knew, introduced him to tastes and textures that had nothing to do with sex, but ended up heightening his already charged libido nonetheless. He'd learned a few phrases in Chinese and laughed with the locals at his poor pronunciation. He'd tasted specially prepared squid and sipped the hottest, most potent sake ever distilled. By the time they returned to her room atop Mrs. Li's shop, they were full and drunk and giddy.

With the box of condoms they'd bought at the first drugstore they found, they'd made love on the throw pillows, then fallen asleep, waking just as the last of the San Francisco fog melted into the night.

Max believed it was his turn to show Ariana something she'd never seen, so after a quick phone call and a stop at his house for a change of clothes, they'd parked near Pier 31 and now strolled up the wooden dock toward slip number 12.

The hushed squawk of night-flying gulls and the gentle clang of halyards and rigging accompanied the splashing ocean to create a musical quiet. Ariana shivered and hugged close to him. She was nowhere near dressed for a night cruise on the bay, but after she learned her lesson in taking his advice, he'd do as she'd asked and warm her.

"You have a boat?" she asked, grabbing his hand as he stepped over a thick rope lying across the walkway.

"Watch your step. Sort of. The boat is in my name."

She nearly slipped on a wet patch of wood. He was tempted to lift her into his arms and carry her the rest of the way, but was going to have a hard enough time explaining Ariana to his brother who waited for them aboard their yacht, the *Oakland Dreamer*.

Ford would more than appreciate Ariana's exotic beauty, enhanced by her clothes and by the glow of having more than one orgasm in the past twenty-four hours. For a moment, Max wondered how many women Ford had carried onto their boat for a midnight liaison. More than likely, his baby brother didn't even bother to cast off. But Max had more to show Ariana than just the soft bed in the master cabin. He wanted her to see the city, lit up and sparkling against the wind-roughened bay—the image he'd first seen as a child that had contributed to making him the man he had become.

"I hope you have a lot of energy, mister. Warming me up will be no easy task." Frustrated with her slippery progress, Ariana tugged off her sandals, wincing when her feet met the chilled wood.

"Maybe you're going sailing with the wrong brother, then," Ford claimed from above.

Max glanced up to find Ford leaning over the flybridge of their sixty-foot cabin cruiser, securing a line Max knew must be important though he had never taken the time to learn much about his floating investment. So long as Ford brought the boat back from charter fishing trips and pleasure cruises in good working order, Max normally ignored the operation all together. Ford wasn't making them any richer, but he was happy and out of trouble, which was the reason Max bought the boat in the first place.

He nodded at Ariana, indicating that this was the brother he'd warned her about and that if she had a clever comeback to his insinuating insult, she was more than welcome to return the volley.

"You must be Ford," Ariana said simply, obviously not wanting to play into their brotherly feud.

Ford slid down the ladder to the main deck, looking every bit the modern-day pirate with his windblown, shaggy blond hair and twinkling eyes. He'd obviously shaved for the wedding that never happened this morning, but he still managed to exude pure rogue charm wearing nothing but a wetsuit. He held out his hand when Ariana came closer. "I'll be anyone you want me to be, sweetheart."

Ariana stuck out her tongue as though she was gagging. "How about being original? That line was banned for overuse about ten years ago."

Zing. Max grinned while Ford faked an injury to the heart, then took her hand and helped her on board.

"My brother told me you were different."

"I said *special,* Ford. Ariana is special. Mind your manners. Your job is simple. Take us out on the bay. You can do that, can't you?"

Ford chuckled and helped them both aboard. In minutes, the dual engines roared to life, a growling echo in a marina normally silent at this time of night. Max freed the bow from its mooring then joined Ariana.

She stood on the aft deck, hugging her leather coat close to her body as Ford eased the boat out of the slip and puttered slowly toward the bay. Max had two choices: pretend to know what he was doing enough to help his brother maneuver out to sea, or practice what he did know—warming Ariana. He motioned for her to come in closer to the cabin where the wind, already slashing against them before they even left the protection of the marina, would be buffered by the fiberglass walls.

"You could have told me we were going out on the bay," she mumbled, only half complaining as he pulled her full against him.

"I didn't want to ruin the surprise. You're not afraid of the water, are you?"

She smirked. "Isn't my fear of heights enough? I love the water. More specifically, I love looking at the water, sailing on the water. But let's not forget that San Francisco Bay is shark-infested."

He leaned down and nibbled her neck, blazing a path across her throat where his chin rubbed against her cleavage. "So I've heard."

She pulled back enough to meet his gaze. "Maybe this boat is shark-infested, too. You should see the look in your eyes. I'm feeling somewhat like shark bait right now."

"You don't look like bait. You look utterly amazing. And you taste...fantastically...delicious." With a sharklike strike, he returned to nipping her neck. She laughed and tugged his hair, the sound of utter freedom urging him. Rewarding him. He shrugged out of his jacket and pulled it around her shoulders. He no longer needed the extra layer to keep the chill away.

He was hot, and getting hotter. The slap of the wind and the spray from the waves as Ford increased the boat's speed into open waters acted like agents of fire, spreading the sensual conflagration until he was sure he'd burn with wanting. He wanted to make love to her. Here. On deck. With the rock of the waves to give rhythm to their instinctual tempo.

And he would. As soon as he got rid of Ford.

They kissed and teased and touched and played until his brother slowed the boat and idled the engine. When Ford climbed down from the elevated helm, he took one look at Ariana and Max as he headed toward the bow to lower the anchor and smiled from ear to ear.

"Lady, I don't know what you've done to my brother, but keep doing it. I haven't seen him this loose since he was six and sniffed a little too much Elmer's glue."

Max socked Ford in the arm as he passed, causing Ford to howl with unbridled laughter.

"Damn, bro! You haven't hit me since you were six, either. When I was a pain," he said to Ariana, conspiratorially angling his hand across his mouth as if Max couldn't hear him, "he used to steal my allowance. Then he'd invest it. T-bonds. Blue chips. I'm not kidding."

Max put his arm around Ari's waist, hoping to shield her somehow from the truth of his carefully planned and executed childhood, which led him to his carefully planned and executed life. "We had quite a portfolio by the time I turned sixteen, if I remember," Max reminded him.

"Yeah, well…" Ford hedged, not the least comfortable with any point conceded, however true. "I would have rather had baseball cards and bubblegum."

"Baseball cards and bubblegum wouldn't have paid for a nice chunk of our college tuition," Max chimed, shaking his head. He loved his brother, he honestly and truly did, but he didn't understand how they could have been raised in the same household. Ford was in a constant state of laid-back, roll-with-the-flow relaxation while Max was in a perpetual siege of uptight, concentrated energy. At least he normally was. With Ariana around, he was acting more like Ford—and he was beginning to recognize the appeal.

Ariana obviously sensed an argument brewing, so she stepped between them while cuddling closer to Max. "Now, that would depend on the baseball card, wouldn't it? People pay millions for some of the rare ones."

Ford's smile defined smugness.

"Don't encourage him, Ari. He's a hopeless nomad as it is. This boat is the only way I keep him in one place." Max glanced out at the expanse of bay and ocean that was his brother's workplace. "Relatively speaking."

"Yeah, well, if you didn't finance my boat, you wouldn't have your own midnight charter cruise and captain, would you?"

"Actually, we could do without the captain."

Ford scanned the sky, which was clear and full of bright, twinkling stars. Not a cloud in sight. Max grinned. He was not in the least bit qualified to captain this boat, but he did know the basics—how to untie the moorings, where to find the life jackets, how to turn the engine and bilge pump on and off and how to use the radio to send an SOS. He doubted he and Ariana would get into any trouble he couldn't handle on his own.

At least, none of the nautical kind.

"I was just leaving," Ford murmured. He lifted the top of a padded seat and pulled out a life jacket, shrugging into it and securing the straps. "I stocked the galley after you called. Ariana, I have a big, warm, hooded sweatshirt hanging on the back of my door. Down the steps, first cabin on your right."

Ariana thanked Ford, then grinned at Max, smirking at the smoothness with which his brother had dismissed her. Yet without a word, she braced her hands on the railings and made her way out of earshot. He and his brother did have a few things to talk about.

"I had a great time at your reception," Ford said by way of getting straight to the heart of the matter. "Got the phone numbers of two bridesmaids and several of Maddie's cousins."

"Then why aren't *you* using the boat tonight?" Max quipped, not entirely sure which part of the truth he wanted to tell his brother.

Ford shook his head. "Who says I'm not already through? But that's not the point, Maxie, and you know it. Who is she?" He gestured toward the cabin. "And where the hell is Maddie?"

Max groaned, then went to the stern to help Ford release the WaveRunner from its compartment to aid his departure. "I don't know where Maddie is, but she's the one who told her parents we eloped. She called me last night, just around midnight, and left a message on my car phone."

"On your car phone? Why didn't she call your house?"

"I suppose she wanted to make sure she was long gone before I even knew she was missing."

"Mom and Dad are going to be disappointed. They really liked Maddie."

"She's not dead, Ford. She's gone to find herself. Her lie just bought her some time. I respect her ingenuity."

Ford nodded, obviously impressed himself. "Man, but the shit's gonna hit the fan when Randolph and Barbara catch on. You should have seen them this afternoon. They played king and queen of the kingdom to the hilt."

Max laughed. His brother had guessed a long time ago that Maddie and Max's decision to marry wasn't because they were in love. Ford had accepted their plan in his usual, laid-back style, somewhat entertained and re-signed to watch the events unfold. "If you came to more family gatherings, you'd know that Randolph and Barbara Burrows play king and queen all day, every day. I'm sure Maddie will return ready and willing to handle them. I just hope she realizes she'd better get back here in a week. I can't disappear forever."

"Sure you can, bro. You just *won't*. Too many deals brewing."

"I'd say 'I have my goals, you have yours,' but that would only be half-true," he quipped. He heard Ari closing a door belowdecks and remembered he had better things to do than berate his brother for the lack of direction in his life. "Don't come back until after sunrise, okay? *Long* after sunrise."

Ford climbed onto the WaveRunner and held out his hand to accept Max's keys. Although it wasn't legal, Ford lived on the boat. If Max wanted him out of the picture for the night, he'd have to relinquish his car and house in trade.

"You still haven't told me who this Ariana is," Ford reminded him while he unzipped a pocket on the life jacket and stuffed the keys inside.

Max considered his next words carefully. What could he tell his brother about this woman that wasn't an intimate secret? A sensual confidence? Wasn't that all he really knew about her? Those things private and personal and not open to discussion?

"She's someone I know," Max answered. "Someone who in one day has shown me more about me…more about this city…than anyone I've ever known. I just want to return the favor."

ARIANA HEARD THE ROAR of a smaller engine and climbed back on deck in time to see Ford skim away on a personal water vehicle. Max was nowhere in sight. Except for the quiet hum of the retreating vehicle and the lapping of waves against the fiberglass hull, the night was soundless.

Then she heard music—cool jazz sung in dulcet tones and accompanied by a saxophone so mournful, she closed her eyes while the emotions rocked her. A moment passed before she heard Max climb down from the helm where he'd turned the on-board stereo.

He looked somewhat disappointed that she'd done as Ford suggested and traded her tight red sweater and sleek leather coat for his battered but surprisingly clean San Francisco Giants sweatshirt, size extra, extra large. The soft fleece swallowed her from shoulders to just above her knees, and though she'd rolled the sleeves at the wrist, her hands were still hidden in folds of gray. But she was warm. And judging by the hungry look in Max's eyes, she was about to get warmer.

"Where's Ford?" she asked, knowing he was gone but fishing for information about the timing of his return.

"I threw him to the sharks."

"Ha, ha. I saw him on the WaveRunner. That's incredibly dangerous, you know. Going out without a wetsuit at night."

"Ford lives for danger, Ari. And he's good on that thing. He's just going back to the dock, where he'll take my car to my house and live a life of luxury, which he won't appreciate. He'll come back in the morning. We have all night."

She couldn't help but smile as she smoothed her hand across the polished railing, then stretched her fingers toward the sky. "*This* is luxury. The night. The chill. The waves and wind and rush of being alone just far enough from the city where we won't be disturbed, but close enough to see the skyline in all its glory."

"Good point. What are we waiting for?"

Max took her hand and led her around to the bow. They were moored just off Sausalito, close enough to see the Golden Gate, yet far enough so they didn't hear the hum and whir of cars and trucks crossing over. The skyline rose like a mountain range of twinkling shadows. Transfixed by the awesome beauty of the city, Ariana barely felt him lead her back onto a cushioned seat until she was cradled in the V between his thighs.

"This is wonderful, Max. Thank you."

"No. Thank you. It's been a long time since I saw the city from here."

The wistful, sad timbre of his voice clued Ariana that more was at play here than the glittering lights of the skyline.

"How long?"

Max pulled in a deep breath, pausing while his gaze became lost in a tunnel of time. "I was nine. My grandparents had come from Florida and took Ford and me on a night cruise, a real tourist tour. We'd been living with my aunt and uncle in Palo Alto and I think they needed a break."

"Where were your parents?"

It seemed a natural question to ask, but the moment the query tumbled from her lips, his chest stiffened. She turned in time to meet his tortured gaze.

"You don't have to answer," she said quickly, regretting that she'd delved into some painful part of his past. Not because she didn't want to know everything about him—she did. She just hadn't expected to stir up such an obviously difficult memory. "I didn't mean to pry."

She grabbed his wrists and pulled his arms tight around her. After a moment, he relaxed.

"It's okay. My parents were back in Oakland. My father drove a cab for a living and he'd been shot by a robber."

"Oh, my God! Max, I'm…"

"He was okay, but he couldn't work for over a year. Mom was a public school teacher and she had to quit her job to nurse him. There wasn't enough money to feed and clothe two growing boys, so we made the rounds of the relatives."

Ariana's heart pumped hard, bleeding for the little boy who'd known a poverty and loneliness she couldn't imagine. Though her family had been stifling to her as she approached adulthood, her time as a child had always been secure.

"No wonder you're such a driven businessman."

Max chuckled, but the cadence lacked any real humor. "You don't know the half of it. My grandparents told us on that boat tour that if my father didn't return to work soon, we'd have to go to Florida with them. They acted like Walt Disney World and sandy white beaches would make abandoning my parents all okay."

He buried his face in her hair, inhaling the scent of her shampoo. She nuzzled back into him. He was baring his soul to her. She wanted deeply to offer at least a silent comfort.

"I was so angry. You should have heard me—nine years old—negotiating a loan with my mother's father, estimating the costs of supporting two boys and then adding on the expenses of a family on disability and welfare. He was so impressed, he brought us back to our parents and took out a second mortgage to help us out."

Ariana's chest eased at the sound of pride in his voice. "So you started working to pay back the debt yourself."

"I sold newspapers, ran errands, collected bottles for deposits and, later, cans for recycling. I learned about investing and the stock market from a banker whose shoes I used to shine. By the time I was in high school, I knew the big bucks were in real estate. So, here I am."

Yes, here he was—a man more complicated than she'd ever imagined, driven by the wounds of poverty and separation from his family to make an indelible mark on the financial world. She could now understand why a marriage of convenience to a wealthy, connected woman would fit with his needs, both professional and private.

"Here we are," he said. "We've got the view, each other, no money worries and six days to enjoy the city."

Realizing he sought to restore the playful mood of their excursion with a lighthearted tone, she rewarded him with a seductive shimmy.

He responded in kind, sliding his hands down her silky skirt. The heat from his palms contrasted completely with the icy wind slithering through the thigh-high slit. He then ventured beneath the hem of the sweatshirt, bunching the material as he inched up past the waistband of her skirt. With the cold air swirling just on the other side of the thick cotton, his hands exuded pure fire. His fingers teased the lower swells of both breasts. When he skimmed her nipples, they were hard.

He sucked in a breath, moaning his pleasure at her arousal. "You're very cold." Nuzzling her neck through her hair, he plucked and pleased and toyed. In one afternoon, he'd learned exactly how to touch her. Exactly how to start that liquid pounding between her thighs, that rainbow euphoria that made her lose her mind.

Then tonight, he'd let her glimpse into his heart—into his soul. A powerful aphrodisiac she couldn't—wouldn't—fight. Nestled in his lap, she could feel the strain of his erection against her back. Memories of making love to him on his balcony—facing the view, with him deep inside her—kicked up her response to his gentle foreplay another notch. If he continued, she'd come right here, right now, with him doing no more than touching her breasts and kissing her neck.

"You're...making me...hotter," she said between gasps.

"That's the idea."

Moisture trickled down, kissing her inner thigh. "Too hot."

"No such thing."

She scooted off the seat long enough to turn around and sling one leg over his thigh, her slit flashing open. "Sure there is. God, Max. I'm so close and we're both still dressed."

He inched through the opening of her skirt. "How close?"

His cat-in-the-cream smile and bold touch made her suck in her breath. She'd made a tactical error if she'd thought that admission would slow him down. Instead, he blazed a trail straight to the center of her need where his wind-chilled fingers met the wet desire he had stirred. She remained standing, half straddling him while he probed and parted her sensitive flesh.

"You feel so slick," he told her.

She braced her hands on his shoulders. "Max..." She could say only his name. Couldn't he see what he was doing to her? Did she really have to expend the energy to form a response?

"Mmm," he answered for her. "Feels good, doesn't it? So soft. So silky. So wet."

When he eased a finger inside her, she bit down a gasp. He played her with deep thrusts, rhythmic and round, rotating his touch until her knees started to buckle. He bunched up her skirt, exposing her to the elements in one cold flash, then yanked her fully onto his lap and pulled down the sweatshirt's hem.

Not once did he stop touching her, stroking her. The sweet pressure built. She couldn't wait.

"Come on, honey. Let me see you lose control. Here. With the city behind you. And me inside."

She shook her head, fighting the flashes of color, raging against the orgasm that was only moments away.

"You're not inside," she protested.

"I will be, sweetheart. Later. But right now I'm not stopping long enough to put on a condom. Not unless you want me to stop. Do you want me to stop?"

With a second finger, he stretched her, prepared her, forcing her over the edge. "No, Max. Don't…stop. Don't…"

She bit down hard as the convulsions began.

"We're in the middle of nowhere, Ari. Let me hear you. Let me hear you come—just from my touch."

She shook her head, but it was useless. Useless to deny Max anything he wanted. Anything at all. She gasped and shouted, unintelligible sounds, sounds she'd never heard spill from her own lips.

Yet judging by the look on Max's face as she collapsed into his arms, the payoff for her surrender would be worth the price.

10

HE DONNED PROTECTION in the time it took for her to catch her breath, then he was inside her, sex to sex, warm and wet and as wild as the bay rocking the boat.

She folded her knees up on the padded bench, drawing her closer; him, deeper. She set the tempo, but he gauged the depth. Splaying his hands on her cheeks, he pulled her mouth to his for a long, tongue-clashing kiss.

"Again. Please." She tossed her head back, crying his name. The sound tugged at him, sexually. Spiritually. She wanted him. Here and now and for no other reason than because they sought and gave pleasure, together. No ulterior motives. No hidden agendas or looming financial payoffs. Hard to the point of pain, he throbbed for release. He could think of nothing else, feel nothing else.

She sat up fully, nearly breaking their intimate link. The cold air stabbed at his bare skin. He clutched her bottom and pressed her down, sighing as heat enveloped him again.

He blinked, realizing he'd closed his eyes in preparation of the rapture. When he glanced up, she was watching him intently, her hands still bracing his face.

She rode him to her own primitive beat, her smile growing as passion stole his sight. But when he felt the end looming, he stole back the driver's seat.

"My turn, honey. Let me hear you again." He twisted, adjusting their position until he could go no deeper. She gasped and cried when he touched just the right spot.

Her shudders pushed him over the edge, into a place where only heat existed. Where the air was hot and thick and nearly impossible to breathe. He came with a mighty roar, his voice echoing across the water. He pulled her down for one last thrust, then held her steady, capturing her mouth as their orgasm ebbed and the cold air returned.

This time, she quaked from the cold, so he bundled her as best he could and carried her downstairs.

In minutes they were nude and nestled beneath the covers of the feathery, queen-size bed. With the cabin lights dimmed, only the stars and the shine from the city through the windows lit their gentle embrace. Shivers came in one strong wave along with chattering teeth that made them both laugh, which led to tickling, which led to touching, which led to one long, soft kiss that eventually drew them into a comfortable quiet.

"I can't believe we've made love this much in less than twenty-four hours," she said, snuggling closer and laying her cheek on his chest. "I'm not usually this horny."

"Must be the company you're keeping," he said smugly.

"No doubt." She twisted her fingers into the patch of hair at the center of his chest. "We're good together. I don't think that happens very often."

Max bit the inside of his mouth. No, it didn't happen very often. Not to him, anyway. Yeah, he'd had flings and affairs from time to time, but never like this, never with such an irreverent, carefree attitude. Never with pleasure and pleasing being his one and only agenda. Even in college, he'd chosen the girls who had the right connections, who could give him an edge in his classes with their knowledge or who could get him invited to the right parties with the right people. Not that he wasn't attracted to them or didn't like them individually, he just decided attraction and basic interest weren't enough.

Even when Maddie had pointed out the shallowness of his actions, he'd chosen to ignore her words. Ariana understood him, fully accepted what it was like for him to have to claw his way to success.

And judging by the way she'd responded, she was okay with his past. And why wouldn't she be? She'd worked her way up much as he had. But she'd also been married once. She hadn't completely ignored her personal life as he had. He couldn't help wondering how any man could have let this remarkable woman go.

"What about your husband? You must have been good together or you wouldn't have tied the knot."

She squirmed, but didn't pull away. "We were very attracted to each other. Rick was a sexy man. Unfortunately, you can't build a marriage on sex."

"Good thing for us," he said, wincing at the callous sound.

But she didn't hesitate to agree, which increased the sting tremendously. "Exactly. And you know, as sexy as he was, he never paid attention to what I liked. I was a virgin when I married him. He barely had to touch me and I'd come. After a while, my orgasms weren't so easy. But he wasn't interested in working on anybody's orgasms but his."

Max pulled her closer, amazed and pleased that she could speak with such candor. "The man was a fool."

She nodded, snuggling closer. "Yeah, that's what I figured out. Recently." Her mouth twisted into an ironic grin. "But by that time, I'd closed myself off to trying a relationship again. All I wanted was work, work, work. Success and more success. Now I've just about gotten what I want...and I've got you, to boot. For now."

Her gaze actually softened when she voiced yet again the temporary status of their affair. He expected something different—a touch of regret, a bit of melancholy. He swallowed a tiny taste of bitter disappointment.

"Don't worry, Max," she reassured him, misinterpreting his frown. "When I make a deal, I stick to it. You and I, we're great. But you have a whole life out there that I don't fit into. Connections and cotillions and million-dollar deals. In a way, I'm sorry Maddie and you didn't work out. She'd probably do that part real well."

"Don't sell yourself short, Ariana. You're a beautiful, charming, intelligent woman. The San Francisco elite would find you as breathtaking and fascinating as I do."

"Is that before or after my fourteen-hour day at the restaurant? When I come home smelling like a kitchen? Or worse, a bar? How breathtaking and fascinating is the woman who just got done mixing your Absolut and Evian? Come on, Max. Let's not weave some dream that won't come true."

Max's logical side conceded her point. They were from different worlds. Unfortunately, his ambitious side knew too well that clever, intelligent, determined people could successfully cross the chasm from one world to another. They only had to have the know-how. The desire.

"You and I are living proof that all sorts of wild dreams can come true," he pointed out. Moments ago, he'd subscribed to the same determination—to keep their affair temporary and brief. But the more he thought about it, the more he resented the emptiness in his personal life. Just this once, he wanted to try something new. Someone new. Ari.

The flash of apprehension widening her gaze told him now wasn't the time to make the suggestion. He'd bared his soul tonight and gained insight in the process. Insight into both of them.

"You're right." She eased her hand down his chest and explored until she found his sex. "We can create wild dreams." She encircled his shaft with her fingers, teasing below with her nails as she disappeared farther beneath the covers, trailing a path of openmouthed kisses over his nipples, down his abs, across his hips. "And they'll come true, all right."

"Ari…"

"Shh…" She let the elongated syllable tease his moistened tip with her hot breath. "No more talk, Max. No more talk."

He couldn't deny his desire any longer. They'd have time for conversation later. Much, much later.

FORD RETURNED TO THE BOAT after 10:00 a.m. By then, Ari had changed into a complete sweat suit and Max had served her a breakfast feast of cheese and canned fruit from a blanket spread on the bow. Ari guessed they'd slept two hours, maybe three. But she'd managed to make sure that each waking moment was filled with either sex talk or sex play and no more discussion of her marriage, her goals or her plans for the future.

Especially any future that included Max, enticing notion that it was. Even Ariana, a consummate dreamer, knew that some things were out of her realm. She couldn't stand to set herself up for something so pie-in-the-sky as a serious relationship with Max only to be crushed when his schedule, her schedule, his obligations, her obligations, his career, her career, clashed and warred and destroyed the special connection they'd formed in the past two days. She was too close to having everything she wanted to let love get in the way. Again.

She guessed that Max's canceled marriage was forcing him to take a long hard look at his life. She respected and admired him for latching on to the opportunity to take stock and consider changes, but dammit, she couldn't afford to let his self-assessments alter her own decisions.

When Ford docked and began his washing and gassing and whatever else seamen did to ready their vessels for the next cruise, Ariana considered saying goodbye to Max and grabbing a cab home. Despite spending an entire glorious night on the open sea, she had a strong urge for space. For just an hour or two.

Max beat her to the punch. "Why don't I drop you off at your place to pick up a change of clothes and take a nap? Then I'll take you out for dinner. Somewhere I'll have to pay some obscene amount of money to get us in since we have no reservations."

"Like a date?" she asked, tamping down a sigh of relief.

"Not *like* a date—a date. Flowers. Small talk. Good wine. No plan. No expectations. Just…fun."

The man was a master of true romance and he had absolutely no idea. Good. Because if he had any inkling of the power he wielded and he decided to seriously train his sights on her beyond this week, she'd be a goner for sure.

"Sounds wonderful. What do you feel like? Italian? French?"

He shook his head, taking her hand as he helped her off

the boat and they said goodbye and thanks to Ford. "Let me surprise you."

She hooked her arm around his waist as they walked, suddenly regretting that she'd entertained the idea, even for a minute, that her decision to be with Max might be wrong. When he concentrated his decision-making powers on her, the results were always incredible.

"It's worked quite well so far," she said.

"Oh, yeah. That it has."

MAX DROPPED HER OFF at the front of the tea shop, kissing her sweetly on the knuckles before she bundled her red sweater and silky skirt into her leather coat and watched him drive away. She hesitated, smoothing her hand against her cheek, imagining his scent still lingered on her skin.

"You're in trouble, girl," Mrs. Li announced the moment Ariana entered, engaging the jangling brass bell her landlady had strung along the top of the door.

"Excuse me?"

Ariana couldn't imagine what she could have done to offend Mrs. Li. They had no standing rules against having a lover stay over and, technically, Max hadn't slept in her apartment anyway. Glancing around the shop, she realized that, except for the three women sitting in the back sipping tea out of earshot, she and Mrs. Li were speaking privately.

"That look on your face. Trouble. Good trouble, but trouble anyway."

Ariana bit her lip and started to walk toward the stairwell in the back until she realized she'd have to pass by Mrs. Li's friends who were clucking over some article in the newspaper. In her experience, that trio was just as intuitive and nosy as the woman who collected her rent. They imparted advice at absolutely no charge, and until today, she hadn't minded hearing their perspectives.

She really didn't mind so much now, either. But she'd rather deal with one matron of experience than with four.

She moved to the counter where Mrs. Li was opening small wooden drawers filled with dried herbs, extracting some with a tiny metal spoon into a paper cup. "Is there such a thing as good trouble?" Ari asked.

"You answer me."

Ariana replayed the past two days in her mind, then went back farther. She thought back to the minute Charlie had deceived her about Max and his wedding, to her discovery of the magazine. The sexually charged flirtation in the bar. The surprise in Max's drink. Deception. Erotica. Illegal drugs. All trouble individually.

All wonderful when meshed together to result in her union with Max.

"Yeah, trouble can be good. Very good."

Mrs. Li nodded, pursing her lips sagely. "That's why trouble is trouble. Can be very good or can be bad. You have to be smart to keep it good." She tapped a finger to her temple and shook her head. "Not smart with your head." She lowered her finger to her chest, still tapping. "With your heart."

Ariana rolled her eyes. She wanted to keep her heart out of this. Her heart usually got her in the bad sort of trouble. "My heart isn't the organ I trust most."

Mrs. Li returned to scooping herbs into her cup. "If you don't trust your heart, it'll get broken for sure."

"It's been broken once. It mended."

Shoving the last drawer closed, Mrs. Li poured the herbs into the center of a sheet of butcher paper, then folded and tucked until she'd created a perfect square packet of her medicinal mixture. "Was it really broken? Or just bruised?"

"I loved Rick," she insisted. Rick had been Mrs. Li's boarder before Ariana came to live with him. Their landlady had baked the wedding cake they'd eaten after returning from the courthouse ceremony. She'd been there for Ariana after Rick left, nursed her with kind words and strong teas and sometimes-silent company until the pain of his abandonment subsided. How could she not know how devastated she'd been?

"I didn't say you didn't love him. But Rick never loved you back, not the way he should have. It's the man's love that truly tears the woman's heart apart, and vice versa."

After labeling the small square packet with a wax pencil, Mrs. Li tossed the order in an out basket and answered the summons from the back table to join them for tea. She invited Ariana, but Ari smiled and shook her head, too intrigued by Mrs. Li's words, too distressed by what might be happening between her and Max, to subject herself to chitchat with the ladies. She accepted the newspaper they were finished with and escaped upstairs as quickly as politeness would allow.

She tore through her living room quickly, not wanting the throw pillows and windows and tea sets to remind her of the decadence she and Max had enjoyed. She removed her borrowed sweats and tossed them into the mountain of dirty laundry on top of the hamper in her closet and dashed into the shower.

She was going to enjoy tonight. She was going to enjoy tonight without thinking about the damage Max could do to her—and she to him—if either of them succumbed to falling in love.

MAX PARKED IN HIS GARAGE, but closed the door from the outside so he could collect his newspaper and Saturday's mail from the boxes outside his front door. His brother, who'd stayed at his home the night before, had no interest in the goings-on of the world if they weren't printed in San Francisco's newest rag, *The Bay Insider,* so he wasn't surprised to see two days' of the more conservative *Chronicle* littering his porch.

After unlocking the front door, Max flipped through his mail while lights flickered on and off as he made his way into the kitchen. As expected, Ford had left a mess. Normally, Max didn't care. But he was all too aware that he'd given his housekeeper the week off, so he shoved his mail in the appropriate cubbyholes and collected the dirty dishes from the table, rinsed them then stacked them in the dishwasher.

He found *The Bay Insider* spread out on the kitchen table that looked down on the rest of Russian Hill through a wall of crisp windows. In a vain attempt to compete with the more venerable, long-established competition from the *Chronicle* and the *Examiner,* recently merged, the upstart newspaper was rife with gossip, innuendo and downright lies. Max scanned headlines as he folded Castro Club Owner Hot for Young Customers. Cruising the Embarcadero for Rich Sex. Then, atop a hazy picture of two people doing something rather up close and personal outside in the fog, he read, Prewedding Jitters?

Max lowered himself into the nearest chair. He forced his gaze away from the photograph—away from the shape of a woman with long, black hair—away from what appeared to be a bare breast peeking out of the heavy fog that curled over an outdoor balcony—and read the short square of text below.

San Francisco won't be shocked by lovers taking
liberties out in the open, but they might raise an eyebrow if they knew which respected, high-powered
real estate broker poised to tear into a city monu-
ment in the next few weeks was entertaining a lady
obviously not his fiancée on Friday night. The shot's
not clear, but the activity is. We can see the Forrest
through the trees, er, fog. Can you?

Holy shit.

Max read the caption again. Then again. He'd committed the words to memory by the time he registered the
sound of the telephone ringing. His answering machine
clicked on before he reached the receiver. The red number
blinking the number of messages changed from twenty to
twenty-one.

Hesitantly, Max lifted the receiver in time to hear Charlie's voice pleading, "…you gotta call me, Max, before
anyone else—"

"Charlie?"

"Max! Damn, where the hell have you been?"

"As if you didn't know," Max snapped. Despite his
horror over the caption in the paper, not to mention the
photo, hazy as it was, he still hadn't forgotten that Charlie's deceptions might have led him to the brink of this
current catastrophe.

Max knew his own balcony when he saw it. And all
that dark hair? Ariana's undoubtedly. Hell, he recognized
her breast. How could he not when he'd spent hours upon
hours in the past two days exploring and enjoying every
inch of her body?

He swallowed, forcing the stone of rage that had formed
in his throat to settle in the pit of his stomach.

"I called her restaurant," Charlie explained. "No one answered."

"They're closed for renovation. You know that, you lying son of a bitch."

Charlie groaned. "Her number's not listed."

"Get your ass over here, Charlie. Now."

Max's mouth twitched as he heard the click on the other end of the line. Almost hypnotically, he dropped the receiver back into the cradle and watched the red number blink and blink. How many of those calls were from Charlie? How many from Randolph Burrows? Or his other investors? How many from the owners of the Pier, the owners he'd enticed to the property? These people were new-monied, upstart capitalists who were more concerned with using this project to buy their way into San Francisco respectability than with the cash they'd make on the development deal. They were a cautious group that had nearly balked at the first sign of controversy over Max's brilliant plan to convert the Pier, currently used for commercial fishermen, into a classy, slick collection of high-end nightspots and shops to compete with the carnival-like tourist draw at Pier 39.

Max backed away from the answering machine. If his ass was going to be chewed out on recorded cassette tape, he sure as hell wasn't going to listen without Charlie there to suffer every word with him. He might not have been on that balcony with Ariana if not for Charlie's lies.

The rustle of newsprint alerted him that he was still clutching the paper in his hand. He scanned the photograph again. Must have been Friday night—the night he couldn't remember.

He couldn't see her face, but he knew it was her. He slumped into a chair by the window and looked closely.

He saw a hand. His hand. Palm flat against the Plexiglas that surrounded his balcony.

Closing his eyes, Max tried to stir up one memory, one sensation that might make this scandal-in-the-making worthwhile. He shook his head, realizing he didn't need to remember the deed to justify the risk. He had the past two days of clear and crisp memories to erase any inkling of regret.

He felt no repentance for one instant with Ariana, erotic or otherwise. But he sure as hell didn't want to lose this deal.

And he didn't want to lose her. Not until the appointed time, when he'd have no choice. They'd agreed to a week-long-only affair, and though he'd already entertained several schemes to see her well beyond the deadline, she'd made it more than clear last night that she preferred they adhere to the original plan. He shook his head and plopped into a nearby chair. When she saw this picture, she might call off their affair right here and now.

When she saw this picture...

Max dashed to the phone, then realized that, like Charlie, he didn't have her phone number. He did, however, know the name of Mrs. Li's shop, so after a quick call to Information, he waited for the connection to go through.

"Lin Li, Herb Shop," Mrs. Li answered in her brisk, efficient English.

"Mrs. Li? This is Maxwell Forrester, Ariana's friend."

The woman chuckled lightly. "More than a friend, I think. What can I do for you? Interested in more of my tea, maybe?"

Max was tempted to ask her if she had one that included strychnine as an ingredient—something he could serve to Charlie—but he didn't know the woman well enough that she'd understand his black humor. He did, however, understand that if he was going to ask her for a favor, he'd better make it worth her while.

"Actually, yes. I'd love to put together some gift baskets for my office staff. Four of them. Assorted teas, cups and such. I'm not sure what goes into one…"

"That's my job. Four baskets. I can do them for tomorrow. How much you want to spend?"

They negotiated a fair price and once Max was a few hundred dollars poorer, he finally asked Mrs. Li to give Ariana his phone number and instruct her to call him right away.

"Sounds important," Mrs. Li commented without bothering to hide the sound of her worry.

"Yes, ma'am. It is."

"Then I'll bring her the message immediately."

Max hung up and stalked upstairs, showered in record time, then stood in a towel scanning his closet while he wondered what the hell he was going to do. Charlie's knock on the door answered his dilemma for him.

"Get in here."

Charlie walked in sheepishly, a copy of *The Bay Insider* neatly folded and clutched beneath his arm. He shut and locked the door behind him.

"No reporters lingering on your doorstep," Charlie announced brightly. "That's a good sign."

"It's Sunday. Give them time. Fix me a scotch and then meet me upstairs. I'm going to get dressed."

He was slightly concerned that Ariana hadn't yet called, but only fifteen minutes or so had elapsed since he'd given Mrs. Li the message.

"You're going out?" Charlie sounded as shocked as Max was, but Max waved away his surprise and bounded up the stairs. He'd promised Ariana a real date. And judging by the chaos she was about to be plunged into, he owed her at least that much. He would pick some out-of-the-way, very dark restaurant—one not likely to be frequented by anyone who would understand the barely hidden references in the photograph's caption.

He'd donned his underwear and a pair of pants by the time Charlie came up with his drink.

"There's nothing in here, is there?" Max asked, eyeing his supposed friend warily to gauge his reaction.

All he saw was confusion. "I put ice... Isn't that how you like it?"

Max swirled the gold liquid. Ice clinked against the crystal. The sound was way too innocent and delicate for the situation.

"Yeah, it's how I like it. Doesn't mean you wouldn't add a little something...like on Friday night maybe? Something to make me relax. Take a certain restaurant owner home? Miss my wedding to your cousin...a wedding you didn't approve of?"

Charlie looked down at his hands, then once he'd strung Max's hints together, shot him an incredulous, offended glare. "What the hell are you implying?"

"Someone slipped me a Mickey on Friday night. Probably laced my beer...that beer *you* insisted we stay late to have."

"Max, man, I'm a schemer, I admit that. I told Ariana a few choice lies to get her to make a move on you...but I wouldn't put something dangerous in your drink. What if you were allergic?"

Max weighed Charlie's logic with his obvious sincerity and the fact that Charlie had a list of allergies as long as the real estate listings he represented in northern California.

"Well, someone put something in my drink."

Charlie hesitated. "Ariana, maybe?"

"No. It happened before she made me that flaming drink, probably before she arrived. Whoever did it knew I was going to be at the bar. And only *you* knew that."

"It wasn't me, Max."

Max glanced at the newspaper, now spread across his bed. Who would have been watching him? Training a camera lens on his balcony at some time after midnight? The fog had obviously been thick that night. It's not as though a neighbor or some passerby could have seen what was happening and alerted the newspaper. A chill ran up his spine and tingled the damp ends of his hair.

Someone had been following him. Was *still* following him? As he toured Chinatown with Ariana? As he pleasured her on the windowsill or made love in the open waters of San Francisco Bay?

The phone rang and Max grabbed the receiver without considering that anyone but Ariana might be on the other end.

Ariana sounded winded and drowsy, as if Mrs. Li had roused her from sleep. "Max, what's wrong?"

"Do you read *The Bay Insider?*"

"The newspaper?" She sighed, sounded more relieved than she would in a few moments. "Yeah, usually. Not today. I was taking a nap. Mrs. Li said you called. I thought something was wrong."

"Something is wrong. Do you have a copy of today's edition?"

He heard a rustle of newsprint, and though he called

her name, she'd obviously taken the receiver away from her ear to grab the paper.

"Here," she said once she returned. "I picked up Mrs. Li's copy on the way up. What's in here that…" Her voice died away before he could explain or warn her. "Oh…my… God."

"Ariana, relax. No one can tell who you are. The caption doesn't even allude to your name at all. Just me."

"Oh…my…God," she repeated. "That's…oh…my…"

With a high-pitched beep, she disconnected the call.

_11_

"DAMMIT! SHE HUNG UP!" Max clutched the phone until he heard the casing begin to crack, then slammed the impotent device on the bed. "I can't imagine what she's thinking right now."

"Call her back," Charlie snapped.

"I don't have her number. And I don't want her landlady asking more questions. I don't want Ari any more embarrassed by this than she already is."

"You don't need to call her landlady." Charlie scooped the cordless from atop the comforter. He punched in *69, the code that would identify the number of the last person who called. He pressed the number for automatic redial and handed the phone to Max.

"You're way too clever," Max groused. "You sure you didn't orchestrate this mess I'm in?"

"Why would I, Max? I'd never hurt Ariana this way. The two of you were supposed to be happy together." When Max scowled at his friend's magnanimous, lofty intentions, Charlie grunted and amended his claim. "I don't want you to lose that deal—or my part of the commission."

As the phone trilled with unanswered rings, Max accepted that Charlie wasn't lying—this time. Sure, he didn't want Max and Maddie to marry and make what Max now knew would have been a horrible mistake for both of them, but Charlie would no sooner jeopardize a deal than he would cut off his right hand.

"She's not answering," Max announced, swearing as he disconnected the call. "I need to see her."

He shot back into his closet, pulled out a crisp, white, button-down shirt, glanced down at his khaki slacks and blanched. Two days ago, his predictable, classically *GQ* casual wardrobe wouldn't have bothered him. But now he'd tasted the flavors of the unexpected, savored the richness of living outside the box. Potential scandal or not, Ariana would never forgive the old Max if he went charging into her apartment as the man he was before.

He dug a little deeper, hissing out a triumphant "Yes!" when he found the laundry Ford had left at Max's house after the engagement party he'd hosted a month ago. He'd had it all cleaned, of course, and, knowing Ford, he didn't even realize his clothes were missing. Well, Max would put them to good use.

He took a long swig of his scotch before unbuckling his pants to change.

"You can't leave now, Max. We've got damage control to plan. Have you checked your voice mail? Have any of the investors—"

"I don't give a rat's ass about the investors right now, Charlie. But if you're so concerned, go to the kitchen to check my machine and then call into my office voice mail." He gave Charlie the password. "But do it quick. I'll be ready to go in ten minutes, and you're coming with me."

"With you? To see Ariana? I'd think I'm the last person she'd want to see right now."

Max shook his head. "Second to last. But you're coming. You're going to tell Ariana—and me—the whole story of your involvement in Friday night. Then you're going to help us figure out why someone was taking pictures of us."

"Will I make it out alive?"

Max turned away and dressed, his expression doubtful. He'd known Ariana Karas intimately for only two days, but he respected her Mediterranean temperament and her justification in letting loose on both of them. *He* and Charlie were about to charge into the den of a wounded lioness, but they had no other choice. He had no other choice. He'd agreed to let her go at the end of the week, but not like this. Not with hurt and betrayal between them. And maybe not at all.

ARIANA READ THE CAPTION again. She'd lost count of exactly how many times she'd read the words—sometimes silently, sometimes aloud—but the exact number didn't matter. Little by little, she'd broken through the haze of her disgrace and realized she was being used.

Not by Max, but because of him. Maxwell Forrester was the "Forrest" the writer referred to. In her opinion, that reference wasn't the least bit clever, but the words were certainly laced with disdain and mockery. Obviously, Max had been working on some controversial development deal, something that angered someone enough to want to dig up dirt and print it in San Francisco's newest daily. But had it angered that someone enough to drug Max and set him up for that picture to be taken?

Either way, she'd been caught in the crossfire.

The risk you take, she told herself, *when you mess with a man outside your world. A rich, famous man.* But hell, it wasn't as if Max was a movie star or a political figure. He was a businessman doing his job. Was someone out to make him look bad and screw up one of his business deals? Or was this just someone's sick idea of a joke?

Well, Ari wasn't laughing.

She tore through the pages of the newspaper for the name of the editor and the number to the newsroom and ripped the masthead out. No use calling today, a Sunday. She certainly didn't want to deliver her oration on yellow journalism to an answering machine. But they'd hear from her tomorrow. Maybe in person.

And then what? They'd know who that breast belonged to, wouldn't they? Maybe they'd print another picture, one that showed her face, run a story about her and her restaurant and her family.

She crumpled the torn piece of newspaper and pitched it across her tiny kitchen into the sink. No righteous indignation for her.

But where did that leave her and Max?

She had no time to consider the big question; her thoughts were interrupted by someone knocking on her door. Just short of pounding, the raps were insistent, hurried. Desperate.

Max.

She shot up from the table, then slowed down as she crossed into the living room. She tightened the sash on her robe. The pink one. The one Max had seen earlier. The one he'd loosened as she sat on the windowsill so he could kiss her ever so intimately. She let the beautiful image flow over her, reliving the sweet sensations, when the knocks started again. She wouldn't fall into his arms for comfort, she promised herself. She wouldn't. They'd already become much closer than she planned in only two days. Maybe now was the perfect time to call things off and escape relatively unscathed.

Maybe…

After a quick peek through the peephole, she flipped the locks and opened the door.

"You got here fast," she said by way of greeting. She'd already turned away and plopped onto the couch before she realized that Max wasn't alone. Charlie sheepishly followed Max inside and shut the door.

"Well, look who it is," Ariana said as she pulled her lapels closer and eyed Charlie from head to toe. "Benedict Arnold, reincarnated just in time to ruin my life."

Max bit back a chuckle and, deep inside, breathed a sigh of relief. If she still had her sense of humor somewhat intact, he still had a chance to repair the damage.

"I asked Charlie to come and explain what happened Friday night."

"I didn't drug Max," Charlie explained quickly, picking that detail out as the most important. Max believed him. Charlie wouldn't do something so dangerously reckless.

"Then who did?" she asked.

Max moved around the coffee table and sat on the cushions beside Ariana. The scent of incense still hung heavy in the room; the scent of sweet jasmine still radiated from her skin. He ached to take her hand in his, walk her through this situation gently, but she clenched her fingers in a tight ball on her lap and impaled him with an impatient look.

"We don't know," he answered.

"Look," Charlie said, practically pleading. "Maddie just asked me to keep Max at the restaurant long enough for her to make her getaway."

"Maddie!"

Max and Ariana shouted the name in unison.

"You *knew* Maddie was going to bolt?" Max asked, needing clarification. He and Charlie had spent the car ride to Chinatown reviewing the business-related messages Max had received and discussing how they were going to ease this situation for Ariana. They hadn't had a chance to go over the facts beyond that. This revelation certainly hit Max unprepared.

He'd assumed Madelyn's disappearance had been spontaneous, but now that he thought about it, that didn't make sense, either. Weaving the tale of the elopement to cover her trail had been brilliant—and required preplanning. He'd known Madelyn for many years and spontaneity wasn't her forte. She'd made quite a few stupid decisions when backed into a corner. "Since when? When, Charlie? When did you know?"

Max was about to stand when Ariana laid her hand on his knee. The gesture wasn't calming, as she'd obviously intended. But it sure as hell stopped him dead. A surge of something electric—a mixture of relief and desire—shot from her warm palm directly into his skin. He fell back into the cushions, his anger inoculated.

"About a month ago," Charlie answered once he realized he was safe and didn't need to shoot for the door. "Maddie wanted to call off the wedding, tell you she'd made a huge mistake, but she didn't know how."

"That's bull!" Max insisted. "Maddie could tell me anything. She knew why we were getting married. Hell, it was her idea! It's not like she was going to break my heart."

"No, but she might have broken up the deal for Pier Nine. At that point, you'd sunk a lot of capital into it and, like it or not, her father and his bank control most of your investment funds. She was afraid that if she called off the wedding, something she knew you'd agree to, Uncle Randolph would take it out on you by torpedoing the deal. She knows how much the Pier means to you."

Max pressed his lips together, silenced by the truth. Luckily, Ariana had questions of her own to fill the void while he mulled over Maddie's collusion in this potential catastrophe.

"And how did I play into this?" Ari asked. "Did Maddie handpick me?"

"No. You were my idea. I've spent the past two years watching Max stare at you, watching him pretend he wasn't salivating every time you walked through the restaurant or stopped at our table. I just figured I'd play matchmaker. That simple. I had the opportunity. I took it."

Charlie stepped forward and knelt by the coffee table, as close to Ari's feet as he could. "I swear on my mother's grave. I just wanted the two of you to be happy."

Ari's ebony eyes narrowed. "Is his mother really dead?" she asked Max, obviously wondering how to gauge his friend's sincerity.

"Since he was twenty," Max answered with a bittersweet grin. "And from what I hear, she was a very good woman."

Ariana's lips twisted into a reluctant grin. "I'm sorry for your loss." Then she grabbed his shirt at the chest, twisting the cotton around her hand. "But if you ever lie to me again, Charlie Burrows—if that is indeed your real name—I'll light you up the same way I do my Flaming Eros, understand?"

Charlie grinned and stood, smoothing out the crinkles in his shirt. "Yes, ma'am."

"So, now what?" she asked, breaking her eye contact with Charlie to lock an expectant stare on Max.

"Now *I* apologize," Max said. "I didn't mean for your picture…"

She pulled her robe more closed. "Let's not talk about the picture, okay? Like you said on the phone, no one can tell it's me." She squirmed and her gaze darted at Charlie, then back to Max.

Charlie didn't miss the hint. "Maybe I should leave you two alone. I'm going to drop by Uncle Randolph and Aunt Barbara's house. See what they know."

Max nodded. None of the messages on his machine were from Randolph Burrows. Ten calls were from Charlie. Two were from his secretary, who read *The Bay Insider* daily, and accurately read through the hidden meaning in the caption, but angel that she was, assumed the picture was a fake. Several others were congratulatory messages from wedding guests who'd gotten word of the elopement and couldn't make the ceremony since the bride and groom weren't going to be there. None yet from any investors or the owners of the Pier. The picture had done no damage—so far.

"Tomorrow is Memorial Day," Max reminded them. "Most offices are closed. We have until Tuesday before we can really find out what's going on. Most of our investors are loyal to the *Examiner* and the *Chronicle*. They won't read *The Bay Insider*. It's too young and hip. But they'll hear the news as soon as they get back to their offices."

"What do you want me to say when they start calling?" Charlie asked.

Max had absolutely no intention of going into the office and handling this himself. Yes, it was probably the prudent thing to do. But since Maddie had gone to all that trouble to create a week-long alibi, he wasn't going to screw things up with Ariana when he still had a chance to make things right.

"I'm going to get the hell out of town like I'm supposed to be. That's what you tell the investors. How could it be me in the picture if I'm in Hawaii? On my honeymoon?"

"You have a very distinct balcony, Max. These people know real estate."

"Then tell them the picture could have been taken a long time ago…before I owned the house. Or maybe it's Maddie and me. Our privacy was invaded and we're outraged. I don't care what you tell them, Charlie, just keep things as calm as you can for twenty-four hours. We'll check in then."

Max turned to Ariana and joined both her hands with his. "That is, if we're still a *we*. You still want to see the city with me?"

With a hint of a smile, Ariana bit her bottom lip imbuing Max with a surge of power and relief that had his heart beating hard against his chest. He didn't know what was happening to him. He'd been putting business and profit ahead of fun and pleasure since he was a child—a child old enough to realize that being poor meant you had little control over what happened to you. He'd been single-minded in his pursuit of wealth, his parents and brother being his only soft spot—a spot that eventually grew to include Maddie and Charlie. And now Ariana. And with Charlie newly married and Maddie exploring the world, Max felt the emptiness in his heart with magnified intensity. He couldn't let Ariana just slip away.

She grinned at him now with a smile half wicked, half resigned. "I think we should concentrate on the outlying areas of the city—those secret spots no one knows about—don't you?"

She still had her sense of humor. She still had her sense of adventure. The woman was unstoppable once she set her mind to something. If he could help it, he wouldn't hurt her again.

The door clicked closed as Charlie departed. A thousand separate concerns ricocheted through his brain. The first was the possibility that the photographer who had caught them on the balcony continued to follow them and had more pictures to share with the press—more ammunition to convince his investors that Max had faked his marriage, was a liar not to be trusted, was a cheat unfaithful to his wife. Who knew what other sickening spins someone with an agenda could put on his affair with Ariana to impugn his development deal?

But at the moment, Max didn't care. The moment his lips pressed against Ariana's soft mouth, the worries of his world dispersed in a puff of smoke.

LIKE TEENAGERS ON THE RUN, Ariana and Max stuffed a few essentials into one small bag, rented a convertible in her name, just in case, and took to the highway. As they pulled onto Highway 1 approaching the Golden Gate, Ariana leaned back into the buttery leather seat and closed her eyes, allowing the stiff wind to buffet her face. By the time they'd passed the tollbooth where people on the other side paid to enter the City by the Bay, she wasn't the least bit concerned with newspapers or scandals or real estate or bare breasts peeking through fog and Plexiglas. Anticipation for her next adventure with Max overrode any and all negative thoughts. She didn't even succumb to that unstoppable sensation of falling she usually experienced just thinking about going across the bridge, much less actually doing it. Max was doing amazing things to her fear of heights—first on the balcony and then at the window-sill. Max did amazing things to her, period.

She didn't remember ever feeling so free, so avid and impatient for adventure, since she'd boarded the plane to California all those years ago. She'd been wide-eyed and open to all experiences then. Ready to cast off the chains of her upbringing. But marriage to Rick had slowly taken most of the fight out of her—forced her to narrow the scope of her vision and energy on career goals only. She'd done damn well for herself, but now she clearly saw all she'd missed.

With Max, she fantasized she could take on the world—and win. If only she could keep Max around for longer than a week. Shaking her head, she forced the thought away. *Not today,* she insisted to herself, knowing that following that train of thought would lead to maudlin conclusions she didn't want to face.

Instead, she focused on the thrill of doing something new, something she'd wanted to do for years. As a restaurateur and bartender, she'd been invited to attend tastings and festivals in nearby Napa and Sonoma Valleys. The tourists in her restaurant raved about the beauty of the wine country, but she'd never had the time to go. Maybe she'd never made the time. Maybe she hadn't wanted to experience the rolling hills and fertile farmland by herself or with only business on her mind.

Thanks to Max, now she didn't have to.

"This is wonderful!" she shouted over the roar from the road. "I can't believe you booked us at a private winery. I've never even been to one that's open to the public! Are you sure your friend won't rat you out to the newspapers?"

"Phillipe?" Max shifted the car into fifth gear, then settled comfortably into a fast cruising speed. "He doesn't give two flips for American politics if it doesn't affect his business. He came to the States from France five years ago with a box of grape plants and a dream. I was the real estate agent who found the winery he bought and built up. People don't do that anymore, you know."

Ariana nodded. "My great-grandparents did, but that was a long time ago. They turned a plywood seafood stand into one of Florida's premier Greek restaurants."

"Your family runs a restaurant in Florida?" he asked, apparently surprised. "Why didn't you stay and run their place? Not that I'm not glad you came here."

She rewarded his considerate comment with a sweet smile. "If I'd stayed in Tarpon Springs, I would never have made it beyond hostess. Women in my family don't make important decisions or give commands—or generally do anything that requires public acknowledgment that you have a brain."

"Which is why you left," he guessed.

"Two weeks after my nineteenth birthday. Don't get me wrong. I love my parents and my brothers. And I really didn't want to go. I admire the sacrifices my great-grandparents made. My parents, too. But, even though they raised me, they couldn't give me the respect I wanted."

Max's frown deepened as her story progressed. "They'll have no choice but to give you that respect once you've made a real splash with Athens by the Bay."

"That's the plan." She hated that Max could read her so easily, but then realized his own background gave him precisely the insight to understand the ferocity and breadth of her goal.

Hard work. Sacrifice. Ingenuity. Those three qualities had turned her great-grandparents' American dream into reality. And she'd learned that those same three elements could go a long way, no matter the goal: restaurants, wineries…true love.

She shook the thought away, choosing to watch Max drive instead. He gripped the steering wheel at two o'clock with his right hand, his left arm was casually draped on the door while he toyed with the side mirror. His choice of clothing surprised her, but she thanked whoever or whatever was responsible for this fashion inspiration. The silky, slate-blue shirt fluttered in the wind, allowing her elongated glimpses at his bare chest. The material pleaded to be touched, smoothed by a woman's palm. And who was she to say no? As soon as they got off this bridge, she was going to find out just how soft and slick that shirt was. And the skin underneath.

They drove across without another word, but the minute Max passed the exit to Sausalito—the small artist colony where they'd been docked the night before—Max asked a question that kept her desire to touch him in check.

"Did you and your husband ever take excursions out of the city?"

He glanced sidelong before putting his gaze back on the winding road, shifting and braking in smooth, fluid motions. He sure managed to mention her former marriage quite a bit. She didn't mind as much as she thought she should. The pain of Rick's rejection truly had faded to near nothing.

"Rick and I left the city all the time. He was a musician. He played gigs from Oakland down to L.A. We even went to Reno a few times."

"So you probably saw more outside the city than you did within?"

She laughed at his assumption. "What I saw was the inside of a ratty van and even rattier clubs. I won't even discuss the hotel rooms. Being a musician is an exciting adventure—for the musician, but not for his too-young, too-inexperienced wife. After a while, I stopped going with him. A little while longer and he was off to Seattle, then Nashville without me—for good."

"So you hung out with your uncle at the restaurant while he was on the road?"

Ariana's heart swelled. Max always seemed to plug right into her, know things about her before she told him. And he showed more concern with how Rick had abandoned her before the marriage was over, somehow knowing that had hurt the most. By the time Rick had left her the divorce papers, the worst was over. The damage had been done long before.

"Stefano was great to me. He gave me a job, taught me to mix drinks, let me experiment with the food. By the time Rick left, Stefano knew I was ready, willing and able to take over for him." She stared at her hands, wringing them softly in her lap to keep her emotions at bay. She'd *so* wanted to run her parents' restaurant in Florida, but they'd made it undeniably clear that the legacy would belong to her brothers. She could work for them as her sisters did, but she'd never run the show. So she'd left for California to find something to call hers and hers alone.

"The distraction of working was much appreciated and couldn't have been better timed," she concluded.

Max switched his right hand for his left on the wheel, then reached over and cupped her hands in his. "But running Stefano's restaurant turned into more than a distraction, didn't it? More than just a temporary means to take your mind off the sorry state of your life?"

The double meaning wasn't lost on Ariana. Their weeklong affair was supposed to achieve the same goal—

provide a brief distraction to take both their minds off the sorry, lonely state of their lives. Scandal or not, she could feel their liaison changing into something much more serious, much more binding than she'd ever imagined.

She tried to pull her hands out of Max's grasp, but he held tight. After he turned his eyes back to the road and allowed a self-satisfied grin to curl his lips, she gave up trying. He wasn't going to say another word about it and he wasn't going to let her go. He'd given her plenty to think about, plenty to hold on to and, luckily, they had a long drive ahead.

12

RANDOLPH BURROWS DRUMMED his fingers atop the grainy black-and-white photograph, grimacing when smudges of ink transferred from the newsprint to his fingertips. He pulled a handkerchief from the breast pocket of his blazer and wiped away the grime.

Too late for that, he mused. He was deep in the grime of scandal, deeper than he'd ever planned to be. Having Max Forrester followed should have produced some evidence of his ill-bred character *before* his daughter got hurt. He'd put a private investigator on his trail the day after Madelyn announced the engagement. He'd found nothing but the vague possibility that Forrester was having an affair with the owner of an ethnic restaurant on the Wharf. The rumored affair had been proved real by this picture, but too late. Madelyn had already run off, obviously humiliated.

Randolph had thought the photograph to be unusable, with the quality so poor and his daughter on the lam. He'd only paid the punk with the camera in hopes he'd find something more damning while he followed Maxwell and his Mediterranean mistress around the city—something

Randolph could use privately to force Maxwell Forrester out of their deal, now that the wedding was off. He had no idea his amateur paparazzi would take his money and then sell the indistinct photograph again to the newspapers.

This was supposed to be a personal matter.

With precision, Randolph withdrew a pair of scissors from his desk drawer and cut out the picture, then placed it in a manila folder that he slid into his briefcase. He needed to find his wayward photographer and yank in the reins. He'd accept nothing less than loyalty, even if he had to pay a hefty price—to which he resigned himself that he'd now have. Somehow, Leo Glass had figured out that there was more at stake in this operation than his daughter Madelyn's honor or a few thousand dollars.

He stood, then tapped the button on his intercom. "James, bring the car around. I'm going to the office."

"Oh, no, you're not!"

Barbara fluttered into the room and poised at the corner of his desk, much like a butterfly alighting on a flower. She held a hat in each hand as if she was just coming into his study to ask his opinion on which one would look better with the flowing blue frock she wore. Damn, but she was one handsome woman. He couldn't help but grin at his wife's expression, a mixture of chastisement and humor. She would do her best to keep him from working today. She always did.

"It's a bank holiday," she pointed out, as if he some-how didn't notice that the stock exchange was closed and he hadn't had to rise before dawn to beat his staff to the office, as was his weekday ritual. "I've made reservations for us to take a cruise on the bay and Magda has packed a beautiful picnic lunch. We're meeting the Andersons at the pier in an hour."

"Darling, that sounds delightful, but I have an urgent matter I must attend to."

"Nonsense, Randolph. How long has it been since we've gone off on a romantic excursion?" There was a slight pout to her grin, but only a slight one. She'd long ago perfected the exact dose of solemnity to add to her sensuous smile in order to get her way. "I suppose all this wedding planning and Madelyn's elopement has me waxing poetic, but we're not getting any younger. So tuck your business away until tomorrow. I allowed you to take your meeting with Charles over that Pier investment yesterday. That's enough money talk for this holiday weekend."

With that, Barbara leaned across the desk, kissed his cheek and retreated, nodding approvingly at the large-brimmed straw hat as she left, deciding entirely on her own. Some retreat, he thought wryly. She'd won that argument, just as she'd won so many others.

No use canceling the car since they were indeed going out, but he did have one phone call to make. He walked around his desk and shut the door. Barbara was still in the dark about their daughter's humiliation and self-preserving deception and he planned to keep her there until he had no other choice. He didn't blame Madelyn for running off and concocting that elopement story to buy some time to save face. In fact, he found the scheme incredibly clever, more so than he'd expect from his daughter, who was naively but endearingly honest and idealistic.

And he couldn't disavow his hand in her naiveté. He'd shielded her from the ugliness of the world, as was a father's right, a father's duty. But Maxwell Forrester had shattered that safe wall he'd built around his one and only child, and for this he would pay.

Randolph certainly had no intention of scuttling the Pier

deal at his own expense. But it seemed someone else had that agenda or, more than likely, it was just this upstart newspaper longing for a local scandal to increase subscriptions. Once he had the situation back under his control, he'd push his philandering, almost son-in-law out of the deal and make him pay for what he'd done to Madelyn.

He'd pay dearly, and from what he could see from the photograph and caption, he'd pay with a lot more than money.

ARIANA LEANED AGAINST the wall in the hallway, allowing Max to work the key to her apartment. It had been a long day—a glorious day. She was still giddy from the windblown ride back from Napa Valley, still dizzy from the bottle of Phillipe's special wine they'd drunk just before leaving. With a borrowed blanket and a basket of cheeses and fruit, they'd found a secluded spot at his winery, shaded from view by rows of blooming vines and fat bunches of grapes. Actually, since Max planned to drive, she'd done most of the drinking. Not enough to get certifiably toasted, but enough for him to nearly seduce her amid the golden Chardonnays. A seduction she had, with great difficulty, rebuffed.

No more making love out of doors, he'd proclaimed, then promptly tried to reverse his wise decision. Since they'd left the city, she'd tried not to think about the photo in the paper and all the potential problems the scandal could cause. He'd resisted her myriad questions regarding who would have the motive for such drastic measures or who would have known how to find them at his house, much less on his balcony. He hadn't wanted to discuss his troubles, preferring to concentrate on enjoying the here and now with her. So they'd toured the winery, watched hot-air balloon races, even attended a wine tasting on board a train that snaked around the lush hills of the valley. But they'd made love only at night, in the guest house Phillipe prepared for them. And during the glorious sexual byplay, they'd barely spoken a word. They didn't need to. He knew what she liked and vice versa.

On the way out to Napa, Max had invited her—oh, so subtly—to consider the possibility that their affair didn't have to end when the week did. That the "distraction" their liaison was supposed to provide could be altered into a real relationship. The offer was so tempting. The potential payoff so great. But if Ariana had learned one thing about relationships, it was that they required sacrifices, compromises, give-and-take. And while she didn't mind enjoying the ebb and flow of sharing Max's life this week, she held tight to the belief that she wouldn't be able to be so magnanimous once she went back to work next week.

Knowing Max, hearing about his rise to prosperity, made her want her dream even more. She'd coaxed a few stories out of him over the past two days, tales of his search for success. She'd heard about how by age twenty-one, he'd graduated with a degree in business. How by age twenty-three, he'd earned his real estate license and was buying and selling properties while he successfully completed his MBA. How he'd met the right people, made the right contacts. And this deal with the Pier—the one he really didn't want to talk about because of its connection to the embarrassing reference and picture in the newspaper—if he managed to pull it off, he'd be a millionaire several times over—his ultimate goal since childhood when he'd realized his family was poor.

Her dream was decidedly smaller, simpler, but no less important. She didn't just want a restaurant to call her own—she wanted a showplace. A unique dining experience that travel guides never overlooked, that the food critics raved over, that the locals enjoyed with the same fervor and comfort as the tourists. She couldn't imagine attaining her goal without selfish, single-minded pursuit—much as Max had employed earlier in his career.

Fact was, he was at the uppermost point of his arc toward success. She was just starting the climb.

"Are you coming inside or does this hallway have some charm I'm missing?"

Ariana turned toward his voice and blinked. The lights inside her apartment were all on; the television was tuned to the cable station playing a very sexy movie she'd been wanting to see. She could even hear the whir and crackle of her microwave making popcorn. He'd obviously gone inside while she stood in the hallway thinking. She felt like an idiot, but the aftereffects of the wine took the edge off her embarrassment.

"I guess I drank more than I thought," she said, sheepishly brushing past him and tossing her purse onto the black lacquered chest.

"You're probably tired. We didn't sleep much last night."

She swept a kiss over his lips before heading toward her bedroom. "No, we didn't. But I'm going to seriously relax tonight, just as soon as I change into my pj's."

"Our relaxation techniques don't usually include sleep," he said, barely managing to cover a yawn with the back of his hand.

"No, they don't."

He arched an eyebrow. "Maybe tonight we'll try something new."

Max shook his head, amazed, as she smiled with anticipation and disappeared beneath the beaded doorway.

He could always depend on Ariana to try something new with him. Something exciting. Something so special he was finally convinced there could be more thrills found with a good woman than with a closed deal or a jump up to a new tax bracket.

And she'd convinced him without trying. In fact, he figured that if she knew the effect she'd had on him, she'd run for cover. He'd had absolutely no trouble keeping Ariana focused on the present during their excursion—no arguments when he declared they wouldn't talk about anything serious and only enjoy the scenery, the view and each other. Unlike any other woman he'd ever met, Ariana was content to keep their interaction casual. And he knew why. If things remained casual, she could more easily say goodbye.

Pushing his disappointment aside, he went back into the kitchen to listen to the microwave. They'd made a deal. She'd stick to it. But would he? Keeping his competitive spirit at bay was hard enough—keeping his growing disappointment under wraps even harder. Not to mention his pride. The realization that he wasn't irresistible was about as easy to swallow as an unpopped kernel of corn.

He didn't often cook for himself or for others anymore, but he could microwave popcorn with the best of them. He timed the intervals between pops, shutting off the power before one kernel got scorched. Gingerly, he pulled out the piping-hot bag and searched for a bowl.

He was just about to shout a question to Ariana when he heard her curse from the bedroom.

"Ah, damn!"

He looked around the corner from the kitchen to the living room, just in time to see her emerge with an overflowing armful of laundry.

"What's wrong?" he asked.

"There's nothing like the real world to intrude on your fun. I have to put a load in the washing machine."

"Can't it wait until tomorrow?"

She shook her head and expertly maneuvered to the door despite the hefty laundry blocking her view. "Not if I want clean underwear."

Max shot to the door and opened it for her, then blocked her exit with his arm. "Who needs underwear at all?"

She sighed. "Great question, but I do like the option. Mrs. Li lets me use her laundry room downstairs, but she needs the machines on Tuesdays. My day is Monday and Monday is nearly over. I'll only be a minute."

He let her pass, but not without bestowing one long, rather wet kiss to show her what she'd be missing if she didn't hurry. She broke away, groaning as she ducked beneath his arm and made her way down the hall to the stairwell. "Promise more kisses like that and I'll make it back in thirty seconds."

She'd twisted the knob and propped open the stairwell door with her foot before he could assist her.

"I can keep *that* promise," he said.

With a smile, she disappeared. Max remained in the hall, staring at the door as it swung slowly closed. He could promise her kisses. He could promise her good loving. Hell, he could promise her the world—and deliver—if she'd let him.

He made his way back to the kitchen, shaking his head. He couldn't let her go. His nature didn't allow for such sacrifice. His heart would no longer accept the emptiness he'd lived with so long. Not now that it knew the fullness Ariana put there, whether she'd intended to or not.

He thought about Charlie. So far as he could tell, his best

friend was an expert on two things—selling real estate and finding him the perfect match. He'd schemed brilliantly to bring them together. Ariana's honest, adventurous spirit effectively broke down a wall Max hadn't realized existed around his heart. But once Ari was inside, as she now was, he felt certain he couldn't let her out. She understood him. Admired him. Wanted many of the same things he did.

And therein lay the problem.

As he pulled open the hot bag of popcorn and poured the contents into the large plastic bowl he found in a cabinet above the refrigerator, he realized only two things stood in the way of keeping Ariana in his life.

First, the photograph. He assumed the whole incident was somehow set up, starting with the drug in his drink. Perhaps someone had been following him for weeks, learning his habits, watching for weaknesses they could exploit into a scandal. Common sense dictated that someone trying to sink the Pier deal had schemed to make him vulnerable to scandal and then planted a photographer to capture the results on film. They'd probably searched for shady business dealings or other dark secrets to exploit, and finding none, decided to concoct their own. Ariana's presence, the timing of their liaison, was nothing more than an accident, a twist of fate.

A wonderful twist, Max thought, popping a buttery morsel into his mouth.

Considering all angles and all possibilities, Max knew there was nothing he could do to stop this potential scandal. He had no idea if more pictures would surface or if his investors would react negatively. For all he knew, the whole matter would die a quiet death.

He also had to consider the second barrier to bringing Ariana into his life for the long haul—Ariana herself. He couldn't fault her reasoning. Her dream was a big one, her goal admirable. But Max knew firsthand the sacrifices that had to be made to make a business work. He could adapt. So she'd work long hours. So did he. So they'd see each other mainly when he came to the new restaurant. He could live with that.

Couldn't he?

Scooping up the bowl and grabbing two long-neck beers from the fridge, he set their feast in front of the television and considered the past two years, when he'd watched Ariana from afar, talking to her only briefly. When she was working, she was entirely focused, consumed with her attention to detail, ensuring that each and every patron of her establishment felt pampered and served and welcome. Every customer was a good friend, every employee family. She was excellent at her job—the best he'd seen in such a casual setting—one reason he'd been drawn to Athens by the Bay in the first place.

Was it fair to ask her to divide her focus? Now, when she was so close to achieving everything she wanted, everything she deserved?

The thought made him pensive. Frustrated. Annoyed as hell. He twisted open a beer and grabbed a handful of popcorn, stuffing his mouth and chewing. He was a genuine son of a bitch. Still selfish. Still self-absorbed. Still willing to bulldoze his way for the sake of his own needs.

Because, dammit, he wanted Ariana in his life, no matter the cost.

ARIANA WATCHED MAX from the corner of her eye, then glanced back at the screen. The sexy, romantic comedy had zero effect on whatever black mood had descended on him while she was downstairs separating the whites from the delicates. He'd barely spoken three words, and while he didn't recoil from her arm entwined with his, he didn't invite any other affection. She tried to console herself with the fact that he was tired and that tomorrow, the first business day this week, could result in a crisis over his Pier deal, but she sensed that his mood had more to do with her.

"Max, what's wrong?"

He turned to her slowly. "You don't want to know." He blew out a frustrated breath. "I'm sorry. I'm being a jerk." He chugged down the rest of his beer, now undoubtedly lukewarm since he'd done nothing but clutch the bottle for the past half hour. "I'll get over it. I'm exhausted."

"I do want to know. Is it the picture? Are you worried there might be more? Worse things could happen, Max. Embarrassment never killed anyone."

He turned and clutched her hands, a smile fighting with the frown that had reigned over his face since she'd returned. "You've got a great attitude. I want you to know that I'm sorry for involving you."

"You've apologized a hundred times, Max. You know I don't blame you. That's not what's wrong."

He glanced aside, then back at her. He wanted to tell her—she could see the signs. Deer-in-the-headlight eyes. Mouth slightly agape.

He wanted to but he wouldn't. Instead he stood, grabbed the empty beers and the depleted bowl of popcorn and retreated to the kitchen. She shook her head. Maybe he was right—maybe she didn't want to know.

Maybe she already knew and didn't want to face the crossroads they'd arrived at—entirely too soon for her liking. While she'd sorted her dirty clothing downstairs, away from Max and his magnetism, she couldn't help but consider how he'd come in and turned her life completely upside down in only three days. All she thought about was Max. All she wanted was Max. While she'd measured out the detergent and sprinkled white powder into the running water, she'd actually imagined what it would be like to live with him in his Russian Hill home. To wake up with him as she had at the guest house this morning, rousing him with soft kisses that led to lazy, wonderful sex. She thought about redecorating his ice-cold living room in Oriental style, merging their homes, merging their lives.

And not once—*not once*—did she think about the restaurant, her long hours, her dream. All of a sudden, her personal goals seemed silly, unimportant and selfish next to the possibility of love. But hadn't she felt *exactly* the same way with Rick?

Max was not Rick, she knew that with the same certainty that she knew she was no longer the innocent child who'd married her first lover for all the wrong reasons. She was older, wiser. And unfortunately, that wisdom included the knowledge that when the week ended and she severed her affair with Max, she was probably letting go of the best thing that had ever happened to her.

"I'm going to go put my stuff in the dryer," she announced, hoping her voice didn't squeak with the sound of tears she could feel coming.

"Need help?" he asked.

She shook her head and pasted on a smile. "No, I can handle it on my own."

She scurried to the door. Laundry, she could do by herself. But the rest of her life? Only three days ago she'd thought she could manage. Now she wasn't so sure.

13

SHE'D BEEN GONE WAY too long. After watching more of the
movie and then realizing he didn't even know the characters' names, Max had flipped off the television and ventured downstairs. He had no idea where Mrs. Li's laundry
room was, but the hissing rush of water filling the washing machine drew him in the right direction.

The intimate space, little larger than a closet, was tucked
in the farthest corner behind the tea shop. A fluorescent
light flickered slightly, casting a harsh lavender glow over
Ariana as she draped damp delicates over the edges of a
laundry basket. The curtain of tiny window, high in the
outer wall, fluttered with a cool breeze.

She worked mechanically, her gaze glossy and seemingly unfocused. But from the crease in her forehead and
the decided dip of the corners of her mouth, Max judged
he was the cause of her contemplative expression. He
couldn't blame her. He'd allowed his somber mood to ruin
the movie, perhaps the entire evening. He decided enough
was enough. If he wanted Ariana to seriously consider ex-
tending their relationship past the end of the week, he'd
better change tactics quickly.

Impulsively, he flicked off the light switch.

"Hey!" she protested, twirling toward him.

He stepped in immediately, closing and locking the sliding pocket door behind him. "It's just me," he reassured her.

Clutching a pair of bright red panties in her hands, she sighed. Light from the alley flashed in from the high window whenever the wind threw the curtains aside, revealing her relieved expression. "I'm sorry I'm taking so long. I was just…thinking."

He took one step closer. "About us?"

The room wasn't large enough to allow her much of a retreat. When the washing machine stopped her from backing up farther, he moved in and pressed full against her. In an instant, he was hard with wanting. But sex wouldn't be enough this time. Not for him. And he hoped she too was tiring of the game of physical pleasure only they both were pretending to play. Truth was, in three short days, they'd built the foundation of a relationship that could either be strengthened by honest emotion or would crumble into nothing from too much hesitancy, too much emotional denial.

They both had decisions to make. And he figured there was no time like the present to begin the process.

"What's to think about with us?" she said flippantly, obviously trying to hide the flustered quiver in her voice with a shrug and a smile. She slipped her arms around his waist and moved to snuggle closer.

He stopped her with a halting grip on her elbows.

"There's a lot to think about, Ariana. A lot to say. You need me to go first? I will."

Her eyes flashed with a fiery mixture of vexation and bravado. She tried to pull away, but he held her firm. She didn't struggle, just lifted her chin higher. "I'm not afraid of you, Max."

"Of course you aren't. You're afraid of repeating the mistake from your past."

"What is that supposed to mean?"

He paused, tilting his head to the side to tell her silently that he didn't buy her sudden ignorance one iota. But to her credit, she didn't back down. She countered his expression with an impatient huff of her own.

Max softened the tone of his voice. "It's supposed to mean that you have a very clear, very defined mission in life—a mission you've already detoured from once with Rick. And here I am offering another side trip."

"Just for a week. And, for the record, I asked you."

"Yes, *you* asked for just the week. Now I'm asking for more." He released her elbows by sliding his palms down her bare arms, twining his fingers with hers and then lifting their clutched hands to his lips. "You fascinate me, Ari. I've never felt so alive." He skimmed his mouth over her knuckles, then tucked her hands beneath his chin. "I can pinpoint, to the minute, the very moment I realized that I couldn't be poor for the rest of my life. I've devoted my life to attaining wealth. And I missed so much in the process."

Her gaze softened. She slipped her hands from his grasp, caressing his cheeks to soften the blow of her words. "But now you have your success, don't you? You have what you wanted. It's easy to change the direction in your life after if you've reached your destination."

He fought to ignore the lulling sensation of her warm palms on his face. Her point was valid and difficult to dispute. But he had to find a way, or he'd lose her for sure. "I wish it was that easy. You're making me realize that money isn't all I've wanted, Ari. Money was just the easiest thing to attain."

She shook her head. "Easy? Don't you think that's an oversimplification? You've worked hard, Max, sacrificed so much."

He shrugged, knowing he'd busted his butt to attain all he had, giving up a normal childhood and countless social interactions in the process. Until Ari came along, he'd convinced himself that his single-minded focus had been admirable. Requisite. It had given him an edge over other entrepreneurs and upstarts. And until Ari slipped into his life—his heart—he'd believed he had much more to accomplish. Yes, he had wealth, but he still considered himself just a poor kid from Oakland who had somehow managed to do well for himself. He'd been lucky. Knew the right people. Right place, right time.

The Pier deal would win him the unqualified self-respect and security he'd truly desired. He wasn't just making money for himself this time, but for the power-brokers of San Francisco as well. He was creating a play-ground for them, with their input as investors. And though the scandal with Ariana could cost him that ultimate tri-umph, right this very minute he simply didn't care.

He searched the depths of her dark gaze, not speaking until he was sure she was listening. With her heart. With her soul. "And I'm going to continue to work hard until I get *everything* I want. It's just that now I want you, too."

Ari sighed, then slipped beneath his arm, darting toward the large washbasin just below the window. She turned the faucets and splashed her face, drawing the moisture through her hair with her wet hands, splattering water across her neck. She sighed again as the cool drops from the tap ran over her skin, though this time the sound resembled more of a coo than an echo of frustration.

Max watched, enthralled, as the droplets kissed her skin. The running dryer infused the air with humid heat, making his breathing even more difficult when Ari shut off the faucet and slowly turned. Glistening, the water dropped off her eyelashes, flowed down her cheeks, throat, breasts.

"You want me? Then have me, Max."

She tucked her hands in the back of her leggings, just enough to stretch open the top of her oversize shirt. She'd left several buttons unfastened so that her thin silvery bra, now spotted and translucent with water, showed him hard evidence of her desire.

"It's hot in here, but we *can* make it hotter," she promised.

Max groaned. "You're trying to distract me."

And her trick was working like a charm. But even her powerful sexuality couldn't overpower his desire to turn their affair in the direction of something more serious, more permanent. As she closed in, she unbuttoned her shirt completely, allowing him to see precisely where the water had drizzled down, over and through her bra. She pushed her shirt off her shoulders, then pressed him backward until the hot metal casing of the dryer warmed through the denim of his jeans.

"Looks that way." She drew her fingers down her chest, her touch manipulating the moisture on her skin, manipulating him just the same. "I'm all wet." She gripped the dryer on either side of him, trapping him in a box of pure heat. "Maybe we can put this appliance to better use."

God, he couldn't resist her. Not when she moistened her lips so slowly. Not when she slipped her hot, wet hands beneath his shirt and up his chest. He whipped his shirt off in time for her to capture his nipples in her mouth. Moisture and heat assailed him from all angles. She kissed and plucked and bit until the oxygen in his lungs thickened into molten need. She unzipped his jeans and guided him out of them, stripping away his boxers in the process, leaving him naked. He hissed when she pushed him back against the dryer, bare flesh to increasingly hot metal. Her devilish grin heightened the thrill.

She thought she'd conceived the perfect means to keep them from talking further, but Max had learned several important things about Ariana in the past few days. One of them was that she was a woman of action. To tell her he cared for her was one thing. Rick had told her, her parents had told her…and then they'd let her down.

To convince Ariana that he was different, he'd need to show her. And he'd use their intense physical attraction as his medium.

"Too hot for you?" she asked, challenge lilting her voice and lighting her dark eyes.

"With you? Never." He snagged a towel from her laundry basket and spread it on top of the dryer. Bracing his hands on either side, he lifted himself up, breathing out loudly as the heat rumbled beneath him. She wanted to have sex? Fine with him. But he'd turn this into a lesson in trust and sacrifice she wouldn't forget.

Hurriedly, he snared her bra strap with one finger and tugged her between his thighs. "But if you don't hurry up, some very important parts of me—two parts to be exact— might get scorched."

"Aw," she said with an exaggerated pout, cupping and kneading him softly, melding the heat from the dryer with a warmth all her own. "I wouldn't want that to happen."

She pushed his knees farther apart with her other hand

and then brazenly cooled his hard sex with a wicked lick,
followed by a breathy whistle. The contrast of tempera-
tures—fire beneath him, humidity around him, the chill
from the fluttering wind from the window and the gentle
warmth of her mouth—clashed into a perfect storm of
pleasure.

When she took him completely into her mouth, the tempest raged. He gripped the dryer, then grasped her shoulders, branding her with the heat of his hands, making her
gasp even as she brought him nearer and nearer to the edge.

"Ariana, no. Ari, I'm…"

His restraint was tentative, and some of it slipped
before he could push her away. He wondered then who
was teaching what to whom. She wouldn't move, wouldn't
stop loving him until she claimed the prize she wanted.
Stubborn as she was giving, she took all he offered, then
caressed him back to earth.

He made a move to slide off the dryer, but she stopped
him with her palm on his belly. "Let me."

She snatched a condom from the pocket of his discarded
jeans, the precise place he'd promised her he'd keep protection during the duration of their affair. She tore open
the packet then set the circle of protection on the washer.
With little fanfare, she ripped away her bra, leggings and
panties, upended the wicker basket and climbed onto his
lap.

With the towel safely beneath him, he scooted back to
give them more room, capturing her breast in his mouth,
loving the feel of her hardening nipple against the softness of his tongue. The gentle reverberation of the laundry
spinning below them thrummed straight through his flesh,
coupling with the feel of her wrapping her legs around
him until he was quickly aroused again. She slipped the

prophylactic on in one quick tug, then moved to help him inside.

She wanted the passion quick. The act fast and frantic and ultimately meaningless. No time to allow the sexual connection to reach her heart. No time for the depth of his passion to touch her soul.

Maybe that's how they'd made love the first night—the night he couldn't remember. But since then their loving had become slower, more attentive, mirroring what he knew was scaring her most.

"Slow down, sweetheart. It's not often I have a beautiful woman straddling me on a dryer. I want to enjoy this."

She bathed his face in a splash of insistent kisses. "Someone could come in and find us."

He stopped her passionate assault by bracing her cheeks in his hands. "No one is going to find us here. It's two o'clock in the morning, the doors are all locked and that window is too small and high for any photographer to peep through." With his thumbs, he stroked from her cheekbones to her lips, skimming her moist mouth, savoring the eroticism of the simple touch. "It's just you and me."

So he took his time, placing sweet, butterfly kisses just above her eyelids, on the tip of her nose, at the lobes of each ear. He stretched her arms across his shoulders, where she laced them behind his neck. Holding her bottom with splayed hands, he kissed a path from her collarbone to her breasts, alternating his mouth from one nipple to the other while his fingers teased and tormented her down below.

"Max, you're killing me," she murmured, only half teasing as he licked a luscious path back to her mouth. He claimed her lips with ravenous want, pulling her closer so he could feel the slick throbbing of her need against his.

"Then we'll both die happy, sweetheart."

God, he wanted to be inside her. Here, now, forever. Blood raged in his ears, louder and hotter than the roll and tumble of the dryer beneath them. Still, he waited, focusing on the textures and tastes of her mouth and skin, biding his time just a minute longer.

She lifted herself and forced the tip of his sex against her, grinning as she realized that unless he moved, her position allowed her ultimate control. He witnessed the flash of power that lit her eyes, the curl of triumph that turned her pouting mouth into a grin.

Sliding one hand between them, she held him stiff against her, both of them breathing in sharply as the sensations rushed and spiked.

"You can have me right now," he told her, making clear the conclusion he needed her to see. Holding out hadn't been easy, but he trusted her to follow his clues to this sweet resolution. "You can have me whenever you want me, Ariana. Wherever. Tonight." He shifted, just enough to slide ever-so-slightly inside her. "Tomorrow." He drew her knees up so her feet were flat against the dryer's control panel, giving her all the leverage, allowing her utter power over their coupling. Utter power over him. "Anytime you want me, I'll be right here."

When he looked up, he knew she understood. Her pupils swelled completely into her irises; her lashes fluttered, polishing her ebony eyes glossy and glossier. Her bottom lip quivered. He hungered to alleviate the shiver with his mouth on hers, but instead he pressed a single kiss on her cheek, drawing his lips upward so he could whisper in his ear.

"Think you can handle all that power?"

With a narrow-eyed gleam that combined determination with desire, he eased inside her. She urged him to thrust and touch her with hot, demanding cries—thrusting and touching him with equal abandon. Hands reached and grasped. Lips clashed. Tongues mated. In a wild instant, they crossed over the edge, her first, then him.

And yet, when the insanity ebbed, Ariana hardly moved. Cradling her cheek on his shoulder, she crossed her legs behind him, drawing her completely against him. He drew his knees up, balancing his feet on the dryer's edge, to brace her back, completing the intimate ball of bodies they formed. And for a long while they sat there, quietly cradled, until a sharp bell signaled the end of the cycle.

ARIANA SNUGGLED INTO the warm sheets on her bed and breathed in the nearly overpowering scent of fresh fabric softener. Without opening her eyes, she grinned. Max didn't know a damn thing about laundry, but he made up for his heavy hand with the Downy by doing delightful deeds with the warmed pillowcases and towels. Yet, as she turned and allowed the morning light to assail her eyes, she remembered the significance that Max's soft ministrations had held. He hadn't just made love with her last night in the euphemistic sense. He'd shown her his love. Lived it. Without the words, yes—he was sharp enough to know that such a declaration would send her running—but he felt the emotion just the same. He'd opened his heart and shown her the contents, forcing her to look inside herself and gauge the depth of her feelings.

And in the bright morning light, she didn't like the results one bit.

She shook her head as she checked the clock at her bedside. Nearly eleven. She groaned, trying to remember when she'd last allowed herself the luxury of sleeping past eight o'clock, even on a rare day off. But Max wore her out.

And she'd enjoyed every minute of it. She knew without a doubt that she could sneak back under the covers and fall instantly asleep.

But at eleven o'clock, the morning papers had been on the stands for nearly half a day. She decided to focus on Max's potential trouble with his investors and his Pier deal rather than on her feelings for Max. She would leave that minefield for another time.

She didn't want to love him, dammit. But as she threw on her favorite pink robe, she had a hard time ignoring the cut-and-dried fact that she most probably already did.

The scent of hot coffee wafted from the kitchen and she found Max there, a barely touched mug chilling in front of him. He looked up from *The Bay Insider* spread out on the countertop. The rage in his eyes answered her question.

"How bad?" she asked simply. She reached for his cup and found it stone cold. He'd been staring at the paper for a long, long time.

"I called my attorney."

"That bad?" She shot toward the paper, but he stopped her by standing and bracing her shoulders with his hands. "I…"

She jabbed a finger into his chest, hoping a good fight would alleviate the nauseating pit of dread rolling in her stomach. "Don't apologize again, Max. Just let me see."

He shook his head. "You don't need—"

She exhaled. "Don't tell me what I need and don't need, Max Forrester. You're my lover, not my protector. It's me they got this time, isn't it? You think I'm not going to see it? You think my not seeing it is going to change anything? You called your attorney, for God's sake. Now give me the paper."

In the seconds it took for him to turn around and re-trieve the offending page and hand it to her, none of the horrific images that flashed through her mind were as shocking as the actual photograph.

This one wasn't grainy. The black-and-white reproduc-tion was crisp and clear. Her, sitting on the windowsill, rapture overwhelming her features, a man's hands—Max's hands—braced on her knees.

She couldn't read the caption. Her eyes wouldn't focus. The paper fluttered from her fingers. Her stomach clenched into a tight stone and her lungs seemed to reject the small amount of air she managed to pull inside.

"Ariana—" Max reached for her, but she stepped out of range, out of the kitchen. In the living room, her gaze darted to the window. She marched over and flung the curtains aside, nearly tearing the material from the rods. When she spun back around, Max stood at the threshold, his hands clenched in fists within his pockets.

"That picture was taken from across the street."

He nodded. "I know. I visited there this morning. For two hundred dollars, Ty Wong gave me the name of the man who paid him exactly the same amount to let him use his window—a kid with a telephoto lens."

She tugged in some air to control the rage boiling inside her. "Who?"

He shook his head, as if the name was insignificant. "Some guy he knows from rave parties. Leo. Red hair. Three lightning-bolt earrings in his left ear. He didn't know his last…"

"Leo?" She couldn't believe this was happening, but the description had been too precise to be anyone but the Leo she knew. "Leo Glass? Leo did this to me?"

"You know him?"

She stalked across the room, pushing past him in her search for the phone. "I should. I sign his damn paychecks." She found the handset and dug her address book out from behind her cookie jar. She flipped to the G listings and was about to punch in Leo's number when Max stopped her.

"Wait. I don't understand."

"Leo is my backup bartender. One of the guys who covers for me when I'm out or in the kitchen or working the dining room."

"How long has he worked for you?"

Ariana shook her head, attempting to push beyond her anger long enough to answer Max's question. She knew she had to act rationally, think about this and work through the hows and whys. But, dammit, right now all she wanted to do was kick that scrawny son of a bitch in his cocky little ass.

"I hired him, I don't know, six months ago."

"He's a good employee?"

She shrugged. He wasn't the best on her staff. He tended to flirt too much with the young female tourists, bucking for bigger tips. Hell, he'd flirted with her one time too many until she'd finally set him straight.

"Was he working Friday night?" Max asked. The struggle on his face, his intense focus on putting this puzzle together into a logical explanation snapped her back to reality. Until they understood, they couldn't protect themselves, couldn't strike back with accuracy. Her anger would have to wait, just until she told Max what he needed to know.

"Yeah. He was tending bar when I got there."

"So he could have slipped that drug in my beer."

Ariana nodded. And if Ty Wong knew Leo Glass from

raves—the late-night, techno-music parties where drugs usually flowed more readily than even alcohol—he had access to whatever had been put into Max's drink.

"Easily. But why? What does he have against you?"

Max shook his head. "You're his boss. What does he have against you?"

The question stunned them both to silence. Leo Glass was somehow connected to both of them, though even from Ty's description, Max could barely remember what he looked like. Now that he knew the punk worked for Ariana, he did vaguely remember the carrottop kid. When Max frequented Athens by the Bay, he usually sat on the outside terrace. In the early mornings, Ray, the manager, usually waited tables. In the evenings, an older waiter named Johnny and his wife—the crusty, but lovable Aida—covered the outdoor crowd. If he'd somehow managed to piss off this Leo fellow, he couldn't imagine how or when. The punk had to have taken the photographs for money— money from someone trying to sabotage Max's life. That he was a regular in Ari's restaurant made him an easy target of Leo's watchful eye. But why would he put Ari in the middle? Why embarrass her? She'd been identified in this caption, along with the restaurant's name and location. Unless she had simply been at the wrong place—with him—at the wrong time.

"Maybe you should get dressed," Max suggested, attempting to pull the address book and phone out of her hand. "We need to sort this out. Figure out this kid's motive. His connection to both of us."

Her nod was nearly imperceptible, but she released the book and phone and disappeared into her bedroom without another word. Max was scanning the open page for the kid's listing when the phone trilled in his hand.

He answered immediately. "Karas residence."

"Max, you gotta get down here!" ever-relaxed, ever-laid-back Charlie barked into the phone.

"I can't...I have—"

"Max, trust me. Whatever is going on there is nothing compared to the crap happening here."

14

AFTER HAILING A CAB to his house to change clothes, Max drove to the office, parked and walked through a gauntlet of screaming reporters who had staked out his reserved spot. Shouting "No comment" as he strode to the bank of elevators to the twenty-fourth floor, he ducked out of the light of the cameras and wondered if these vultures had found Ariana.

Reluctantly, he'd left without her, but she'd out and out told him that she needed time to deal with this alone—to find Leo so he could be dealt with. Max highly suspected that a plan of retribution was forming in that incredibly sharp brain of hers, but he didn't ask for details. He'd asked her to wait for his return before she did anything and had elicited a tentative agreement. He forced his focus to quelling the catastrophe Charlie had screamed about on the phone.

The reception area of Forrester Properties was eerily quiet. The young girl who took care of the phones and greeted clients was suspiciously absent from her post. Max fought a growl as he made his way through the maze of cubicles and offices his agents used. Those on the phone were talking in hushed whispers. The rest gathered in groups of two and three, talking frantically until they saw him. Then silence thundered in his ears. Charlie, waiting for him in his office, effectively undid the quiet with his instantaneous, frenetic shouting.

"Randolph and his core investors have been calling all morning." Charlie slammed the door behind him. "Aunt Barbara showed up, bawling her eyes out, wondering where the hell her daughter is, wondering how she'll deal with the humiliation of having her daughter dumped by a philandering cheat. What am I supposed to tell them?"

Max took a deep breath and poured a cup of coffee from the carafe behind his desk. He nodded, trying to remain cool, trying to center on something simple—like how impressed he was that his secretary filled the thermos when he was supposed to be on vacation. He took a sip, slightly disappointed that she hadn't laced the drink with something stronger than cream and sugar.

"Don't tell them anything," Max answered once the heat of the coffee dissolved the baseball-size pit in his stomach. "I'll handle this."

"You're back in the game? For good?"

Max shook his head. Now that Ariana had been pulled into his mess, or he into hers—he wasn't sure which since they both had been targeted by the same jerk with a camera—he had no intention of leaving her to deal with the backlash alone. "I'm here now for damage control. But I'm out of here by tonight. Ariana and I have a photographer to find."

"Where is she now?"

Max shrugged and fell into his leather wingback chair. "She said she was going to find her uncle."

"You don't believe her?"

"Ariana has a mind and a will of her own. I called my brother and asked him to keep her company, but she was already gone by the time he arrived at her apartment."

For now, he'd give her the space she needed and handle things from his end.

"First order of business," Max directed, snatching a pen from a leather-trimmed cup and jotting notes as he spoke. "Find Madelyn for Barbara. Your aunt doesn't deserve to be worried. I assume you told her that Madelyn is fine, that *she* chose to run away on her own?"

Charlie nodded. "I told her. I also put a call in to Maddie's cell phone. She'll check in when she gets the message. She never intended her quest for independence to hurt anyone, least of all her parents. She lied about the elopement to save face for them, not for herself. She thought a week of downtime would lessen the blow."

"Maddie didn't know *The Bay Insider* was going to get involved. What about the Darlington Group?"

Charlie tugged a chair closer to Max's desk and fell into the stiff cushions. "Ambrose wants us to meet as soon as possible. He doesn't give a shit what you do with your private life, but his brother isn't so liberal or forgiving."

As if Max needed anyone's forgiveness for finding the woman of his dreams. But he put aside his comments, just as he'd put aside his emotions, for the time being. Max had become adept at suppressing his feelings to focus on business. He'd always considered that a talent until Ariana pulled it on him this morning. Urging him to the office had been an effective means of keeping her heart safe for another day. But the sooner he handled this crisis, the sooner he could find her.

"Bottom line?" Max asked.

Charlie leaned back and stared at the ceiling. "They

don't want any more controversy associated with this project. They came to San Francisco to live, Max. They want to be perceived as part of the community, not 'heartless interlopers who shanghaied a historical landmark for commercial rape.'"

Charlie quoted a line from *The Bay Insider*'s latest editorial with clear disdain. He and Max both knew that the paper's opinion was crap. Pure bleeding-heart, antidevelopment crap. Worst part was, through the course of this deal Max hadn't had a clear enemy on whom to blame the propaganda. Not one neighborhood or civic group had formed to fight the development. Not one individual had come out as a leader in the opposition. He'd been fighting the phantom "general public" as reported in the news— until now.

He dug into his briefcase and extracted the offending newspaper, turning to the masthead to read the name of the editor. Donalise Parker. Never heard of her. The reporters who'd covered the deal in the past and who'd interviewed him for the slanted stories they'd printed had each been different. All young, all hungry and not one with the savvy or experience to orchestrate the level of hostility he'd been contending with.

But printing a photograph of Ariana rated as an act of war, especially when the caption left no question as to her identity. They'd not only printed her name and the location of her business, they'd implied that she was the reason for Saturday's canceled Forrester-Burrows wedding. Though written tongue-in-cheek, the commentary thanked Ariana for breaking up not only a marriage but also one of the "most offensive real estate transactions the city has ever faced."

He swallowed his rage with another sip of coffee, forcing himself to tear the editor's name out of the paper without ripping the newsprint to shreds. He handed the jagged scrap to Charlie. "Call the Darlingtons and your uncle Randolph and set up a meeting for three o'clock. Then call this Donalise Parker and tell her I'd like to speak with her. Right away."

Charlie scanned the clipping. "You're going to talk to the newspaper editor? Why not the owner?"

Max grabbed his phone to dial his lawyer again. He wasn't going to march into the offices of *The Bay Insider* with a full patrol from Gonzalez, Oehler and Powell, Attorneys-at-Law, in tow. He'd handle this himself. However, he wasn't foolish enough to confront the press without a strong dose of legal advice.

"Because the owner is some European conglomerate just making the move into media." A few phone calls on the way over had netted him that knowledge. "They dole out the cash, but they don't mess with the content. I've got to find out where this opposition is coming from...why they're stooping to personal assassination in order to stop us dead. The Pier was a rotting pile of smelly, barnacle-encrusted wood that no one cared about until we came in with a plan not only to make some money, but bring more people to that area of the Wharf. Until today, I thought *The Bay Insider* was just stirring up trouble for the sake of stirring up trouble, like the media often does. Now I'm not so sure."

"You think they have another agenda?"

Max flashed him the picture of Ariana, briefly, before folding the newsprint into a tight rectangle, photo-side down.

"Go make those phone calls. I want to check in with Ari."

Charlie rose and walked toward the door, his shoulders slumped and his gait sluggish. He turned before he grabbed the doorknob, wincing as if he finally realized the price this mess was costing Max's lover. "How is she holding up? She's gotta be humiliated."

With Charlie well across the room, Max felt safe to turn the newspaper over and run his hand over the offending picture—even though his friend and a majority of San Francisco had already seen and dissected the photo *The Bay Insider* chose to print. Though snapped in profile, Max could easily superimpose the other side of her face from memory. Her eyes had been closed. Her mouth open, lips shaped in a delicate O. The breeze fluttered her hair, tangling the dark strands with the ruby curtains, creating an image he suddenly realized was incredibly aesthetic. Her beauty—exotic, wild—belonged in a gallery…to be admired, not disdained.

She didn't deserve this. And he wondered if he deserved her.

"She's angry. Furious. The guy who took this picture works for her."

Charlie stalked back to Max's desk, his whisper echoing his shock. "At the restaurant?"

Staring, Max conveyed the implications of this too-coincidental-to-be-a-coincidence turn. He wasn't a big fan of conspiracy theories, but he couldn't ignore the facts. He and Ariana had become an item, he thought, purely by chance. Leo Glass was either a brilliant mastermind or the luckiest son of a bitch in San Francisco.

"Yeah, and right now, he's M-I-A. As soon as I've taken care of the Darlingtons and the investors, we're going to look for him and find out who he's really working for."

Charlie's face skewed with skepticism. "You sure Ariana isn't already looking without you?"

Max shook his head, denying himself the frightening images that scenario presented. "No, I'm not sure. I'm not sure of a lot of things. But I intend to be—very soon."

ARIANA STRETCHED HER NECK from side to side, then in one full rotation winced as kinks and cricks popped from her vertebrae. It had been a long morning. A long, fruitless morning. Leo Glass had apparently disappeared off the face of the earth. She had a good idea where he'd surface next, delaying her retribution until late tonight. Waiting, doing nothing, wasn't an option she preferred. Doing nothing meant she had to think, and her thoughts ultimately drifted to Max.

"Here, drink this."

Her uncle poured a shot glass of crisp, clear ouzo and slid it toward her. His lined face and tanned, stubbled jowls bore none of his usual good humor this morning. Even before Ariana sneaked in through the restaurant's back door, eluding the reporter who'd staked out the front entrance, he'd seen the photo that had the Wharf in an uproar. She could only imagine what comments and crudities his cronies had tortured him with. By the time she'd arrived, he'd dismissed the crew that had been dismantling and storing equipment in preparation of the upcoming construction.

It was just the two of them. And though Ariana normally didn't imbibe alcohol before the evening hours, she did as he ordered and swallowed the liqueur in one quick gulp.

He let her regain her breath before he posed his first question.

"Do you love this man?" Stefano asked.

That wasn't the question she expected.

She tipped the empty glass over her lips again, hoping a dash more ouzo would help. "I've only known him—really known him—for a few days."

Stefano's expression portrayed his disbelief. "Ari, time doesn't matter. You married your first husband after knowing him less than that."

She nodded. "And we know how that turned out."

His expression was incredulous. "Rick may not have deserved your love, but that didn't change how you felt about him. I'm not asking you if this affair with Max Forrester is going to last beyond next week. I'm asking if you love him."

Ariana toyed with the empty shot glass, twirling her finger around the smooth lip, recalling with crystal clarity how she'd done the same to the glass she'd served Max's Flaming Eros in just before she touched him for the first time.

"I can't fall in love with him. Look around us!" She gestured to the near-empty room that had once been a cluttered, vibrant bar. The mirrored shelves behind her uncle were almost completely bare. The tables and chairs and bar stools, save one or two, had been dragged away and stacked in a moving trailer parked around back. "We're about to dive into some serious debt here. I can't—*we* can't—afford to be distracted now."

He nodded as he cleared away her glass, but she could tell he wasn't buying her argument. He came out from behind the bar and dragged a battered stool beside hers, taking her hand in his as he sat. "Love is the ultimate distraction, isn't it? But you know I loved your aunt with all my heart. From the instant I set eyes on her, I didn't want anything else but to make love to her…all the time. That was 1955," he clarified with a pointed finger on the bar.

"Is that why you married her so quickly?"

He chuckled, flipping off his battered captain's hat, then setting it back down at an angle that looked rakish and dashing, even though he was long beyond seventy and had put on a good sixty pounds of extra weight. But until the day she died, Sonia Karas had watched her husband with adoring eyes. Ariana had seen their love for herself. She imagined that her aunt Sonia hadn't stood a chance of escaping this man's charm.

"Three days we knew each other." He rolled his eyes heavenward as he recalled the tempest of their whirlwind romance. "Her father would have hung me from his largest fish hook if I hadn't produced that marriage license."

Ariana laughed with him. They both knew the stories, knew the history of the forty-five year marriage during which Stefano and Sonia had worked together side by side, all day, every day. They'd had their arguments—loud ones, passionate ones—but they'd never tired of each other, never lost that spark of respect and desire that even strangers could see. They'd never even spent a night apart—not since their wedding on the run from Sonia's father and half-dozen brothers.

For a while, Ariana had hoped she'd find something similar with Rick—something exciting and forbidden and wild. They'd had the desire but never the respect.

And with Max? Even in the face of horrible humiliation, Ariana still considered him a remarkable man. Full of integrity, honor. His instinct to protect and avenge her was strong, and yet he managed—only at her request—to rein in his natural inclination to find Leo himself and beat the living daylights out of him. By simply trusting her to find Leo herself, respecting her need to retain some semblance of control, he'd shown her once again that he was more than worthy of her love.

"So? Do you love him?"

She laid her palm over her uncle's hands, relishing the warmth of his weathered experience. No sense running from the truth any longer, at least not with her uncle. He'd been her only family since she'd come to San Francisco. And after all the grief she'd caused him over the photo, she at least owed him some honesty.

"Yeah, I do. Something fierce. Isn't it awful?"

"Awful? Ari, that's wonderful!"

"How is it wonderful?"

Stefano shook his head. "He's a smart man who worked hard and made good. Don't think I didn't check him out a long time ago, when I first noticed him making goo-goo eyes at you."

Ariana wasn't the least surprised that Stefano would find out all he could about Max. And it wouldn't have been hard since Max came in the restaurant all the time.

"Yeah, well, making a success of himself in this town means a lot to him. He goes to charity functions and all the right parties. I need to be here, where my dream is. A wife should be with her husband."

Stefano snorted. "Yeah, you were with Rick. You used to call the clubs and book his shows before he got a promoter. Used to inventory his equipment. Hell, girl, you used to help lug his speakers in and out of that beat-up van. You were a damn good wife by your definition. Where did it get you?"

"Divorced. Single. Which is maybe where I should be. I have dreams of my own, Stefano. You know that more than anyone. I can't give them up."

"Is he asking you to?"

"Max? No! Of course not. He'd never ask. He just figures we'd find a way to make it work."

Stefano nodded and stood, dragging the stool with him
and stashing it in the bare alcove that had once been their
hostess station. "You're afraid to fail again, Ari. Afraid to
have your heart broken. That's nothing to be ashamed of,
but it's also no reason to be stupid. If you love this man, if
you believe he loves you, then you're a damn idiot to walk
away."

Stefano huffed when he finished his tirade, just to make
sure she was paying close attention. Then he waited…for
her to agree? Ari sighed, joining Stefano in the alcove
after lifting her stool and stacking it atop his. She knew
her uncle was right. Knew only a "damn idiot" would let
a man like Max go. And even though she'd claimed for
years—including the first night they'd made love on his
balcony—that a fear of heights was the only thing she was
scared of, she knew now she'd been telling Max a big fat
lie.

She was afraid of falling in love again. Of getting her
heart broken yet again. Of losing herself in a man after
she'd fought so hard to gain her independence after her
divorce. And she also worried that this fear was one she'd
never overcome.

"Stefano, I'm sorry if I embarrassed you with that photograph. We should have been more discreet."

Draping his burly arm over her shoulder, he led her
toward the back office. There was work to be done today,
and none of it could be completed at the restaurant. "I'm
your uncle, not your father. You don't live in San Francisco
for fifty-five years without developing some tolerance for
unusual behavior. You don't worry about me."

He kissed her on the cheek and she knew the incident was done. "Thank you."

His "you're welcome" was a chesty grunt. "So, do you need any help making this matter right? I know a couple of mean sailors who might be looking for some extra cash."

Ariana laughed, not doubting for a moment that Stefano did indeed know someone she could pay to break Leo Glass's legs—and his camera—for little more than a night's worth of tips. "Thanks, Uncle Stefano. I'll keep that in mind."

He kissed her other cheek, then unlocked the back door and checked in both directions for any sign of trouble, waving her through once he was certain the coast was clear. He pressed a set of keys into her hand. "Take my truck and do what you have to do. Leo doesn't know who he's messing with."

That might be true, but, for that matter, neither did Max Forrester. But after tonight they'd both know. And maybe she'd know herself. As she skipped over a puddle and ducked around a trash bin to where Stephano parked his truck, Ariana realized that she couldn't deal with Max and his suggestion that they extend their affair until she first dealt with the contents of her own heart.

15

ARIANA'S FIRST INSTINCT was to hold her breath. Pungent smoke, thicker than fog and ripe with marijuana and tobacco, drew the multicolored haze into a sickening swirl. Sweetened by the overpowering mixture of cheap perfumes, colognes and sweat, the air stung her eyes and burned the back of her throat. But she carefully kept a disgusted snort to herself. This world of raves and music wasn't hers, but she needed to exist here long enough to find Leo Glass.

Ty Wong had assured her that Leo would be at this party. And after infiltrating several rave parties and dance clubs all night, she just wanted to find his scrawny, deceitful butt, force the whole truth out of him and leave.

To go back to Max. Back to adulthood. Back to worrying about the contents of her heart rather than the safety of her body.

"There. In the corner."

Ty pointed toward a shadowed spot far from the front door of the abandoned building the teens and twenty-somethings had commandeered for the rave. Techno-music blared from speakers that probably cost more than her apartment. Girls in barely-there tank tops and hip-hugging capri pants chatted between sucking on pacifiers and drinking bottled water by the gallon. Guys made the rounds, a few hanging tight to helium balloons, some made from inflated condoms. Ty had already explained the uses and reasons for such odd sights, incongruous and childlike. Pacifiers. Balloons. Toys used to play with drugs like Ecstasy, the psychedelic of choice with this partying set.

This wasn't her world, thank God. She preferred her ecstasy to be of the sensual kind. The kind Max gave her rather than some chemical wrapped in a pill.

Ty started to walk away, but she grabbed his arm. "Where do you think you're going?" she asked, delivering her toughest sneer to the reed-thin excuse for a man she'd been forced to take on as her guide.

"I told you I'd help you find Leo Glass. I did that. I'm outta here."

She didn't release him, even when he tugged. "You still want me to ask your uncle *not* to throw you out of your rent-free apartment?"

He stopped struggling. "Hey, man. That was the deal."

"Well, man—" she poked his chest, not surprised to instantly meet the feel of bone through his T-shirt "—then you better get Leo for me and bring him outside. This place stinks. I need air."

Ty hesitated, but nodded. The strands of hair he'd dyed blue swung into his face. Until she got an explanation from Leo Glass, if not his head on a platter, she would manipulate Ty however she could. It had been a long time since Ariana had been this angry. Unfortunately for Leo Glass and Ty Wong and anyone else who got in her way, she was going to settle this score on her own terms.

That's why she'd left without returning Max's half dozen calls. At the time, she told herself she had to prove to Max that she could take care of herself. He was so powerful, so commanding, so at ease in the world of giving orders and orchestrating events to his advantage. But after the first descent into this foreign social world, she acknowledged that her fear of falling in love had sent her running from Max. She was afraid of trusting again. Loving again.

Once certain Ty was doing as she requested and wasn't trying to sneak out a side door, she made a beeline for the exit. She took a deep, invigorating breath of garbage-scented air outside, thinking it the freshest fragrance she'd inhaled in a long time. She stepped toward the truck she'd borrowed from her manager, Ray, when she heard her name shouted over the residual pounding of music from inside.

She turned, expecting to see Leo. Instead she found Max. She should have realized he'd find her. That he wouldn't let her get away so easily. Her admiration for this man warred with her need to put this matter to rest on her own.

"Max? What are you doing here?"

"Looking for you." He shoved his hands into the pockets of his jeans, rage firing his green eyes and tempered only by the unmistakable softness of relief. "I know you said you needed to find Leo on your own, but...these parties aren't safe. Ford and I have been all over town looking for you. What were you thinking?"

She bit back her anger when his tone altered from concern to condescension. She didn't need Max following her, tracking her down, playing knight in shining armor to her damsel in distress. She'd taken damn good care of herself so far. She didn't need his rescuing. But, God help her, his concern felt like a soft, wool blanket on a wet, cold night.

She pushed the warmth away. "How did you find me?"

Max glanced over his shoulder. Ford, lingering on the sidewalk beside Max's Porsche, waved. "My brother is very good at finding people."

"Yeah, well," she murmured, impressed despite her annoyance. "I should have let you throw him to the sharks when I had the chance."

"Probably." Max chuckled. "Did you find Leo?"

She glanced behind her at the battered steel door of the building, barely lit by the glow of a nearby street lamp. The parking lot was full of cars. At least twenty kids hung out on the weed-infested blacktop, sitting on the hoods, talking and laughing and having a much better time than she was.

"He should be coming out any minute."

Max nodded, then scanned the area as he took Ari's arm and led her into the light. Gazes darted at them from all directions and conversations stopped.

"You look like a cop," she pointed out, gesturing at his clothes. He was dressed casually in faded jeans, a polo shirt and dock shoes, but he still looked out of place in this setting.

"Sorry, my oversize Tommy Hilfiger outfit is at the cleaners."

His attempted joke succeeded. She chuckled, briefly imagining Max in baggy jeans slung low on his hips, boxers peeking out at the waistband beneath an oversize T-shirt and a sideways ball cap. She liked him better in his jogging clothes, or in those sexy, tailored suits. She liked him naked most of all, but now didn't seem the time to admit her preference.

The door behind them opened and Ty emerged. Ariana turned, then sought Max's gaze.

"Please let me handle this, Max. Leo betrayed me most of all."

He hesitated, but then nodded and stepped back into the shadows. Close, but out of sight. Her heart swelled. Max trusted her, even though his own success with the Pier deal could be on the line.

She suddenly felt like a fool. Not because she had absolutely no idea what to say now that Leo was approaching, but because she'd let one minute pass without realizing how much she loved Max Forrester. Yeah, he'd found her when she'd wanted to confront Leo alone, but he was backing away, giving her control, just as he had when they made love. Just as he had since the very beginning, whenever she wanted to take the lead. She'd simply been too afraid to see that, unlike her family, Max trusted her to make good decisions. And, unlike Rick, he didn't need to control her choices in order to elevate his own sense of power.

"Well, if it isn't San Francisco's sexiest homewrecker," Leo said with a slur, kicking up gravel as he shuffled closer. She defensively held up her hands, palms up. She didn't think Leo would strike her, but she had a strong suspicion he might lose his balance and topple over. Ty poked his head out of the door, then slinked back inside.

"Hello, Leo," Ariana greeted, her tone even. Once certain of his balance, she slid her hands into the pockets of her leather blazer. "You're not an easy guy to find."

"Can't say the same, can you?"

She conceded his point with a shrug. "You got me. You got me good. Care to tell me why?"

He rolled his eyes and chortled; his breath nearly knocked her a few steps back, but she held steady.

"Easy money. The old man wanted the inside scoop on that Forrest guy, and he paid cash."

"Old man? What old man?"

"Burrows. The bank guy."

Ariana shrugged. The only Burrows she knew was Charlie, and he was in real estate. Oh, and Maddie.

Wait a minute. Wasn't Maddie's father, Randolph Burrows, the president of First Financial? Ariana glanced over her shoulder at the shadow where she knew Max lingered, where she was certain he could hear every word they spoke. He stepped slightly forward into the light. The rage in his eyes easily bored through the darkness.

She turned back to Leo. "Randolph Burrows put you up to this? Did he say why?"

"Something about his daughter. Something about Forrester cheating on her or some shit. I don't know. I don't remember. I just know I was supposed to get pictures of the guy with some chick, any chick. But the man was a fuckin' monk—until I placed that roofie in his drink, until you came along. You're one hot piece of ass, you know that?"

Ariana clenched her mouth tightly closed, willing her dinner to remain in her stomach and her hands to remain by her sides. "Yeah, you told me that once, remember. I set you straight about talking trash to me. I don't suppose my lecture had anything to do with this?"

Leo only laughed. "I saw you watching Forrester all the time. Heard his friend talking about fixing you two up. Pairing you was fuckin' brilliant, don't you think? Brought you both down at the same time."

"Brilliant," she begrudgingly agreed. She'd always suspected Leo Glass was a smarmy type, but so long as he showed up to the restaurant on time, worked his entire shift, got the orders right and was polite to the customers, she'd been a satisfied boss. She'd forgiven his one breach of decorum, ascribing the crude come-on that she barely remembered to a case of youth and hormones.

This time, he'd crossed the line. But she held back her retribution until she had the final piece of the puzzle. "And the newspaper? Did the old man arrange for the photos to be printed there?"

Leo clucked away her suggestion. "Hell, no. He wanted to keep the whole thing private. But I'm no idiot. I *do* read. I knew the press was all over Forrester for that thing with the Pier, so after I collected from the old man, I went to see the editor with a second set of prints."

The hollowness in her chest expanded as more and more anger burbled up from the pit in her stomach. As Leo had said, it had all been too easy. Ruining her reputation and Max's deal. Well, it was just as simple for her to put a crimp in Leo's future. "I hope you got paid well…since you're unemployed."

"You can't fire me!"

She tilted an eyebrow, but didn't say another word. She sure as hell could fire him. "Already spent your payoff, didn't you?" she asked.

His glazed eyes betrayed him. Leo was back where he'd started from. Good.

"Doesn't matter," he spat. "I can get another job."

She nodded. "Yeah, you can. However, unless you want me making sure your new boss knows all about this incident, you're going to take us back to your apartment and watch us burn whatever is left of your film."

Max didn't miss the "us" she purposefully placed in her demand. He stepped forward and waved for Ford to join them. Not only wasn't she stupid enough to go anywhere with Leo without protection, she no longer wanted to.

She'd proved her point. To him. To herself.

Being in control, being strong and independent, wasn't all it was cracked up to be. She'd won with Leo, but the victory was somehow hollow without Max at her side.

Leo cursed the minute he saw Max.

Max placed a protective arm over her shoulder and, this time, she allowed the warmth of his concern to flow through her.

"Ari, why don't we let Ford take Leo home for that little fire party. You and I have someone else we need to see."

She pushed the button on her watch, her weary eyes widening at the hour. "It's 3:00 a.m., Max. Do you think Maddie's father wants to see us in the middle of the night?"

"I don't much care what Randolph wants at this point." He skimmed his hand down her arm, then back up from wrist to cheek, as Ford led Leo to Max's car. His caress ignited a burning deep within her, incinerating her residual anger at Leo's self-serving actions.

"You handled Leo incredibly well," he murmured.

She leaned her face into his palm, reveling in the soothing feel of his skin against hers. Max was a balm more potent than any of Mrs. Li's teas, more intoxicating than the ouzo her uncle served. She wanted nothing more than to take him home and show him, as he'd shown her, that she was more than willing to find some compromise that would make their relationship work beyond the end of the week.

But they had one stop to make first. One last piece of the scandal to put to rest.

THOUGH THE CLOCK in the Porsche read three-thirty, the windows of the Burrows mansion in Nob Hill were ablaze with light. Max hadn't called ahead, preferring the element of surprise to ensure that Randolph told him the entire truth of his involvement with Leo Glass, Donalise Parker and the scandal that had nearly ruined his relationship with Ariana, not to mention the development deal at the pier.

But Charlie had beaten him to the punch. Max pulled up behind Charlie's car and parked the truck Ariana had borrowed from her uncle. Max hoped his friend was there because he'd heard from Maddie—and that the news was good.

The butler opened the door shortly after Max knocked, not the least ruffled by greeting visitors in his pajamas and robe. He ushered them into the study and offered freshly brewed coffee from a silver serving set.

"Mr. Burrows will be down momentarily," the butler assured them, then left.

Ariana stood in the doorway, surveying the opulence of the house with wary eyes. "So this is what old money looks like."

"Some of the oldest in the city," Max verified while he poured and mixed two cups of strong java for both of them. He handed her a cup and gestured for her to sit. She shook her head, taking her first sip without moving farther into the room.

Max couldn't help but grin. She wove her way through raves and clubs with ease. She handled Leo with conviction and control. But Randolph's wealth gave her pause.

He recalled with all too much clarity the intimidation he'd faced the first time Maddie had brought him to her parents' home. He understood perfectly what Ariana was thinking as her gaze scanned the antique furniture and original artwork. *I don't belong here. I don't fit in.*

"Money is money, new or old," he assured her, cupping her elbow with his palm and leading her to a leather love seat tucked near the window.

"Leo betrayed me for money."

"The quest for cash can make people do all sorts of stupid things." Since knowing Ariana, he'd honestly begun to see that truth with painful clarity. Most of his stupidity had luckily harmed only himself. He'd missed out on so much—experiences and emotions Ariana had shown him over the past few days. Adventure, risk, desire. Love. But of all the places in the world to admit that to her, inside Randolph's study wouldn't do. They'd put this episode to rest and then move on to what he now knew to be the more important things.

"Do you think that's why Randolph got involved with Leo?" she asked. "For money?"

Max shook his head. That scenario didn't make any sense. The money to be had was with Max and the Pier deal—the deal Max had brought to Randolph's attention nearly a year ago. But without a doubt, Randolph and Leo had nearly ruined everything.

He and Charlie had met with the Darlingtons and the other investors earlier as planned, and performing their best tap dance, had soothed the uproar. Max hadn't had time to worry about why his former father-in-law-to-be had missed the gathering. The meeting had run long and he'd barely made his appointment with Donalise Parker of *The Bay Insider*.

"No, but money is the reason *The Bay Insider* printed the pictures. Increased circulation, just as we suspected. No big conspiracy there."

"You found Donalise Parker?"

Max downed more coffee. "She wasn't happy meeting me, but her largest advertiser was a client of mine."

And that fact had given him the idea of how to handle the newspaper once and for all.

"And she verified what Leo told us?"

"She paid him for the pictures and wrote the copy herself. Her paper appeals mainly to the young crowd, and she wanted to reach a bigger demographic. The development controversy, the sex scandal with a major player—too much titillation for her readers for her to pass up on."

Ariana set her cup and saucer down on the side table. "Then what's to keep her from sending someone else after us?"

Max grinned, knowing Ariana would enjoy his tale as much as he loved telling it. "I brought along a copy of the classified section of her paper. I carefully pointed out all the real estate agents' ads—all the agents who were friends or acquaintances I could easily persuade to suspend their advertising dollars. Her tabloid stood to lose some serious cash flow."

Ariana clapped her hands on her knees. "You didn't! I love it. But aren't real estate ads tiny? How bad could that really hurt them?"

Charlie entered the room at that moment, shaking his head and chuckling since he knew the rest of the story firsthand. "You should have seen him, Ariana. He saved the big gun for last."

Max shrugged off Charlie's compliment, but pride swelled his chest all the same. Though he wanted to find out what Charlie was doing here at nearly four in the morning looking as if he'd been here for a long while, he chose to finish telling Ariana this story first. Easing her mind took precedence over everything else. *She* took precedence over everything else.

"The investors I organized for the Pier deal run the gamut of the financial world," he explained. "Bankers like Randolph. CEOs of major corporations. Brokers. I just showed Ms. Parker a letter we'd hashed out at our meeting that promised to cancel approximately fifty percent of her entire advertising revenue if she didn't cease and desist her personal attacks."

"We should have thought of it the first time they complained about the Pier deal," Charlie groused as he poured coffee for himself.

Max clucked his tongue. "Now, Charles. That wouldn't be fair. Silencing the press, denying their First Amendment rights with blatant blackmail."

His holier-than-thou tone didn't fool Ari one bit. "Isn't that what you did anyway?"

Max set his coffee down and then did the same to hers. "As far as I'm concerned, Donalise Parker forfeited those rights when she printed that picture of you." He took her hands in his, massaging her fingers. He realized then that he couldn't stand being near her and not touch her. No matter what happened in the next few days, he couldn't possibly let her go.

"Luckily, Ms. Parker agreed to my terms. And as soon as we find out what Randolph had to do with all this…"

Randolph stormed into the study at the sound of his name. "…You can go back to having your sordid little affair with impunity." His voice brimmed with tightly controlled annoyance, softened only by the pure exhaustion that reddened his eyes.

Max stood, taking Ariana's hand as she rose beside him. "Watch what you say, Randolph," Max warned. His tone was even, but the threat was clear. "The one who made our affair sordid was you."

Randolph stopped, dead still, and Ariana watched as the two men squared off and psychologically and physically took their corners. Randolph strolled to the other side of his desk. Max pulled her with him and then offered her a seat directly across from the massive antique table. Ariana didn't want to sit, but when Max silently insisted by turning the chair toward her, she didn't argue.

He remained standing, as did Randolph. Charlie stayed at the sideboard, idly stirring his coffee, which Ariana knew for a fact he drank black and with no sugar.

"I want you off the Pier deal," Randolph demanded, slamming his fist on the leather blotter.

Charlie's eyebrows rose over wide eyes.

Max hooked his thumbs on his belt loops.

"It's my deal, Randolph. I personally recruited every single investor, including you. Why would I back off now, when I stand to make millions? Was that your scheme? To force me out?"

Ariana watched Randolph fume at Max's confidence, his easy, level tone and utter disregard for the older man's command. Randolph's nostrils flared like a raging bull's, but he folded himself into his chair, gripping the armrests. "You've humiliated my daughter, my family."

"I would never do anything to hurt Madelyn," Max said evenly.

Randolph growled. "You didn't love her!" he insisted. "And you were going to marry her anyway. For her money. Her position."

Max took that moment to sit. He couldn't argue that point with Randolph, Ariana knew. But Max did care for Madelyn and, in many ways, Ariana was grateful. His caring for his friend, no matter how selfishly motivated in the beginning, had played a hand in bringing Max and Ariana together. Knowing that talking about his feelings for Maddie would be difficult for him with her there, she laid her hand over his and gave his knuckles a little squeeze.

He rewarded her with a tilted, grateful grin. "I loved Maddie enough to try and make her happy. She only wanted to marry me to please you and Barbara. But she came to her senses and changed her mind. She didn't want to jeopardize the Pier deal by canceling the wedding, so she pulled a disappearing act and asked me to lie low until she could tell you the truth herself. Obviously, you found out sooner, thanks to Leo Glass."

Randolph winced at the mention of Leo's name. "Did he tell you how he broke our deal by selling the photographs to the newspaper? The humiliation Barbara has faced! Both of us! This is exactly what I suspected would happen." He wagged his finger. "I knew your uncouth ways would come back to denigrate this family. I only wish Madelyn had come to her senses sooner."

Max swallowed whatever bitterness Randolph's reference to his past caused. "Why didn't you warn her about me before? We were engaged for six months."

"I encouraged Madelyn's relationship with you because of Barbara. For whatever reason, my wife likes you. I couldn't openly oppose you without proof of your coarse character."

"So you hired Leo Glass."

"I hired a private investigator. Your business dealings were all legitimate, but you spent an inordinate amount of time at Ms. Karas's restaurant. Mr. Glass pointed us in the direction of your affair."

Ariana had remained silent long enough. "What affair? Max and I had never even been alone together until Friday night."

"Yes, my dear." Randolph said with a condescending nod. "You slept with the groom on the night before his wedding. How genteel of you."

She started to stand and protest, but Max stilled her with one glance. A glance that said, "Let me." He'd deferred the Leo situation to her. Fairness dictated she give him the same consideration with Randolph. Besides, she really liked seeing Max so coolly in control. When his dictates weren't leveled at her, the power was a real turn-on.

"You don't mean to be disrespectful to Ms. Karas, do you, Randolph? By now I'm sure you know that we weren't having an affair before Friday." Max shot his gaze, neither accusatory nor angry, to Charlie. "And you also know that Ms. Karas thought I was the best man, not the groom, on Friday night. And that Madelyn had left immediately after the rehearsal dinner. And that Leo slipped something into my drink."

Randolph huffed. This man didn't like being thwarted any more than he liked being wrong. "Leo told me about your liaison shortly after Madelyn called to announce your supposed elopement. I knew then that she was lying and assumed it was to save face after your rejection. I decided to use the pictures to force you out of the Pier deal, as payback for hurting my daughter. I didn't know until Madelyn called tonight that she'd been the one to cancel the wedding because she didn't love you. But the newspaper's involvement was Leo's doing alone. I wanted this to be a private matter."

"Well, that didn't happen and neither will my abandoning the development of the Pier." Max stood. He'd obviously heard all he came to hear. He glanced at Randolph, who remained seated, then held out his hand to Ariana.

"Randolph, let me give you a piece of advice. Next time you have a concern over your daughter, why don't you actually break down and have a conversation with her? Talk to her instead of trying to just take over and micromanage her life. That's why she left, you know."

As he let out an exhausted sigh, Randolph's shoulders sagged. "So I've learned, the hard way." He locked gazes with Ariana, but whatever he intended to say to her caught in his throat. He turned back to Max. "I'll call each of the investors today and assure them of my support of the deal—my support of you, Maxwell."

He attempted eye contact with Ariana again. "Ms. Karas, I'm not certain there's anything I can do to compensate you for your unfortunate involvement."

Ariana's dark eyebrows arched above wide eyes. "Speaking to me with respect is a very good start, Mr. Burrows. But other than that, no, there's nothing you can do." She stood and extended her hand, but pulled back briefly just as Randolph was about to accept her handshake. "Wait, there is one thing…" She took his proffered hand and held it firmly in hers. "I ran away from my father, from my family, for much the same reasons Maddie ran from you. But I did it when I was a lot younger."

The regret in her voice was a sound Max hadn't heard before. She'd always talked about her emancipation with a tinge of romantic adventure, but comparing her circumstance to Maddie's showed him the sacrifice she'd made in running away. He braced a hand on her shoulder.

"Show your daughter some respect when she gets back, Mr. Burrows. She cooked up her engagement to please you. She ran away to please herself. You'd better give her a reason to stay home, or she won't. You'll lose her forever, and that's not good for either of you." She pumped his hand gently, obviously as aware as Max was of the moist glaze that had formed over the man's eyes.

"Come on, Uncle Randy," Charlie said, breaking the somber mood with the endearment, "let's go check on Aunt Barbara."

Without argument, Randolph released Ari's hand and followed his nephew out. They shut the door behind them, leaving Max and Ari alone.

"Well," Ariana said with a sigh. "That's that. No more photographers. No more lies. What do we do now?"

Max encircled her waist with his arms and tucked her against his chest. "I have an idea, if you're not too exhausted."

She leaned back just far enough to look into his eyes. "Too exhausted for one of your ideas? I can't imagine."

16

WITHIN HALF AN HOUR, Max was weaving his way up the road to the top of Twin Peaks in a borrowed pickup with Ariana snuggled beside him. The hills, the second and third tallest vantage points in the city, were nearly deserted in the early-morning hours. A few joggers huffed toward the top. A group of bicyclists congregated toward the bottom, stretching and checking their bikes in preparation for a grueling uphill run. Max had heard about the dazzling panoramic view of the city from here, but he'd never seen it. And with the dawn, he anticipated the sights would be magnificent. Though not nearly as magnificent as the woman beside him.

He drove until he spied a quiet and secluded spot on the hill, well beyond the paved spaces earmarked for tour buses and tourists.

Daybreak was close at hand, but the skyline still sparkled as they parked. Ariana dug a blanket out of the compartment behind the seat.

"Uncle Stephano used to take Aunt Sonia here all the time," she explained. "It's supposed to be a stunning view."

Ariana pulled her jacket closer and bounded out of the

truck before he could tell her the only stunning view he needed could be had by looking at her. She released the latch on the flatbed and climbed aboard, tossed open the metal trunk and then spread a second blanket for them to sit on.

"This is your way to beat the cold?" Max got out of the truck, somewhat disappointed that she planned to rely on thick wool rather than good loving to heat their chilly skin.

She made a show of looking both right and left. For the moment, they were alone. But that could change at any moment. "I've had my fill of public displays, Max."

He climbed onto the truck bed. "Can't argue that point."

He sat with his back against the cab and held out the other blanket until Ariana snuggled in beside him. She held a bottle of wine and two glasses.

"Your uncle is one prepared guy," he quipped.

Ariana laughed as she dug for the corkscrew and adeptly popped the cork. "Stephano only donated the use of his truck. I brought the wine. After I found Leo, I was planning on surprising you at your house."

He accepted the full glass of something dark and sweet-smelling, but only swirled the liquid while she poured her own glassful and then set the bottle aside.

"You shouldn't have gone after Leo alone, Ari. And I'm not saying that because I want to control you or tell you what to do…"

"I know."

"E-excuse me?"

She grinned at his sputtered response. "I'm obsessive about doing things my own way. I'd like to say it's a hard habit to break but, truth is, it's a reflex I've developed after getting hurt. First by my family not trusting me to run the restaurant. Then by Rick not trusting me to breathe without his direction."

"Things happen," he said, adjusting the blanket so he could slip his arm around her. "It's human nature to protect yourself any way you can."

"Even at the expense of love?"

She locked her gaze with his. Max saw the hopeful uncertainty lingering in her eyes and recognized the emotion as exactly what he was feeling himself.

"Love is the first thing we seem to sacrifice," he admitted. He most definitely had—in the past, but not anymore. "Pretty stupid, huh?"

She glanced down into the dark depths of her wineglass. "I don't know if it's stupid or not."

She took a sip, then twisted around to abandon her glass on top of the metal trunk they were leaning against. When she turned back, her expression was so stricken, so utterly confused, Max couldn't bear the agony of watching her not know that he loved her, that he was willing to sacrifice everything he owned, now and in the future, to have her love him the way he loved her. With his hand still behind her, he pressed her flush against him and captured her mouth before she could say another word.

Over the past four days, they'd touched a thousand times. Each press of lips, each act of intimacy, had paled compared to this simple kiss. He wanted nothing more than to hold her, feel her connected to him. A part of him. Forever.

She pulled away, her eyes sad. "I can't do this, Max."

"Can't do what?"

"Pretend I don't love you!"

His heart swelled. "Who asked you to?"

"No one. You. Me. We were supposed to be together only for this one week. How can we make it work beyond this? I can't give up the restaurant."

"And I'd never ask you to."

"So you want to have a relationship on stolen moments? Breaks from the dinner crowd? How about when you get bogged under with construction at Pier Nine? I'm just organizing the renovation of one restaurant and I can't believe how much time and effort and energy it takes."

"You know, for someone who can instigate some incredible spontaneous excursions, you think too much."

"I think too much?"

Max couldn't believe the words forming in his brain. Since he'd known Ariana Karas, he'd become another person, a better person. The man he had been destined to become before his quest for financial stability overtook his life. He wasn't fooling himself. Accepting these changes wouldn't be any easier for him than they would be for her. But he was willing to make the effort...if she was.

"We'll make it work."

"How?"

"I don't know exactly. And that's the beauty of it. We don't have to know. I didn't know anything about Chinatown until you took me on a tour. You didn't know we were going out on the bay until I took you to the boat. But we had wonderful adventures without a plan." He set his wineglass next to hers, needing both his hands to capture her cheeks, hold her steady while he convinced her they could make this work. "We'll *both* have to change our ways, Ari, not just you. I love you too much."

"You do?"

"Didn't you know that? Couldn't you tell? I've never loved anyone before, Ariana. And you know what? I'd go back on food stamps if that's what it took to have you in my life. All these years, I never really understood my parents. How they stayed together when they had nothing."

"But they didn't have nothing," she said.

He nodded, able to agree with all his heart now that this

week with her had taught him the truth. "They had love and passion. Commitment. We could have that, too. We can have everything we want."

"I'm afraid, Max."

"Of course you are. So am I. It's great, isn't it?"

A glow of new sunlight pinkened the sky just behind Max, adding a phosphorescent glow to the challenge in his eyes. She swallowed, tasting the lingering wine, remembering the feel of his kiss. "'Great' isn't the word I'd choose. I don't like being afraid."

Max's mouth twisted into a mischievous grin. "That's because you're afraid of too many things."

She gasped loudly. "What? There's the fear of heights and the fear of…" What? Loving him? No, that didn't really scare her at all. The act was elemental, natural to the woman she'd become over the past few days. Was she afraid of losing herself in Max the way she had with Rick? No, that wasn't it, either. Max loved her, respected her. He'd never allow her to abandon the dreams and ambitions and quirks that made her who she was.

As the dawn brightened, the impatience in his gaze grew more and more obvious. She tugged her bottom lip with her teeth. She feared losing him, but one glance into those dark green eyes and she knew that her fear was completely unfounded.

"You won't leave me, will you?"

He only shook his head. That's all she needed. The rest she knew with her own heart.

"Okay, then I'm just afraid of heights."

Max's mouth twitched, then he stood quickly, drawing her up into his arms with a bounce. "Let's see if we can't take care of that one, too."

"What?"

Before she could react, he swung her up on top of the

cab of the truck. Parked on the precipice as they were, she glanced down and felt as if she was about to tumble onto the slowly waking city.

"Ack! Max!"

He let go of her long enough to climb up beside her. Their combined weight dented the top with a metallic pop.

"Oh, God!" she gasped. The man was insane! Wonderful, handsome, giving beyond belief, but certifiably crazy.

And so was she. Crazy in love.

"Don't worry about the truck," he assured her, grabbing her by the waist when her legs failed to move. "I'll buy Stephano a new one."

"I'm not worried about the truck. Yes, I am. Is the emergency brake on? Max! We're going to fall."

He moved her in front of him and wrapped his arms around her waist. Curving his body around her, he buried his face in her hair, inhaled, then nuzzled her neck. "Too late. I've fallen for you, Ariana Karas, and there is nothing you can do about it."

She closed her eyes, focusing all her attention, all her rioting nerves, on the feel of him holding her, steadying her, erasing the overwhelming dizziness caused by the vertigo, until all that was left was her light-headed reaction to being in love.

"If that's the only falling you plan for us to do today, then I'll survive."

His chuckle renewed her sense of impending danger. "I want you to more than survive, sweetheart. Open your eyes."

"They're open," she lied.

He cleared his throat. "Ariana, do you remember the last time you wouldn't open your eyes when I told you to?"

"When we made love on the balcony," she admitted, hardly needing to think to recall the sensual means he'd used then to convince her. "Wait a minute! I thought you didn't remember that night?"

Her eyes flashed open in protest, just in time to catch the wiggle in his eyebrows. "Little bits and pieces have been coming back, mostly in dreams. All of them so decadent I thought they might have just been naughty fantasies."

She huffed back into the safety net of his arms. "You should have told me."

"We have a few days left of our wild week. I thought I'd show you."

He pulled her fully against him, his hard arousal pressed to her back. One arm held her steady, wrapped protectively across her midsection while his other hand wandered down her thigh, then up, skirting beneath her blazer over her ribs.

"I thought we were done making love out in the open, Max."

"Who's making love?" he asked innocently. "I'm not making love. I'm just touching you, holding you, showing you the city in the dawn of a new day."

Though the sensations of his touch made her vision hazy, she picked out a few famous sites they'd yet to visit. The top of the pyramidlike Transamerica Building. The round, nozzle shape of Coit Tower. The vast green expanse of Golden Gate Park. But with Max's hands wandering, brushing over her breast, skimming the top of her waistband, she couldn't think of any sight more attractive than that California king at his house.

She twisted around until she faced him, rocking unsteadily despite his tightly coiled embrace. Her fear of heights was obviously going to take a little longer to overcome than her fear of falling in love. And she'd never felt freer in her entire life.

"We've got the rest of our lives to see the city, Ari. I just want to see you. Naked. In my bed, your bed, anywhere."

"Anywhere?"

He laughed. "Don't tempt me. I'd make love to you right here if I had my way. Maybe I am an exhibitionist at heart."

"And that's just one thing I love about you," she said with a smile.

He kissed her deep and long, until she nearly forgot they were standing on the cab of a truck parked at the top of the hill. With the wind and the warming sun, she imagined they were floating on a cloud.

"What I really want is for you to marry me." He whispered the proposal in her ear, then leaned back just enough to gauge her reaction.

Only she didn't have a reaction. She didn't know what to do or what to say. She'd never dreamed…never guessed. "Max, that's a big leap. Are you sure?"

"I wouldn't have asked if I wasn't sure. Take the leap with me, Ariana. I promise we'll make it."

Ariana lifted herself completely into his arms, then jumped up and wrapped her legs around him while shouting like someone who'd just won the lottery. She didn't care who heard her. She didn't care who saw. She was going to marry the man she loved with all her heart and soul. And knew their union would last for a lifetime.

Because she knew firsthand that Max was a man of his word.

* * * * *

Harlequin Blaze™

COMING NEXT MONTH

Available August 30, 2011

#633 TOO WILD TO HOLD
Legendary Lovers
Julie Leto

#634 NIGHT MANEUVERS
Uniformly Hot!
Jillian Burns

#635 JUST GIVE IN...
Harts of Texas
Kathleen O'Reilly

#636 MAKING A SPLASH
The Wrong Bed: Again and Again
Joanne Rock

#637 WITNESS SEDUCTION
Elle Kennedy

#638 ROYALLY ROMANCED
A Real Prince
Marie Donovan

You can find more information on upcoming
Harlequin® titles, free excerpts and more at
www.HarlequinInsideRomance.com.

HBCNM0811

REQUEST YOUR FREE BOOKS!
2 FREE NOVELS PLUS 2 FREE GIFTS!

Harlequin *Blaze*

red-hot reads!

YES! Please send me 2 FREE Harlequin® Blaze™ novels and my 2 FREE gifts (gifts are worth about $10). After receiving them, if I don't wish to receive any more books, I can return the shipping statement marked "cancel." If I don't cancel, I will receive 6 brand-new novels every month and be billed just $4.49 per book in the U.S. or $4.96 per book in Canada. That's a saving of at least 14% off the cover price. It's quite a bargain. Shipping and handling is just 50¢ per book in the U.S. and 75¢ per book in Canada.* I understand that accepting the 2 free books and gifts places me under no obligation to buy anything. I can always return a shipment and cancel at any time. Even if I never buy another book, the two free books and gifts are mine to keep forever.

151/351 HDN FEQE

Name _____ (PLEASE PRINT)

Address _____ Apt. #

City _____ State/Prov. _____ Zip/Postal Code

Signature (if under 18, a parent or guardian must sign)

Mail to the **Reader Service:**
IN U.S.A.: P.O. Box 1867, Buffalo, NY 14240-1867
IN CANADA: P.O. Box 609, Fort Erie, Ontario L2A 5X3

Not valid for current subscribers to Harlequin Blaze books.

Want to try two free books from another line?
Call 1-800-873-8635 or visit www.ReaderService.com.

* Terms and prices subject to change without notice. Prices do not include applicable taxes. Sales tax applicable in N.Y. Canadian residents will be charged applicable taxes. Offer not valid in Quebec. This offer is limited to one order per household. All orders subject to credit approval. Credit or debit balances in a customer's account(s) may be offset by any other outstanding balance owed by or to the customer. Please allow 4 to 6 weeks for delivery. Offer available while quantities last.

Your Privacy—The Reader Service is committed to protecting your privacy. Our Privacy Policy is available online at www.ReaderService.com or upon request from the Reader Service.

We make a portion of our mailing list available to reputable third parties that offer products we believe may interest you. If you prefer that we not exchange your name with third parties, or if you wish to clarify or modify your communication preferences, please visit us at www.ReaderService.com/consumerschoice or write to us at Reader Service Preference Service, P.O. Box 9062, Buffalo, NY 14269. Include your complete name and address.

HB11B

Rafael de Luca had been in bad situations before. A crowded ballroom could never make him sweat.

These people would never know that he had no memory of any of them.

He surveyed the party with grim tolerance, searching for the source of his unease.

At first his gaze flickered past her, but he yanked his attention back to a woman across the room. Her stare bored holes through him. Unflinching and steady, even when his eyes locked with hers.

Petite, even in heels, she had a creamy olive complexion. A wealth of inky-black curls cascaded over her shoulders and her eyes were equally dark.

She looked at him as if she'd already judged him and found him lacking. He'd never seen her before in his life. Or had he?

He cursed the gaping hole in his memory. He'd been diagnosed with selective amnesia after his accident four months ago. Which seemed like complete and utter bull. No one got amnesia except hysterical women in bad soap operas.

With a smile, he disengaged himself from the group

around him and made his way to the mystery woman.

She wasn't coy. She stared straight at him as he approached, her chin thrust upward in defiance.

"Excuse me, but have we met?" he asked in his smoothest voice.

His gaze moved over the generous swell of her breasts pushed up by the empire waist of her black cocktail dress.

When he glanced back up at her face, he saw fury in her eyes.

"Have we *met?*" Her voice was barely a whisper, but he felt each word like the crack of a whip.

Before he could process her response, she nailed him with a right hook. He stumbled back, holding his nose.

One of his guards stepped between Rafe and the woman, accidentally sending her to one knee. Her hand flew to the folds of her dress.

It was then, as she cupped her belly, that the realization hit him. She was pregnant.

Her eyes flashing, she turned and ran down the marble hallway.

Rafael ran after her. He burst from the hotel lobby, and saw two shoes sparkling in the moonlight, twinkling at him.

He blew out his breath in frustration and then shoved the pair of sparkly, ultrafeminine heels at his head of security.

"Find the woman who wore these shoes."

Will Rafael find his mystery woman?
Find out in Maya Banks's passionate new novel
ENTICED BY HIS FORGOTTEN LOVER
Available September 2011 from Harlequin® Desire®!